Leslie Marshall has wri~~tt~~ publications, including t~~he~~ *Simple* and *InStyle* maga~~zine~~ contributing editor. She gre~~w~~ and now lives in New York

Praise for *A Girl Could Stand Up*:

'An atmosphere of crazy cheerfulness . . . undercut by moments of poignancy . . . a pleasure to read'
Daily Telegraph

'Exotic and bright'   *Daily Mail*

'Hard to tear yourself away . . . poignantly funny'
Prima magazine

'A must for Kate Atkinson and John Irving fans'
Glamour magazine (a Must-Read selection)

'Reality and imagination blur . . . in this coming-of-age tale . . . magical'   *Mirror*

'A promising novel of infectious élan'
Independent

'*A Girl Could Stand Up* is a ride through a fun house – playful, startlingly saturated with colour and light and sound . . . irrefutably true'   *O* magazine

'Fast-paced and deliriously dizzy'   *Elle* magazine

'This coming-of-age story is a page-turner that will disarm and charm. A stand-out talent'
People magazine

www.booksattransworld.co.uk

A GIRL COULD STAND UP

Leslie Marshall

BLACK SWAN

A GIRL COULD STAND UP
A BLACK SWAN BOOK: 0 552 77190 2

Originally published in Great Britain by Doubleday,
a division of Transworld Publishers

PRINTING HISTORY
Doubleday edition published 2003
Black Swan edition published 2004

1 3 5 7 9 10 8 6 4 2

Copyright © Leslie Marshall 2003

Set in 11/12pt Melior by
Falcon Oast Graphic Art Ltd.

Black Swan Books are published by Transworld Publishers,
61–63 Uxbridge Road, London W5 5SA,
a division of The Random House Group Ltd,
in Australia by Random House Australia (Pty) Ltd,
20 Alfred Street, Milsons Point, Sydney, NSW 2061, Australia,
in New Zealand by Random House New Zealand Ltd,
18 Poland Road, Glenfield, Auckland 10, New Zealand
and in South Africa by Random House (Pty) Ltd,
Endulini, 5a Jubilee Road, Parktown 2193, South Africa.

Printed and bound in Great Britain by
Cox & Wyman Ltd, Reading, Berkshire.

Papers used by Transworld Publishers are natural, recyclable
products made from wood grown in sustainable forests. The
manufacturing processes conform to the environmental
regulations of the country of origin.

To Kate and Robert

Contents

Acknowledgments

While working on this book I have been blessed to have many family members and close friends who have offered me their constant love and support – not to mention no small cache of fine raw material. Without them, and their quiet but rock-solid assumption that I could do anything I set myself to, I would never have persevered.

Carrie Tuhy, Martha Nelson, and Charla Lawhon are three brilliant magazine editors who have become great friends. Over the last decade they have kept me laughing and writing and solvent—no easy combination. They have also taught me that even Real Simple People can dress InStyle. Many thanks for everything girls. And woof!

I am permanently addicted to the astonishing beauty of the Beaverkill Valley, where so much of this book was so happily written, and forever grateful to Larry and Wendy for all they have done to preserve and share this wilderness paradise.

It has been a pleasure and an honor to be published by Grove Press, and especially to have the wonderful Joan Bingham as my editor there. Joan believed in Elray from the very first, and has done much to make sure she stands up, straight and tall. A special thanks also to Lindsay Sagnette at Grove, for all her astute suggestions and good-natured help.

For the amazing Tina Bennett, my agent at Janklow & Nesbit, I reserve a standing ovation. Her support and enthusiasm and editorial suggestions are always so artful and on target that they feel more like an internal than an external source of inspiration. Her understanding of what I am trying to do often exceeds my own, as does her patience. Tina and the wise and witty Svetlana Katz both worked tirelessly to make sure this story found its way to readers. I will never finish thanking them.

Finally, a salute to Billy, my own wild boy whose mind and heart and spirit I so admire, and to Josephine, Beatrice, and Marshall, the most spectacular people I know. Thank you for letting this book live with us for so long, and for making me get it out of the shoe box and into the world.

Prologue

Sometimes when I am alone in this house I turn invisible. I disappear. It starts with a strange shiver, an almost electric current that rattles through me impatiently as if it has more important places to go. Just as the shiver subsides, I too begin to evanesce. Quietly and rapidly, as traceless as an unfinished thought, I fall in with the ions that ricochet from wall to wall in this, my home. I de-atomize into a sweet mist of selflessness. Then, from a fine high orbit of mock omniscience, I watch the stories that have taken shape in this house – a house where I have lived for all thirty-three of my years.

I enjoy evaporating to a wide, anonymous place – perhaps because I have always been a compulsive cliff walker, one of those spiritual Peeping Toms who long to peer into any and every abyss that yawns. The same impulse that caused me to test my flesh against the blade of a fine knife when I was very young has attracted my older self to more abstract edges – the divide between men and women, between love and work, between love and hate; the lethean border between this world, the one we all share for a while, and those other worlds of who knows what comes before and after.

Omniscience, that quiet perch between existence and nonexistence, is a delicious edge. As a child when I flew to this perch, I called the stories I watched my 'mind movies.' Today I still thrill every time I feel the desire to judge evaporating, and a story line spreading through me, erasing me from myself. But lately, whenever I feel the rumble of near nonexistence rattling through me, something else happens too. Yes, these days when I am tempted by anonymity, I immediately think of Rosie and Valentine, my very own Romulus and Remus. I think of them, and I think of the child that even now may be watching from my womb. And then I remember how important it is not to simply disappear. I remember how terrible it can be when people slip away. I remember that while I am here, I must fight to stay.

I have noticed that no matter how badly they may break the rules — of justice, of narrative, of so-called real life — all stories long to hoist the pirate flag of themselves upon the wind. Today I sit down to write some of the stories I have lived and watched in this house. It is not just that I want all the pieces gathered in one place, on paper, as a record. I also want to reassure those who might care that although I may seem to disappear from time to time, I, Elray Mayhew, am very much alive. Others have come and gone, but I am still here. I am still here, and I will hold on as long as I can. We are all honor-bound to hold on as long as we can. And then, if we're lucky, when we do disappear, the best that was in us may still survive. Just listen.

Part One

The Big Scream

Follow me back to a day twenty-seven years ago, to the moment that will serve as my beginning. Return with me to an afternoon that has come to feel more like a geological event than a segment of time – to an incident that over the years has metamorphosed into such a communal piece of property, the very bounds of narrative self blur and then dissolve as I approach. Indulge me as I step outside myself and into blissful omniscience for a moment and turn back to the day when:

Elray

Elray was under the house, the part of it that had no basement, lying on her belly in the cramped and musty crawlspace with her face pressed against the dirt. It had been three days since her as yet uncelebrated sixth birthday. Three days since the accident. Two hours since the still, almost airless moment when her parents, Barkley and Jack, had disappeared forever into the quiet and unremarkable ground of Washington's Montrose Cemetery.

Overhead people were moving, clacking their shoes across the floors in dotted lines like the paths that chart explorers' routes on maps. Elray took a deep breath of the stale crawlspace air. It was good air, old air. The same air that had been there when Elray and Barkley and Jack had looped their own footsteps through the open spaces of the house, garlanding the rooms with the private patterns of their family dance. The same hard earth had been there too. Elray shifted her weight and opened her mouth slightly so that the bitterness of that earth could creep at the edges of her taste. Then she tried to whisper to them: 'Mama, Daddy. Barkley, Jack.' No sound came, of course. She had forgotten – she kept forgetting – about her dead voice. Elray slid her tongue forward for a quick rude scoop of dirt and mimed the names one last time as the bitterness blossomed. 'Barkley. Jack.'

Soon someone would miss her, and come looking.

Elray knew that. But she would hear them calling first, and she would have time to scuttle out of the crawl-space back into the sunlight, and act like she had just stepped outside to throw a peach pit into the hedge where it belonged. These people upstairs were pretty slow. They didn't notice much, didn't remember much. Not one of them had remembered her sixth birthday party, or noticed the bright ziggurat of presents stashed in the hall closet. Elray had discovered the presents, of course, and she'd seen the colorful paper plates with matching cups and napkins that were still sitting in the pantry in their plastic wrapping. She had been painfully aware of the big chocolate cake on top of the refrigerator, getting stale in its white box. Last night when no one was near she had even climbed up on the counter to peer in at the cake. She had admired the little miniature merry-go-round and tiny Ferris wheel and toy clowns pressed into its chocolate top, and the way her own name, ELRAY, had been scripted in big letters that erupted into clusters of pink roses with the beginning E and the ending Y.

Barkley and Jack had had everything ready. They had remembered her birthday. But now they were gone and only all the other people, the ones who didn't remember or notice, were upstairs. It was not a handsome crowd. Grown people turned into monsters when they cried; their faces went rubbery, and their eyes bulged as if they were eggs about to hatch more little sad rubbery monsters. Nearly everyone had been a cry-monster at some point today. Even Elray's Auntie Ajax, usually so full of energy and jokes, had looked at her from across the room with shimmery eyes, and then had let loose a long sad hiccup.

Elray wiped her tongue on her sleeve. The dirt had lost its good bitter flavor and was just bad grit in her mouth. Some ginger ale might be nice. Perhaps she should go upstairs and get a little drink in one of those pretty party cups, and walk around and try to make one of the dumb grown people take the hint. She could hold the cup up and wave it, as if to say: 'Do I have to save all of these cups for my BIRTHDAY PARTY, or can I have some ginger ale in one now?' She would find her Uncle Harwood. She hadn't seen him crying. He wasn't his normal silly self, he hadn't walked on his hands and said the alphabet backward for her yet. But at least he wasn't weepy. He was wearing the camera, taking pictures, the way he always did. If Barkley had been there, Elray knew what she would have done. She would have laughed at Harwood and said, 'Oh cut it out, you old shutterbug.'

This vision, the picture of Barkley and the sound of her voice scolding Harwood, came to Elray so clearly she decided to rewind it and run it again. It was nice to have Barkley around, even in a mind movie. 'Oh cut it out Harwood, you old shutterbug,' Barkley said, and then she tilted her head back and gave her brookwater laugh. Uncle Harwood's camera flashed right back at her and then, for just a second, there were magic blue pinwheels of light twirling on Barkley's teeth and in her eyes.

Elray had been going full tilt on the mind movies lately. All sorts of things had been coming and going on screen, but the story that kept coming back and starting itself over and over was the story of Thursday morning, her birthday morning, just three days ago. It was a good movie. It always began the same way, inside her head, with the sunlight melting on her face and making patterns like tree branches on the insides of her eyelids. Then the lids lifted, slid upward the way shades on airplane windows do, and the day with all its special birthday potential came slowly, deliciously into focus. The October air was apple-clean, and carried the promise of breakfast bacon. The sunlight was brassy and loud, and danced around Elray's bedroom as if impatient for her to rise.

In the movie Elray thawed from sleep into consciousness of all this and hit the ground running, her bare feet slapping across the cold wood floors with loud thwacks, her child's voice rising from a tickle in her chest and sailing forth with the hearty acquisitive flush of one who is ready to receive.

'Mama! Daddy!' She called for them. It was her birthday. She had called her parents and there they both were, in the kitchen and hard at work. Barkley was pouring hot water over the coffee grounds, moving carefully around the edges of the inverted pyramid, washing the coffee down the slopes. Jack was turning the bacon, intently. They both looked up and grinned.

'It's a Birthday Thing!' said Barkley.

'It's a Birthday Thing with no slippers!' said Jack.

'Happy birthday, Birthday Thing!' They said it together, and then they swooped down in a whirl of arms and faces and squeals that left Elray breathless, seated at the breakfast table before a large pink package with a gray ribbon. Elray stared at the package, and the package, it seemed, began to grow. The longer she stared, the larger the package grew and the pinker it turned, until it was shaking and rattling before her, straining at its restrictive gray ribbon with the groaning song of a big boat under sail. Then BOOM – the package exploded in a cloud of pink dust. When the storm of cardboard and paper settled, there sat a pair of black high-top sneakers. Brand new, in Elray's size.

The sneakers were a perfect fit and made an auspicious birthday beginning. Elray had wanted them badly and now, as she lay stretched across the backseat of the car, riding to her surprise birthday outing with Barkley and Jack, she propped her feet on the window ledge so that she could admire the way the shoes punctuated the ends of her legs. The little white crescent moons across their toes made the sneakers look happy to be there too.

In the front seat, Barkley and Jack were dropping hints, trying to make Elray guess where they might be headed.

'Is it the beer factory again?' Elray asked, remember-ing her birthday outing the year before. The three of them had walked in the cool shadow of big vats that stood on top of tall pipes like metal trees, surrounded by a pungent thick smell that made Elray want to grab the air and squeeze it into shapes. Her favorite part had been when the bottles filed past like soldiers to get their cap hats.

Barkley looked across at Jack with narrow eyes. 'No,' she said. 'Last year was your daddy's pick. This year is my turn. Keep guessing, Kumquat. This is something really exciting.' Barkley slid Jack another slit-eyed look. 'Something really exciting for CHILDREN.'

'The zoo?' Elray tried to hide the sadness that lives in that word, but it came out pretty flat anyway. So she tried it again. 'The zoooouo?' This time it came out like a crazy train whistle. Still not a happy sound, but luckily Barkley was already shaking her head and wrinkling her nose and saying, 'No, no, no. Keep guessing.'

Not the beer factory, not the zoo. Oh God. 'The Bay Bridge?' Elray's father had a theory about one of the exact-change booths on the big Bay Bridge that led across the Chesapeake toward the beaches. The spirit of his dead mother, Elray's Granny Mayhew, some-times inhabited a certain booth there, he said, and on a good day you could get a hot tip on which horse to play at the Laurel Racetrack if you counted the seconds between when you dropped the money in the basket and when the automated gateway lifted to let you through. Once Elray and Barkley had suffered through seven and a half round trips over the bridge in the course of an hour and a half because Jack claimed to be piecing together information on the whereabouts of some family silver that had mysteriously dis-appeared about the time of Granny Mayhew's death.

'Is it the Bay Bridge?' In the mind movie, Elray usually repeated her question in a tiny pushed-away voice. Partly because the car was already slowing and turning, lurching downward and to the left, kicking up a drumroll of gravel that seemed to signify arrival somewhere – somewhere that was much too soon to be the Bay Bridge. But her voice was also pushed away because it was right about here that this particular mind movie, in the three days it had been running, always started to unravel on Elray. The picture began to stutter and flicker and finally faded away altogether.

But not on that long-ago now famous afternoon, it didn't. Not as Elray lay in the crawlspace. This time the reel kept rolling. The colors brightened, if anything, and the focus grew sharper as the car turned down a driveway toward what appeared to be a cluster of castles. Flags were flying from turrets and towers in every direction. To the left was a wild, looping railroad built high on stilts. The air was full of tinny music and sugary smells and disembodied screams.

'It's called Glen Echo,' said Barkley. 'It's an amusement park. Happy birthday.'

First they all sat in a giant teacup, like three giant sugar cubes, as it whirled around and around. 'Hold on, Crumpet,' said Jack.

'You,' Elray said back at him. Then she stretched out a foot and poked at his knees with a new high-top to check if his sugar-cube legs were starting to dissolve yet.

'Goodness,' said Barkley, clutching at a purple scarf that the wind was trying to steal. 'Pretty wild teacup, this one.'

Next they visited a booth where they were outfitted with little fishing rods. When they cast the rods over the counter, the woman in charge bent over and left her bottom in the air for a long time. Finally, just as there was a mighty tug on Elray's line, the woman reappeared, red-faced and yelling, 'Hey! Youse got something!' Sure enough, when Elray worked her reel to take in the slack a little plastic monkey came dangling into view.

They rode the merry-go-round, with its bobbing

bored beasts, and they went fishing again, this time by aiming Ping-Pong balls at the narrow necks of little glass globes that held real live goldfish. They had to lean way over the barrier fence to aim, and even so the Ping-Pong balls kept bouncing maddeningly to the ground. But finally Jack got it right, and a ball bobbed on the surface above a startled fish.

'What will you name him?' Jack asked as he handed the little glass globe to Elray.

'What day is it?' Elray squinted through the glass at her prize. 'And how do you know it's a him?'

'It's Thursday, and I don't.'

'Then I'll call him Friday,' Elray said. 'Lily says Friday is fish day.'

'What's next?' asked Barkley. She had just bought a beehive of blue cotton candy, and Jack and Elray paused to watch her eat it and to consider her question.

'Hey, little family.' A tall elderly woman in a long gray flannel coat took advantage of their momentary indecision to approach them with a Polaroid camera. 'Can I snap a quick picture? You look so happy today. *Quel beau poisson!*' the woman said, admiring Friday. 'May I?' she asked, holding up her camera. 'I'll take two – one for me and one for you?'

They huddled together, Elray holding Friday up in front and Barkley holding her cotton candy behind her back, while the woman took two Polaroids. A moment later Elray watched as the image of her family, newly expanded by the addition of Friday, came into bloom against an empty white background. She stared at the photograph the woman offered her and then stuffed it into her coat pocket.

'What's next, Elray?' Barkley asked again as she returned to her cotton candy.

'This one,' Elray announced as she grabbed Barkley and Jack by their knees and pulled them toward a dark stone cottage set into the hill. A pretty blue light, like angels' hair, shone from the door of the cottage.

'That's a grown-up one. Tunnel of Love,' said Jack. 'You won't like it.'

'This one,' Elray insisted. It was her birthday, her day to call the shots.

Inside the cottage a line of wooden boats bobbed in a narrow canal. The boats were twirled at the ends like elves' shoes, and bumped against each other gently, like livestock.

'Hi-ho! A gondola for the lovely trio of lovebirds,' cried a small man who looked like a big version of Elray's plastic monkey. He jumped down from a seat high along one wall and gave a little bow as they entered. 'Here we go. The finest in my fleet.' He helped Barkley and Elray and Jack into the front seat of the boat, and then carefully settled Friday in his glass globe on the back seat. 'Bon voyage,' he called as he climbed back to his high seat and waved a grimy monkey hand. The gondola lurched forward with a grinding, creaking groan and splashed down a ramp and into the canal. 'Hey, you devils,' the voice of the little monkey man echoed after them as the boat slipped away from the harbor of light inside the cottage and into the dark underworld of the Tunnel of Love. 'Now don't you do anything I wouldn't do.'

At first the only sound around them was the silken swoosh of water parting, the only sight in the darkness the almost indistinguishable darker mass of the curled bow some six feet ahead. But then the boat tilted sharply to the right, and a bright light flashed on a big black and white cow as it rolled down a grass mound toward the boat. Loud cackling and a frenzied 'Moooooo! Mooooo!' exploded the silence. Moments later, as suddenly as it had appeared, the cow was gone. They were back in the dark with only quiet water sounds.

'Tunnel of Love?' Barkley hissed.

Elray felt Jack's shoulders shrugging a response on her right. 'Tunnel of Weird. Whatever,' he whispered.

'The black and white cows are called Holsteins, Elray. They're very gentle, usually dairy cows – that is, they give us milk.'

'I know,' Elray said as she let the darkness and water noises wash over her. 'I bet this is what it feels like to be an eel.'

The boat had begun to climb some sort of hill. It labored noisily upward, occasionally slipping backward for an ominous few inches before catching and moving on, until finally it leveled off and lights sprang on all around to reveal a range of pointed mountain-tops on either side of the canal. Goats as big as the mountains grazed on some of the peaks, and in one valley a little girl who would surely grow up to be a giantess rocked mechanically up and down on the handle of a huge butter churn. As they neared the girl the lower half of her frozen smile dropped and a loud yodeling reverberated through the tunnel: 'Yo-Da-Lay-Eee-HOO, Yo-Da-Lay-EEE-Hoo!'

Elray flinched at the noise and turned to Barkley. 'Is that Heidi?' she asked.

'I guess so.'

'She's big, isn't she?'

'Yes she is.' Barkley glanced through the half-light toward Jack. 'The mountain air must be good for her. She seems to be doing monstrously well.'

'I'll say,' said Jack. 'Heidistein.'

But the boat was already leaving the mountains behind now, heading downhill and back into the inky eel-dark, and as the yodeling faded away the water noises seemed almost friendly, like welcoming kisses from a dog. Or was it that there were new water noises? Closer water noises?

'Oh yuk!' Barkley jumped on Elray's left. 'Jack, there's a leak in this boat! I've got water all around my ankles.'

'Me too.' Jack was splashing his toes up and down noisily. 'It all sloshed forward when we headed down the mountain, I guess. Must be the spring thaw.'

'Jack, really. Don't joke. We could catch pneumonia, or capsize and drown,' Barkley scolded. She was slapping her toes up and down in the water now too, but she paused to check on Elray. 'Kumquat, you keep your feet up high and dry.'

Elray snatched her knees to her chin and felt her new high-tops. Whew. Dry as a bone. She patted them and tucked them underneath her.

'Ah, the Tunnel of Love,' Jack said with a sigh. He was reaching behind Elray to find the back of Barkley's head. 'Don't worry, my sweet,' he said. 'We seem to be heading for the warm dry tropics now.'

It was true. Exotic birdcalls had begun to sound from the darkness ahead of them, and a faint rosy glow was spreading from around the next bend. But the boat seemed to be slowing down. Yes, it was definitely slowing down, and Elray was becoming worried that it might come to a halt, might never make it around the bend to the land of birds and light and who knew what other surprises.

Or was it the boat that was losing steam? The story had been playing so vividly, for so long, that Elray had forgotten that it was only a mind movie. She couldn't bear for it to stop – not now, with such a tantalizing adventure shimmering around the next corner, not with Barkley and Jack waiting there in the movie, waiting for her. Elray shut her eyes against the crawl-space shadows, against everything outside her head, and tried to pull the movie back. She concentrated on the slap slap swoosh of the water against the sides of the boat. She let the dank, sweet smell of the tunnel flow through her nostrils into her head and down deep to her lungs. She felt the awkward lump of her high-tops tucked snugly underneath her, and the slight hum of warmth against each shoulder that let her know Barkley and Jack were there.

Creeeeeak. The boat was moving again, slowly but steadily, gaining on the warm halo of light up ahead. The birds were hooting and cawing just inches from their ears now, and then the boat tilted abruptly again as it headed into another tight turn and WHOOSH!

They had splattered down a short ramp and landed in a pink and green and orange world that could only be Paradise. Palm trees lined the shores on either side of them and lifted their thick green fronds upward gracefully in a welcoming arch overhead. Big-beaked birds of all colors populated the trees, and little grinning monkeys hung by their tails here and there. Wrapped around the trunk of one tree was a bright snake with a big smile – the friendliest snake smile Elray had ever seen, for it had squared-off people teeth, not the pointed fangs most other snakes had. Twinkly sounds, as if from whole armies of wind bells like the one that hung on Elray's own back porch, made a pretty background chorus. And in a midnight-blue patch of sky there blazed the brightest, most beautiful moon Elray had ever seen. It was a crescent moon, with soft pinks and blues in it, and it was swinging lightheartedly in the night sky, somersaulting playfully in a most unmoonlike manner.

'Ah, Eden at last,' said Jack, pointing to the snake. 'Do you like this garden, Elray?'

'I love it,' Elray said, staring upward, transfixed. 'Look at the moon. It's dancing.'

But Jack had turned to Barkley. 'How about a little original sin, Eve,' he whispered as he leaned toward her. And at that moment, as Barkley and Jack exchanged a loud kiss behind her head, Elray's moon did a spectacular flip in the sky and began to descend toward her, as if it too wanted a kiss.

'Oh Moon.' Elray leaned forward and reached up to catch the cuddly mass of soft cottony light. 'Come here, Moon!' It was almost there, almost in her arms, when Elray felt the flash of pain against her right arm. This moon was not soft; it was burning hot and hard. And it was a rude moon. It had sailed right through her open embrace to the bottom of the boat.

And then it happened – the whole world exploded.

Everything – the moon, Barkley, Jack, the boat, the mind movie and even Elray herself, the real Elray who had been in the crawlspace watching the mind movie – everything exploded and was consumed by a rushing, searing fire that burned without sound or light but with violent perversions of each. Its blaze was blindingly loud, deafeningly bright, everywhere and nowhere at once. It raged and it roared in a way that had to end but that obviously could never stop.

For the longest time Elray, like everything else, was simply obliterated. But then slowly, slowly some faraway remnant of something inside her began first to catch at a rhythm and then to superimpose logic. Finally Elray thought she understood what had happened. The entire world had become a train. A runaway train; a runaway train on fire; a runaway train on fire rushing rushing rushing through a tunnel. A runaway train on fire rushing rushing rushing through a tunnel and she, Elray, was a part of it all. She was a part of the rhythmic pounding of the wheels on the track, a part of the infernal heat of internal combustion gone awry and, most of all, a part of the hollow wail of the train's whistle that came streaking now, like a long sad banner, above everything else.

Ajax

Ajax topped off her glass of white wine in the kitchen before heading into the hall to begin her search in earnest. 'El-RAY,' she hissed in a loud whisper. Where had the child gone? That useless boob Harwood had been put in charge of her for ten short minutes, and already he'd lost her. Christ. Life was shaping up to be one major pain in the butt.

'Elray sweetie, where are you?' Ajax hissed again, not wanting any of the guests to hear. That was all she needed – for some Nosy Parker to notice that she'd already misplaced her new ward. All the busybodies who had been making such an unbearable fuss, shaking their heads and rolling their eyes and heaving great sad sighs, would cluck the roofs of their mouths positively raw over that one. No thank you.

She headed upstairs, pausing to take a preventive gulp from her now too full wineglass and shifting as much of her weight as she could to the hand that held the banister. Her feet were dying. She had wedged them into a pair of black evening pumps that she hadn't worn for years – a decade or more, she'd guess. In fact, as she glanced down at her right foot arching for the next step, she realized exactly when she had last worn these shoes. It had been almost exactly fourteen years ago, on the Halloween that marked her twentieth birthday. The same night she had stood on top of a table in a divey little jazz club on the Lower

East Side and insisted on doing an impromptu rendition of Cole Porter's 'Love for Sale.' Ajax shuddered and looked down again at her shoes, which suddenly seemed dangerous. She twisted out of them and pushed them aside. Yesterday had been Halloween and her thirty-fourth birthday. The co-incidence was a little too close for comfort. She did not want to put on any wild shows today, not for any-body, least of all the lugubrious crowd downstairs.

'Elray honey, it's Auntie A – HEE-YUK – jax.' Oh damn. Those noisome hiccups. 'Where – HEE-YUK – are you, baby?'

As if the poor little thing could answer even if she wanted to. Wasn't it just like tragedy to throw some totally unnecessary trick in on top of a major act of brutality? It wasn't enough that Elray had lost her parents, but she had to lose her voice too. Now the lost voice would serve as a daily reminder of the lost parents.

The doctors had been so silly, the way they were all baffled by the child's condition. At first they had been convinced it was a side effect of a lesser electrical shock Elray must have suffered at the moment of her parents' electrocution. Enthralled with the miracle of Elray's survival, they had searched eagerly for evidence of exactly how close a call it had been. A blown-out larynx seemed just the thing. But then they had been unable to find any physical or medical evidence to support their theory of electrical shock, or to find any other explanation for why Elray should be unable to speak.

Ajax could tell them where the child's voice had gone. It had been spent in that last ungodly scream, the bloodcurdling yowl that so many witnesses had come forward and testified to hearing, once news of the accident had spread. Some of the witnesses had been a full quarter of a mile away when they heard it. One woman – a favorite with the local TV news – had been at the very top of the Ferris wheel, virtually in the treetops, when the sound reached her. Ajax would never forget the sight of the woman's simple face puckered up in an effort to describe the sound, or the ridiculous words that finally came to her: 'It jes' pickled my innards,' she said. 'Turned 'em to jelly.'

Well, screams like that weren't screams of the voice. They were utterances of the spirit, laments of the soul. Ajax knew that much. When people strayed too close to a line where this world is bounded by some other, they often lost a piece of themselves in the process. Mountain climbers with their frostbitten extremities were a simple, purely physical example of this. Just imagine the hazards to body and spirit of venturing where Elray had been. Elray had traveled to the brink of this world and peered over the edge at the unknowable. She had teetered on that edge as her parents flew past her into some other world; perhaps she had even watched them take some new form. She had stood there, and chances were she had been tempted to follow. But Elray had come back. That she should return speechless was perfectly understandable to Ajax. The child had obviously suffered a form of spiritual frostbite. There was no sense fussing over the lost part. They should just be grateful she had made it back at all.

'Elray honey, bang on the wall or the floor or something. Give me a hint where you're hiding,' Ajax pleaded. She was standing in the big upstairs bathroom, talking to her own reflection over the sink. HEE-YUK! Damn hiccups. They were so undignified. Weren't hiccups also, now that she paused to think about it, potentially fatal? Surely she'd read in some very reliable source that a prolonged case of hiccups could result in death. It was something about every hiccup being a miniature heart attack, on an itty-bitty scale, so that when they just kept coming, one after another for hours and hours, hiccups could stack up to be as lethal as a real heart attack.

HEE-YUK. Oh God. Ajax couldn't afford to die. Not

right now. She leaned over her wineglass and took as big a swig as she could manage upside down and backward from the far side of the rim. Then she straightened up and confronted herself in the mirror again, turning to present a three-quarter profile that minimized her nose and Adam's apple. She drew in her breath, held it, tensed her cheeks and pursed her lips slightly. Not so bad for an old queen in her mid-thirties. She was decent; the bones were still there.

And then, for just an instant, it was Jack who looked back at her in three-quarter profile. Jack, her dear, now dead, baby brother. Jack, who had always had the same features as Ajax, though much prettier and finer, had looked out at her with limpid green eyes that said: 'Elray. Where is she?'

Ajax exhaled with a gasp that was part groan. The wine and the day, with all its thudding sadness, were mixing badly, and she could feel the tears coming. The reflection in the mirror – now a dumpy, true likeness of herself once again – swam in a haze before her, blurring in a way that allowed her to notice for the first time that the surface of the mirror was speckled with dozens of little white flecks. The result of an overly enthusiastic toothbrushing session, no doubt.

As she reached instinctively for the sponge on the counter the little flecks – probably some of the final handiwork of the now deceased Barkley and Jack – seemed inexplicably sad to Ajax, and she surrendered entirely to her tears. There she was, mid-scrub and mid-sob in a swaying wailing dance of grief, when suddenly – as abruptly as if someone had pulled her plug – she stopped. She stopped because she had to. She was in pain. Something fierce, something very sharp had risen from somewhere beneath the house, maybe even from hell, and stabbed her. Slowly she understood that the sharp thing was a sound, and that the sound was a scream. And then, seconds later, she understood something else. This scream had positively pickled her innards. Turned 'em to jelly.

Harwood

Harwood was in the hall closet. He had shut himself in there on purpose, ostensibly to reload his camera. But in fact he was seeking refuge from the sea of sad faces, the buzz of trivial exchanges that had dogged him all day. The entire weekend had droned on in the same way – obligatory introductions followed by obligatory condolences, over and over again, until Harwood had felt himself on the verge of doing something very silly or very rude or very both. After a pit stop at the crudité platter he had walked around with a string bean tucked behind each ear for a while, but even this – and he was sure that at least three people had noticed – had failed to get a rise from anyone. Feeling himself primed to take more drastic action, he had checked himself into the hall closet instead.

How could Barkley have done this to him? That's what Harwood kept asking himself. And who were all these people? Surely not friends of hers, or even of Jack's. Though he had to admit he didn't know his brother-in-law's family that well, they had never seemed exactly conventional or dull, not in the way these people were. One look at Jack's fruitcake brother Ajax would disabuse anyone of that notion.

Harwood had meant to stay only a minute in the closet, just long enough to catch his breath. But it was so lovely and quiet and dark in there, and the almost animal smell of coats and boots had produced in him a bear urge to curl up and hibernate. Layered beneath the smell of leather and fur was a secondary scent, a sporty undertone of mink oil and racquets and aging tennis balls. It had seemed to Harwood, as he closed his eyes to track it better, the lingering essence of happier, more carefree times; if only, he couldn't help thinking, life had proceeded as it should have. He would be bonefishing in Belize right now. He would have finished his assignment for the magazine yesterday, when the tubby country-western singer and his entourage packed it back to Nashville, and today he would have been on his own, free at last to wield the rod and spare the lens. If he closed his eyes, he could almost feel the tug in his palm as some monster hit and ran, hear the zizzing of his reel, smell the salt and the sun and the raw sport of it all.

God, how he longed to be there. Not just because bonefishing was one of the finest ways he could imagine to spend a day, but because if he were there it would mean he wasn't here. Meaning there would have been no need for him to be here, no accident, no emergency call summoning him home. None of all this dark sad mess.

Someone was coming. Harwood froze, uncertain whether he should dive and hide behind the rack of coats, casually exit the closet or simply stay put. He opted for the last, mostly by default, and soon the clatter of approaching high-heel shoes was accompanied by a raspy whisper that he thought he recognized. 'Elray,' it hissed. 'ELLL-RAY!'

It was only Ajax, looking for the child. The fool should just leave the kid alone for a minute. A little while ago, when Ajax had asked Harwood to take charge of Elray, Harwood had looked his niece straight in the eye and asked, 'Would you like to go read a story with me?' and held up one finger. Then, holding up a second, he'd asked, 'Or would you like to go play by yourself?' Elray had immediately held up two fingers and flashed Harwood the biggest – in fact the only –

36

smile he'd seen on her little urchin face since he'd arrived late Friday night. Then she'd made a beeline for the front door. Smart kid. He'd been tempted to follow.

Now Ajax was clunking through the house, obviously in the early stages of a low-grade panic, looking for Elray. Harwood knew he should step out of the closet and put Ajax at ease, but a part of him was hoping that Ajax might come to him instead. A thorough search would mean opening the closet door and looking inside. If that happened Harwood would jump out and yell 'BLAH-HAH-HAH' right in Ajax's face, and then watch to see what effect this had. Maybe Ajax would reward Harwood with something really rich: 'Okay Davey, you beast. Come *out* of the closet.'

Ajax had been making a point of calling Harwood by his Christian name, David – and every diminutive version thereof – instead of using his surname, as the rest of the world did. Probably it was an act of retaliation, launched in response to Harwood's refusal to use feminine pronouns, or the prefix 'Aunt,' when referring to Ajax.

Whatever the reasons, it was a good thing their enforced coexistence could draw to a close as soon as this funeral was over. The tragedy, with all its attendant decisions and arrangements to be made in such short order, had stretched them pretty thin. There had been no time so far for the one thing they might have shared – grief – and their ideas about everything else had proved radically different, to say the least. None of it had been easy, but if Harwood could just make it through today, with all its formalities and guests, there would be only the appointment with the lawyers tomorrow morning, and then he could go home. That meeting would not be pleasant, but at least he and Ajax were in complete agreement, for once, on how it should be handled.

Harwood had thought back again and again in the last few days to that evening, several years ago now, when Barkley had called him and made her request in such a serious voice. Harwood had laughed and quickly agreed. Of course he would take Elray if anything ever happened to Barkley and Jack. It had seemed an easy enough promise to make at the time, but then he had never imagined for an instant that it was one he might have to keep. Not even when Barkley, in that same phone call, had tried to insist that he take some time to consider the responsibility such a pledge carried. Harwood, anxious to hear the customary lightness return to his sister's voice and to move on to more interesting topics, had brushed aside her reservations and assured her she could consider the matter settled.

Ajax must have been similarly shortsighted when the same request came his way, because he had seemed absolutely undone by the prospect of parenthood when he came to pick Harwood up at the airport three days ago. 'I love Elray, I really do,' Ajax had whined, dabbing at his eyes with a white, lipstick-stained handkerchief. 'But me, a MOTHER? It's just not possible.'

It certainly wasn't. And it was equally inappropriate to imagine that Harwood, who was rarely in his New York apartment for longer than three days between out-of-town assignments, could provide adequate child care. Barkley and Jack hadn't thought this one through very logically. But it was too late for them to rethink it now. Harwood and the crazy Ajax would have to do that for them.

Speaking of whom, where had Ajax gone? Harwood had heard him stump upstairs a few minutes ago, but he hadn't come back down yet. Harwood was still in his closet, so all of the guests were milling about on their own, without either 'host' tending to them.

Harwood heaved a great sigh and prepared to exit his hideaway. But as he reached for the doorknob he paused. Another smell was coming to him. It had been nagging gently at him, but now, as he moved toward the door and his feet stirred against something on the closet floor, the smell insisted on itself. It had nothing to do with overcoats steeped in the smoke of autumn leaf fires, or the gymnasium-tinged aroma of sports equipment, or, for that matter, anything you might expect from a closet at all. It was something much more pungent, something highly exotic but tantalizingly familiar. What was it? A fruit or a spice or an aftershave? It was so obvious, Harwood knew he knew it, he could almost name it. It was . . . it was . . . kumquats!

Harwood stood blinking against the shock of the closet light he had just turned on and stared triumphantly toward his feet. Sure enough. There, perched on top of a bulging shopping bag, sat a basket of kumquats. A pink ribbon had been tied around the basket and a little white card wedged into its load of fruit, and even as he reached toward it Harwood felt a double-edged stab of apprehension. Already the grinning face of an eight-year-old Barkley was before him. It was Christmastime, and her cheeks bulged with the kumquats she had loaded into each side. 'I eat 'em whole,' she said as best she could with what was left of her mouth. And then she bit down savagely, gleefully on the fruit.

Harwood extracted the little card from the basket, noticing as he did so that the top kumquats were getting slightly moldy on their undersides, where they came into contact with the fruit below. 'Some kumquats for my favorite kumquat of all. Happy 6 to Elray! Love, Mama.' He read the card and wedged it gently back in place. Of course. It had been October 29, Elray's sixth birthday. Neither he nor Ajax had remembered. Harwood felt something hard and round, something about the size and shape of a kumquat, forming inside his throat. Then, as he bent over to return the basket of fruit to the shopping bag, the blood and heat came rushing to his neck and head as if some internal gasket had blown. The bag was crammed with brightly wrapped gifts, all carefully tagged.

From far far away, as if through the longest of long-distance lenses, Harwood watched his hands reach into the bag and close around the top package – a large trapezoid in gaudy purple and gray paper. He didn't want to touch the package; he sensed that he shouldn't. But he was powerless to stop. He watched his hands ease the package out of the bag, and then, as the last curlicue of ribbon pulled itself free, the alarm went off. It sounded instantly and accusingly, in a piercing blast that seemed almost too fierce, too urgent to be a sound.

Elray

Just when it seemed nothing would ever change, something had climbed onto the side of the runaway train that Elray had become. It was rattling at the windows, banging on the doors, dragging at the wheels. Then came a terrible screeching jolt, and Elray was back in the crawlspace under her house, lying on her side, staring up into the mascara-smeared face of her Auntie Ajax.

Ajax was shaking Elray's shoulders and weeping and calling her name, over and over. The rhythmic pounding of the train had shrunk down and was lodged now inside Elray's chest, where it still beat wildly against the solid ground beneath. The howl of the train whistle came blasting now from Elray's throat. It went ricocheting around the low-ceilinged crawlspace, banging against the stone foundation of the house in a wild relentless scream that Elray could not, for the life of her, silence. Even after other people began gathering in the crawlspace, filing in through the little lattice door, Elray still couldn't stop the scream. Until she saw her Uncle Harwood, standing at the very back, holding one of her birthday presents. And then as suddenly as it had seized her, the scream let her go.

'My birthday present,' Elray said, looking right at her Uncle Harwood. 'That's mine.'

Part Two

The Crawlspace Years

Crawlspace Day

So my story begins itself. Outside the bounds of my own narrative voice, inside the spiraling crescendo of a howl that, on that day almost thirty years ago, seemed larger than life itself. Over the years my bellow was deemed a historic landmark and nicknamed, by those of us who were involved, The Big Scream – because it marked the explosive and violent creation of our new universe. As a result of the events on that first and historic Big Scream afternoon, when I was growing up I always had, in addition to Easter and Christmas and all the big days the whole world shared, my own special holiday, called Crawlspace Day. I celebrated it every year with my Uncle Harwood and my Aunt Ajax, on November 1. The three of us celebrated it together, to mark the day that our lives became entwined.

The fact that Crawlspace Day also marked the date of my parents' burial may make the occasion seem ghoulish to some, and hardly prime holiday material – especially when you consider the nasty way my parents died. But for Harwood and Ajax and me, the holiday, with its name and all its special significance, crystallized in a good way, naturally if fiercely. It was one of those lessons about the way life can turn itself inside out. A battered prize we carried off the battle-field of our bad times.

It was Ajax, I think, who first saw the power of that

day, and understood that the dark cannot and should not be forgotten any more easily than the bright. It was Ajax, at any rate, who decided to throw me a second seventh birthday party, three days after my first and real seventh birthday party, and exactly one year after the day my parents began their forever naps in Montrose Cemetery.

On the morning of that original Crawlspace Day — although none of us called it by that name yet or knew that it would be the first of many — Ajax appeared in my second-floor bedroom wearing faded workman's cover-alls and one of those miner's hard hats that have little flashlights attached to them. It was highly uncharacteristic dress for my Aunt Ajax, who generally stalked life in layers of muted silks, gunboat-sized high heels and a cloud of loud perfume.

'Up an' at 'em, EL-RAY.' When she spoke, Ajax's voice was a surprise too, for she let it scrape the very bottom of her register. Since my Aunt Ajax was really my cross-dressing Uncle Ajax, it was a rumbling bass boom that greeted me.

'Up an' at 'em, kid,' she growled. 'We're going groundhoggin'.' After she had helped me find my blue jeans, a sweatshirt and my beloved black high-tops, Ajax produced a smaller miner's hat and settled it on my head. Then she took me by the hand and led me down the stairs, out the front door and around to the side of the house.

As we approached the hinged section of wooden lattice that gave access to the space below the front porch, I saw that it was propped open, and that the shadowy entrance thus offered was festooned with party streamers. Ajax and I pushed our way past the bright curtain of crepe paper, Ajax stooping awkwardly, and into the musty world that lay below the porch. Before my eyes could adjust to the dark, Ajax had switched on the light on her hat, and then she reached over and switched on mine. From farther ahead, deep in shadows, a third light came alive in answer to the beams of our own, and as we moved toward it I saw that it shone from a hat worn by my Uncle Harwood, who was seated cross-legged on the ground. Before him was a low table set in a festive manner and piled high with presents.

Even now I can remember the peculiar sensation that came over me as I moved toward Harwood, how everything felt mysterious and familiar at once. A thrill was building backward inside me, growing smaller and more condensed as it grew more powerful, until finally it lodged itself in my chest as a specific, physical humming. It was as if I had swallowed something compact and heavy, like a shot-put disk, that despite its weight had a wondrous buoyancy that might carry me upward and diffuse me through the airy skies and heavenly realms above.

'Happy Crawlspace Day!' said Uncle Harwood, inadvertently christening a tradition. Then there was the bang of a champagne bottle uncorking as Ajax let out a whoop and Harwood handed me my first present.

Soon after this my memory of the first official Crawlspace Day explodes into a kaleidoscopic memory of many Crawlspace Days, a mosaic that is itself shot through with bright shining shards of the original day – the day of my parents' burial and The Big Scream – that had brought the tradition into being. Over time I was able to retrieve some pieces of that experience for myself, with gentle prodding from Ajax and Harwood; others were supplied by them, in response to my questions. I dragged every detail out of them about where they were, what they were eating, what they were thinking when they heard my Big Scream. I was fascinated by these fragments. I studied their every detail, rerunning each until I could splice all of the bits together into a narrative that had the grainy texture and jerky play of a newsreel or a historic film clip. Eventually some sections of the afternoon even returned to me with all the subjective throb of vivid personal memory.

Even today I have only to shut my eyes briefly, for instance, and I can be back in that moment on the day of my parents' burial when I looked up in confusion at the crowd that had gathered around me in the crawl-space under our house. My first sensation is one of extreme embarrassment at being the focal point for so many sets of eyes, and my anxiety deepens as I realize that the siren blast ringing in my ears is the high shriek of my own voice. It is pitched in a tone of desperation that is truly ridiculous, not to mention way out of scale for any panic I feel.

As I struggle to close the noise down Ajax, who is kneeling beside me, lifts my shoulders to cradle me in her arms. But the sound refuses to stop. So I stretch a huge grin across my face, as if to signal that everything is really A-OK, and wag my hand from side to side at everybody in the waving style of people who ride the floats in parades. Still the hideous wail comes sailing forth.

It is only when I spot my Uncle Harwood, standing at the back of the crowd near the crawlspace exit, that the scream abruptly, and seemingly of its own accord, ceases. Harwood is holding a colorful package in his hand, and when I see this the same forces that had been squeezing the awful scream out of me take over again as I sit up and reach toward him.

'My birthday present,' I hear myself say, in a voice that I am chagrined to note has an accusatory edge. 'That's mine.'

A loud silence follows. For the three days since the accident I have been mute. Physically unable to speak. But any surprise I myself might feel at the mysterious return of my voice is quickly eclipsed by my Aunt Ajax's decidedly more dramatic response. 'She's speaking!' she screams as she wraps me in a death grip that nearly chokes off my air supply and makes bright spots flash at the edges of my vision. 'She's talking again! Harwood, you ass! Get over here!'

Within minutes Ajax has shooed away all the

48

onlookers, including a Mr Peters who keeps insisting, 'But I'm a doctor. You know, a medical doctor,' and she and I and Harwood are alone in the crawlspace. I have torn open the package Harwood was holding when I spotted him, and am just settling down to attack several more that he has run back and retrieved from the house. The three of us, Ajax, Harwood and myself, sit on the hard, slightly damp dirt floor of the crawlspace while I greedily strip the pretty wrappings off each package, maintaining a nonstop monologue all the while.

'This is Mrs Hedgehog,' I explain, waving a small stuffed hedgehog doll dressed in a checkered apron in their faces. 'I already have Mr Hedgehog. He's a carpenter. He's upstairs.' And then, as I uncover another in the series of French comic books that was my passion: 'Oh, Tin-Tin. He's my favorite. I haven't read this one.'

Occasionally Ajax interrupts me to read the message on a card she has rescued from the wrappings as I carelessly toss them aside. 'This one is from "The Sandman," Elray,' she tells me as I unwrap a pair of blue flannel pajamas that have yellow sharks swimming all over them. 'Who's he?'

'Oh, you know.' And I sing them a bar from the 'Sandman Lullaby' that my mother sang to me every night: "He scatters the sand, with his own little hand, in the eyes of the sleeping chillll-drennnn."'

And so the orgy continues, ending finally when Harwood reappears from one last trip to the house carrying a basket of slightly overdue kumquats and my birthday cake, with all its little candles alight.

For a long time I kept all my presents from that belated sixth birthday party on the afternoon of my Big Scream on a special shelf in my room. I propped the Polaroid of Barkley and Jack and me on our last day together, the one the old woman had taken, beside them. It was not just that the presents represented my last tangible exchange with Barkley and Jack; I also credited them with having somehow cured the awkward muteness that had settled on me after the accident. I came to equate the three days during which I could not speak with the time it must have taken Barkley and Jack to travel from their life here with me to wherever it was they went. It seemed to make perfect sense. Obviously the moment they were no longer in transit they had sent me back my voice, which had followed after them like a lost puppy. And then they had arranged to have my birthday presents delivered.

Gathering String

It was to commemorate the confluence of all these events – the return of my voice, the belated celebration of my sixth birthday, the end of my life with Barkley and Jack and the beginning of my time with Ajax and Harwood – that Crawlspace Day evolved into a yearly tradition in our house. It was to commemorate The Big Scream – the explosive creation of our new universe – that we gathered. Although originally the holiday had the trappings primarily of a second, bonus birthday party for me, it quickly became as much a celebration of my parents, and an investigation into the people they had been. Ajax, Harwood and I would sit in the mote-filled half-light under the porch, eat and drink, open presents and tell every story we could think of about Barkley and Jack.

At first it was Ajax and Harwood who did most of the talking, in response to my questions, and I who listened. In this way I began to compile my own mythology of Barkley and Jack – as children, as adolescents, as young adults and, finally, as my parents. I could recite by heart the story of how a ten-year-old Ajax had once placed an apple on the head of his trusting younger brother, my father Jack, and proposed a game of William Tell. I flinched as I imagined the sudden stab of betrayal that pierced Jack with the head of Ajax's first arrow, which lodged not in the apple on Jack's head but in the ungenerous flesh around his ribs. I could feel the liquid fury that then sent Jack chasing after Ajax with his little George Washington hatchet, plunging like a mad Visigoth through the thickets of Glover Archbold Park for more than three hours.

I knew as if I'd been there myself the various stages of rising panic the young castaways Barkley and Harwood felt as they drifted on a raft of four lashed-together telephone poles they had found bobbing in the shallow surf of Chesapeake Bay. I suffered with them the first tingle of an adventure turning sour as the leeching heat of the summer sun beat down and the shoreline and its familiar landmarks grew irretrievably smaller and smaller. Then came shivers and chills as the sun disappeared, leaving them only darkness and the ice fire of their own sunburns. And finally the rush of their relief, only slightly more intense than that of their shame, as a dim glow of light turned into a Coast Guard boat that had been sent to rescue them.

I read and reread the script of *The Importance of Being Earnest*, paying particular attention to the lines of Algernon and Cecily. 'I don't think that you should tell me that you love me wildly, passionately, devotedly, hopelessly,' I'd say, playing Barkley as Cecily. 'Hopelessly doesn't seem to make much sense, does it?' And then I'd imagine how one night, as she delivered these lines under the unforgiving stage lights of her college theater, she looked up into the face of Jack as Algernon and saw, as if for the first time, the intelligence of his green eyes, the hard line of his jaw, the catlike power implied by the arc of his neck. It was in this play that I also found a clue as to why, in blatant disregard for the little green sign at the end of our block that read 'High View Street,' my parents had referred so often to our 'house on Half-Moon Street.'

Occasionally I found the language and the confidence to contribute my own Barkley and Jack stories to our Crawlspace Day sessions. These were not so much real stories as snapshots – like the one of Jack packing snow into a saucepan and heating it on the stove to get hot shaving water one winter when our pipes had frozen; or the one of Barkley serving socks, dipped in batter and deep-fried, for breakfast one April Fools' Day. Ajax and Harwood seemed to take as much delight in these simple images as I did in their tales, for they asked me about them over and over. All of these scenes, theirs and mine, took on that patina that comes to memories revived time and time again. Each acquired all the formality and symbolism of a medieval tableau; each could be pulled out of storage, dusted off and admired at will.

Over time, after I was sure I had extracted every story Harwood or Ajax or even I could remember about Barkley and Jack, I began using Crawlspace Days as a kind of ongoing archeological dig for anecdotes about other missing family members. (Both Harwood and Ajax, I had discovered, would answer questions in the crawlspace that they dodged above ground.) It was in this way that I first became intrigued with my long-dead Granny Mayhew, my father and Ajax's mother, Amanda Baer Mayhew. Although all my other grand-parents – my Grandpa Mayhew and my mother's mother and father, Grandpa and Granny Harwood – were also dead, they had gone at fairly advanced ages from comparatively common causes: cancer, pneumonia and lupus, respectively. Granny Mayhew had died young and violently. Just like my parents. Ajax and my father had been only twelve and eight when she was snatched from them, the sole and tragic victim of a freak fire that broke out in a local steak house late one New Year's Eve. It seemed to me that Granny's bad luck, like that of my parents, had been of the cruelest and most arbitrary kind. The poor woman had stepped into the ladies' lounge at Blackie's Bar and Grill only moments before a kerosene heater in the lounge malfunctioned and exploded, thereby blowing her to bits and starting a huge fire.

Perhaps it was nothing more than my predictably morbid child's curiosity that caused me to pester Ajax for every detail of this sad event. I begged her to tell the story again and again, and to explain once more how a few of Granny's teeth, badly charred but still identifiable, had been all that remained of my ill-fated relative by the time a cleanup crew could pick its way through the ash and debris that had been Blackie's House of Beef. How Amos Mayhew, Granny's husband and my grandfather, had testified that his last glimpse of his beloved wife had been the shimmery glimmer of her turquoise silk suit as she disappeared toward the ladies' lounge. (He had been standing at the hatcheck at the time, waiting for their coats, and had already asked the doorman to bring their car around so they could head home.) How only moments later a horrible explosion shook the floor beneath his feet, and how smoke then came roiling through the rooms and a steamroller rush of stampeding people came pushing, shoving, dragging him out the door.

Or perhaps I embraced these details of a similar but distant tragedy because they gave a kind of sideways access to my own elusive tragedy. In theory I had witnessed my parents' death. Yet when I tried to summon a memory of the event, all I could find was the formally scripted, third-person mind movie that had played for me in the crawlspace on my Big Scream afternoon. I could not connect to it emotionally. At the mere mention of Granny Mayhew, on the other hand, my eyes filled with tears. I was overcome by a power-ful and sad vision of the scene on the street outside Blackie's on that fateful New Year's Eve so long ago. I watched the panicked crowd of survivors sifting through itself and subdividing into little groups of loved ones, all huddling together, gaping at the raging fire that had nearly claimed them. Then I saw my grandfather – tall and slightly stooped, two coats draped over his arm, his face already settling into the sad and hollow-eyed look that stares out from every photograph of him taken after Granny's death. I watched as he moved impatiently through the crowd, calling 'Amanda? Amanda?' in a voice that was not quite completely bereft of hope. I understood that as they combed the night air his eyes were trying desperately – as they had never tried for anything before – to conjure up a patch of turquoise silk.

Although my Aunt Ajax would usually plod dutifully through this fascinating piece of family lore that I so frequently requested, I felt she had a very bad attitude about Granny's tragic end. 'Bad timing. Stupid, humiliatingly bad timing,' she would mutter. 'Imagine getting blown to bits because of your bladder.' The attitude seemed strangely impatient to me, especially coming from Ajax, who showed such talent as a tender heart.

'She didn't know there was going to be an explosion and a fire,' I would always argue in defense of the grandmother I had never met, perhaps betraying some sensitivity on the topic of freak accidents in general. 'She didn't know it would be fatal to pee at that exact moment.'

'She shouldn't have been out so late, using public bathrooms,' Ajax would snap back, shrugging her shoulders. 'She should have been home with her children instead of pounding down the whiskey at some joint. She was exquisite-looking, I'll give her that. Why, half the world was in love with Mama because of her looks. But her inside was not so pretty. Christ, five out of seven nights you could have found her knocking them back at Blackie's. There or at the track.'

Despite Ajax's obvious disapproval, over time I cultivated a special reverence for this dead grandmother of mine. And then, after one Crawlspace Day when Ajax let it slip that Granny Mayhew had once performed as a dancer, the deal was sealed. Ajax could counter with all the sourball criticism she liked. For me Granny Mayhew had achieved the same exalted status that Barkley and Jack enjoyed. In some ways she almost seemed to be a gift from my dead parents, a vision that had arrived as compensation for their departure. They had sent back my voice, after all, and they had arranged to have my birthday presents delivered. And then they had sent Granny Mayhew to perform as my personal Isadora Duncan — a dazzling figure who pirouetted and cartwheeled across the screen of my imagination in a fabulous turquoise silk suit.

Starting Over

What a struggle our first year together must have been for Ajax and Harwood. It was not just that they had to figure out what to do with me and how to launch themselves on a mission of legal revenge for the grisly deaths of my parents. I now realize that for the two of them the worst of it must have been having to deal with each other.

After my Big Scream on the day of the funeral, Ajax made the hero's leap. She turned her back on her blissfully adult existence, with all its New York City trappings (two-bedroom walk-up in Gramercy Park, part-time dabbling in amateur theater, biweekly bridge gatherings, longtime live-in boyfriend named Virgil), and moved right into our big run-down house in the Cleveland Park section of Washington, D.C. Then she set about the task of mothering me with a vengeance. In retrospect I can recognize that Ajax's enthusiasm and thoroughness were both admirable and touching, and perhaps a necessary part of the almost magical capacity my uncle-cum-aunt had for recasting herself in life. At the time, however, my aunt's style registered as more than a little annoying. Determined to do things exactly right, she acquired every book she could find on parenting and child care and began to work her way systematically through each. Often I would come home from school to find her elbow-deep in paperwork, meticulously mastering all kinds of techniques and information that had little or no application to her situation with me. Upon arriving home one afternoon I found her stretched out on the sofa in the front room, breathing heavily. Rennie, the maid from across the street whom Ajax had recruited as her coach, was kneeling beside her, reading from a manual and chanting, 'Pant, pant, BLOW. That's real good, Miss Ajax. Pant, pant, BLOW.' For the next week the two of them could be found working together at the sofa every afternoon, until finally Ajax felt she had mastered the Lamaze technique of childbirth.

Another time I came home to find that all of the pillows and animals that made my bed my bed had been moved to its unclaimed twin on the far side of the room. 'Rotation time!' Ajax announced to me gaily as I stood looking puzzled, my head swinging back and forth between the two beds. 'You've had the window bed for quite a while, dearie. You'll have a much happier life in the long run if you learn to share with your siblings now.' Because she spent nearly every waking moment of our first few months together buried in one or another of these manuals, Ajax tended to forget about me – the living, breathing reason for her new obsession – and such simple needs as meals and clean laundry. I quickly learned to scavenge for myself in the kitchen. The laundry I didn't care about.

I knew better than to question Ajax herself about such tactics. Instead, I learned to wait until my Uncle Harwood's next visit. It was on one such occasion, I remember, when he had just returned from a photographic shoot in the rain forests of Brazil, that I decided to get to the bottom of the sibling issue. Harwood had arrived laden, as he did from all his trips, with a stash of small presents for me, and we were sitting together in the front room, on the very sofa where Ajax had rehearsed giving birth, admiring my loot. There was a necklace made of porcupine quills and cacao beans and other exotic seedpods, a pair of bookends that looked like ringed slabs of stone but that Harwood explained were really petrified wood, a fist-sized rock that had been split down its middle to reveal the surprise contours of a fossil fish inside and, my personal favorite, a stuffed piranha, its mouth open to reveal its wicked teeth.

'Friday's going to love this guy,' I told Harwood as I placed my finger cautiously between the piranha's jaws. Friday was my pet goldfish who had, like me, miraculously survived the accident that took my parents. A piscine reminder who wiggled his way through our hearts for years. 'I'll share him with Friday. Is Friday my sibling?'

Harwood laughed and said, 'Well, he could be, in a sense I guess, if you'd like. But no, not really.'

'What is a sibling, really?'

'Well, a sibling, really, is a brother or a sister. A human one.'

'Do I have any?' Harwood looked at me strangely then.

'No, Elray. You don't. You are what's called an only child.'

'Then why do I have to share?'

I was by no means unaware of my betrayal as I led Harwood upstairs to show him the elaborate share system that had been imposed on me by Ajax, and I regretted my actions later as I sat on the stair landing listening to the argument that raged between the two of them in the kitchen.

'That's not a lesson in sharing,' Harwood was shouting. 'That's a system of denial, denial of the worst kind — purely wrongheaded, arbitrary, insane. Are you insane, Ajax? I thought you were just a silly old queen, but are you completely, criminally insane?'

'David, please lower your voice and please DO NOT speak to me like that.' I knew Harwood would hate that, being called David. And Ajax was using her most theatrical voice, the one she generally reserved for reading aloud or for imitations of people she disliked.

'It's all very well for you, David. You come blowing

in from some macho trip wrestling anacondas in the jungle, or some week-long hard-on shooting bathing bimbos in Waikiki. You throw your wampum at the child, take a quick look around and tell me everything I'm doing wrong. Then you piss off again. Well, I'm here every day, pally poo. Every day. What do you know about raising children on a day-to-day basis?'

'A lot more than you, it would seem. You haven't even mastered the basics.'

'And what is that supposed to mean?'

'Like nutrition – food. Bread and eggs and bacon. These are Elray's wonder years, you know. Look at this friggin' refrigerator.' I heard the suck and squeak of the refrigerator door swinging open. 'Let's see. What have we got in here? Two gallons of cheap jug wine, a moldy lump of Gorgonzola – mmmm, I'm sure Elray just loves a tidge of Gorgonzola with her nightly quota of rotgut wine. Six cans of baby formula. Baby formula? What the hell is that for? And in the drawer: a basket of putrid kumquats. Kumquats? . . . Oh no. Ajax, tell me these aren't what I think they are.'

'Of course they're what you think they are, David, and they're staying right there. Don't you dare touch them. That's their drawer, in perpetuity.'

Arguments like these were not uncommon between Harwood and Ajax; in fact, they were quite regular that first year when we were all starting over together. But this one seemed to have had a particular effect on Ajax, for in the following months she did indeed turn her focus to nutrition. Diet books and health-oriented cookbooks began to supplant child care books in the daily barrage of mail-order packages that arrived at our house. The refrigerator, formerly an object of such ridicule with Harwood, now bulged with tofu, wheat germ, buttermilk and bricklike loaves of whole-grain breads. From the not-quite-shut mouths of its jam-packed drawers the wild leafy tops of strange tubers came creeping out, and lining the racks along the door were jars of fresh-squeezed vegetable and fruit juices, most of them in the murky orange and squash colors of Gauguin's palette.

The pursuit of proper nutrition launched Ajax on a secondary obsession, gardening, and by spring the only level section in our jungle of a backyard had been tilled and planted in neat rows. The fact that the empty seed packets at the end of each row promised a harvest of vegetables most of whose shapes I didn't recognize and whose names I couldn't pronounce in no way diminished my primal thrill at the triumph of tiny green shoots pushing up through the black earth. I developed a new admiration for my aunt, the visionary who had wrought this magic.

In the heat of her horticultural fever, Ajax also planted dozens of flower beds along the sides and front of the house, the effects of which could be measured satisfyingly as passersby out for their Sunday stroll began to slow down and cast long, curious looks at our formerly scruffy yard. 'Silly goggle-eyed newts,' Ajax would snort as we sipped lemonade and watched them from the front porch. 'You'd think they'd never seen a creeping fig in bloom before.'

I remember it was at some point during this period that Ajax's reading on the care and feeding of plants and the care and feeding of children became entangled. When she stood me in the bathtub to trim the lank locks that spilled in a dozen different directions from the seven cowlicks that swirled on my head, she spoke of the benefits of regular pruning. When a pair of pants or a T-shirt seemed to grab me a little too tightly, she'd cluck her tongue and say, 'You need repotting.'

The extremes to which Ajax's mental fluidity sometimes took her were exhibited in the worst of these horticultural and nutritional mix-ups, a cross-pollination of theories that inspired her to make me drink the water from vases after their bouquets had headed south — 'recycling the essential elixirs of

61

nature in full bloom,' she called it. Fortunately our flowers were all homegrown, rather than commercial cut flowers, which might have been treated with chemical boosters, so Ajax's potions, though putrid and swamplike, were relatively harmless. I think.

'It's ready, dearie. Drink.' Auntie A would stop me in the shadows on the stair landing and hold up a green glass vase that had recently showcased tulips, or a tall white porcelain pitcher that had held branches of lilacs. Always, when she pressed the vessel to my lips, it was awkward, and often, between us, we misjudged and the liquid would come spilling down my chin and neck, leaving guilty wet blotches on my shirt. Then Ajax would cluck and dab. 'Precious juice for precious girl,' she'd mutter. 'Mustn't waste a drop.'

I put up with this unpleasant ritual in part, I think, because I was a naturally polite child, but also because, on the off chance that Ajax was actually on to something, I didn't want to miss my shot at immortality and perfection. Later, after rinsing my mouth to purge the foul aftertaste of floral bilge, I would retreat to the privacy of my room and stare at myself in the mirror over my dresser, watching for the stirrings of new and wondrous powers. Of course, I never saw anything much, although once, after sampling the distillation of several dozen irises, my pupils grew huge and black like bullet holes and my head felt breezy, as if it might be floating at the top of a long stem.

The House on Half-Moon Street

During that first year following my parents' death my Uncle Harwood's visits, originally intended as monthly check-ins, had been growing longer and more frequent. The front bedroom he had staked out as temporary headquarters slowly accumulated more and more Harwood flotsam – an exotic jumble of camera equipment, outdoor gear, magazines and scraps of correspondence that I found irresistible. Every time Harwood took off on another trip I felt an edge of happy anticipation on the flip side of my sadness. I knew that as soon as his taxi disappeared around the corner of our street, I would run upstairs and let myself into his room, where, with the reverence and care of an archeologist on a breakthrough dig, I would sift through the surface debris, admiring all the old familiars and mentally cataloguing anything new.

Harwood always complained about the time he was having to spend in D.C., of course, and made a point of blaming it on some newly discovered aspect of Auntie A's incompetence. I will never forget the day he discovered Ajax feeding me one of her floral potions, because it triggered one of his most vehement and, as it turned out, most significant fits.

'Jesus, Ajax! Are you mad?' he screamed. Ajax and I were standing at the far end of the second-floor hallway and Ajax was administering a vase of dead roses when Harwood stepped unexpectedly from his room.

He grabbed Ajax by her peach-colored cardigan and pushed her toward the wall. 'STOP THAT IMMEDIATELY!'

Then Harwood dropped Ajax and whirled toward me with equal intensity. 'SPIT THAT OUT, ELRAY! OUT!'

I had already swallowed my tiny sip of rose juice, but I tried to spit anyway. A sad web of saliva hit the hall floor.

'Oh God.' Harwood groaned and began to pound me on the back. 'Don't worry, sweetie, it's going to be all right. YOU!' He glared at Ajax, who was rearranging herself haughtily in the hall mirror and examining the red marks around her neck. 'You idiot.'

'Beassst!' she hissed back at him as he steered me past her and downstairs to the kitchen, where he forced me to drink a mustard-water concoction that was far worse and caused me more discomfort than anything Ajax had ever fed me.

'Good girl. Get rid of it all.' Harwood was holding me over the kitchen sink and patting me on the back as I retched. 'Next time Ajax tries that trick you just let me know, okay?'

I nodded my assent between gags, although I had no intention of obeying. Not if it meant more mustard water. 'But what . . .' I paused and gagged feebly for dramatic effect. 'What if you're not here?'

Harwood's face was right against mine as I said this, and I had to back away quickly because of the way his nostrils and lips flared. I thought he must be getting ready to puke too.

'Elray,' he said. 'I will be here. Whenever I can be, I will be here.'

A week after the incident with the rose water, Harwood sublet his New York apartment and officially moved in with Ajax and me. Because my uncle had been called away on assignment at the last minute, Ajax had to oversee the movers as they carried all his possessions from the van to the house. What a field day she had.

'Oh my. More African fertility totems?' Ajax vamped coyly past one of the movers as he dumped yet another life-sized sculpture in our living room. 'Harwood, you rogue.' She spun around the sculpture as if they were dancing and it had twirled her. 'I never would have guessed.'

Sculpture, books and darkroom equipment – those were Harwood's contributions to our house on Half-Moon Street. My Auntie Ajax had already imported some of her own prized possessions, which could be politely described as belonging to the diaphanous/eclectic school of decor. She had brought in bolts of rich fabrics that she festooned around the windows, and even along the back and down the legs of one hall table. Her collection of small boxes (lacquer, crystal, pewter), Canton china and alabaster fruit lay scattered casually through our downstairs rooms, where it looked as if a very lazy Easter Bunny had been forced to work inside on a rainy Easter day. In positions of power over the sideboard in the dining room and above the fireplace in the living room she had hung two faded tapestries – one of two male angels recumbent on a cloud luxuriating over a feast, the other of an armor-clad knight riding off to battle with a pack of hounds in tow.

Although it may be difficult to imagine, the layering of Harwood's and Ajax's possessions atop those left behind by my parents did not add up to interior design disaster. My parents' theory of home decor had been sheerly functional – they had furnished our house with a few necessary items, such as beds and chairs, and filled the remaining space with stray furniture they inherited and were too lazy to figure out whether they really needed or wanted. Both Harwood and Ajax seemed to have collected only unnecessary items, and from opposite ends of the taste spectrum. The final effect was odd but composed. There was a balance, even an offbeat elegance, to the three households combined that would have been lacking in any one of them alone.

As it turned out, the sculptures that Harwood had brought with him were his own work. They were all life-sized human figures, slightly abstract but definitely human, in a variety of upright and seated postures. Often they had an arm or a leg akimbo. Ajax and I had fun, when they first arrived, arranging them in different configurations in the living room and library, and their effect was quite convivial – as if an around-the-clock cocktail party was taking place in our home. At first Harwood muttered vague disapproval of this playful display of his work, but eventually he dropped the subject and the sculptures became permanent party guests.

During the first month or two following his official 'arrival,' Harwood was a whirlwind of activity. By the end of this period he had transformed our basement into his own domain, just as Ajax had established the grounds surrounding our house as hers. Harwood began by carefully clearing away the now dormant laboratory where my father, a compulsive tinkerer and amateur inventor, had worked on all his peculiar projects. My uncle and I spent a few days together admiring and testing all Jack's devices before labeling them and stowing them away in a far corner. (My personal favorite will always be the miniature but lethal electric guillotine my father designed to behead his cigars, a finger-sized contraption replete with a gruesome blood-red paint job and a little red Christmas bulb that lit up when the blade made contact with the base.) With my father's laboratory respectfully dismantled and archived, Harwood set about reorganizing the emptied space to accommodate his own obsessions. At the end of the basement where there were no windows, he set up his darkroom, with all its tongs and trays and bottles of potent-smelling fluids. I loved standing beside him as he worked there in the eerie glow of the safety lights, and for me life held few greater thrills than those magic moments over the developing tray when a faint shadow first appeared on blank paper and then, with the clarity and speed and force of speech, announced itself as a distinct image. (Oh most mysterious threshold between invisible and visible!)

At the other end of the basement, where big windows looked out onto the backyard and Ajax's vegetable kingdom, Harwood set up his sculpture studio. Ajax had stubbornly refused to move the washer and dryer that occupied one corner in this light-filled end of the basement, and over the next months I watched with delight as a series of worker-women sculptures, featuring a burly figure not unlike Ajax in a variety of laundry- and garden-related duties, took shape. This time it was Ajax who clucked with disapproval when Harwood and I decided the new sculptures made a poignant subgroup of worker-guests in the eternal party upstairs. But in the end I think she was secretly pleased by her clones. To me, all of Harwood's sculptures helped fill our house with life. They caulked the joints and seams as we bonded as a new family. Sometimes late at night, when Ajax and Harwood were asleep, I would sneak down and sit on the stairs halfway between the first and second floors. I could swear that rising to me from the pitch dark below came the soft murmur of voices and the festive clinking of ice swimming against glass. The good times were gathering. We were beating down the sadness. I could feel it.

Hansueli

I was never sure by whom or why the decision was made, but not long after Harwood moved in I found myself scheduled for regular appointments with a Dr Hansueli Mueller. At first I was perplexed by our strangely calm and polite sessions. Every Tuesday and Friday afternoon Ajax would drop me off outside the bland oatmeal-colored apartment building where I would let myself in the glass doors and take the elevator up to Dr Mueller's narrow little waiting room and its uncomfortably straight-backed chairs. After a few minutes one of two doors would open and Dr Mueller, who must have been at least seven and a half feet tall, would stoop over and stick his head through.

'Hell-oh Elray,' he would say. 'Kom on in, vy don't chu.' (Cliché-ridden as it now seems, the psychiatrist I was sent to back then was in fact Swiss.) Hansueli, as he insisted I call him, would then motion me toward a wingback chair on one side of his office. I always settled myself there as quickly as possible so that I could enjoy the show as this flamingo of a man folded himself into his own wingback chair on the far side of the room. He would begin his long descent and his head would sink down down down as his knees rose up up up until the latter finally came to rest just below his eyes. His face, perched there atop the big inverted V of his stick legs, looked birdlike too – dominated by a beak of a nose with round eyes set close by on either

68

side and topped by a thatch of sandy hair that sprang up like head feathers.

'So. How are your onkles zis veek?'

The first time Hansueli asked me this I thought he was asking after my ankles, and I stared at my feet in confusion before answering, 'They're fine. Fine.'

'So. You are all dare togedder now. You, und Onkle Ajax und Onkle Harvood. Is zat fun times?'

Oh. *Uncles*. 'Mmm-hmmm. Yes. Fun times. AUNT Ajax gardens. Uncle Harwood makes pictures and sculptures. Sometimes I help.'

'Oh. *Aunt* Ajax. Dat's nice.'

After a few conversations like this, I began to feel very sorry for Hansueli, who obviously had so little going on in his own life that all he could do was ask silly questions about mine. Here was a man in dire need. He needed someone to help him discover talents of his own, to help him strike out and forge a new life. After a little probing I learned that Hansueli spoke five languages – German, French, Spanish, English and Russian – which seemed like something of a talent to me, and I decided to focus on it. I insisted that we conduct our sessions in French and Spanish, scheming that this would give Hansueli a boost of confidence and keep me from dying of boredom.

As it happened I was right. Soon we were chattering away in basic French and Spanish, and my desire to learn new vocabulary seemed to increase the range of topics we tackled. I actually began to look forward to our appointments, and Hansueli seemed happier too. He took to fixing little meals – usually a bowl of hot soup and a bottle of cold Coca-Cola – for us to eat while we talked and laughed our way through an hour that seemed to be getting shorter and shorter as the weeks went by. I learned that Hansueli had a beautiful Spanish wife and a little eight-month-old baby. His passion was sailing, and when he had worked in Spain, where he and his wife met, they had lived on the coast. Almost every afternoon he would leave work early and they would sail to some nearby cove or island where they would drop anchor and enjoy a picnic supper of bread and cheese and wine.

It sounded like a pretty good life, and I could not understand why Hansueli would have left it to come work in the oatmeal-colored apartment building in Washington, D.C. But I never pressed him on this, sensing that only something ugly or tragic could have precipitated such an undesirable move.

Hansueli, I could tell, exercised a similar restraint whenever he touched on the circumstances of my parents' death. He approached the subject regularly but always briefly, hovering over it with the delicacy of a hummingbird before darting off again. I was sympathetic to his curiosity — I was, after all, very curious myself — and I wanted to assure him that I did not feel tender on the topic, only ignorant. I had had the story of Barkley and Jack's electrocution explained to me, and I thought I now understood the mechanics of how the neon moon had dropped through my arms into the bottom of our leaky boat and then sent deadly shocks up through their legs. I understood this, and that I had been spared. But I didn't remember the incident, not in the ordinary way you remember things. I had the mind movie of our last day together. And then there were only the after facts. Barkley and Jack were definitely gone. And there, on the underside of my right arm anytime I cared to turn it over and look, was the pinkish crescent moon-shaped brand left by the passing touch of its neon counterpart.

'Zat's your burn from dee accident?' Hansueli asked about the scar once when he noticed me rubbing it. He always gave himself away when he was straying into territory where he felt awkward, because he slipped into English, his least fluent language as it turned out. 'What do you think of when you see it?'

'*Rien. Les couleurs, les bruits,*' I answered in French, knowing that I would not find words in that or any language to tell him the truth. That sometimes, like

70

right then, when I ran my fingers along the moon-shaped welt on my underarm, Barkley and Jack spoke to me, sent me messages.

HE SEEMS LIKE A NICE MAN. Barkley was talking. BE POLITE, CRUMPET. ASK HIM ABOUT HIS BABY. ASK IF THE BABY IS WALKING YET.

'*Marcos, pequeño Marcos? Está caminando ahora?*' I found myself using Spanish to ask after Hansueli's son Mark, perhaps because I knew that this was the language he and his wife used in the privacy of their home.

'*Ah sí, sí, sí!*' A big smile washed away the worried look on Hansueli's bird face. '*J'ai voulu te dire toutle de suite, mais je l'ai oublié. Ce matin il a pris ses premiers marches!* How did you guess?'

I touched my scar once more and smiled. BOY OH BABY BOY OH BOY. Barkley was laughing. BET THAT'S A CUTE SIGHT, DON'T YOU?

Rena

The first time Rena Guilfoyle came to our house Ajax mistook her for the Avon lady and slammed the door in her face.

'Not today you don't! No siree, sir. No suckers here today!' Ajax barked at Rena through the slammed door, and stomped back to the kitchen, where she was cooking up a big pot of sorrel soup. From my post on the sofa in the front room I could hear Ajax simmering in the kitchen – 'The nerve of that woman, THE NERVE!' she kept repeating – and if I tilted my head back slightly, I could also see Rena as she pulled a little slip of paper from her purse, studied it, studied our front door, shrugged and knocked again.

'It's not that Avon woman,' I called out to Ajax, after looking our visitor over carefully. 'This one's taller, and funnier-looking. And she's not carrying any suitcases.'

In fact, Rena did bear some resemblance to the woman who, about three weeks earlier, had held Ajax spellbound for hours while she explained the wondrous contents of an army of little jars and boxes that she pulled out and spread across our living room floor. Ajax – amazed, convinced and grateful for the opportunity – had bought one of almost everything, at considerable expense, I gathered from her later grumblings. That same evening, when Ajax secluded herself in the bathroom for the inaugural application

72

of a series of miracle creams that promised to restore a twenty-year-old's translucence to her skin, she opened one magic pot after another only to find that every one was entirely empty except for a small folded scrap of paper in each that bore the same message scrawled in a tiny pinched hand: 'Ha Ha Ha. VANITY THY NAME IS FOOL.'

After her initial storm of outrage had subsided, and after the Avon agency had explained that yes they had heard similar reports and even had suspicions about a disgruntled former employee but really they could not be held responsible for every bootlegging con artist in the world, Ajax decided to adopt what the two of us privately referred to as a 'Lady Fustian' on the whole incident. *Lady Fustian's Rules for Young Girls* had been one of the essential primers Ajax had latched onto in her first exuberant months of parenting. In Lesson Five of *Lady Fustian*, in a chapter entitled 'Qui S'Explique S'Accuse,' Daisy, the young star of all twelve lessons, finds herself in a predicament while strolling down a seaside boardwalk with friends. The fact is, she feels her underwear slipping off. Slowly, inch by inch, it is sliding down her legs. But Daisy, the essence of etiquette, strolls coolly on until her lacy bloomers reach her ankles and finally drop to the ground.

This Fustian dilemma was one of our favorites and Ajax always slammed the book temporarily closed over one hand at this point and shouted her question at me with great intensity: 'AND WHAT, YOUNG LADY, WHAT DOES A WELL-BRED GIRL THEN DO?'

'SHE WALKS PROUDLY ON!' I would shout back triumphantly. 'WITHOUT A DOWNWARD OR A BACKWARD GLANCE!' And then we would open the book again and turn the page to admire the big color-plate illustration that showed Daisy, in her long high-collared hooped dress, strolling nonchalantly down the boardwalk. Her head was held high, she had a friend on each arm, and about six feet behind her lay the lacy, already anonymous panties.

So this was the kind of 'Lady Fustian' that Ajax decided to take on the Avon incident – treating it as too tawdry an affair to acknowledge – which is probably a lucky thing for Rena, who might otherwise have had a fist instead of a door in her face on that first day she came to visit.

'It's really not her,' I shouted again to Ajax on that day. 'The Avon lady had a scooped-out dish face like a pony; this one has a pointy chin and a pointy nose.'

Ajax appeared from the kitchen carrying a big spoon that was dripping sorrel soup. 'Are you sure?' She peered through the window at Rena, checked her watch and then gasped. 'Oh Mother of Mary. Oh shit!' She rushed to the front door and threw it open.

'Miss Guilfoyle? My deepest apologies. I mistook you for a merchandizing whore. Do come in.'

Rena nodded politely and stepped inside, ducking slightly as though used to bumping her head.

'Not to worry. 'S quite understandable, really. I've had my whorish moments. But, as you yourself said, "Not today." Is that sorrel soup you're dripping? How lovely!'

Whether it was because Rena spoke with the remnants of an Irish brogue – an accent Ajax always described as 'shivering with literary nuance' – or because Ajax was trying to compensate for her rude behavior earlier I'll never know. But my usually crusty aunt took to Rena Guilfoyle more immediately and more emphatically than I have ever seen her take to anyone else, before or since. Within five minutes of Rena's arrival – or, I should say, of her welcome – she was seated at the dining room table with Ajax and me, slurping appreciatively over a bowl of sorrel soup. Ajax had uncorked a 'quiet little chardonnay' that she'd had on reserve in the back recesses of the icebox, and an almost reunion-like mood had taken over.

Rena, as it turned out, was a lawyer with Morris and Montague, the company Ajax and Harwood had chosen to handle the liability suit we were pressing

74

against the amusement park where Barkley and Jack had been killed. Already we had run through five or six attorneys from this company, all of whom had been rejected by Ajax because of 'unforgivable frailties' that ranged from 'chinlessness' to 'soullessness.' Finally, in a moment of exasperation, the senior partner overseeing the case had presented Ajax with what he called a 'pig book' that listed and pictured all the attorneys employed at the firm, and had suggested that she make her own choice. Her choice had been Rena Guilfoyle, who, according to the pig book blurb, 'had joined the company recently after a brilliant and highly publicized career in Dublin, where she triumphed as prosecutor in the famous Finlay case, involving a series of fatal poisonings executed by an internationally renowned chef.'

The fact that Rena's pig book bio read more like an Off-Broadway theater blurb than a summation of legal talents surely appealed to Ajax. And then, of course, the thirty-year-old Rena's looks were pretty dramatic too. She was very tall (almost six feet) and big-boned, but very narrow and tightly knit at the same time – a combination that gave her an almost frightening aura of barely contained power. Her hair was long and dark, and fell across the angular geometry of her high brow and cheekbones conspiratorially, like a half-drawn curtain. This perpetually furtive, secretive look was intensified by the darkness of her eyes and eyebrows, which were wide-set in a level horizontal line that accentuated the failed symmetry of the vertical line her nose and mouth should have composed – but did not.

I spent a lot of time analyzing Rena's looks in this way after first meeting her because Rena, like just about everything else in our house, became a source of fierce contention between Ajax and Harwood. By the end of our impromptu sorrel soup luncheon, Ajax had fallen into a deep swoon over Rena. The meal had started with the two of them exchanging measured, somewhat formal compliments, but by the time Ajax came pirouetting from our kitchen with a dessert of raspberry fool held on high, they had advanced to the squealing, rapid-fire rapport of eighth-grade bosom buddies. Rena's stint as prosecutor in the case against the poison-happy Irish chef had introduced her to some very arcane cooking techniques, which even Ajax, despite all her study of nutrition and herbal remedies, had not yet come across. The two were swapping some rather sinister recipes, and joking about the good use they could put them to, when I finally excused myself from the table and disappeared upstairs.

That evening when Ajax announced to Harwood that she had hired another lawyer to handle our case, she described Rena as 'physically, intellectually and emotionally the quintessential perfect woman.'

'Picasso-face' was how Harwood chose to describe Rena, after he finally met her, and this was the nicest thing he had to say about her. When I asked him to explain his nickname, he pulled down volume two of Brenner's *History of Art* and showed me how the women in Picasso's *Les Demoiselles d'Avignon* had sideways noses and asymmetrical eyes. It was true. They did look a lot like Rena when Rena got to talking too fast.

'Rather be Picasso-face than a Soutine-face, like that sorry little parboiled thing you brought home the other night.' Ajax always defended Rena against Harwood's slurs, and once, I remember, she hit back with this comment on an overnight guest of Harwood's whom I was not supposed to know about. Of course, I did know about the 'parboiled thing' – she was a waitress, I think, because I found a little black triangular apron with white scalloped edges in Harwood's room later that week. I knew about her, and I knew about all the others too. But I pulled my best elsewhere look when Ajax's indiscretion caused Harwood to stare first at me and then at her. 'You may have a point' was all he said, but from that day on Harwood dropped the Picasso nickname and instead referred to Rena as 'Spider Woman' or 'Can-Opener Nose' or 'Bossy Boots.'

I remained undecided as to whether Rena's looks fell on the scary or the beautiful side of exotic, but I welcomed what quickly became her regular visits because, unlike the legal colleagues who had preceded her, she lavished quite a bit of attention on me. The others had always met privately with Ajax and Harwood, either in our upstairs study or downtown at their offices. Occasionally they would call me in and sit me down for a few minutes and ask, in patronizing baby voices that I found insulting, stupid questions like 'Do you remember your mommy and daddy, sweetie?' or 'You miss Mommy and Daddy, don't you?'

Barkley and Jack also found these sessions annoying, and if I kept my fingers lightly on my scar, they would regale me with such rude comments about my inquisitors that I would get the giggles and be unable to respond to questions.

OOH! THIS GUY SMELLS LIKE MONKEYS IN THE ZOO! GET 'IM OUTTA HERE! Jack screamed one day when a balding lawyer named Mr Kramer was questioning me earnestly. 'Monkeys in the Zoo' had been Jack's name for the insidious stink that developed when we forgot to empty the pan that attached to the underside of our refrigerator to catch condensation as well as stray drippings from leaky foods.

TELL HER TO GO POUND SAND IN HER BLOOMERS Barkley whispered to me when a sinewy blonde named Astrid made puppy-sad eyes at me and asked if I'd had any scary dreams lately.

But Rena was different. She had a style all her own. 'This little innocent holds all the keys, all the answers,' she announced to Ajax and Harwood in our first official meeting together after she had been hired. She had me stand in the center of our living room and, resting one of her long-fingered hands on my head, spun me around like a toy doll.

'This little girl is our map to buried treasure. We're going to look to you for clues, Elray, and we're going to dig dig dig until we find our treasure. If we have to dig from here to China, we'll get there. Right, Elray?'

I looked at Rena hesitantly, and touched my scar.

HMMM. SHE CERTAINLY KNOWS HER GEOGRAPHY. Barkley was intrigued, I could tell. I wondered if she, like me, was thinking back to the afternoon when I set about digging a big hole in our front yard in an effort to test the assertion that if you blasted straight through the earth you'd come out in China. I wondered if she also, like me, had glanced inadvertently across the room just now at our National Geographic globe, which still bore the scars of another experiment in which I hammered the tip of a barbecue skewer in at Washington, D.C., and out again in Upper Mongolia.

THIS COULD BE INTERESTING was all Barkley said. GO AHEAD. LET'S SEE WHAT COMES NEXT.

'Right.' I nodded to Rena. 'We'll dig and dig. To China if we have to.'

'Brrrrrrilliant!' Rena sounded like an Irish Tony the Tiger, and as she sprang across the living room and began to rearrange our furniture she looked a little like one too. 'Okay, let's have at it. Where shall we start? I always say at the heart of the matter, *in medias res*, is best. How about we start at Glen Echo, in the Tunnel of Love.'

Rena had dragged a love seat to center stage. 'This can be your boat,' she said with a flourish that actually reminded me of the little monkey man in the Tunnel of Love in my mind movie. 'And this . . .' Her words came in strained gasps as she dragged first one and then another of Harwood's seated sculptures over and positioned them on the love seat. 'This . . . can be . . . phew . . . Barkley. And this . . . can . . . oof . . . be Jack.'

Harwood, who had stood up as if about to say

78

something when Rena first started dragging furniture around, finally sprang into action here. 'No way!' he announced. 'You ARE NOT going to do this. Are you mad? Come on, Elray, let's get out of here.' He'd stretched his hand out behind his back, reaching in the direction where I had been only a few moments ago, just before he began to speak.

But I was already gone, listening to Jack and moving across the room to take my place on the love seat between the two statues. HEY, THIS RENA REALLY IS WILD. Jack was laughing. PLAY ALONG FOR A WHILE. HAVE SOME FUN.

'Actually, THIS is Jack,' I said as I sat down, pointing to the sculpture on my right whom Rena had misdubbed Barkley. 'And THIS is Barkley.' I pointed to the sculpture on my left. 'And we need a backseat, for Friday to ride in.'

'Friday?' asked Rena.

'Friday, yes, Friday her goldfish,' answered Ajax, who was already halfway out the door on her way to get the fabulous Friday himself.

'I don't believe this. I simply can't believe this,' Harwood stood muttering to himself as Ajax returned with Friday and placed him on the ottoman that Rena had set up as a backseat for the boat. 'I won't stay and watch this. I won't.'

'Bye-bye, Davey,' Ajax called to him sweetly as he headed for the door.

'Yes. Bye-bye, Davey dear,' Rena echoed wickedly.

'Oh. Uncle Harwood.' I called after him too, because Barkley had sent me a message to deliver. He stopped and turned to me expectantly. 'Barkley says: TAKE IT EASY, HAR-HAR. DON'T GET YOUR KNICKERS IN A TWIST.'

Harwood's face sucked in on itself when I said this, as if someone had opened a valve at the back of his head to deflate it. I felt bad. I had meant to cheer him up with a little word from Barkley, and I was sure she had meant it to be teasing.

'Only a story, only a story,' I said quickly, using the

password Harwood always used to reassure me when, in the midst of one of the long tales of adventure he spun so well, it sometimes happened that I began to take things a little too seriously and to get upset. 'Only a story,' I said once more, and it seemed to take effect this time, because his face filled out again and he came back into the room and sat down.

'Barkley would say that, wouldn't she.' He said this to me quietly, intensely. He looked like a little boy.

'Yes.' I smiled at him. 'She would. She did. Just now.'

Postcards from Afar

In this way it came to pass that, in our first session with Rena, I confessed to the very thing that I had promised myself I would never tell anyone. That Barkley and Jack seemed to be hanging around, ready to talk to me from time to time. I don't know why exactly I had been so determined to keep this a secret, because what I discovered after Rena and Ajax came swooping across the room and pried the information out of me was that it really didn't matter whether or not anyone else knew about it. It was what it was because it was there for me. Rena and Ajax wanted to believe me, I think, or they at least wanted me to believe that they believed me. But the experience wasn't theirs. It had nothing to do with them. It wouldn't touch them, and they couldn't touch it.

What did happen once the scar-conduit cat was out of the bag, so to speak, was that they – Barkley and Jack – started to talk to me a lot more. The three of us started to have a lot of fun during Rena's sessions, just as Jack had hoped we would. As I have mentioned, I had no real memory of the accident, just the mind movie of the events that led up to it, which was rather stylized and more like a documentary I could watch if I chose to than like a memory itself. During the re-enactments that Rena organized we would always eventually make our way to the moment of the accident itself, at which point Rena would ask: 'And then what, my darling? What else can you – or can your parents – remember?'

I had no memories to share with Rena, but if I rested my fingers along my scar I sometimes got messages. Many of them were utter nonsense, juvenile concoctions designed to ram the outrage button as fiercely as possible. But I would pucker my brow and turn to Ajax and Rena and repeat, verbatim, whatever had been dictated to me by one or the other of my parents.

'IT WAS AWFUL,' I would recite. 'EYEBALLS POPPED OUT AND FINGERNAILS FLEW OFF AND HOT BLOOD CAME SQUIRTING FROM EARS.'

Or: 'YES, A SHAFT OF BLINDING WHITE LIGHT DESCENDED FROM ABOVE AND WHIRLED AROUND MAMA AND DADDY LIKE A VEG-O-PEELER. IT CUT THEM INTO LONG COILED RIBBONS AND THEN THE RIBBONS SLID UP TO HEAVEN LIKE SNAKES.'

Sometimes, however, my parents spoke more solemnly. Then their voices took on a different quality, and their words came rumbling like distant thunder through my arm, stacking sentence upon sentence into the urgent monologues that I will never forget. Monologues that haunt me still.

LOSING YOU WAS WORSE THAN THE LOSING OF OURSELVES, Barkley told me. AH, THE RIPPING TEARING SEARING PAIN OF YOU SLIPPING, IN ONE SECOND AND AFTER YEARS OF CAREFUL AND TENDER EMBRACE, RIGHT THROUGH OUR FINGERS. I KEPT LOOKING FOR YOU, MY ONLY BABY GIRL THAT I HAD LOVED AND SQUEEZED AND LOOKED UPON EACH DAY WITH HEART-SWELLING WONDER, MY MIRACLE OF FRESHNESS IN THIS PLODDING THING CALLED LIFE.

The emotion packed into my parents' pronouncements sometimes made me uneasy, but I was gripped by a morbid curiosity about the physical sensations the two of them had experienced during the accident and in the world where they were now lodged. I listened carefully to these more serious messages, and committed their words to memory. Later I reviewed their language and scanned it line by line for tidbits.

WE DROPPED FOREVER THROUGH A TERRIBLE EAR-ROARING

HEAT BEFORE WE FINALLY LEVELED OFF, GENTLY AND LOGICALLY, LIKE BIG HOT-AIR BALLOONS WHEN THE BALLAST GOES OVERBOARD, Barkley told me. I COULDN'T BELIEVE I WOULDN'T BE ALLOWED TO DROP OUT OF MYSELF FURTHER, THE PAIN — NOW NOISELESS — WAS STILL SO HOT AND SO GREAT, THAT SAME RIPPING SEARING TEARING PAIN OF LOSING YOU.

I FLOATED FOR THREE DAYS, CONSUMED IN A VACUUM-PACKED PYRE OF DRY-BONED HEARTACHE. I THOUGHT THAT WAS ALL THERE WOULD EVER BE. BUT THEN I HEARD A SCENT — A SWEET AND PUNGENT SCENT — COME SHOUTING OVER-HEAD LIKE TRUMPET BLASTS. BEFORE I COULD NAME THE SCENT, A SOUND TOUCHED ME. IT WAS THE UNMISTAKABLE SHUFFLE OF FOOTSTEPS BRUSHING ACROSS MY FACE. I FELT THE FAT BITTER BLOSSOM OF DIRT SMOLDERING IN MY MOUTH, AND I REALIZED THAT IT WAS THE FAMILIAR AND EXOTIC SHOUT OF KUMQUATS THAT HAD FILLED THE AIR LIKE A TRUMPET SERENADE. I HOWLED WITH HAPPINESS THEN FOR I KNEW THAT I HAD FOUND YOU. OR AT LEAST I HAD FOUND THE MOMENT WHERE YOU, MY ELRAY, WERE STILL ALIVE AND MOVING OXYGEN.

When I heard this I understood that Barkley had first been reunited with me under the crawlspace, on the day of her own funeral, on the very afternoon of The Big Scream. It seemed that she hadn't just sent my voice back, she had delivered it personally.

When Jack said, DO YOU HAVE ANY IDEA WHAT A BITCH IT WAS WIRING THIS CONNECTION? I understood that my father, the compulsive tinkerer, had brainstormed the mechanics of our communication system. EVERY CIRCUIT WAS SCRAMBLED, he complained. FOR A LONG TIME I HAD TO JUST STUDY THE PIECES AS THEY CAME FLOATING IN, LIKE FLOTSAM THAT WASHES ASHORE AND TELLS THE BROKEN STORY OF A TERRIBLE SHIPWRECK AT SEA. THANK THAT TRANSMOGRIFIED LITTLE CHUNK OF FLESH ON YOUR ARM, BABY. THAT SAVED THE DAY.

I was possessive of these longer communications from my parents, and very cautious about how much I shared with Rena and Ajax and Harwood.

'It was like a big bonfire of the heart,' I translated Barkley's monologues as simply as possible. 'They miss me terribly,' I'd say, or 'Did you know your senses get rewired when you're dead? Smells make noise, sounds touch. Language is edible.'

Following all my 'reports from the far side,' ridiculous and serious alike, Ajax would go pale and sit down. Rena would scribble furiously in the little black book where she kept all her notes, occasionally looking up to ask a question like ' 'Scuse, please. What's a veg-o-peeler?' And Harwood – who had decided, after his initial disapproval, to stick around for these sessions after all – would sit in the far corner and stare gloomily into space.

Even the Rena sessions that didn't spark communication with Barkley and Jack – and there were many times when I would lay my left hand against the underside of my right wrist and feel nothing more than the extra-smooth contours of the scar itself – were fun, and for this I must give all credit to Rena. She managed to turn what others had made a tedious, sad and seemingly impossible business – the legal pursuit of compensation for my parents' electrocution – into a compelling and exciting game. She presented it to us as our own private treasure hunt – with one obvious treasure being, of course, the fat wad of dough we might collect from the amusement park. All four of us – all six of us, actually, if you give Barkley and Jack their due – got caught up in the challenge of gathering the clues and stringing them together into what we hoped would be an invincible legal strategy.

For me the whole process was strangely exhilarating and liberating in another way. Always before, on the rare occasions when people other than Ajax and Harwood dared to mention my parents at all, they cast sad pitying looks my way that left me feeling ashamed of the way life and I had failed each other. When Rena spoke of Barkley and Jack and the dramatic end they'd met, I felt like the luckiest girl in the world. For who else had such clever parents, parents who could take a powder with such fantastic style?

Apples and Oranges

Although Auntie Ajax was my aunt, she also was my uncle. I never really thought about this but I knew it, in the quiet interior way that children always instinctively know all the big dark truths that adults always think they have so brilliantly concealed. I knew this big dark truth about Ajax, and I approved of the way she had chosen (once again in keeping with Lady Fustian's parable about boardwalk-bound underwear) to step away from that truth. It was nobody else's business. And I happened to agree with Ajax. She made much better sense as an aunt. After all, I already had an uncle. What I could use, among other things, was an aunt.

By the third year of my new life with Ajax and Harwood I had become very comfortable with the way things were working out on Half-Moon Street. But I also, gradually, had become aware that the world at large had its own ideas, different ideas, about families. About how boys and girls and mothers and fathers should act. For some time I had sensed that this outside world was peering at the household I called home through a long lens of low-grade disapproval. I had felt the nudge of this disapproval in the pinched smiles that mothers of my schoolmates flashed at me and Ajax through the closed windows of their cars when they came to pick their children up from school. I had seen it in the eyebrow haiku shop clerks exchanged when Ajax and I were out on a 'repotting spree,' getting new clothes for my weedy body. Most of all, I had heard it slithering like a small and nasty reptile through the simple question other children put to me time and time again when they met Ajax: 'Is SHE your MOTHER?'

The symptoms of the world's disapproval were everywhere, but Rena was the first one to come right out and state the matter flatly, to our faces. She put it to us one day – boldly, loudly, in a way that couldn't be ignored. She was standing on the coffee table in our living room and performing, TV evangelist style, into a microphone that had been wired to our stereo system. Rena often resorted to special effects or theatrics of some kind to get into new or difficult topics in our so-called strategy sessions. In fact, the sessions were more like experimental theater than any kind of legal preparation. It was something we had become accustomed to over time, and even enjoyed. In this particular meeting Rena had cast herself as a preachy, southern-born defense attorney, deep in the heat of cross-examination. It was essential, Rena insisted, to anticipate what tactics the defense lawyers might take when we finally went to court. (We were all beginning to wonder if this mythic court battle would ever really come to pass. The lawyers for the amusement park had approached Rena several times with offers of settlement, but each time she had turned them away with a snort – 'Dream on, you corporate pimps!' – and insisted we continue to prepare for court.) So there Rena was, on the coffee table, evangelizing an offensive defense.

'What must it do to a young girl?' Rena wailed. 'I ask you. To be raised by two men, one of whom insists he is a woman? What must it DOOOO? Think on it, y'all. 'Coz I want an ANSWER.' Rena's Irish brogue gave her attempt at a southern drawl an interesting texture, but accent aside, the significance of Rena's point must have hit home, because Ajax immediately put down the sweater she was knitting for me and looked up nervously.

'Oh my. But really, THAT has nothing to do with THIS,' Ajax said, folding her hands quietly in her lap. 'Does it? I mean, one is apples and the other is oranges, wouldn't you say?'

'Whooooeee, child!' Rena slapped her thigh, tipped her head back and lobbed her microphone across the room toward me. Just as I was reaching out to catch it she gave a yank on the cord with one hand and the microphone snapped right back into her other hand, pretty as a sinner returning to God.

'That's an adaptation of a fly-fishing trick I learned in the Ol' Country, Elray,' Rena stage-whispered with a big wink. 'Teach it to you someday.' Then she whirled back to hit Ajax with another blast of evangelical outrage.

'Let me get this straight,' she said quietly. 'You, Mr Andrew Jackson Mayhew, are going to sit there in that pretty lavender dress with the fine PANSY flowers bursting into bloom all over it, you are going to sit there with the matching lavender barrettes sticking up like donkey's ears from your nest of fake hair, and you are going to try to tell me that YOU KNOW APPLES FROM ORANGES? Whooooeee, child, GET out!' Rena's last exclamation lost its volume halfway through because Harwood had moved across the room to switch off the stereo.

'Rena. Ajax.' Harwood looked at each of them and spoke in a near whisper. 'This is an issue we need to discuss, but Elray needn't be included. Have some sense.'

'Hallelujah! Glory glory. Alistair Cooke has risen from his armchair and walks amongst us!' Rena exclaimed as she jumped down from the coffee table and dropped to her knees at Harwood's feet. I'd seen this kind of thing happen before, when Rena burrowed a little too deeply into one of her impersonations and seemed almost to get stuck there. 'Alistair, Alistair my dear,' she pleaded. 'Yes, 'tis an issue we need badly to discuss. But don't be a nitwit.' Then she stood up and brushed the dust from her knees and I could see that – thank God – she was sliding back into just plain Rena. 'How many times have I told you?' she snapped. 'Without Elray we are nothing. Nothing!'

With this they all three turned to stare at me, and I'm afraid that when they did they must have caught the look of amazement that was plastered across my face. But the look was not there for any of the reasons they probably all assumed. I certainly wasn't surprised by Rena's theatrics, which were standard fare in our sessions. And, as I mentioned, the confusion over Ajax's sexual identity was hardly new or shocking to me. No, what had spread the look of disbelief across my face, what was resounding still in my ears with the avalanche boom of a slot machine jackpot, was the name Rena had just used: Andrew Jackson Mayhew. I had never heard it before, and I had always assumed that Ajax's name was a two-pronged tribute to a compulsion she had to scrub surfaces clean and to a cleaning agent of the same name. Since living with my aunt and uncle I had noticed that clutter could mount and overtake every drawer, shelf and closet in our house, but never grit. Ajax, who had a knack for pulling a damp sponge out of thin air the way some magicians will pluck coins from behind ears, made sure of that.

Knowing this little phobia of my aunt's, I had let myself slip into a simple and clumsy assumption about her name. As I rolled my tongue again and again around the syllables – Andrew Jackson Mayhew – what amazed me as much as anything was my own stupidity. I had never even paused to wonder if there could be any other explanation for my aunt's name or what, if Ajax was a nickname, her real name might be.

Then another wonder hit me. Andrew Jackson. A. Jacks. A-jax, L-ray. 'Ajax! Oh Ajax!' I shouted excitedly. 'You're just like me!'

Before I could explain myself Harwood was groaning and rolling his eyes at Rena. 'There. Try that one in court. Oh boy, this is just great. Ladies and gentlemen of the jury,' Harwood said as he gave a low sweeping bow and brushed the floor with the back of his hand, 'here come the worms.'

All I had meant by my outburst was that I suddenly understood that Ajax's name was a contraction of her first and middle names, just like mine. For as long as I could remember I had been called Elray, and I was even enrolled that way at school. But my real name – and I tried to keep this my own dark secret – was Logan Raintree Mayhew. It was a terrible name, an awful name. Mayhew was Mayhew, and unavoidable, but the rest of it was entirely my parents' fault. The Logan part was for the airport in Boston where they had met, and Raintree was my mother's mother's maiden name. Logan Raintree Mayhew. They could have named me anything in the world, and this had been their choice. I can only assume that my parents eventually realized their error themselves, because it was they who collapsed the whole monstrosity into the almost equally weird 'Elray.'

'I mean our names,' I quickly tried to explain to the three faces that had turned in unison, as if controlled by a single brain, to stare across the room at me now, serious as heart attacks. 'Ajax and Elray. The nicknames are like secret codes for the real names. And with them, we can be boys or girls.' Another groan came out of Harwood at this, and the three faces exchanged glances. Then Rena took charge.

'Okay. Conference time,' she said, drawing four chairs into a tight circle in the center of the room. 'This is the very matter I wanted to get out on the table today, and I see we are ready for a good straight-forward discussion now. So, all fireworks and fun aside, let's get to it.'

'Elray, this is the deal,' Rena continued. 'Ajax likes to dress up and pretend to be your aunt.'

'I know,' I said, nodding. 'She's a good aunt.'

'But Ajax is not your aunt, she is your uncle. She is Andrew Jackson Mayhew, your father's brother, your uncle. And lots of people outside this house would say it was a bad thing for her to pretend to be your aunt. A bad thing for you to see.'

I didn't like this. I thought Rena was being unnecessarily blunt, and right in front of poor Ajax. 'But they're outside the house,' I explained, patting Rena's hand a little impatiently. 'They don't need to see anything. Ajax is a good aunt, and she's a good gardener too. And she's a very very good scrubber. Right, Harwood?' I was desperate that Ajax not have her feelings hurt.

'Right.' Harwood lifted his tired head and nodded. 'You're right about that, Elray.'

A moment of quiet hung over the little circle our heads made, and then Rena exploded: 'Brrrrrrillllllliant!'

The rest of us looked at each other and cringed in our chairs. We knew by now that whenever Rena delivered this particular expression with such enthusiasm it meant that some new scheme was hatching inside her hyper Irish head. 'You're brilliant, Elray,' she began to sputter. 'This just might work.'

Rena did in fact have a scheme, and as she laid it out for us it became clear that the first part of it, anyway, impacted mainly on Ajax. Ajax, Rena insisted, would have to start dressing and acting like a man whenever she stepped out in public. I was to drop the prefix 'Aunt,' and to try to use male pronouns when speaking of Ajax to anyone outside the house – even to Hansueli. We would all have to help each other in this elaborate ruse, this plot to fool the world into believing that Ajax was in fact a man. Otherwise, Rena explained to me earnestly, people outside our house might try to take me away from what they saw as an inappropriate home. (At the time I couldn't imagine who would possibly care enough about me or my situation to go to such lengths, but not long afterward

I would remember Rena's fears that afternoon and understand that they had not been entirely paranoid.)

As it turned out, the second part of Rena's scheme impacted heavily on me. Given its intrusive habit of minding other people's business, she said, the world was sure to worry about what she kept calling my 'lack of female role models' at home. To disarm such charges before they could be made, she suggested that I promptly be withdrawn from the public school I had been attending and enrolled in the Cathedral Academy for Girls, an Episcopal preparatory school just down the road.

I had my own thoughts, visceral and immediate, about this part of the plan. I had seen the Cathedral girls walking to and from school in their Black Watch plaid skirts and white blouses, their knee socks and brown oxfords, their sticklike arms laden with big books. They traveled in packs, like maggots. They were spineless sissies, I knew it.

'I have females at home, Rena,' I argued. 'I have you, and I have Ajax.'

'I AM YOUR LAWYER, and nothing more. You must never forget that,' Rena scolded. 'Or we are really cooked. And don't you remember what we have been talking about here all afternoon? Ajax is NOT a female. Not to the outside world.'

'Amen! Effing-A, A-MEN!' Harwood, who usually sat silently through any sessions he attended until he reached some mysterious point – a moment only he could understand – when he stood up and left the room, was on his feet now and thumping Rena enthusiastically on the back. 'I'm with you all the way, Rena baby. For once you're talking sense, on every count. Ajax has got to act like a man, Elray has got to go to a good girls' school and you've got to be our lawyer and nothing else. No more evangelical sideshows, no more Ouija board crap. Fantastic. When can we start, right now?'

Rena had pinched her eyes closed and hunched her

shoulders against Harwood's back-thumping. When he finally stopped his pounding, she cracked open an eye and squinted at him curiously, as if she'd never seen him before. 'Yes,' she said quietly, smoothing the shoulders of her blouse back into place. 'If you've finished tenderizing me, I think we might start now. Right now.'

Dressed to Kill

Within only a few weeks Ajax and Harwood had pulled me out of the public school and enrolled me at the Cathedral Academy for Girls. I tried everything I could think of to prevent this move, including faking a veto vote from Barkley and Jack. 'They say: "IT'S MUCH TOO EXPENSIVE AND WE'LL ALL GO BANKRUPT AND STARVE,"' I lied, unaware at the time that my inheritance from my parents and from my grandfather Amos Mayhew was substantial enough to cover both private schooling and basic living expenses.

There seemed to be no way out; I was to be a Cathedral girl. But as brutal as I found the adjustments I faced during my own transition, my heart went out even more to Ajax as she struggled to become – at least publicly – what the world seemed to want her to be: a man. Her wigs, of course, were the first props that had to go. As it turned out Ajax had pretty good hair of her own – slightly receded around the forehead, it's true, but otherwise ample and of a reddish-blond hue that was quite attractive. With the help of a handsome young Brit named Gary, who made several house calls that first month and who always dressed in a way that reminded me of the soldiers in *The Nutcracker*, Ajax learned to style her locks into a kind of hair helmet that she found acceptable.

Next came the problem of wardrobe. The notion that Ajax might shop for herself in the men's department of some store was simply too mortifying for her even to consider, so instead we ordered her a lot of men's clothes from catalogues that I dug up in Harwood's room. To help get past the strangeness of what felt to her like an exercise in cross-dressing, Ajax tended to pick highly specialized men's gear. 'If I have to wear a costume,' she said, 'for God's sake, let it be a real costume.' For a few months she paraded around in jodhpurs, jacket and boots, as if fresh from a morning of foxhunting. Then one day, in the back of a catalogue put out by a fly-fishing outfitter in Scotland, she found an offer for men's kilts, with full dress regalia, in colors for every clan. She ordered one of each.

'MacGregor today, is it?' Rena always remarked on the plaids when she came to visit. 'Very handsome, very handsome indeed. But I still think the Graham greens become you the most, Ajax. Lord, but you're a heart-stopper in the Graham greens.'

Perhaps I felt so attuned to Ajax's misery during this period because so much of my own unhappiness sprang from a radical change in daily uniform. At the public school, where I had been free to wear anything I chose, I invariably dressed in a T-shirt, blue jeans and black high-top sneakers. Every morning I now found myself buttoned into the Black Watch plaid skirt that was the Cathedral Academy's mandatory uniform. And every morning, as I stood looking down at my knees bobbing like doorknobs just below the hem of the stupid skirt, I felt something inside me die.

Ajax sensed my humiliation. 'Look what's become of us,' she said to me one day with a smile as she held out her own plaid kilt with one hand and pointed to my skirt with the other. 'Couple of ninnies, the two of us, eh? But you know what?' She moved in conspiratorially, and bent toward me with a whisper. 'This is actually battle dress, for war,' she hissed. Then she took off the little dagger – the skin *dubh* – she always strapped around her calf when in her kilts and knelt down to buckle it around my calf instead. She had to go get scissors and punch a new hole in the strap to make it fit. 'There,' Ajax said to me quietly. 'Wear it inside your knee sock, as a secret. Don't let anyone else know.' Then she hooked her arm in mine and we danced a fine war jig, right there in the front hall, before I stepped out the door and strode off to battle at school.

From then on I wore the little dagger every day, and the feel of it, snug against my leg inside my sock, did give me a comforting edge of individuality as I waded down the school halls through a sea of small figures that were otherwise indistinguishable from my own. But nothing could quell the hollow dread I felt rising in me at the notion that this smoothly groomed and squealing-voiced community, this so-called female-ness that I saw all around me, was the destiny the world saw as mine. I was nine years old, in the fourth grade, and I had never before thought of myself as female. It wasn't that I'd thought of myself as male either. Like some distant and anonymous crane operator in the sky, I had been too busy working the controls of my machine to consider the issue of its – or anything else's – gender.

But now Rena, Ajax and even Harwood all seemed to be obsessed with this problem of female versus male behavior. It was a distinction that puzzled me. I took a close look at the students who swarmed through my new school, hoping that en masse my sex might exhibit some noble or at least distinctive qualities that were innately its own. But I could see little difference between these girls and the children – both male and female – who had been at my other school. These girls talked smarter – or perhaps I should say they talked richer, and older. From the things they said you'd think they already knew everything and had every-thing they might ever need. That they still lived at home only to keep an eye on naughty parents who couldn't be trusted to behave. But I knew otherwise. I'd watched these same tough talkers at the end of each school day as they rushed out the door toward a queue of Volvo station wagons. I'd seen the way their arch school looks drained out of them as they ran, the way their faces went all soft and smooth as a baby's when it's snug and asleep in its cradle. I'd heard them calling to whatever big fuzzy family dog they had – a 'Shadow,' or a 'Bear' – as it sat thumping its tail, steaming up the window in the way-back.

I wasn't sure exactly what Rena meant by 'female role models,' but I knew these girls weren't it. They were silly baby maggots, just as I'd thought. Still, I couldn't put the troubling question of gender-appropriate behavior to rest. I kept turning the matter over and over in my head, as if simple agitation might shake loose some answer. A few times I even tried resting my fingertips on my scar during these meditations, hoping one of my parents might weigh in on the subject – but the only time I heard anything at all the two of them seemed preoccupied with other things.

DON'T STAND THERE STOMPING YOUR HIP BOOTS AND SHAKING THAT BIG WET NET AT ME LIKE THAT, I overheard Barkley saying one day. IT'S NOT MY FAULT YOU GOT SKUNKED THIS MORNING. JUST LOOK AT YOUR HAIR! WHY, IT'S DOWN TO YOUR SHOULDERS. I BET YOU HAVEN'T EVEN HAD IT CUT SINCE THE ACCIDENT, HAVE YOU?

NAG ONE, WORRY TWO, NAG ONE, WORRY TWO, Jack answered in a singsong voice a second later. It was the first time I had ever heard the two of them talking to each other instead of directly to me, and I felt a tickle of eavesdropper's guilt running like a lost beetle up the back of my neck. Still, I couldn't keep myself from listening.

SIT IN A HEAP AND SPIN SORROW, LIKE SOME SAD SPIDER, Jack continued. BRING ELRAY DOWN TO THE WATER. THEN WE'LL CATCH SOME FISH.

FISH, FISH, AND MORE FISH! IS THAT ALL YOU THINK ABOUT? Barkley sighed.

OH! DON'T SPEAK OF OBSESSION, MY MONOMANIACAL PRETTY! Jack whispered back. He sounded so close, I could almost see my dead father: his jaw clenched, his teeth bared, his hair (as Barkley had just inadvertently told me) straggling down to his shoulders. GO BACK TO YOUR EASEL, DEAR, he said. GO PAINT FOR THE NEXT FORTY-TWO BILLION YEARS.

My scar station went suddenly static right after this exchange. I got the impression that wherever they were, Jack was fishing a lot and Barkley painting. That was okay. But it upset me that both of them also seemed to be worrying and bickering about me.

After fretting over this for a while, I decided to mention my eavesdropping information to Hansueli. The two of us had lapsed into a frank and easy friendship, conducted mostly in English, at this point. After listening to my concerns about my parents, Hansueli clucked his tongue and gave me some calming advice: 'Oh my. It is so selfish uf parents to argue in front uf dare chiltren, Elray. So unfair. You must try not to listen to dem, my dear. For one ting, day are dead. But more important, try to remember that day are who day are, and dat you are you and only you. Quite separate. Just step yourself right out of dare loop. Ta-dah! Like dis.' Then Hansueli pulled his long tall self upright and with a huge grin executed a simple but evasive sidestep across the floor. Minutes later the two of us were pirouetting together in happy evasive circles all around the room, and I could feel a physical lightening around my neck and shoulders as I literally sidestepped my parents' troubles.

Because of the success of this discussion, at my very next session with Hansueli I finally found the nerve to broach the still unanswered and very troublesome riddle of male versus female behavior. What seemed to me to be the perfect opening for the topic presented itself while we were watching home videos of Hansueli's son Mark – a pastime that had become one of our favorite ways to spend our hour together.

'Look, look, look! He's about to do it. Here it comes,' Hansueli paused in his reach for another handful of popcorn and whispered to me excitedly. The three-year-old Mark was cutting up on screen, standing in Hansueli's backyard and doing a floppy-jowled imitation of an infamous national politician, nodding his head and wagging the peace sign with both hands. Tucked under Mark's left arm was the unmistakably lumpen form of Raggedy Ann.

'That's a girl toy Mark's carrying, right?' I asked.

'A "girl toy"?' Hansueli asked back. 'It's a doll, Elray. A doll. Kom on, English is your native language. Remember?'

'Right, right. A doll,' I said impatiently. 'But what I mean is, Mark's a boy, right? Doesn't he have any male role models at home? Or is he just going to be a girl instead?'

Admittedly it was a clumsy way to pry open an awkward subject, and at first Hansueli was a little huffy: 'Uf coorse he has a mule rale midel at hume!' he snapped, his accent going haywire as it always did when he was upset. 'He haz me, his FODDER. Remember?' It wasn't such a smooth start, but after a few minutes I managed to calm Hansueli and we settled once again into the kind of shorthand, frank exchange we had gotten so good at. I told Hansueli about Ajax's new kilts. I told him how I needed to wear the skin *dubh* strapped to my calf to offset the humiliation of my school skirts.

'I'm going to tell *you* something, Elray,' Hansueli said as he warmed to his subject. 'But you must never tell anyone you heard dis from me – I might lose my license.' He leaned back and opened his mouth to catch a popcorn kernel he had tossed in the air. Then he continued. 'We are all uf us androgynous – boy and girl, mixed togedder – at some level. Just like we are all clinically schizophrenic – two different people or more, in one body – at some level. You, you are both androgynous and schizophrenic at slightly higher levels than what the world might like. But so what. You're having a goot time, right? Enjoy yourself. I, as your doctor, say just enjoy yourself. Forget about the girl stuff or the boy stuff. Have fun.'

'But what about all those female girls at my new school?' I asked. 'What do I do about them?'

'Don't even tink about dem. You just make sure you drive the tennis ball down dare throats, okay? Now let's watch a little more uf my Marky-boy. My crazy, doll-toting girly Marky-boy. What do you say?'

'Lights, camera, ACTION!' I answered. Then I settled back comfortably in my wingchair, happy to know that for a while at least I could just shove all the world's apples and oranges far far away and over the cliff, back into the abyss, where they belonged.

Family Document:
Ajax's Letter

Let me pause here, and as a palate cleanser offer the following family document, one of several letters I found in Ajax's desk drawer a few years ago. A strange thing happens when people put a pen to paper: We get hints of how huge the submerged portions of most lives are. I always thought I knew my own family and my own story as well as anyone could, but there were big pieces I missed. Written by Ajax to her friend Virgil in New York, this letter was returned to Ajax unopened. She never reopened it, but she kept it — which is why I was able to break the seal and read the letter myself several years later. Every time I read Ajax's letter, her words slay me. I am moved by how much she gave up for me, by how entirely mine she made herself. I feel a nostalgic rush for the sweet and innocent childhood she so generously provided me.

My dear Virgil:

How I long to have a letter from you and just a few scraps of news about you and our dear life that I miss so much. I keep hoping things here will settle down and give me a chance to slip away for a short visit – but it seems there is always some new crisis. Elray needs new school shoes or Harwood picks up a rare tropical flu on his travels and arrives home in a coma. The lawyers want to meet to try to discuss possible settlement terms or a gasket in the washing machine blows. (Incidentally, to give you an idea of how surreal real life can be here in the nation's capital, the washing machine repairman's name is Mr Mister. Do you love it?) All my life I've listened to intelligent people talk of leaving the crazy kinetics of New York for a 'simple life' elsewhere, but I swear that when I think back on my lovely times with you on Lafayette Street, the vision is positively pastoral compared with the gear-grinding frenzy that my life has taken on in this, a so-called 'quiet residential neighborhood' in a much smaller town.

Of course much of the chaos I feel comes from my having landed smack dab in the middle of 'motherhood' after so many years of perfecting my style as a domestically feckless adult. In fact, Virgil, I think you might be quite astounded by the life your old chum Ajax is leading these days. For instance, I serve dinner at home every night – and I'm not talking the home-pressed-gravlax-followed-by-boeuf-en-daube-and-accompanied-by-ninety-two-bottles-of-pink-wine type of affair that you and I used to pull off biannually as paybacks for the other 360 dinners we ate out each year. I serve a nutritionally balanced meal of simple unsauced substances that a small girl can first look at without wrinkling her nose and then maybe even consider eating. I GROW a lot of the simple substances I cook. Seriously. A few years ago if you had asked me what 'dirt' was, my first answer would have been 'a particularly juicy nugget of gossip,' and then I might have hazarded 'the prehistoric forerunner of pavement' as a secondary definition. But almost every day now, weather permitting, I'm up to my elbows in the real thing: clumpy, funky, worm-laden soil. I dig in it, I aerate it, I fold in loam and fertilizer, I pack it tenderly around the roots of plants and sometimes I even talk to them – the dirt and the roots – as if they are the team and I am the coach. 'There you go,' I say. 'How does that feel? Pretty good, am I right? Now get in there and go go go.' What I am saying is, I garden.

And cooking and gardening aren't even the half of it. I attend parents' nights at school, field days, bake sales, Christmas pageants, Easter plays, PTAs and prize days. I make Halloween costumes and I shoot hoops out back. I play Monopoly and Clue and, oh my but this one bores the very breath out of me, Parcheesi if I must. I do laundry by the bale, dishes by the barrel. And this is sure to finish you off: I do breakfast every day. I swear. At 7 A.M. In other words, Virgil, I am a Mom. I can just see your doubting face. But it's true. Hearing me describe all this, do you wonder, as I so often do, how it could have happened? How a middle-aged gay man who has fought against and finally found a comfortable niche outside society's accepted norms of gender and family can possibly have embraced so emphatically this the biggest cliché of all, the role of American Mom? I myself am mystified by the phenomenon. And in such moments I am surprised not just to find myself living in a place where I never expected to live and doing things I never knew I could or would want to do, but also by the overwhelming sense of inevitability that pins me to this new life of mine. The situation feels surreal and mundane. I'm like a character in one of those weird psycho shows who finds herself walking, in this the real world, through a landscape that previously she has visited only in dreams.

But whoa, now. Let me pull back a little. Things are getting a little too probing. Especially for someone like me, who, as we both know, prefers to skate the surface of life – at least conversationally. 'The Hans Brinker of thinkers,' as you always liked to tease me.

But that's another strange thing, Virgil. Even that part of me that drove you so crazy, that dodgy way I used to get whenever life turned serious, seems to be changing. Notice how I began this letter with a perky account of my new madcap 'daily life' as if it were a letter home from summer camp. And then, quicker than even you could ever say, 'Waiter, more tequila,' I took a dive down to the dark me me me waters of what does it all mean. That's so unlike the old Ajax, don't you think? And yet I'm doing more and more of that these days. In fact, here I am writing a letter and doing it. What's next? I don't know. I've been thinking about it all quite a lot lately. ('Perhaps that's the problem . . .' Yes, I can't help hearing you and your wisecracks all the time still, sweetie.) I have been thinking and I've decided that perhaps the sessions with Rena – she's the lawyer handling Elray's case and she's inventive and smart and very handsome to boot, you'd adore her – have something to do with my new tendencies to 'delve' in areas where once I would have preferred to 'glide.' Rena is always after us to 'dig dig dig,' as she puts it, and she doesn't mean out back in the potato patch with a trowel. She wants us to go deep into our memory banks, down into our psyches and even into our dreams. Of course mostly Rena wants Elray to go to all these places, but I think some of her tactics are rubbing off on me. Partly because it is such a moving sight, watching my brave little Elray dive headlong into the dark pits and then seeing her reemerge with some big nasty – to use a Rena phrase – in tow. It's just amazing.

In fact, if I'm going to be honest about it I'd have to say that Elray probably has everything to do with the ways that I myself – not just the circumstances of my life – have changed recently. I find this a little embarrassing, that a pint-sized gum-snapping girl has taught me what in almost forty years of living I had failed to learn for myself. But in a way that's what has happened. It's because of Elray that I'm seeing and feeling things differently now. I guess I find this awkward to admit because I was so convinced for so long that I never wanted children – I mean, you and I obviously wouldn't be having any together. And it never occurred to me to adopt. But as it turns out, now that I've been 'ambushed' by parenthood, children – or a child, at least – may have been just what I've needed all along. I guess for me, you'd have to invert the old adage and say: In responsibilities begin dreams.

Oh dear. Have you tossed this letter in the trash yet? I know you must be ready to and I apologize, but I want so much to explain to you what is happening to me down here. You see, it's as if I'm connected for the first time. Everything fits together in some way that it never has before. Take this afternoon, for instance. The simplest kind of afternoon really, a pretty spring day so I decided to walk over to Elray's school and surprise her when she got out. Harwood was home earlier than expected from a wilderness stint in Manitoba, so he decided to join me. The two of us walked over together, leaning into the series of dogleg turns and secret shortcuts that Elray insists is the only route worth taking to her school. Along the way we had a low-grade bicker going about whether or not Elray should continue to see Hansueli, an all but useless shrink Harwood found for her. (Since he hired the shrink, Harwood of course thinks him indispensable. I maintain that Rena does all Hansueli's

106

work and more.) We were just chewing quietly on this topic, the way you might roll a blade of grass between your teeth on a fine sunny day, and at the same time keeping a running tab of how many dogs we saw along the way – a canine tally Elray insists upon.

'That makes fifteen, right?' Sharp-eyed Harwood pointed to the front window of a house we were passing where a small live ball of fur was banging against the glass from inside. Presumably it was barking, although the only noise that came to us was a muffled knocking.

'Do interior sightings count? I'm not sure,' I said. I wasn't trying to take anything away from Harwood, I really just didn't know the rules.

'Of course they do,' said Harwood. 'A dog's a dog.'

'Okay, okay,' I answered. 'Yes, then fifteen.'

We walked on in silence, just soaking up the spring air and counting dogs, until we took the last left turn and we were standing at the bottom of the driveway watching a regatta of little girls come sailing downhill. Every time the double doors of the gymnasium swung open, sharp little yelps and cries would escape and drift downwind toward us.

'Sounds like an aviary in there,' I said.

'Yep. And here comes our little bird,' Harwood answered.

Then Elray was standing beside us, hip-hopping from foot to foot and flapping her elbows and smiling up with her urchin face. 'Hi, hi, hi,' she said. 'Harwood, you're back! How many dogs on the way over?' Twenty-three, we told her.

It was too nice a day not to do something special, so as soon as Elray had changed from her school shoes to her high-tops the three of us walked over to the Bishop's Garden – a quirky, Gothic-style garden that is owned and maintained by the nearby cathedral – and wandered up and down its paths. Elray kept taking great gasps and holding her breath. (This is the latest in a series of exercises she does for some crazy

'invisibility' club she's started. I don't really understand it, and as far as I can tell the only 'invisible'
thing about the club is some imaginary fellow club
member named Raoul, whom I hear a lot about. But I
leave it alone. Kids have to have their secrets, you
know.) Harwood was walking backward in front of us,
dodging in and out of the boxwood and shooting
pictures, trying to finish up a half-used roll from the
Manitoba trip. And I was having just the best time,
poking through the flower and herb beds, identifying
plants and telling Elray stories about them. I pointed
out the pennyroyal, rue, feverfew and horehound and
explained how they had all been on the Emperor
Charlemagne's plant list – how they had been valued
for their medicinal and odor-masking properties in
medieval times. I showed her the Glastonbury thorn,
brought to England by Joseph of Arimathea, and the
Atlas cedars from Lebanon and the fine stand of tall
Irish yews, which symbolize immortality. I kept
pulling up information, like an unexpectedly long set
of roots, from some rich and fertile place inside me I
didn't even know I had.

Is any of this making any sense? Can you see at all
what I mean when I say that things are fitting together
differently, better? Everything is smaller and quieter
than my life was in New York, but the pieces fit
together in a way that feels bigger. It all makes sense
and gives me great pleasure.

Oh my dear Virgil. As I read over this silliness I have
been writing to you my overwhelming sense is of how
much I miss you, and of how much I've failed you.
Who else could I ever talk to in this way and have a
prayer that they might understand me? I feel the sadness of missing you, and I feel the sadness of having
missed having with you the very thing I'm trying to
describe here. It was, I can see now, all my fault that
we didn't get there. It was all my fault, and I apologize.

I'm going to sign off now, with a hex on Rena
for having nurtured in me this awful tendency for

self-scrutiny. I used to be such a champ at avoiding it on any level that went deeper than a makeup mirror. How did this happen?

Much much love to you, darling, and just a little bit less to all the others. I really do miss you terribly, and I really will try to visit soon. When I do, do you think we could play a little bridge? Nobody, I mean but NOBODY, plays down here.

Your everloving Ajax

Part Three

The Invincible Heels

Raoul

A drama teacher I studied with in high school used to say that every scene has its subtext, its hidden agenda. As an actor, she insisted, you had to understand that subtext and absorb it – simply and organically, like a sponge breathing water – before you could so much as walk onstage without betraying your craft. I spent months as an adolescent trying to find the subtext in various characters I portrayed on the dusty black boards of our high school stage, and years as an adult trying to get a visual version of subtext into every frame of every film I ever shot. But for some reason, only recently, with the help of that fabled perspective called hindsight, have I been able to see a startling truth about the role of subtext in my own life.

The fact is, for a long time following my parents' death my life was nothing but subtext. I had the subtext of my daily life with Auntie Ajax and Uncle Harwood, a kind of wacky echo of a real family life I had had with a real mother and a real father. I had the subtext of my weekly meetings with Hansueli, where we performed a polite do-si-do around all the issues we both knew we were meant to be addressing. I had the subtext of my supposed 'legal' sessions with Rena, where we actually targeted and attacked the very same issues Hansueli and I ignored. Woven sporadically above all these subtexts, like some crazy medieval descant, were my messages from Barkley and Jack.

These were becoming so rare and so fragmented and so cryptic, I didn't like to think about what my parents must be up to in their other world.

For the longest time I had subtext galore, but I had no text proper. I had no text proper, that is, until I met Raoul. Raoul Person (and that really is his name) and I first came eye to eye crawling on our bellies in the bowels of the Washington Cathedral – 'ground-hoggin',' as Auntie A would have called it. He was thirteen, I was twelve, and each of us, unbeknownst to the other, had taken on the self-appointed task of exploring, conquering and claiming as our own the eerie subterranean world of crypts that lay below the glorious soaring public spaces of the cathedral.

As a student at the Cathedral Academy for Girls I had been logging a lot of time in the cathedral's public spaces – for chapel services, school plays, recitals, flag days. While I had remained coolly indifferent to the rituals themselves, I had been gripped by a near obsession with the building in which we performed them. On days when I had free time after school, or on weekends when my hours were entirely my own, I would wander over and lose myself in the big vaulted spaces of the cathedral. I loved the delicious way my footsteps came echoing back at me a beat later wherever I went, magnifying my solitude and at the same time implying that perhaps I was not alone. I grew scornful of the stubby lay-shadow I cast in the outside world – how could it possibly compete with the long angular shadow of myself that went rocketing up the stone walls of the cathedral, as if my soul itself were on an express launch to heaven?

Working systematically from the basement level up, I set about exploring every shadowy nook and testing every door behind which my school functions had not yet taken me. After an unpleasant encounter with a janitor whom I inadvertently caught napping behind the altar in the Bethlehem Chapel, I started wearing my purple and white Glee Club gown on my cathedral bivouacs. My theory was that this costume would make me appear legitimate, and in fact, I never was challenged again. On the few occasions when I actually encountered someone, they moved aside so quickly and deferentially that afterward I was tempted to cast an eye backward to see if I had sprouted angel wings.

I was in the fifth grade when I began these explorations, and within a year and a half I had become completely fluent in the labyrinthine system of hidden passages and narrow winding stairways that led from one chapel to another, from the nave to the balconies, from the balconies to the tiny ledgelike pulpits at the base of the rose windows, from the rose window pulpits up up up the tower to the bell chamber in the sky. How I loved to race through these dark and secret arteries, my hand skimming the smooth cool of the stone walls, the back of my neck tingling from the vast amorphous terror that came snowballing toward me through the vacuum of quiet I left behind. To keep the terror at bay I concentrated on the steady flick flick flick against my fingertips that marked the seams where one massive stone block abutted another. I concentrated on the meter of the stone seams, and I repeated over and over inside my head, for no logical reason except that I had chosen it as my confidence chant, the name of a Pakistani exchange student who had once attended my school: 'Phampam Bihram Bacti. Phampam Bihram Bacti. Phampam Bihram Bacti.'

By the middle of my sixth-grade year I felt sure I was one of the world's foremost experts on the cathedral. But by this time I also had to admit something else. As thorough as my explorations had been, there was one needling challenge that I had yet to face: the world of the crypts. The rumor of the crypts – an allegedly vast and shadowy underworld of the cathedral – had knocked around my school for years, but their exact purpose and how one gained access to them had always remained vague. One of the most compelling things about the rumor of the crypts was the corollary rumor that the biggest alligator in the world lived in a lake in their depths. It lived down in this dark and dank underworld guarding the religious treasures that were stored there and, it was said, growing fat off a diet of mortal sinners who were tossed to it by Reverend Tucker, a tall concave priest who always carried a flute and talked to himself nonstop as he crisscrossed the cathedral close.

In the course of my explorations I had come across a little locked door at the back of the St Joseph of Arimathea Chapel, which, my knowledge of the building's layout had combined with my instincts to tell me, was the only logical choice for entry to the crypts. Twice I had gathered my courage and set out to check behind the arched door, but each time, as I pulled out the jackknife that I used to pick the cathedral's standard-issue dead-bolt locks, Barkley and Jack, in a most unprecedented manner, had interfered. In the past I had always had to touch my scar before my parents could be heard. But the first time I tried to enter the crypts my little crescent moon-shaped brand began to itch and burn slightly; when I touched my scar I found Barkley waiting there, shouting a crazy, incoherent version of my own confidence chant: PHAM-PAM BIHRAM BACTI PIMPIM BAHRIM BICTI POM PAM POM POM BAD BAD STOP STOP DON'T!

It was typical of Barkley that, feeling the pinch of a crisis, she would begin to blather her version of what she thought I might say. It stirred up a very old memory of mine, of the way, when Barkley was driving me somewhere in the car and had to stop suddenly, she used to shoot her hand out in front of my body as she muttered something like 'Aw-oh. No. No owies please, Mama. Get back.' As I stood in front of the little door at the back of the St Joseph of Arimathea Chapel that first time Barkley's language was scrambled, but her panic came through loud and clear. I backed away and immediately left the building, I was so spooked.

Another month passed before I approached the door again. When I did, it was Jack who intervened, screaming so loudly that my arm began to shake. My little jackknife, its blade drawn, clattered to the floor and lay spinning there, shiny and guilty as a murder weapon.

HADES YES! HELL NO! STOP RIGHT HERE! WE WON'T GO!

Jack was chanting this with such a savage intensity that I couldn't suppress the vision that came of him as a maniacal cheerleader, dancing through flames on the sidelines of some underworld football game. Even after I had retreated to the boxwood quiet of the nearby Bishop's Garden and plunged my arm into the wishing well to cool its aching heat, he kept whispering HELL NO! WE WON'T GO! in a low shaky voice until finally he fell silent and then began to snore loudly.

For a few months after this my curiosity about the crypts was muted, to say the least. But nothing gnaws more viciously at a young and still ambitious soul than the private knowledge of a small failure of nerve, and over the next weeks all my wanderings through the cathedral, previously a source of such heart-pattering thrills, suddenly seemed flat and mundane. I trudged down hallways and up stairs like a janitor with too big a job. The stone around me looked like cement, the air smelled overused and all the dramatic shadow play of darkness and light – which before had bristled as a kind of secondary architecture inside the rooms themselves – bled together into a flat gray nothing.

I knew I had to go back to the arched door at the back of St Joseph of Arimathea, and after thinking it over carefully I came up with a plan. On February 2, Groundhog Day, I approached the little door once more. I was wearing one of Ajax's long black leather gloves, which reached to the elbow on my right arm, covering my scar, and I had wrapped the glove snugly with silver duct tape. As I stood at the door I opened the blade on my jackknife – and nothing happened. I pushed the tip of the blade against the dead bolt and slid the bolt back. Nothing happened. I slowly eased the door open, drank in deep drafts from the tunnel of darkness within, and still nothing happened – except that I felt a strange surging sense of confidence shoot through me, as if bee stings were leapfrogging up my veins.

Apprehension, once conquered, can become a powerful source of energy. From the moment I overcame my last hesitation and stumbled through the dark to discover that the crypts did in fact exist, I became obsessed with mastering everything there was to know about this underworld. My task proved to be no small feat, for, as I soon discovered, there were crypts, subcrypts, sub-subcrypts and even, if you were very brave and not susceptible to claustrophobia, a kind of shallow pit in one area that could be called a sub-sub-subcrypt. The first or highest level of crypts was fairly innocuous, for there were water pipes and wires and fuse boxes that lent it the familiar look of a domestic basement. (Never mind that waiting for you in the first big room on this level, stacked from floor to ceiling on a bleacherlike assembly of boards, was a grinning audience of stone gargoyles.) But as you moved downward the levels got progressively darker and more confining, and also, it always seemed to me, potentially more dreadful in the class of secrets they might hold.

On that day when I first bumped into Raoul, I was in the sub-subcrypts, three levels down, belly-crawling through a narrow tunnel that led from one cavelike room on the north side to another, smaller cave-room. At such a depth I was already primed for dark doings; my antennae were out for strange forces. What I saw when I first bumped into him were Raoul's eyes, and what I immediately thought was that I had finally – and unfortunately – found the alligator. I had managed to put the rumor of the alligator out of my mind during my first crypt probes, but on that day when I found myself looking at a gleaming set of eyes I remembered everything instantly. I assumed my number was up. Forgetting temporarily about the glove I always wore into the crypts to block out Barkley and Jack, I reached instinctively for the scar on the underside of my right arm, hoping that someone would be hanging around with some timely piece of advice – or at least of sympathy. But the section of tunnel I was in was particularly narrow and I could not even maneuver my left hand, which was wedged under the left side of my body, over to my right arm.

'Oh shit.' I said it under my breath. And then I immediately regretted saying it because as far as I knew this profanity as much as anything I had ever done made me a mortal sinner and therefore fair prey for my tunnel mate. Before I could think I had said it again. 'OH SHIT!' Only louder this time.

There was a terrible pause, and then the alligator spoke: 'Swearing won't make it any different. You're stuck.'

The instant I heard Raoul's voice I knew this was no alligator. The voice was too young; it fell in that anonymous range between the bell-like clarity of a child's voice and the irrevocable sad weight of an adult voice. Also, there was a slight drawl. Even if alligators could speak, I was pretty sure they wouldn't drawl.

'If you relax it'll get better. Panic makes the body swell. Try taking a deep breath.'

Hesitantly, I did as I was instructed. I hadn't thought of myself as physically stuck, just as circumstantially in what Ajax would have called a 'pickle.' But after a few deep breaths my left hand did come free and I felt more on guard, readier to deal with whatever might be about to happen.

'Thanks,' I said. It seemed like a peaceful, non-committal offering.

'Hey, no problem. You're stuck, then I'm stuck. You're blocking the only way out far as I know.'

These last words lingered almost visibly, like a sub-title, in the silence that followed, and I latched onto them with the same soul-reviving relief that a cliff-hung climber must feel when a long-dangling foot finally settles into a solid toehold. The owner of the eyes was either very cagey or not too well-informed.

'Oh really? As far as you know?' I had meant to ask this indifferently, but a note of triumph must have crept into my voice, for a response came quickly and it crackled with impatience.

'Yes, really. But if you know something different maybe you'd be good enough to share it. That, or unstick your butt so I can get going. I've been watching you squirm this way a long time. Who are you anyway?'

The directness of the question took me by surprise, and the revelation that I had been watched, and for a long time, made me itch with embarrassment. The sweet, table-turning shift of power I had felt on the brink of executing had been utterly ambushed.

'I'm Elray,' I said flatly. 'If you back up about fifteen feet into the cave-room behind you I'll show you another way up to the next level.' Then I wiggled down the tunnel after the retreating eyes, maintaining a healthy distance all the way.

This was how Raoul Person and I met. Back in the cave-room we stretched out and took a good look at one another, and I discovered that Raoul was no crypt spirit but just another child like me. Except a boy. He wore black high-tops like mine, and he had a miner's helmet, like the one I wore on Crawlspace Days and for most of my crypt visits. As it happened I did not have my miner's light turned on that day, because of a new discipline I had recently instigated in which I forbade myself to turn the light on when traveling through the sections of crypt that seemed to activate my fear glands the most. I couldn't bear the little butterflies of dread that still stirred in me sometimes –

the way they grew larger and larger and then went banging around my chest like crazy bats, using up all the air in my lungs. I was determined to get rid of them, and I knew that the surest way to drive off any kind of terror was to court it.

Raoul had turned his light off as well that day, the moment he spotted me, in order to spy more effectively. When we got to the cave-room we both, as if by unspoken agreement, set our hats on the floor and turned on their lights. I'll never know if Raoul was as disappointed as I by the ordinariness of what he saw. Probably not, because I at least was dressed peculiarly.

'What are you wearing?' He scratched at his boy hair, and tipped his head sideways as if a different angle might somehow help the vision of me make sense. 'And what happened to your arm?'

I looked down at myself and then crossed my arms in self-defense. 'I am a member of the Glee Club,' I announced, as I swirled my Glee Club robes self-conciously. 'I sing. And my arm, this arm . . .' I uncrossed my arms and pushed the glove-and-tape-encased right one out in front of me. 'This is my wooden limb.'

'A wooden arm? Oh, my God. HOW EXCELLENT!' Raoul cried.

Thus, with the help of a minor deceit on my part, was my friendship with Raoul happily launched. The lie about my arm made things a little awkward at first, because Raoul was so curious about all sorts of bother-some technical details – like how I'd lost my real arm, how the fake one attached, how I made the fingers work so well – and I had to think fast to explain them. Like any good liar I drew shamelessly from true experience when spinning my answers and relied on a few basic psychological moves to camouflage obvious gaps. 'I was in a terrible accident with my parents,' I said and then stared at the ground. I let him drag some of the introductory details from me, and then dropped the bomb that my parents were now dead. That shut his questions down pretty quickly, and soon I was able to shift to the far more fascinating matter of what he was doing down here in the crypts, and whether or not he knew more about them than I.

We quickly established our mutual knowledge of basic crypt geography – the gargoyle room, the two immense 'cemetery' rooms where the walls were lined with ash-filled urns, the costume room filled with religious vestments of every size and color and the candle room, where an army of huge candlesticks lay scattered haphazardly against the walls, as if all the torchbearers in history had gone on break for lunch. Then we began to probe each other to test a more arcane expertise. I hinted at the heating duct system, and Raoul knew all about it. Raoul asked if I had seen the 'saloon,' and I knew instantly that he meant the high shelf along one wall that someone had lined with empty Dewar's scotch bottles. We continued in this way, getting more and more petty in our challenges – resorting even to graffiti sightings – until Raoul finally said: 'What about this other way out? Are you going to show me?'

I had been half hoping he would have forgotten my reference to an alternate exit from the sub-subcrypts. I was feeling possessive of my crypt secrets. But it was too late. I looked him up and down.

'I don't know if you're going to fit,' I said. He was a little taller and thicker than I. 'You might get stuck forever. Plus I think there are rats in there. If they know you are stuck they sometimes bite.'

Raoul stared back at me and shrugged. '*Que sera, sera*,' he said. 'That's what I always say in situations like this. Let's go.'

I led him back to the far corner of the cave-room we were in, to a spot where a tunnel dropped to the pit-like sub-sub-subcrypt area. 'This way,' I said, settling my miner's hat on my head. 'Down here.'

'Holy cow.' He was impressed. 'It goes down? Down deeper? Wait a second,' Raoul said, and then he did something extraordinary. First he put his hat on the ground and then he lay down himself, flat on his back, with his arms crossed over his chest. He closed his eyes.

'Hey, what are you doing?' I asked. 'Are you coming?'

'Shhhh. Be quiet.' He cracked one eye at me to say this and then he closed it again. 'Leave me alone for a minute. I'm dying.'

It was probably only about five minutes but to me it seemed like an eternity that Raoul lay there dying. His breathing in and out got longer and smoother until finally it seemed either to have stopped or to be moving only in one direction, as if all the air in the world was emptying into one set of bottomless lungs. His body grew stiller than any stillness I have ever seen. His face went smooth. He changed color.

I looked at him and I knew that he was dead. I knew this absolutely, and yet then, a moment later, there he was on his feet again, strapping on his hat and smiling at me. 'All set,' he said. 'Let's go.'

I must have looked at him strangely, for he shrugged and gave me a strange look back. 'I'm all set,' he repeated. 'I'm dead and ready, ready for anything. You know, to be invincible you have to do what you have to do. I have to preempt. I have to be already dead.'

Earlier when I said that my life was all subtext until I met Raoul this is what I meant. It was with Raoul, and with his help, that for the first time I recognized something that was really all mine. It was something I had been working on for a long time without even knowing it: the art of invincibility. In all sorts of vague and unarticulated ways, I had been trying to build invincibility into myself. And so had Raoul.

If I had thought about it in advance, I might have said that to discover someone else embarked on what was meant to be one's own private quest could only belittle the challenge and muffle the glory. But for me, discovering Raoul as a fellow knight in the crusade for invincibility seemed to make the cause even nobler. Is it possible that all grand efforts, even those we undertake when very young, eventually require an audience of some kind if they are to actually amount to anything?

At any rate, from that first day when Raoul articulated for me what it was we were both after, the intensity and focus of my life changed dramatically. The two of us began to pool our strategies for the pursuit of invincibility, and to devise special tests and rituals for each other. Most of these we carried out in the crypts at first, but soon our friendship spilled over into above-ground territories – a development that proved slightly awkward for me at first, until I got used to wearing my 'wooden arm' disguise in public. Raoul went to the Luckwell Friends school, about a half mile up the road from my own, and many afternoons we would meet in the Apollo Pastry shop halfway between for an invincibility meeting that evolved, over the weeks, into a highly stylized and ritualized event.

We began by ordering an assortment of luscious pastries and, always, a pint of raspberry sorbet. These we carried back to Raoul's apartment, which was near the cathedral and usually empty, and therefore preferable to my house. En route to the apartment we maintained a stiff-legged, zombie walk and repeated my chant – 'PHAMPAM BIHRAM BACTI, PHAMPAM BIHRAM BACTI' – over and over until we reached the halfway point, where we switched to a chant that Raoul claimed aided invincibility: 'I-OH-WAY PO-TA-TOE, I-OH-WAY PO-TA-TOE.' I was a little dubious of this one at first, but he swore by it, and the cadence was familiar, so I went along with him. When we got to Raoul's building we walked in silence past the doorman and into the elevator. Then, the moment the elevator doors closed, Raoul would hit one high note, and I, who had a slightly more accurate ear, would hit a note a halftone higher or lower. We would ride up in our shimmering discord until the moment the doors opened onto Raoul's floor, when we again fell silent.

Inside the apartment we spread our treats out on his mother's silver tea tray. I can't remember how this next part of the ritual evolved — perhaps because our goodies were courtesy of Apollo Pastry — but Raoul and I would then stretch out like gods feasting on Olympus and, using a little leather bag of stones his father had brought back for him from Turkey as our players, we would reenact the battle of Troy.

'More ambrosia?' Raoul, in a godly act of supreme indifference, always paused to offer me more lemonade just when we reached the moment when Hector was to be killed.

'No, thank you. A little nectar, please,' I invariably replied as he filled my glass. Then we would kill the stone that was Hector and pop it into the leather bag and drag it around the walls of Troy seven times.

One day in the middle of this ritual, out of a heightened awareness of the fatal weakness of another of our warriors, Achilles, Raoul and I seized upon a name for our two-man club: the Invincible Heels. In a solemn and symbolic gesture, we cut a hole in the back of our left high-top sneakers and clipped away the exposed section of sock. Then, dizzied by our brilliance, we stepped out into the twilight of a rainy April night and went loping through the streets of our city, happy just to feel the cold air against our brave bare left heels and to know that it was in fact sweet bold invincibility that was pounding like glory itself through our veins.

The Art of Dying

Two important strands of self began winding together for me once Raoul and I became the Invincible Heels. One, as I already mentioned, was that for the first time I had a primary text – a partner and an agenda that I had chosen and that were really mine. The other piece of me that took root during my times with Raoul I can trace back to a particular afternoon. It was an afternoon like any of the many we were spending together at the time, except that on this particular afternoon I thought of a little movie camera I owned and for the first time I knew exactly what to do with it.

The camera had been presented to me by Ajax and Harwood a few years earlier, on the Crawlspace Day that marked my tenth birthday. The three of us were all sitting around our little crawlspace table under the house when Ajax handed it over. 'You have such wonderful mind movies you always tell us about,' Ajax had said, blushing with the shy triumph that sometimes overcomes people when they know they are about to do something that will please someone else very much. 'We thought you might enjoy making real movies.'

I remember how I did love, at first sight, the look of the little black box that was the movie camera. I was thrilled by the cool touch of it against my cheek as I looked through the viewfinder. But for the life of me I hadn't a clue what to do with this new toy. It seemed

126

so laborsome to try to translate the movies that already played so vividly in my own head into something that other people might enjoy. Besides, I liked having those visions as mine and mine alone. For a while I tried to surreptitiously film a few of our Rena sessions – they seemed to me a kind of ready-made theater. But Rena had an absolute fit when she realized what I was doing. 'What can ya be tinking, girlie?' she bellowed at me in her wild Irish brogue that always came on strong when she was upset. 'Supposing tose reels were to fall into ta wrong hands? Into enemy hands?' Then she tore the film from the camera and dumped it in the trash.

After this incident the little camera had snoozed, lonely and untouched, in my sock drawer for a long time until I had what I thought was another brain-storm. 'You know, you and Harwood have great mind movies too,' I announced to Ajax one summer day. The two of us were on the front porch, cutting back the wisteria vines that were threatening to clasp our front door forever shut in their tendril embrace. 'You just have yours when you're asleep.'

This was the simple truth. For almost two years Ajax and Harwood and I had been having what we called a China Summit every morning over breakfast. The China Summits were so named because in her early 'dig dig dig to China' sessions Rena had urged us to sift through our dreams, like gold panners, for any clues that might lead us to our treasure. Partly in response to this, and partly because it turned out to be a fun way to start the day, we began recounting to each other over breakfast, as minutely as possible, the details of any dreams we had had the night before.

After a few of these breakfast summits I had begun to realize something about myself that Ajax and Harwood must have realized about me right away. It seemed I didn't have dreams, or at least not the normal, vaguely if bizarrely narrative dreams that others had. I had only what I called Curtain Pulls, and what Ajax eventually nicknamed TA-DAHS. These consisted of a simple but dramatic moment when a white sheetlike material was lifted away from my brainscreen to reveal either a brand-new color – one I had literally never seen before – or nothing at all. Until I knew better I was perfectly satisfied with these simple night visions: 'New color last night,' I'd announce happily over my breakfast cereal. Or: 'Nothing there. The cupboard was bare.'

But after I started hearing stories of the wild worlds that rollicked through the snore palaces that my aunt and uncle became each night, I began to feel a little sorry for myself. I couldn't believe all the delicious nuance and rococo detail that Ajax and Harwood unfolded for me over breakfast some mornings, and I began to take an almost jealous interest in every little twist of costuming and plot.

To compound my sense of dream deprivation, Ajax and Harwood each had a kind of recurring or serial dream story that played for them on a regular basis. New episodes of these were always my favorites, for details that might have seemed incredibly wacky and arbitrary within the play of your basic one-shot dream took on an eerie and inevitable logic within the narrative of these ongoing sagas. Harwood's epic involved a long and bloody trench war with the Chinese – a fact that lent a purely coincidental secondary significance to the name China Summit – and was cross-webbed with several subplots of treachery and espionage. In Ajax's nightlife, she made recurring appearances as the dashing female sharp-shooter Plinky Tupperwein, who, with her husband, Ad, was on a world tour with a Wild West show. Annie Oakley, the lesser but more successfully marketed markswoman who was the bane of Plinky's existence, usually made guest appearances, and inevitably the episodes would build to a showdown between the two rivals in which they tried to outdo each other's amazing tricks. They would shoot cigarettes from the mouths of sitting dogs, bottles from the hands of little babies and even, in one tense scene, crab apples off each other's heads as they sped past on bicycles.

While it didn't seem right to try to make real films from my own mind movies, the serial dreams of Ajax and Harwood seemed to me to be just the right stuff. To my surprise, they didn't object when I confessed my idea – in fact, they even seemed interested in helping. But from the first the project was hobbled with impracticalities. We simply didn't have the numbers needed to stage the China War effectively, although we did get a few good close-up trench scenes, including one in which Harwood, as an American officer, slithered in to slit the throat of Ajax, a Chinese-American who had turned traitor and was trading secrets to the enemy. We also got a few nice takes of Annie and Plinky, starring Rena and Ajax, respectively, but unfortunately these, like the China War project, involved an almost constant volley of gunfire, and the neighbors began to get annoyed. Finally the police arrived one day and put an end to our backyard shootings – of guns and film.

Once again the camera was retired to my sock drawer. I pulled it out again, briefly, during the period when I was struggling with the problem of girl versus boy behavior, to see if I could capture the crux of this enigma on film. My inspiration to try this had come from a little volume Harwood had given me on the history of film, in which I read about Eadweard Muybridge and his breakthrough analysis of animal locomotion using still photography. I stared again and again at Muybridge's frame-by-frame dissection of horses, birds and apes in motion. If he could get to the bottom of animal locomotion using still photography, I reasoned, then perhaps I could unravel the secrets of human behavior – specifically male versus female behavior – using moving photography. Unfortunately my thinking was naive, vague and, worst of all, theory-heavy – attributes that I have since learned are all anathema to good film.

The movie I ended up making was nothing more than a simple montage of different groups: a clique of my classmates gathered in a hall, a flock of geese grazing on a lawn, a busy anthill, a band of male priests striding across the cathedral close, a troop of firefighters on their truck, a pair of raccoons descending our gutter pipe. After watching it, Ajax – in an uncharacteristically unsupportive mode – condemned my effort as resembling 'a bad ad for life insurance.' So I put the camera away once more, for good this time – or so I thought.

Then one day Raoul and I were in my attic, taking turns practicing dying in two little coffins we had constructed out of heavy cardboard boxes. I looked over at Raoul as he lay pale and still in his coffin, his hands in a gentle cross of surrender over his chest. Outside a cloud passed and I watched the way the sunlight came shouting in through a nearby dormer window and then spilled itself all over Raoul, as if it were celebrating the sight of him lying there, deader than dead. I watched this in the same way I always watched my mind movies, and at that moment it hit me. The camera was the perfect tool of invincibility. With it, you could be there but not be there – the very duality, after all, that was the key to all forms of invincibility.

'Helium!' I called to Raoul, using my Invincible Heels nickname for him and forgetting that at the moment he was dead and couldn't answer. 'Helium, I'm going to make a movie of you dead and you can watch it and learn to die better. Then you can make one for me.'

Raoul didn't say a thing or even move a muscle just then, of course, because he was long gone. But when he returned I explained my idea to him again, and after a few moments of brow-furrowing he nodded his happy approval. 'Good thinking, Tree,' he said, using the Invincible Heels nickname he had chosen for me a few months earlier when, in a Mutual Confession of Vulnerable Secrets session, I had disclosed that Logan Raintree was my real name. ('Helium' was the fruit of an earlier session in which he had confessed a constitutional inability to burp.)

'Nice thinking, Tree.' He said it once again, and then he took my nice thought one step further. 'You know, if the camera was there to watch us, we could try dying together. That might be good, don't you think?'

'Die together? No such thing,' I answered. 'Think about it. Contradiction in terms. Won't work.'

'Well, we could die at the same time then,' said Raoul. 'Alone, but at the same time.'

Always before when Raoul and I had practiced dying, we had been careful to take turns — to leave a witness in the land of the living. Raoul, of course, had died alone and with no witnesses many times before he met me, but for some reason we had sensed that the dynamics of the situation might be irrevocably altered if we both tried to pull the stunt at once. Thus, when Raoul suggested that we die at the same time and let the camera be our witness, he was deliberately bumping us up a notch on our self-assigned invincibility obstacle course. Because of this, and no doubt because of the presence of the camera, we prepared much more elaborately for our double-death film debut than we ever had for our casual individual deaths. We clipped an assortment of flowers from Ajax's most exotic beds and lined our coffins with them. We gathered all the candlesticks we could find and positioned them around the scene, a constellation of mourners. For a while I was worried about an appropriate sound track, but then we found an old 78 recording of a ragtime number entitled 'The Insouciant Ghost.' This seemed just right.

'It shouldn't sound too perfect,' Raoul said as we listened again and again to the recording, trying to pick what would make the most effective opening and ending passages. 'It needs a limp.' Then he took out his pocket knife and carved a clean but deep scratch across the surface of the record. This seemed to me a brilliant touch, perhaps because the little hiccup the scratch gave the melody reminded me of the comforting flick flick flick of the stone seams against my fingertips as I ran through the narrow and dark passageways of the cathedral.

Finally the moment came when we set the camera on its tripod, lit all the candles, started the old windup Victrola we had found in a back corner of the attic, pushed the film button forward and prepared ourselves to climb into our coffins and die. We stood together briefly in front of the camera first, to give a short farewell speech, delivered antiphonally.

'Sometimes in the Pursuit of Invincibility you must preempt,' said Raoul.

'Sometimes, you must die,' I said.

'To die well you must master noble and quiet surrender,' said Raoul.

'Be both pebble and feather when you let go and drop,' I said.

Then we climbed into our coffins and quietly, nobly dropped dead. We knew by then that a presumption of success often can induce the thing itself, and in a gesture of bold optimism – an assumption that we would, as usual, be able to resurface in life – we carefully rigged the camera to allow only five minutes of filming before the reel ended. We certainly didn't want the anticlimactic, not to mention mawkish, scene of our awakening to spoil our fine tutorial on dying.

The first sense to come back after you have been dead for a while is smell, and the first thing I remember after leaning back into my coffin and dropping, fast as a pebble and whimsical as a feather, into the black wash of the dead is the sensation that my nose, at least, was once again alive. Alive and curious, aroused by the hooligan scent of something burning. Sounds come back next, and for several moments I was convinced that I heard someone knocking, insistently.

Perhaps they were trying to escape the fire, I thought. Then everything else came swimming back and I was upright, fully alive, brushing flower petals from my clothes and smiling over at Raoul, who was sitting there, a little pale still, but also definitely fully alive. The smell was coming from one of the candlesticks, where a low-burning candle had ignited a little wad of paper that had been used to wedge the candle steady in the candlestick. The knocking was simply the Victrola needle, riding the end of the record, which was now finished. We were alive again. The camera, our witness, had done its job.

The Art of Dying, as we decided to title this cinematic effort, pleased us immeasurably when we got it back from the developing plant and sat, once again in the privacy of the attic, to watch it. As it turned out, what fascinated us most as we replayed the little film again and again was not the vision of our corpses, but the short farewell remarks we'd made in the beginning.

'I don't think we could die any better than we did there,' said Raoul. 'We're pretty good.'

'Yeah, we are,' I agreed. 'But we could use a little practice in the parts where we have to be alive.'

With this new challenge in mind, we decided to make a whole series of films – a series we referred to collectively, if somewhat ponderously, as the Library of the Invincible. Planning the series really only meant fitting the camera into all the rituals we had already devised to test and strengthen ourselves. But the fact that at the end of all our efforts we could claim the prize of a finished film, something decidedly more tangible than the whirling ambition of our own psyches, seemed to give our crusade for invincibility new life and validity.

Cryptograms and Domesticating Fear were the next two films we made after *The Art of Dying*. The first of these chronicled the various adventures we had pursued in the cathedral crypts and, quite frankly, temporarily invigorated an activity that was beginning to take on the flat emotional contours of routine. We encountered some tough technical challenges while making this film – how to achieve the appropriate lighting and how to hold a camera steady while wiggling through a narrow tunnel. Parts of the finished product were a bit rough, but still the film had its moments.

Domesticating Fear starred the pet snakes Raoul and I had taken on jointly after confessing a mutual loathing for these reptiles. The invincibility lesson behind this film – and, of course, behind our original acquisition of the snakes – was that to smother fear you must embrace it. By the time we decided to film our snake collection it had become more of a general reptile collection, consisting of two big red-tail boa constrictors, a medium-sized rock python, an anaconda, three iguanas, two caimans and one very unthreatening turtle. This was our third film, and in an effort to give it the symptoms of a narrative art at play, I decided we should open with a moody shot of Raoul's face appearing in the backseat of my family car as he wiped away heavy steam that had completely fogged his window, and then close with a shot of me sitting in the backseat of Raoul's family car as my clear window gradually steamed up completely and hid me from view. (Creating the steam was a challenge in itself, requiring many pots and pans of boiling water all over the floorboards of the car.) In between these artsy bookends were sequences we filmed in a neighborhood bamboo patch that satisfied our vision of a jungle setting, featuring each of us handling the various pets. I stood stoically while our python Pauline slithered around my shoulders and neck and deadened the flesh on my face with the delicate touch of her flickering tongue. Raoul cradled the caimans while they greedily snapped lumps of raw hamburger from his palms. In one very odd sequence, I remember, I allowed Raoul to place a live rat on my head while

Steve, the largest of the boas, was wrapped around my neck. Steve must not have been too hungry at the time, for he tightened only slightly around my neck, and to this day it is the feel of those little rat feet clutching my hair – not the rippling power of snake flesh – that still gives me a shiver.

The next and, as it turned out, final installment in our Library of the Invincible was a film we called *Free Heeling*. This consisted of scenes shot during the Invincibility Walks that Raoul and I tried to take every Wednesday night, conditions permitting. Wednesdays were Book Club Night for Raoul's parents, Poker Night for Ajax – and for Harwood, if he was in town. That's how the adults in our respective homes presented it to us, anyway. Raoul and I, once we discovered the happy coincidence, called Wednesday nights Stew Night, for it turned out that on such evenings all four of our caretakers could be trusted to imbibe so heavily that by about midnight or so, when they finally retired, they fell like lead into a deep and irresponsible sleep. Their fuzziness was our freedom – or so we told ourselves. In fact, I probably could have slipped from my bed and out of the house almost any night of the week if I'd wanted to. But by restricting such outings to Stew Night, Raoul and I gave the exercise the pleasing structure and drama of ritual.

'All systems snore,' we would announce to each other when we met on these nights, as prearranged, at 1 A.M. at a corner halfway between our homes. Occasionally one of us – usually Raoul – would be unable to make it, because of an unexpectedly sober adult, and the mission would abort itself. On the nights we both made it we would set off at a slow jog down the long hill that took us away from all the houses we knew so well, away from the neighborhood that looked almost rumpled, it was so familiar. We went loping down the hill and then right onto the wide flat avenue that led downtown, into the unsleeping night-stew of the city. Here windows were always lit, but never with a friendly glow; footsteps of passing strangers reverberated like gunfire in the night air. Smells were different — they were all scorched around the edges, as if the world was an empty pan that had been left too long over a hot burner. The people we saw out and about downtown didn't talk to one another — they spat little twisted pieces of gristly language out of the sides of their mouths, at no one in particular. The night was thick with flying chunks of this tough talk, and with disembodied moans and shouts that came slashing through the darkness like invisible swords. Raoul and I never needed to consult about which streets would test our strength the most. We could sense a good battle zone in the way the hair lay along the back of our necks. We never talked about what was actually happening there; we preferred to keep the exercise abstract.

Usually on these walks, Raoul and I would separate and stalk the night demons alone for an hour before meeting up again and heading home. But to get footage for *Free Heeling*, we had to move together through the streets, taking turns filming each other in scenes where our invincibility might be at play.

To our surprise, we found ourselves in tougher situations when we moved through this world as a team than we had ever encountered when we traversed the streets alone. Perhaps it was the camera that made us more noticeable, or perhaps our two-ness bumped us from lost-child to gang-youth stature in the wild and watery eyes of the native night prowlers who seemed now to stare at us from every stoop and alleyway. Before we had traveled in what felt like an inviolate if not invisible zone — a zone, we naively told ourselves, that our remarkable powers had carved out for us. But now, as we moved down a street separated by twenty paces but still clearly linked, faces came swimming toward us from all directions. They came floating down and hung there, right in front of us, like fallen and infected moons.

'What is you? Kid reporters?' asked one man who dropped out of the sky. Then he fell backward with a noise like a rooster crowing and began to whirl around us like a dust storm.

'Make way for the Soldiers of Democracy,' cried another man as he swept the pavement in a low bow and raised on high the paper bag he clutched.

'Here kiddie kiddie kiddie. Here pretty little kiddies.' A woman's voice came purring through the night, trying to lasso us in its honey-velvet flow. 'Come here, kiddies. Let me fix your hair.'

We knew better than to let ourselves really hear any of this, and I think I remember these scenes now only because Raoul and I watched them over and over later, on film. I do remember that it took all my Heel training, whenever I was in the lead and Raoul was following with the camera, to simply march one foot in front of the other and to keep moving, slowly and deliberately, down the street. And of course I remember the night, even though its most dramatic moments went unfilmed, when instead of feeling that I was braving it through a barrage of the usual verbal scatter-shot I felt more as if someone had snuck up and slipped a big grenade into my sock.

On that night a man stopped his car and left it idling by the curb while he followed three steps behind me down 15th Street. 'Hi, I'm Bill Rogers,' he kept repeating. 'My name is Bill Rogers.' For minutes that felt endless I walked on without looking back, but then I felt my left shoulder go dead, heavy and dead as wet sand, and I knew it was because this man Bill Rogers had reached through the night and touched me there in a way that was wrong.

'My name is Bill Rogers,' he said again, and when he spun me around to face him all I could see was a web of gray saliva moving over small mean teeth and an Adam's apple that was pumping wildly, as if a mouse was trapped there in his neck. I shut my eyes and arched backward and broke all the Night Rules. 'Raoul!' I screamed. 'Raooooooooul!' I let loose the cry again, and it flew straight and hungry as an arrow through the filthy black air.

Then it was Raoul's touch that was upon me, quiet and steady. It was Raoul's one arm that slipped around my shoulders and his other arm that scooped behind my knees, and his two arms together that lifted me up and away from the ghoulish face that called itself Bill Rogers.

'Excuse me, Mr Rogers. Come on, Tree,' said Raoul. Then he walked quietly, calmly away. He carried me all the way down that street, back toward home.

For weeks after the Mr Rogers incident I was mortified and depressed. I was tortured by the double shame of knowing not only that I had failed, but also that Raoul had not. Instead of admiring his strength and feeling grateful for what amounted to a rescue on his part, I hated him for it. Instead of thanking him for remembering in a crisis the rules that I myself forgot, I avoided the subject altogether and set about the silent and mean-spirited task of catching him at some failure of his own.

After the incident we had decided, somewhat arbitrarily, that *Free Heeling* was a finished film – a wrap. Without ever addressing the matter directly, we also came to the unspoken understanding that Invincibility Walks themselves were outmoded and unnecessary, a practice of the past. Our dying sessions had ground to a similar halt once we had *The Art of Dying* in hand, and we almost never went to the crypts anymore. Most of our snakes were dead or lost. It seemed that all of our rituals and exercises were suffering a very literal form of artistic execution – we were killing them off by translating them into film.

'I wonder what makes religious ritual so enduring,' Raoul said one day when we were sitting in his living room, brooding over the matter. We had just finished a rather lackluster session of reenacting Troy – a Heels ritual we had not tried to film yet.

'Duh?' I blubbered my fingers against my lower lip. I was still smarting with a general sense of failure, still resentful of Raoul's rescue of me, and I sometimes leapt a little too emphatically when I thought I saw an opportunity to prove myself superior in some way. This was exactly the case here, and even though I immediately sensed my overkill, I kept right on going; I ran the red light. 'Let's see. Ever hear of immortality? Maybe religious rituals don't die 'coz God don't die,' I said in a cartoon dunce voice, as if I were some idiot bear about to light a match to check for gas in the bottom of a gas can.

And a moment later the whole situation exploded in my face, just as it would have for the cartoon bear. Raoul shot me a reverse-zoom look.

'You can be such an annoying little stump some-times, Tree. You know that?' His words dropped to me from a cold and far-off place, but I could still hear the hurt and the truth in them.

'Invincibility IS immortality, and vice versa,' he said as he sighed and looked at the floor. 'I'm going out to shoot some hoops. See you later.'

Then he laced up his high-tops and left me there, sitting in his parents' living room, poking at a pile of Turkish stones. Stupid little stones that only minutes earlier, I swear to you, had been the bravest, most noble warriors you could possibly imagine.

End of a Reel

This may be fallout from a career in film, but my
memories from the early autumn of my ninth official
Crawlspace Day, the Crawlspace Day that marked my
fifteenth birthday, remind me of images that fall at the
end of a damaged reel. Scenes pulsate with alternating
excesses of darkness and glare, as if the sun is having
a temper tantrum in the sky, refusing to behave and
just make day like a good ball of fire. Normal patterns
not just of light and shadow but also of cause and
effect seem disrupted. A virus of unpredictability
infects everything, including my own behavior.
Perhaps this is why, for once that year, when everybody at my school started talking about where their
family would be going over the long three-week
Christmas break, I jumped right in and talked of travel
plans myself. Almost everyone else was going out west
to ski, it seemed, or to some sunny Caribbean isle. I
decided to spread the word, quietly and matter-of-
factly to anyone who cared to ask, that I was going
to Russia. With Harwood, possibly forever. I had
researched and written a long paper on this country
for my geography class the year before, so I felt well-
equipped to field any impromptu questions that might
arise before or after the alleged trip.

With this silly invention about a trip to Russia I
inadvertently trapped myself into pushing a second
small fib, in addition to the old nonsense about my

wooden arm, on Raoul. He and I had been seeing less and less of each other as the weeks passed, partly because of the awkwardness that had grown up between us after he had rescued me on the night of our last Invincibility Walk, and partly because he was getting more and more involved in sports and having to stay later and later after school. When Ajax and Harwood had asked me for the first time whether there was anyone I would like to include in Crawlspace Day that year, I had briefly considered inviting Raoul. I thought the ritual, which I had never told him about, might impress him. In the end, however, I decided against inviting him, mainly because to do so would kill what was rapidly becoming one of the only frontiers Raoul and I were still exploring together – namely, pretending that he didn't exist.

Every time Raoul had come to my house in the past – and during the heat of our filmmaking this had been almost every day – we had taken great pains to sneak him in secretly, past Ajax and anyone else who happened to be there. It just added a little zing to things. We would creep up to the attic – to practice dying or work on a film or whatever – and while up there we'd remain constantly alert for the sound of ascending footsteps.

If we thought we heard someone approaching, Raoul would run and dive into one of several hiding places we had established for him. Then, when the door pushed open and Ajax or Harwood stuck their head through and said, 'Hi, Elray. What-cha doing?' I would answer, 'Oh nothing. Raoul and I are just working on some Invincibility Exercises.' Whoever had come to the door would look at me and then look around the room and finally say, 'Oh, okay. Well, dinner's almost ready. Come down soon.' Or something like that.

It was a pretty simple trick but for some reason it gave us enormous pleasure, and Raoul and I would roll across the floor in hysterics after the door had closed again and the footsteps had retreated. 'Dinner's ready,' one of us would sit up and say, and then we'd both collapse into laughter again. Even after all our other rituals had begun to fail us we continued with this practical joke, and then in our search for new rituals we decided to expand the joke. We decided 'to explore new territories of invincibility using the ruse of nonexistence,' as we described it in our Invincible Heels journal. Our new exercise consisted mainly of stashing Raoul in places in my house where he could be a secret witness to the routines of my life. I closed him into the wood box in the living room a few times, I remember, where he lay stiff-armed and spied, through a peephole we had drilled ahead of time, on our afternoon sessions with Rena. We also hid him behind a stack of blankets in the linen closet on an evening when Ajax and I were watching movies in the upstairs TV room, but this, he complained, was dull.

'You guys don't say anything, you don't do anything,' he said. 'I'd rather just watch TV myself.'

Once he stationed himself on the back stairs that emptied into the pantry just off our dining room and stayed there throughout a long and festive dinner party that Ajax threw for Rena and two friends of hers from Ireland. As the dinner guests worked their way through a half case of wine, Raoul and I had a good time too.

'What do *you* think of the Panama Canal situation, Elray?' one of the Irishmen turned and asked me at one point.

'I don't know. Let's ask Raoul,' I suggested.

'And who, my dear, might Raoul be?' he leaned toward me and asked.

'Her invisible friend,' Ajax whispered, and then she burst into giggles. 'The two of them practice Invisibility Exercises together.'

'Indeed!' the Irishman howled with an absurd happiness. 'By all means, then! Let's ask Raoul!'

'Let's ask Raoul!' became the rallying cry for every hotly debated issue at the table that night. At times the dinner guests were all shouting it so loudly that Raoul himself could join in from his post on the stairs, and no one – except me, of course – ever noticed.

Our original plan had been that at times I would secrete myself in a similar fashion somewhere in Raoul's apartment, so that I could spy on his family and flex my own fledgling powers of nonexistence. But every time I tried to make a specific date to do this, Raoul came up with some excuse. His parents were away, the whole family was going out to his grand-mother's farm for the weekend, the only good hiding closet had been locked and he couldn't find the key – he always had some reason why it wouldn't work.

Doors were quietly shutting all around Raoul and me. I could feel it. All my efforts to protect what was left of the Prospero's island where the two of us had wandered so happily for so long seemed doomed.

Since Raoul didn't even know about Crawlspace Day, let alone that I had been thinking of inviting him to it, there was no need for me to feel guilty about deciding to exclude him. But that's what I did feel when I ran into him unexpectedly one day as I was standing on the sidelines of the playing fields at his school, dreading being sent into a hockey game where girls from my school were pitted against girls from his. Raoul and I rarely acknowledged each other at public gatherings, but that afternoon I looked up and there he was, running right toward me with a huge smile on his face. It was his Helium smile – a smile that reminded me of the bright look he'd given me on that long-ago day in the sub-subcrypts when I first told him I had a wooden arm. Remembering this fib, and the fact that as far as I knew he still believed it, I quickly slipped my right hand into my jacket pocket.

'Hey, Tree,' he said. 'I hear you're going to Russia? Is it true? My God, that's so superior.'

I looked at the little flecks of mud splattered across Raoul's outdoor-pink cheeks and the way his eyes were shining, and I couldn't bear to surrender this, the first glimpse of real admiration I'd seen on his face since the night I had failed on 15th Street. I hesitated for a split second, but I knew what I was going to do.

'Yeah, I guess so,' I said. 'Looks that way, anyway.'

'That is so great. That is incredible. When do you leave?' he asked.

'Oh, you know. Christmas Day, or right after Christmas probably. It's still a couple of months away. It's up to Harwood.'

'Incredible. You should really try to get to Siberia, check it out,' he said. He was staring at the ground now, trying to dislodge a stone from the mud with his toe. 'I bet it's amazing – great terrain for invincibility practice.' He looked up with a smaller version of his big smile. 'We should get together, do some practices before you leave. Gotta make sure all your systems are in top form for this trip, right?'

'Right.' I nodded back at him, and then I looked down at the ground myself and tried with my own toe to uproot the rock he had now abandoned. By the time I looked up again Raoul was gone. Just another schoolboy in a blue shirt at the far end of the playing field. As I watched him climb the hill and disappear into the asphalt haze of the school parking lot I realized the finality of what I had done. I had left myself with only one option now. I had to turn Raoul away. I had to pretend – oh terrible irony – that he was invisible. That he didn't exist.

I set about my grim task immediately. I stopped checking behind the loose stone in the St Joseph of Arimathea Chapel wall where in the past Raoul and I used to leave messages for each other, usually proposing a meeting time and place for an Invincibility Exercise. I was saddened by the image of the little slips of paper I imagined must be piling up there. I changed my route to and from school, walking almost an extra mile in each direction, and I even took to doing what no one in my house had ever done – I locked the doors at night.

I knew these tactics were having an effect when one evening in late September Raoul broke all the rules and telephoned my house.

'There's someone named Raoul on the phone. For you,' Ajax said to me. She was standing wide-eyed in the doorway to my room, watching me carefully. For the few calls that had come for me in the past she had stood at the bottom of the stairs and yelled, 'El-RAY! Tell-la-phone!' I looked up casually from my book. I was reading *To Kill a Mockingbird*, I remember, and as I faked a deliberately lazy appraisal of Ajax's kilted silhouette it struck me that she would make a fine Boo Radley.

'It must be a wrong number,' I said, without pausing to consider how many other Elrays there could be in our city. 'I don't know anyone named Raoul.'

Ajax gave me a funny look and said, 'All right, dearie. If you're sure.' I had plenty of time during her slow descent to the phone to change my mind, but I didn't. I heard the low murmur of her voice as she said something briefly into the receiver, and then I heard her footsteps as she moved from the front room back to the kitchen. I returned to my book.

About half an hour later the phone rang again, and sure enough I heard Ajax climbing the stairs again after answering it. 'This time it's someone named Helium,' she said to me as she appeared in my doorway. 'For you.' That just about broke my heart, to think of poor Helium trying to get through to Tree. But once again I shrugged my shoulders and went back to my book.

'Never heard of 'im,' I said. 'Wrong number.'

'What is going on, Elray?' Ajax asked. 'Some kind of practical joke?' When I didn't answer or even look up from my book, she clomped back downstairs, faster this time, and disposed of poor Raoul again. The phone didn't ring for me again that night. Or, for that matter, for a long long time thereafter.

Return of the Native

No matter how well you may think you can plot the probable course of your own life, some turns just cannot be scripted. I learned this on a hot night in mid-October when I awoke from a dead sleep with the words of my own old Invincibility Chant in my ear: 'Phampam Bihram Bacti.' I lay very still in my bed.

'Phampam Bihram Bacti.' It wasn't a dream – someone was actually chanting. I sat up on my elbows and blinked into the darkness. It didn't seem possible. Raoul was there. Despite all my efforts to accept the fact that he did not exist, Raoul was kneeling beside my bed, chanting into my ear. 'Phampam Bihram Bacti.'

'Raoul?' The light – or, rather, lack of it – was such that the features of his face were just visible, as if through a shroud.

'Tree.' Something about his voice – a mannish tone around the edges – shocked me. The combination of his kneeling posture and earnest tone confused me further; I had to suppress a church urge to cross myself, or to say 'Amen.'

'Raoul, what are you doing here?' I said instead, and then winced at my boldness. It was such a direct and practical question.

'So many things are happening right now, I think you need recharging,' Raoul leaned over and whispered into my ear. His breath was so warm it felt

146

liquid. 'Me too, Tree. I need recharging. Come on. I've got an idea for a new exercise I want to tell you about.'

Seconds later I was on my feet and getting dressed, pulling on my jeans and high-tops, while Raoul moved toward the door and stood with his back turned discreetly to me.

'Ready?' I asked, as soon as I was in fact ready. Raoul turned toward me and shot me a look, an unforgettable look. He raised his eyebrows as if to say 'You talking to me?' and in that split second something crystallized for me. We had reached a crossroads, I realized. Raoul and I were entering new terrain, redrawing boundaries. I had not yet allowed myself to wonder what stroke of fortune had brought Raoul back to me so unexpectedly, like a dream in the middle of a hot Indian summer night. I had no idea what 'exercise' he might have in mind. But I knew that I was desperate to hold my own in this new adventure. I needed to be both decisive and unpredictable. Strong and mysterious. Immediately. I didn't have a lot to work with, standing there in the dark in so many ways. So I improvised with what came naturally. As Raoul reached to open my bedroom door for our exit I stepped forward and stopped him.

'Raoul, this way,' I said. I took him by the elbow and led him across the room, out the window and onto the roof.

On the roof the night air, so dark and so outside, made me more of my original self. I didn't need to speak in such a situation, only to do. With a confidence and fluidity that even now it pleases me to remember, I slid down the slope of the roof and leapt like a member of the squirrel nation into the embrace of the big sycamore tree in our side yard. It was hardly fair. I had exited my room this way so many times, drilled again and again by Rena, who had taught me the maneuver as an emergency fire escape, that the movement felt as comfortable and safe as pounding out my half of a 'Heart and Soul' duet on the piano.

147

As I stood in my tree I still didn't need to speak. I just needed to catch Raoul's eye. I did this, and a moment later he was sharing a tree limb with me. My bold self shivered and lost its bearings somewhat as the tree trembled and shifted around the odd treasure of its new occupants.

'I love surprises,' said Raoul as he inched toward me, Brailling his way along branches above him and beneath him with his fingers and his toes. 'You're so full of surprises, Tree.'

'Are you talking to me?' I said and shot him my own raised-eyebrow look. 'Or to our escape route?' Then, in an impeccable demonstration of gravity, I dropped to earth.

Seconds later, like a monkey with a magnet in his belly, Raoul had dropped down right beside me. 'I'm talking to you. I'm talking to this Tree,' he said. He paused and then, as if to make his point, he placed the tip of his index finger ever so lightly at the base of my neck.

The tables were seesawing so fast I felt seasick. Now it was Raoul's turn to say nothing and mine to follow as he took me by the hand and led me away from my house out to the street. His step was decisive and I felt lamblike in a way that displeased me. He knew where we were going. I didn't. I looked down at my bare and obviously real right arm, now attached by its hand to Raoul. Let go of the old, I told myself. New terrain. Take charge.

'Actually it's so funny you're here, because I too have an idea for a new exercise,' I announced brightly. This was a lie. I didn't. I had let go of one untruth, my alleged wooden arm, only to launch another.

Raoul stopped and looked up at a streetlamp that was casting a weak halo the color of grapefruit into the dark night. Then he looked back at me.

'Really?' he said. 'What a coincidence. How cool. Do tell.'

'Are you all ears?' I asked. It was not a very

sophisticated stalling strategy, but I was desperate.

'I am. I'm all ears,' said Raoul, turning to face me squarely in a way that I found just a little intimidating – as if he could turn out to be the kind of person who might misunderstand or even rob me. 'I'm ears, ears, ears,' he said as he gave me a small smile and tapped the tops of his real-life real Raoul ears. 'So spill.'

'Well then – oh you probably won't like this, but—' I began and then stopped. I looked downward and rolled a small stone with the toe of my right sneaker. My mind was racing, desperate to find something outrageous that would be right at the intersection of possibility and invincibility. A moment later I looked up and smiled at Raoul with the quiet calm of the supremely confident. I was such a lucky luckless girl. I had it.

'It's a nice warm night. If you have time, I thought we might swim across the Potomac, just above Great Falls,' I said sweetly. As I watched Raoul's eyes widen with surprise and enthusiasm everything fell into place in my world. Blood and oxygen began to move through my systems at top speed and the wild roar of triumph pounded in my ears.

'Oh I do have time for that,' said Raoul as he reached for my hand again. 'I definitely have time to swim across the Potomac with you. Very superior exercise, Little Tree.'

In my exhilaration at my last-minute save I didn't pay much attention to where Raoul was leading me, and I was surprised when it turned out to be to a blue Pontiac station wagon parked in the puddle of light made by the streetlight Raoul had stared at earlier. I looked from the car to Raoul.

'It's my dad's,' he said, reading my look.

'Who's driving?' I asked.

'I am,' said Raoul.

'But you – you're not sixteen. You don't have a license!' I hoped I was right. It would be too humiliating if Raoul, in addition to all his other superior achievements, had somehow circumvented the laws the rest of us abide by and become a legal driver.

'I know. But I almost do. I'll be extra careful. It can be a part of the exercise.' He patted my shoulder in a way that left no room for argument.

As I opened the front passenger door and climbed in next to Raoul I felt I was experiencing the modern miracle of the automobile for the very first time. The dials and gauges on the dashboard looked so scientific, and when Raoul turned the ignition key the answering roar of the engine sounded both victorious and threatening. I thought of Orville and Wilbur Wright and focused on trading my apprehension for a spirit of adventure. I looked up at my house, inside which the adults whose driving skills I had taken for granted for so many years were innocently sleeping, and felt a small rush of remorse.

Then we were moving through the streets, very slowly and carefully as Raoul had promised, on our way to the Potomac River and the adventure that I had pulled out of my hat to defend my standing as a full-blown Heel.

'Do you think these exercises really make us stronger?' I asked Raoul as we rolled out MacArthur Boulevard toward Great Falls Park. It was my second uncharacteristically direct question of the night. Raoul reached over with his right hand and put it lightly on my left knee. He was such a touchy person suddenly.

'I'm not sure, but I really like doing these exercises,' he said. 'Something is building – I'm not sure if it's invincibility, but something big is building.'

I nodded. 'Maybe you should keep both hands on the wheel,' I suggested. He took my advice. 'Aren't we almost there?' I asked after an awkward silence.

'Yes, almost. But do you realize what we're passing right now, Elray?'

I looked through the window to the left and to the right but saw nothing unusual or familiar. The moon was out, but only intermittently. Whenever it went behind the clouds it became very dark. I wondered, in fact, if we'd even be able to see our way to swim across the river when we got there. I began to worry that in my competitve bid for Heel status I had maybe set the bar too high.

'We just passed Glen Echo, Elray. The amusement park.' Raoul turned toward me and announced this so solemnly that the only possible reaction was laughter.

'Glen Echo? Echo . . . echo . . . echo . . . *Ecco la*!' I babbled, as I wriggled in my seat and giggled and slapped at my knee. 'Ecco puer,' I said, pointing to Raoul. 'And Ecco Glen Echo,' I added, sweeping a hand across the windshield out toward the big dark uncaring night that somewhere nearby, evidently, held Glen Echo. I was embarrassed that, despite having spent as much time as I had thinking about Glen Echo, I had no idea where it physically was. 'Actually, not such an amusing park if you ask me,' I finished, surprised by the sudden upset I felt. 'Better keep your eyes on the road. I'm not that anxious to be reunited with my dead parents.'

Raoul looked at me strangely but said nothing. His silence made my recent antics seem even sillier, and I found myself longing suddenly for the cool wrap of night water all around me. The quiet embrace of the Potomac was just what I needed. It would wash me out of myself and maybe even away into some other life altogether. I felt a stab of genuine excitement over the challenge I had so nonchalantly thrown out for Raoul. Forget Glen Echo, wherever it was. Raoul and I were about to swim across the Potomac together, on a semi-moonlit night, with the roar of Great Falls smashing, crashing nearby. I really was a lucky luckless girl.

At Swim-Two-Braves

The first surprise Raoul and I encountered when we arrived at Great Falls Park sometime after midnight was that we were by no means the only cowboys out and about on that warm October night. The parking lot held about fifteen cars, and a couple dozen or more people were milling about, smoking cigarettes and drinking beer and leaning up against their fenders with a look that fell somewhere between casual and criminal. I felt a familiar old prickle up the backs of my legs as Raoul and I walked past them, the same old tickle I used to get on Invincibility Walks through downtown late at night.

'Who are they?' I hissed at Raoul as we started down the path that led out of the parking lot to the river itself. 'What are they doing here?'

'Got me.' Raoul shrugged. 'Drug dealers? Gregarious young runaways? Insomniacs Anonymous?'

'There are so many worlds we don't know about,' I said, sighing and shaking my head.

'Like the world of bugs, and how they feed,' said Raoul as he slapped at his neck.

'Like the world of giant snapping turtles that bite off swimmers' toes, and the world of leeches and poisonous water snakes,' I countered, hoping to up the ante and get our fears focused on the exercise at hand.

'Like the world of bottom muck and invisible centrifugal sucking eddies,' said Raoul.

'Like the world of smithereens of things past that churn in perpetuity at the bottom of the Falls,' I said, cutting to the chase.

'Good one,' said Raoul. We both fell silent then, for we needed to concentrate on the trail before us, which was just barely visible when moonlight fell through the canopy of trees overhead. When the moon ducked behind the clouds, as it did for one long stretch, our pace slowed dramatically as we picked our way gingerly past tree roots and rock outcrops that in daylight we would have skipped over like goats. On several occasions one of us would slip or stumble, and the other would pause and mumble 'Okay?' before moving on. Once something large, probably a deer, shot out through the brush in front of us and I jumped and shouted 'Oh!' and grabbed Raoul's arm in a way that made us both laugh when we recovered from the fright a moment later. Although it was neither easy nor difficult, normal nor strange, the night hike through the woods with Raoul seemed to me about as good a way as I could imagine to pass one's time on earth.

Before I was ready for the hike to be over it was. We reached the river's edge, and as we did the moon came out in all its glory as if to salute us. The last scraps of clouds drifted off the edge of the horizon and left us standing in a world that was all about light and all about darkness at the same time. It reminded me of a charcoal etching, and I allowed myself to imagine that sometime later I might sketch this scene, this moment when Raoul and I stood in the serious moonlight at the water's edge on the brink of a new adventure.

'Here we are,' said Raoul, which was really the only possible thing to say at that moment.

'Yes. Here we are,' I said, ending what I assumed would be our last conversation before we sprang into action. But we stood there for a few minutes side by side in the silence – or in the near silence, for as soon

as we stopped talking the voice of the river blew up
and came rushing all around us. It covered us with its
lapping sounds and slapping noises and trickles and
gurgles and splashes. From somewhere way off to the
left came a roar like wind trapped in a chimney. The
Falls.

Now that it was definitely time to proceed I found
that I was definitely reluctant – not because of the
water or any dangers or discomforts it might pose, but
because of the gargantuan, totally unanticipated problem of what to wear into the water. Neither Raoul nor
I had packed a swimsuit; we had not known until the
last minute that we would be swimming. Stripping
down was out of the question, but paddling across in
waterlogged jeans seemed equally absurd.

'What are you going to swim in?' I asked, shocking
myself yet again with my bluntness.

Raoul looked up at the moon and squinted. Then he
bent down and began to untie his shoes. 'I think I'll
just wear my shorts. Have dry clothes to drive home
in,' he said without looking up. 'How about you?'

It really wasn't fair. His boxers were the sartorial
equivalent of swimming trunks in terms of body
revealed. It really wasn't fair, and he knew it. Girls
always got the short end in these matters. 'I think I'll
wear my shirt. And my underwear,' I said as I bent
down to untie my high-tops. I felt myself getting
almost angry as I pulled off my socks and shoes and
wriggled out of my jeans, but the surprise of how cool
the night air felt against my bare legs took me out of
smaller matters and put me back on track with the
adventure at hand. I really didn't feel like swimming,
I realized. I felt like building a fire and huddling
beside it.

'Shall we discuss strategies?' I asked as I crept
toward the edge of the woods to stash my pants and
shoes behind a tree. When I turned around Raoul was
so close I jumped.

'Yes,' he said. He was standing very straight, not

even a foot away from me. The moonlight falling over his bare shoulders gave him accidental Indian charisma; coincidentally, his blue boxers had canoes all over them. 'Yes,' Raoul said again. 'We definitely should discuss strategies. And I think we may need to lie down and die before this one. Just to be thorough.' He stretched a hand toward me and I took it. Then the two of us walked to the river's edge and lay down on our backs side by side on the gravelly beach.

'Strategies first, dying second?' Raoul asked.

'Yes,' I answered.

'Okay. Let's pick a landmark on the far side, well above the Falls, and keep it in sight as we swim, so we don't get disoriented,' Raoul said.

'Right. Let's make the moon promise to stay out, so we can see our landmark,' I said.

'Let's stay very near each other in the water.'

'And maintain cheerful, pleasant conversation?' I asked.

'Or should we maybe recite something?' Raoul answered my question with a question.

'Phampam Bihram Bacti?' I did the same.

'Well, maybe when we're anxious. But not the whole way,' said Raoul.

'How about we try not to get anxious,' I said, and I meant it. Anxiety could be a killer on a truly danger-ous outing like this one. 'Remember, the water magnifies everything.'

'So does the dark,' Raoul pointed out.

'Like a tongue against a chipped tooth. So if you start to feel anxious, remember everything is less than it feels.' I hoped I didn't sound stupid or didactic.

'Well, almost everything,' said Raoul as he squeezed my hand very hard and wriggled a little closer on his back. 'Some things may be as big as or bigger than they seem. The good things.

'Are you ready?' he added after a short silence. 'Shall we die?'

I gave his hand a return squeeze and nodded. It had

been so long since we had died together, I felt almost nostalgic as we drifted down into the black wash. Maybe this is enough, I thought as we dropped and dropped. Maybe it should end here. We don't need the Invincibility Swim across the river, or even to return to our lives at all. This is what tonight is really about. Dying together. Forever. So peaceful.

'Tree?' I had forgotten how unbelievably calm you get when you are dead. Raoul was up on one elbow, leaning over and talking to me, but I couldn't react yet. I was still too comfortably gone. 'Tree.' He leaned closer and stated rather than asked my name. I stared up into his eyes and they were such a familiar resting place I couldn't tell if they were young or old, his or mine, alive or dead. I couldn't speak.

'Hey, little girl? Are you alive yet? Can you stand up?' The questioning tone was back in the voice that was Raoul's, and the eyes in the face staring down at me were quite obviously Raoul's now, and the whole Raoul package of boy was most definitely alive and not dead, not to mention nearly nose to nose with and on top of me.

'What?' I found my own voice and my own live self. I found my muscles and sat up, tumbling Raoul slightly sideways as I did. I am not a little girl, I thought. I am big and I am brave. I am an Invincible Heel. 'Last one in is a rotten egg,' I whispered into Raoul's ear as I jumped to my feet and dashed into the river.

I heard a wild Indian whooping and an explosion of splashes behind me as Raoul followed suit and then we were both launched, waterborne and gliding like torpedo puppies through the moonlit river in the middle of the night.

'It's so warm,' I said to Raoul as he swam up along-side me. 'I thought it would be freezing. Didn't you?'

'It's so soft and pleasant. This is fun,' he answered.

'Oh God, Raoul.' After we had been swimming side by side for a few minutes I stopped forward motion and turned toward him, treading water to stay in place. 'We never picked a landmark on the far side.'

'I did,' said Raoul. 'That big tree, the one with two arms that go up like goalposts. It's just above that really big rock with the whitish face on the far shore – so that's sort of two landmarks. See them?'

Raoul had stopped swimming too and was treading water right beside me. At first I had no idea what he was talking about, but then I spotted the tree and the rock – once you saw them you couldn't not see them. Raoul had one-upped me yet again. He had remembered to put our strategies conversation into play and he had identified the perfect landmark.

'Good job. Let's go,' I said as I moved into a very businesslike crawl. I needed to leave behind the moment and the spot in the water where I had felt my inferiority rise up in me so familiarly, and I needed to drive off the nervousness that was building in my chest. The water felt colder to me suddenly. The far shore looked at least as far away as it always had. After a few minutes I paused again; I really wasn't that strong a swimmer. And I hated the crawl.

'Is it my imagination or is the water getting colder?' I asked. My voice was embarrassingly breathy from the exertion of my swim.

'Well, it's definitely deeper and moving faster as we get out here in the middle. And it's probably colder too,' said Raoul. 'Come on, Tree. Keep swimming, like you were before. We're shifting too far downstream. Look where our landmark tree is now. We can't afford to stop and talk.'

When I looked up and across the river it took me a while to locate our goalpost tree, it was so much farther to my right than it had been only a few minutes earlier. 'Let's go,' I said as I began to swim toward the tree as fast as I could. Raoul fell in beside me. As we swam side by side our fingertips or shoulders or feet bumped occasionally, which was reassuring rather than annoying, as it would have been in almost any other circumstances. At one point Raoul tugged my shoulder, and when I lifted my face out of the water and turned to him he said, 'Slow down. Steady now. You'll wear yourself out. We still have a long way to go.'

I looked across the water and saw that we had gained very little on the farther shore, not to mention on our landmark. The roar of the Falls was definitely louder. My heart began to drop down toward the river bottom, and it seemed possible it might take me down there with it.

'Oh Raoul,' I said as I tried to find his buoy face and read its expression as it bobbed on the surface of the water that wanted to swallow me. 'Raoul?'

'Keep swimming, Elray. Come on,' he answered sternly as he reached for my hand and tugged me forward.

My arms and legs obeyed and began to move me forward again, but my mind began to race in other directions. How had I landed in this river? I wondered. Why? It had been my own brilliant idea, I reminded myself, born of a vainglorious desire to have the upper hand at all times. Or at least to have it as often as possible. You reap what you sow, I told myself, as clichés and half-truths began to swirl around in my head like a batch of hungry river currents. And the problem with feeding on the exhilaration of death-defying adventures is that you have to actually defy death. As I turned my head mid-stroke to grab a gulp of air I cast a quick glance behind me to the shore we had left behind – our cute home shore with all those cute drug addicts in the cozy parking lot that held our adorable car, the one we had nicked from Raoul's father – and I gasped. With the moon high in the sky over the riverbank we were heading toward I could barely see the shore we had left behind. And we had picked no landmark on our shore of departure. There would be no turning back. We had to swim forward, and swim hard. This time it was I who reached out across the night to tap Raoul.

'Do you think we're cooked?' I asked him. 'Just tell me.'

'Keep swimming. Follow me,' he answered as he flipped onto his back. 'Remember: Water and darkness magnify. Everything is less than it feels.' He was making use of another Invincibility Ritual, in which we sometimes reversed lines we had exchanged earlier. Raoul was a truly great Heel.

'Well, almost everything. Some things may be as big as or bigger than they seem. The good things,' I answered. I remembered how Raoul had squeezed my hand so hard when he had said this to me less than an hour earlier. We had been so safe and dry and with our long lives still ahead of our young selves then.

'Keep swimming,' said Raoul. 'Follow me.'

I settled into as steady and strong a stroke as I could right behind Raoul, but there was no question that we were losing ground against the current. The Falls were getting nearer and nearer. They were beginning to sound as huge as they were. I tried to ignore their existence, just as I tried to ignore the complete exhaustion that was spreading in a dull ache through my less and less responsive body. The water felt like molasses now as my arms slapped sloppily round and round in a lazy imitation of a windmill. My flutter kick was a groggy joke. A nursery song began to run through my head: 'The old gray mare she ain't what she used to be, ain't what she used to be, ain't what she used to be.' I allowed myself to sing a few bars out loud. I waited to hear Raoul's voice joining in. Hadn't he suggested that we recite something during our swim? Well?

'Raoul?' I called out into the darkness, which seemed to be darker and more menacing now. 'Raoul!' I called out again, and the panic I heard in my voice made me realize how scared I was. Not for myself, as it turned out, but for Raoul. Where had he gone? Was it possible that while I had been paddling like a ninny and indulging myself in semimorbid fantasies, he had actually gone and drowned? It happens so quickly, so quietly – I remembered how many times I'd been told that about drowning. Bloop. Someone gets in trouble and – bloop – they're gone.

'Raoul! Where are you? Answer me!' As I screamed this into the night adrenaline went pumping through my body and I began to locomote through the water as I never had before in my life, scanning the surface the whole while for a glimpse of Raoul. A vision of how I imagined my Grandfather Mayhew must have searched through the night crowd outside Blackie's House of Beef for my Granny Mayhew volunteered itself. Hoping against hope – what exactly was that phrase supposed to mean? Wasn't it hoping against fear? I remembered something else I hadn't thought of for a long time – all the mornings after my sixth birthday when I had tiptoed into my parents' bedroom hoping to find them right there, groggy but alive in their beds. It is an awful thing to lose people by accident. What was it about my family? I couldn't let this happen again.

'Raoul!' I called out once more into the night, on the verge of tears now. As I looked toward the far shore to orient myself I realized the complexity of my situation. The moon had disappeared. I had about six feet of visibility into the night. A mist had developed and was shifting in gauzy patches across the surface of the water. The roar of the Falls was so loud it wiped almost everything else out. Raoul probably couldn't hear me. I could barely hear myself, even when I shouted. I understood with sudden clarity that my only option was to keep swimming as hard as I could. Immediately. Diagonally upstream, against the current. That was my new compass point. I set my mind and my body into unified forward motion.

Be a machine, I told myself. A swim machine. Everything is less than it feels, and machines feel nothing anyway.

I swam and I swam, without any idea if I was making headway or losing ground. I reached as far forward as possible with my fingertips with each stroke, hoping against hope with each reach to find the touch of Raoul's invincible heel somewhere ahead of me in the night. It was the hope that was loaded into each reach that kept me going. He was somewhere in this water, and I would find him.

'Raoul!' My lungs felt like they were going to burst from the effort of swimming, but I found enough air to loose another howl into the night. The wind had picked up now and my howl traveled about two feet before boomeranging right back into my face. It was too discouraging. Swim, swim, swim, I told myself, but I could feel my resolve ebbing. I was dutifully doing the breaststroke now, but feeling almost sleepy. The water had taken on a most pleasant texture – the chill and the wetness had gone out of it. I swallowed a yawn. The sound of the Falls was like white noise, swallowing everything else. 'Here comes the Sandman, stepping so lightly, stealing along on the tips of his toes.' The lullaby Barkley used to sing to me every night came back to me from long, long ago, and I smiled. 'Good night,' I said to no one in particular, and I closed my eyes.

A moment later, however, I opened them wide and let out an involuntary yelp. Something had brushed against my arm. My desire to swim toward whatever or whoever it might be was so intense that at first I could not move my arms or legs at all. I slid a foot underwater in a state of paralysis before my limbs took the message and began to flail me up and forward. Within seconds I had landed in a rude collision with something – something hard. I felt pain along my right shin and my left ribs, but it was nothing compared with my relief. I was no longer alone. I had found something. I clutched it to me and felt along its length to decipher what it was that had come to rescue me. I was happily entwined with – a tree. I lay my cheek against its rough bark and rested. 'Hello, tree,' I whispered. 'Hello, tree.'

I think I must have fallen asleep briefly there in the embrace of my tree, because the next thing I remember is awakening with a shock to the sound of the tree talking back to me. 'Elray,' it hissed. 'Ellll-ray! ' I looked around in confusion and began to sort things out. The moon was in the sky again, and I could see. That was huge good news. The shore was not so far away now – I really had made progress across the river. That was also good news.

'Elray, please!' I squinted into the middle distance and scanned the surface of the water. It had not been the tree talking, I finally realized. The voice was too far away. My heart jumped. Could it be Raoul? I looked and looked and finally I saw him, or saw his face rather, floating like a second moon, about thirty yards upstream and very near the shore.

'Elray, let go and swim,' he shouted as he gestured wildly downstream. 'Now!' I shifted my gaze in the direction he was pointing and nearly stopped breathing. The Falls were even closer than the land, and I was headed right for them.

'Let go of the tree, Elray! You have to let go and swim,' Raoul shouted. I understood that Raoul was right, but I couldn't move. My muscles seemed to have locked into living rigor mortis in their clasp around the tree.

'I'm coming,' I shouted back. 'Don't worry. I'm coming.' But in fact I was not – I could not. I didn't think things could get worse, but they did. Raoul began to swim toward me. He lowered his face and began levitating across the surface of the water in a powerful crawl, straight toward me.

'Go back, Raoul! I'm coming, I swear! I'm coming!' I shouted, frantic now. I still couldn't let go of the tree. I tried, and I just couldn't. We were stuck together. But it was absolutely out of the question that Raoul would try to come anywhere near me. 'I'll meet you on shore, right over there,' I shouted, sobbing now as I tried to nod with my head in the direction of the shore. It was only about thirty yards away, this shore, this simple stretch of rocks and mud that also represented safety, survival, life. But it might as well have been on the other side of the moon. As I watched it slipping horizontally past me I was reminded of a strip of film threading through a projector. It was a comforting image. This was my life, I thought. And we have come to the end of the reel. That's all. A hypnotic calm spread through me. 'Good-bye,' I said out loud.

I was about to close my eyes and rest my head against the rough bark of my tree once more, this time to take my eternal rest, when I remembered the real urgency of my stuation. The real reason for my tears just a few mintues ago. Raoul. As I looked up and out into the night again I saw that he was right there, within a few yards of me. Trying to rescue me from the death I had just so calmly decided to embrace.

'Raoul, get the hell out of here! Leave me alone,' I shouted. 'Go away.' I was furious now, and as he continued to swim toward me I reached out to strike him, to push him away. My right fist hit the water, and only then did I realize that I had allowed this hand of mine to release its grasp of the tree. I was balanced on the edge of all edges. If I held on to the tree with my left arm I was headed to the land of the dead, in a matter of minutes if not seconds. If I followed the lead of my right arm and let go of the tree, I might still make a bid for the land of the living. But 'might' was the operative word here. There was a huge struggle and no guarantee of where I might land if I tried to follow my right arm. I might fail, and wind up where my left arm would have taken me anyway. There would be no struggle whatsoever and a guaranteed destination if I followed my left arm. Left arm it is, I thought. Instantly I felt the relief and calm that come with huge decisions that are made for a second and final time settling over me like a big warm blanket. But not for long, for just as I was lifting my right arm toward the tree and toward my decision, a water demon or something very like one shot up from the depths and wrapped the arm in its viselike grip.

It was Raoul. As he held my right arm and pulled me toward him he stretched me once again along the same edge I had just been straddling, but in a new and more painful way. In that splitting second I learned how dramatically moving alone versus moving with others can change the trajectory we choose through life. I knew Raoul would never let me roll over the Falls and to my death alone, and I knew I could never let him come with me. I had to let go of the tree, I had to hold on to Raoul, I had to try to survive.

'Jesus, Elray. What the hell are you trying to do?' Raoul had both arms around me now, and he was sobbing against my neck. 'We have to swim! Swim!' he shouted. A second later, with a fierceness that still shocks me to remember, he twisted me onto my back and hooked his arm under my chin and across my chest and began to haul me toward shore.

'Raoul, let me go! I'll swim by myself,' I called out to him. But if he heard me he paid no attention. I tried to wriggle free – I had no idea if I would actually have the strength to swim or not, but having Raoul drag me along and possibly get himself killed as a result was out of the question. I wriggled some more, but this only caused Raoul to tighten his grip around me.

'Be still, Elray, or I'll kill you,' he muttered. He was holding me so tightly now I really had no choice but to be still. In fact, just breathing was difficult at times. I thought I might pass out. I tried to concentrate on being buoyant, light, manageable, since it seemed to be the only contribution I could make to our efforts. I watched the water sliding over my legs and away in ribbons off the tops of my toes, and as I lifted my gaze upward and out I saw my tree in the distance, its up-reaching branches silhouetted against the moonlit sky. Evidently it was stuck, right at the lip of the Falls. I felt a stab of remorse, mixed with the shame of my betrayal. Poor tree. It had tried to rescue me and I had abandoned it. A moment later, in jerky slow motion, the tree began to stand up out of the water, resuming its original posture as if in final salute to the now finished life it had once had on land. Then it nose-dived in a silent timber right over the Falls. I am watching what would have been the arc of my own ride to oblivion, I thought. For the first time I felt both the narrowness of my escape and a fierce desire to live.

Raoul, as it turned out, was the hero of all time. I felt a rock bump against my back and then against my foot. We were in the shallows, almost on shore, just barely above the Falls that had gobbled my tree. Raoul loosened his grip across my chest, but he held tightly to the back of my shirt as we both rolled onto our hands and knees and clawed our way from rock to rock against a still strong current onto the muddy flats of the mighty Potomac. We collapsed onto the un-believably dear surface of the earth, flat on our stomachs, cheek to cheek with sweet muddy beach. We lay there in silence, exhausted. I'm not sure if we actually passed out or fell asleep – but we closed our eyes and fell, at any rate, into a zone of semi-consciousness that allowed our shocked systems to slow down and recover from the experience we had just been through. Wherever it was we went, it was one of the sweetest, deepest rests I have ever had.

When I opened my eyes again the sun was just rising, and as I looked around and took my bearings I moved rapidly through a sequence of intense emotions. The first was one of awe for the beauty of the light and the scene before me. Mist was rising in delicate puffs off the dark, mysterious river and draped like a winter muff along the graceful arc of Great Falls, which now, from land and by day, looked scenic and grand instead of ruthless and hungry. Raoul was sleeping beside me with his arm flung across my chest, as if he were still hauling me to safety through dark water; his hair was wet and matted in crazy swirls and there were little twigs and pebbles stuck to his bare torso. I felt a surge of love for him, followed by a blast of shame at my own unworthiness and failure as a Heel.

A moment later I became physically as well as morally self-concious. I couldn't imagine what I must look like. I reached up and tried to smooth my own matted hair, but it was impossible. I looked down at my bare legs and saw a confusion of cuts and scrapes and bruises, including one pretty good gash along my right shin. Nice. I tried to sit up, to slip quietly out from under Raoul's arm, but a stab of intense pain on my left side stopped me. Gingerly I pulled up my shirt to have a look, and discovered a huge swollen scrape with a funny bump in the middle. Broken ribs. I pulled my shirt down again.

'You're here,' Raoul said as he woke up and looked across at me with a huge smile. 'Hooray! And I'm here. Hooray! We made it.'

'No thanks to me,' I mumbled. 'Sorry, Raoul. I'm really sorry. You're the greatest, I'm the worst. I owe you everything.'

'You were just pushing things to the very edge, right?' Raoul smiled. He was still half-asleep, I decided. 'Nice job, Elray. And by the way, don't ever expect me to call you Tree again. I now hate trees.'

I smiled too, but I kept quiet. The more I remembered of our night swim, the more I wished I had in fact died. Raoul had saved my life, but I was not worthy of having one. I certainly wasn't worthy of having him. I stood up abruptly and began to brush the sand and other debris off my arms and legs.

'We didn't think this through so well, did we?' I said sourly. 'How are we supposed to get home? I'm never going in that river again.' It was true – our planning had hardly been flawless. Our car and all our clothes were on the other side of the river, not to mention in another state.

'From here forward is a series of small problems,' said Raoul, as he moved to stand up too. 'We have gone head-to-head with the big challenge. And now that we've actually survived it, I have to admit: It was the best yet. Brilliant idea, Elray.'

'Not so brilliantly executed, by me at least,' I muttered, unable to rise from my swamp of self-loathing.

'Don't be so tough on yourself. You were pretty great,' said Raoul. As he moved toward me, however, he stopped suddenly. 'Jesus,' he said as he took a good look. 'You really got knocked around out there. Are you okay?'

'Of course I am,' I said, burning with shame now and stepping away from him. Then, in an effort to turn the conversation back to the only real triumph I could claim (namely, having had the idea for this insane river swim in the first place), I asked, 'By the way, what was the Invincibility Exercise you were going to suggest to me when you came by last night?'

'Oh, it's not really worth mentioning right now,' Raoul said. He looked troubled, and for a second I fantasized that maybe he never really had one in mind at all.

'Come on,' I said. 'I'm sure it's great. What is it?'

'Well, now I think it's not such a good idea. What we just did is much tougher. It would be backsliding,' said Raoul.

'Tell me,' I insisted. I was loving this.

'Okay, here goes,' said Raoul. 'I thought it might be very interesting to go back and ride together through the Tunnel of Love at Glen Echo. That's all.'

I stared at Raoul. I was exhausted and humiliated. But this was too much. This was the final straw. For years this same, very obvious Invincibility Exercise – my return to the Tunnel of Love – had been lurking in the shadows, waiting for me to acknowledge it properly. For years I had been on the brink of suggesting it to Raoul, but the timing never seemed quite right. Now, in addition to my dignity in general, he was snatching this very private piece of intellectual property from me.

'Oh, Glen Echo? The Tunnel of Love? I've already done that at least a dozen times, all by myself,' I lied, and for good measure I loaded my voice with disgust. 'Try again.'

'Really?' was all Raoul said at first. He was brushing the debris off himself now, very carefully, very deliberately. Then he straightened up, took a step toward me and looked me dead in the eye. 'I guess it was on one of those rides that you got your real arm back again, eh?' was all he said.

We both knew that was the end. We looked around the beach for a minute, as if to make sure we hadn't forgotten our briefcases or some other crucial item we'd need that day at work. Then we began to pick our way through the underbrush, away from the river and out toward civilization. When we eventually reached a dirt road, Raoul approached me, as if to make a plan. But I stopped him.

'Go away,' I said angrily, holding out my palm like a traffic cop. 'Good-bye. Forever.'

Raoul turned on his heel, his perfect invincible heel, and I watched as the world's finest Indian brave walked away from me forever, into the sunrise in his blue boxers. Then I turned in the opposite direction, without any idea where it would take me, and walked away myself.

Part Four

The Vertical Bog

Harwood Gets Drafted

Low self-esteem is as dangerous a substance as any hard drug to have coursing through the body of a young person, and in the weeks that followed my final break with Raoul my self-loathing nearly killed me. I had failed so miserably on our last Invincibility Walk. I had proved myself a sniveling poseur on the adventure travel front. Russia – what a farce. I had humiliated myself, not to mention nearly killed both of us, on our swim across the Potomac. And then, just for good measure, I had put out another needless lie, about having returned to Glen Echo. All the sweet reflexive invincibility I had worked so hard to build over the years was gone. My skin itched with self-disgust. I was ready to die – and I felt like something of an expert after all my attic practice. But in the end some spark of pride, some fighting reflex, propelled me to soldier forward. I had to get back on my feet, resurrect my self-respect. I hatched a plan with this as my goal.

I knew very well why I had jumped into my defensive lie to Raoul about having already revisited Glen Echo: It was because for many years the necessity of making this pilgrimage had been haunting me. Now I understood that actually undertaking this challenge, alone, might be my only hope of reconnecting with a bearable version of myself – and maybe even with Raoul. I had to return to Glen Echo and ride again through the Tunnel of Love, to retrace the journey that had snatched my parents away. My exercises with Raoul had taught me about the power that gets loaded into simple actions that are given the contours of ritual – how routinized movement through the physical world can uncover a secondary map, a system of short-cuts to the world of the spirit. A return trip to Glen Echo had all the ingredients of ritual at its finest. Although I knew that I had to undertake the challenge alone, I had learned enough about ritual in general to understand that I needed some kind of an audience: an objective observer who could lend formality to the event and ensure that I was not just imagining it. It was not unlike the dynamic in effect when Raoul and I had first practiced dying – success and survival seemed much more likely if we did it one at a time while the other watched.

After considering my options I decided Harwood would be my best choice as an unwitting accomplice. Harwood was expert at denying the emotional content of life. If he felt it, he rarely showed it or shared it with anyone. He always turned a cold shoulder on any intimations of the spiritual in our sessions with Rena, so I believed he would be likely to remain levelheaded if dangerous or strange conditions prevailed. Because Harwood had always been less attentive to me in general, I believed that during my exercise he would also be easier to keep at a distance than either Ajax or Rena.

Crawlspace Day seemed the obvious setting for a launch of my Glen Echo project. Thus it happened that on my ninth Crawlspace Day, which marked my fifteenth birthday, as we were all sitting around the stone table that Harwood had carved and presented to me a few years earlier, I found myself the center of sudden and rapt attention. Our shoulders were more crowded together than usual, because for the first time I had invited an outsider – Rena – to this secret holiday, my annual extra birthday celebration.

'So, what do you think?' I asked, babbling nervously after laying out my plan. 'Don't you agree that it's time for me to put all this sadness behind me? Next year I'll be old enough to drive, after all. I think I should pass through the Tunnel once more to exorcise, you know, my demons. And then I can say good-bye to Barkley and Jack forever. And Harwood, you can be my escort – I mean, you can drive me there and drive me back. Since I don't have a license yet. Make sure I make it in one piece.' I had been tracing the bas-relief scorpion that Harwood had chiseled into the tabletop to acknowledge my birth sign as I spoke, and as I finished I parked my finger at the tip of the scorpion's stinger and pretended that it was my pressure there that made the silence grow longer and louder all around us.

'Wow.' Harwood, my targeted accomplice, finally broke the quiet. 'Hmmmm. I'm not so sure about this. I'm not so sure,' he said. 'Ajax? Rena? Nothing to say? You two are so wild about reenactments – I'm surprised you haven't thought of this one yourselves.' Harwood took a sip of champagne and looked across the table at them. I didn't need to look around to understand how much tension was building there, like steam in a kettle, and I wasn't at all surprised when Ajax's voice hit the underside of the porch floor overhead in a hot squeal.

'Whoa now, Lewis and Clark,' she said. 'Maybe you two would like to put this little expedition up for discussion before you present it as a fait accompli? Revisit Glen Echo and the Tunnel of Love? That sounds about as jolly as a tornado party in a trailer park. No thank you.' She poured herself more champagne, overfilling her glass slightly so that a small stream bubbled down to the table, where it darkened a patch of stone into a prettier, green-flecked color. As Ajax bent over her glass either the champagne bubbles got to her or she was more upset than I thought, because when she looked up her eyes had filled with tears.

'What a stupid, stupid idea, Harwood,' she said. 'Obviously you and Elray have cooked this one up together behind our backs. Why on earth would we want to take Elray back to that awful place?'

'Actually, this is the first I've heard of it,' Harwood snapped back. 'And who said anything about "we"? It's Elray's idea, and Elray seems to want this to be something she and I do alone. Just the two of us.'

This is fascinating, I thought as I watched quietly. Probably how world wars start. Ajax's wrongheaded attack had produced a reflexive counterattack from Harwood, who was now defending his right to participate in a plan he had never really approved of in the first place.

'Just the two of you? You're going to ride through the Tunnel of Love alone with Elray? What about me?' Now Rena had piped up, contributing her first words since we had gathered for the crawlspace celebration. She spoke with such urgency I sat up to get a better look. Rena had pushed her beach chair back from the table and was leaning way forward, her chin almost touching the table's edge. Her back was very stiff and slightly arched, and she was resting her hands on her knees in a sphinxlike pose.

'What do you mean, "What about you"?' Harwood asked Rena. 'What about you? How should I know about you? You're supposed to know about you, right?' He shrugged and swirled his glass so the little pool of champagne in the bottom sloshed up the sides. I looked from Harwood to Rena and back. Strange feelings were brewing here in the crawlspace. I looked at Ajax. She was making what Harwood and I called her needle-nose face: an austere look she put on only when very angry, a look that stretched the skin over the bridge of her nose so tightly that it turned white. She pulled my birthday cake toward her and lopped off a second, rather large piece for herself.

'Guess what, Harwood,' Ajax said as she primly

licked icing from her fingers and then, not so primly, took a huge bite of cake. 'You're not.'

'I'be na waaaath?' said Harwood, making fun of Ajax's full mouth.

Ajax swallowed and then spoke carefully. 'You're not going back to Glen Echo with Elray,' she said. 'That's what you're not.'

'Damn straight!' shouted Rena as she pulled her chair back to the table and reached for more birthday cake herself.

'But it's my idea. I want to go. I have to go. And I want Harwood to accompany me.' As I heard myself say this, I cringed. I was always surprising myself in the crawlspace, forever blasting forth before an idea had worked its way through my brain. 'No one can stop me.' My mouth finished its spree.

Another big silence followed as everyone stared at me again, and this time it was Ajax who spoke first.

'Okay Elray,' she said. 'Shall we talk about this? Is this something you actually want to do? This macabre replay, this return to the Tunnel of Deprivation?'

We did talk about it then, and as we did the poor little crawlspace, where normally such a tender mix of merriment and nostalgia had prevailed, echoed instead with arguments and accusations. The biggest problem, if I remember correctly, was that Ajax and Rena had hurt feelings because they had not been invited.

'No offense intended. It's just that Harwood is the natural choice here,' I said, telling more or less the truth for once. I was beginning to regret having announced my plans so publicly, and to wonder why I had thought I needed an audience at all on my Glen Echo pilgrimage, when Harwood came to my rescue.

'Ladies, ladies,' he said. (Harwood had been referring to Ajax as a female more and more often lately, I'd noticed, even though he never used to and even though we had all agreed to try not to anymore.) 'Surely you have more important things to do? Rena, I thought you were going crazy in preparation for our upcoming court date. And Ajax, you're always after me to do more one-on-one outings with Elray. Right?'

'Harwood?' Ajax folded her forearms on the table and squared her considerable shoulders. 'Just tell me this. I'm still not convinced this isn't a conspiracy between you and Elray. Where did this brilliant field trip idea really come from?'

Harwood had been rubbing his brow the way people in ads for aspirin always did. When Ajax asked this question he stopped and looked up with the same big smile these people always wore later, after they had taken their pills. He shot me a stern look, and then turned back to Ajax and Rena.

'Ladies,' he said again. 'Okay, you've beaten it out of me. I'm going to confess. I hate to name-drop, but Barkley suggested the trip. You know how excited everybody gets when Barkley talks to Elray? Well, the other night, Barkley decided to have a little chat with me, and in the course of it she suggested that Elray and I go back to Glen Echo. And she seemed to think it would be best if the two of us went alone.'

I looked at Harwood. I didn't know what he was up to or why he was taking my side, but it was working. I saw Rena and Ajax lift their eyebrows at each other and suck in their cheeks.

'Oh really?' Ajax said, leaning toward Harwood now. 'This was Barkley's idea? You were "talking to her" the other night and she suggested this visit, this grisly return to the scene of her own death?'

Harwood nodded, and grinned. He knew he had them. Rena and Ajax couldn't question the validity of a message from Barkley, not right there in front of me. Not after our family history on the topic. For years Rena and Ajax's ready indulgence and interest in every detail of my communications with my parents had been a source of predictable upset for Harwood. 'Why do you encourage this sad fantasy?' he would always ask. 'It can't be healthy. Encourage the child to move on, to forget.' In the middle of such confrontations he often would storm out of the house, sometimes trying to take me with him (though not before he had listened to every word I said if I was reporting something from Barkley, I'd noticed). Perhaps now that my bulletins from the far side had dwindled to an almost nonexistent trickle, Harwood felt he could safely turn the tables. That afternoon in the crawlspace he just leaned back in his chair and smiled at all of us.

'Oh, my. Oh well then. You should have said so in the beginning,' said Ajax, turning back to Rena. 'If it was Barkley's idea that changes things a great deal. That makes it very different, doesn't it, Rena?'

Rena nodded a yes to Ajax, but the look she sent Harwood said something much fiercer. 'That's really sweet,' Rena said to him, without changing her eyes. 'How nice for you that you and Barkley can talk together, can work these things out.'

'Yes. Well. In so many ways, Rena, I'm a very lucky man.' Harwood flashed his widest, most camera-ready smile at her as he said this. And that ended my ninth Crawlspace Day and the debate over my proposed outing to the Tunnel of Love at Glen Echo. Harwood and I were going, and going alone. Case closed.

Que Sera, Sera

As it turned out, Harwood and I had to wait a while before making our visit to Glen Echo. The first complication was that Rena and Ajax — and I think they were just playing for time here, hoping I'd drop the idea — insisted that to return on a date anywhere near the anniversary of my parents' death would be tempting fate. I snorted at this, but by failing to take action I inadvertently agreed. I sank to new levels of self-hatred as I detected a reluctance to embark on my self-prescribed invincibility test.

I was determined to get to Glen Echo, but as Thanksgiving and then Christmas loomed I found myself obsessed with another problem: how to get us all out of town for at least a week as cover for my fib about a trip to Russia. Although I never expected to see Raoul again, I couldn't bear the idea that he might find me out in this lie. With great difficulty I convinced Ajax to organize a last-minute Christmas trip to Key West, where Harwood and I would be able to fish while she and Rena swam in the ocean and sunbathed and read books. Off we went.

The Key West trip was the first time I could remember that we had all been away together for an extended period, and while we were gone something in our house on High View Street changed. I sensed it immediately upon our return. It was as if some invisible dark force had taken up residence in the shadows and corners, a meanness that was now waiting for an opportunity to pounce. Ajax, easily the most sensitive among us, was the first to react. Our first night at home she just fell apart. She stood up in the middle of dinner and went upstairs to her room and shut herself in, weeping.

'What's wrong?' I asked Harwood.

'Nothing. Something that came in the mail has upset her. It's a personal matter,' Harwood answered. The expression on his face did not encourage further inquiry.

'What's wrong with Ajax?' I asked Rena when she showed up in a fluster a few hours later and immediately went speeding upstairs to Ajax's room.

'Nothing, Elray,' Rena answered from the stairs with a big fake smile. 'Postvacation letdown? Or maybe premenopause? Ajax is getting on, you know. And life's full of rough stuff. Don't you worry – everything will be fine.' Then she finished clumping upstairs and shut herself in with Ajax.

There was no doubt about it: The grown-ups were stonewalling me about something. Something pretty bad, it seemed. But in the end their decision to keep me in the dark worked in my favor, for it served as a kind of last straw. Marginalized on every front, I had no choice but to get myself to Glen Echo and relaunched on a path of forward, invincible movement.

On a blustery morning in April when the whole city seemed stampeded by gypsy winds, I got my way and Harwood and I set off for Glen Echo. As we left High View Street in Harwood's bomber – an old Plymouth convertible he had bought the previous spring in a fever of teenage nostalgia – Ajax and Rena stood on the front porch and waved good-bye. Somewhat abjectly, it seemed to me.

'Maybe Ajax and Rena should have come,' I said with a sigh as we headed down Massachusetts Avenue and then out MacArthur Boulevard. 'It seems mean, doesn't it?'

Harwood stepped on the brakes and pulled over as if to stop. 'Shall we go back?' he asked. 'Maybe this is a mistake.'

'No, no. It's not a mistake.' I recognized the look that was collecting on Harwood's face, around the edges of his eyes and in his brow. I wasn't sure why the look was brewing right now, but I knew that it promised a storm of fierce and irrational anger. I also knew what I had to do to stop it.

'You are so good to indulge me in this adventure,' I said. 'You're the only one I could ever include on something like this.' I was learning how to handle bottled-up boys.

'Well, it's not entirely my kind of outing, I have to confess,' said Harwood as his face smoothed and he moved the car out again. 'But I guess I should be flattered to be invited. So here we go.'

'Right. Here we go. By the way, whatever inspired you to say that it was Barkley's idea that we take this trip? You hate that kind of "hocus-pocus," as you call it.' I watched Harwood carefully. I had never really pressed him about his sudden and glib ad-lib that day in the crawlspace, but I was curious.

Harwood wrinkled his nose and stepped on the gas. 'I was just trying to get you what you wanted. Besides, you and I don't get many adventures alone. You don't really think I've ever talked to your dead mother, do you?'

'I don't know.' I shrugged my shoulders. 'You talked to her a lot when she was alive, didn't you?' I was intrigued by the combination of jumpiness and open-ness in Harwood, couldn't resist picking at it. He just slid his big eyes in my direction and said nothing at first.

'Do you know how much you remind me of your mother sometimes?' he asked after a few minutes. It wasn't really a question, so I didn't bother answering. We were passing a graveyard just then anyway, and I was holding my breath, waiting for the sight of a white house to free me to breathe again. We were on a fairly barren stretch of road, and it was a long wait before I could let out all the old air and suck in a big whoosh of the new.

'Tell me something about her. Tell me something about Barkley I don't already know.' My demand came rushing out on the tail end of the gasp the graveyard had produced. Harwood was silent, so I kept silent too. I knew when not to press my luck. I waited.

A few minutes later Harwood pulled the bomber over to the side of the road, alongside a shed that advertised night crawlers on a hand-scrawled sign outside and Budweiser on a neon sign that hung in the one dim window. He pulled five dollars out of his pocket and thrust it at me. 'Go buy us a six-pack of beer,' he said.

'What kind?' I asked, as if that was my big concern. Actually, it was.

'Whatever. Your choice.'

'I don't drink beer, remember?'

'Just grab a six-pack, Elray. Hurry up.'

Five minutes later I was back in the car with a six-pack of cold Budweiser – the advertising had worked, at least on me. As I lined the beers up on the floor-board between my feet, self-appointed bartender for Harwood, I began to absorb what a truly fine day it was, and to feel a prickle of adrenaline up the back of my neck and behind my ears. The big airy sky, courtesy of the open convertible, definitely contributed, and as I opened a beer for Harwood and handed it to him I allowed myself one prodding syllable: 'Well?'

He looked over at me strangely, as if he too had just sniffed the possibility of some sweet new adventure, and then he took a noisy gulp of his beer.

'Do you know what this reminds me of?' he asked. 'Being here in this car with you?'

I shook my head.

'It reminds me of an afternoon I once spent with

your mother, when we were both teenagers. Your mother and I went cruising in an open car on a fine day much like this one. A long, long time ago. She was not quite sixteen. Just a few months older than you, Elray.'

I waited.

'It was the afternoon of your Great-Uncle Minor's funeral.'

'Uncle Minor?'

'Uncle Minor. He was our mother's little brother, Tom. We called him Uncle Minor because he was so much smaller and quieter than Mother's older, loud-mouthed, fat army sergeant brother whom we called Major Jim. Anyway, it was a gorgeous June day in the little Poconos town where Uncle Minor had lived. It was a day not unlike this one – the sun was blazing and the air was delicious, fluid and cool against your skin so that walking felt like swimming. We had buried Uncle Minor and we were back at his house, wandering around outside with the other guests, when Barkley spotted Uncle Minor's old convertible. It was an outrageous, ugly, turquoise Studebaker. In mint condition.

'I was dying to take that car out for a spin, but I would never have had the nerve to ask – especially not on Uncle Minor's own funeral day.' Harwood paused to laugh. 'But your mother, she had a genius for delicate situations. I'll never know how she did it, but she got the keys. Came cartwheeling across the back lawn toward me and waved them right under my nose. She made me beg to come along as a passenger, and she didn't even have a driver's license yet.' Harwood paused again, as if this might be the end of the story, but I didn't say anything. I knew from Crawlspace Days that it was better not to interrupt Harwood when he was reminiscing.

Sure enough, Harwood soon started up again. 'Of course, eventually she did let me take the wheel. And then as we went squealing around the big turn by the cemetery where we had just planted Uncle Minor, Barkley stood up and leaned forward over the windshield and shouted, 'All aboard, Uncle Minor!' She tipped her head skyward and began to sing '*Que Sera, Sera*' at the top of her lungs. She could be such a nimnut sometimes.'

Harwood fell quiet once again, this time because he really had finished. But the end of his story had thrilled me. Raoul and I, on the brink of some big invincibility challenge, used to break the tension by capering about and singing the very same song – '*Que Sera, Sera*' – in thick Spanish accents. The coincidence of my mother's performing it when she was about my age pleased me. I wanted a more complete picture. I couldn't keep myself from prodding again.

'What was Mama wearing?' I asked.

Harwood was quiet for a long time before he answered. 'She was wearing the leaf-green dress she had worn to my graduation earlier that summer,' he finally said. 'Her hair was streaming out, all around her head. Like a drowned person's.' Then he turned to look me in the eye for the first time since he'd started his story. 'Could you pass me another beer?' he asked.

I opened a third beer for Harwood and he let me have two sips before I passed it over to him. The story was definitely over now. We sat quietly for a few minutes and then, as we pushed to the top of a long hill, I couldn't resist the urge to rise, to stretch into the dome of bright sky overhead and sing a little myself.

'*Que sera, sera. Whatever weel beee weel beee,*' I sang, with a thick Spanish accent the way Raoul and I always had. I was laughing. It was easier to think about Raoul now that I was here, headed for Glen Echo with Harwood. It was easier to forgive him for making such a fool of me. '*Que sera, sera,*' I launched into another verse, singing louder this time and making what I thought were very Spanish arm movements toward the sky. But a moment later Harwood was tugging at me, yanking on my shirt so fiercely that I had to sit down.

'What are you doing? What are you singing?' he asked. Maybe it was just my eyes readjusting, coming out of the bright sun and back into the car, but he looked pale. Pale and scared, I realized, and the realization made me feel powerful. I pulled the half-empty beer bottle out of Harwood's resistant fingers and took a long slow drink from it while he watched.

'What were you doing up there?' he asked again. 'Who are you? Tell me.'

I moved my face right up against his and started whispering the song's lyrics, and doing all the arm movements too. *'Que sera, sera,'* I sang softly. *'Whatever weel beee, weel beee. The future's not ours to see. Que sera, sera.'*

Harwood gave me more of his eyes than he should have while I sang, and we almost went off the road once. Then he reached out and held my chin gently with his right hand. 'You're my baby girl, aren't you,' he whispered. 'You're my darling baby spooky Barkley-Elray girl, aren't you. Grab me another beer, baby. And then you go ahead and sing.'

I opened Harwood another beer but I didn't really feel like singing anymore. He offered me a sip but I didn't really want that either, so instead I leaned back and let the wind slice across the top of my head. The beer and the twisting turns we made as the road narrowed were putting me in a good groggy haze, and as I lay there with the wind caressing the top of my head and the memory of Harwood's touch still on my chin, I felt happily bracketed by the two sensations. Confident that life still held plenty of adventure, plenty of mystery.

'Harwood?' I looked over at my uncle with that fuzzy fondness that comes near the edges of sleep. I sensed that we were almost at Glen Echo, but I could barely keep my eyes open. 'Harwood, which would you rather be: invincible or invisible?' I was not really expecting an answer. Harwood smiled and let out his liquid laugh, the one that always reminded me of something long-ago and sweet – I think maybe of my mother, his sister.

'I don't know, Elray,' he said. 'You and your mysterious buddy Raoul are the big Invisibility experts, right? You tell me.' We laughed together then, for just a minute, for different reasons. Then Harwood turned his attention to the road again. I turned to my window and thought for one sad second about my sweet invisible invincible Raoul. Oh well. *Que sera, sera*, I told myself as I dropped into a brief but deep car sleep.

Into the Mystic

When I awoke the first thing I saw was the back of
Harwood's khaki trousers, just outside my window.
The little red string that had opened the cellophane
wrap on his cigarette pack was stuck to the seat of his
pants, so I reached out to brush it away. Harwood
jumped slightly when I touched him and moved himself sideways, and when he did I got an eyeful of the
view he had been blocking. A tall stucco wall painted
with a sequence of colorful scenes – underwater; deep
forest; cloud-laden sky – filled the immediate fore-
ground. Just visible above the top of the wall was an
assortment of turrets and towers – the very same
turrets and towers that I remembered from the mind
movie of my fateful ride with my parents. Was it
possible that Glen Echo was a real place after all, and
that it did still exist? Why had no one brought me here
before? I felt a strange yet familiar sensation building
inside me, a leaden lightness. Perhaps this was a
dreamscape I had entered. Could I finally be having
a full-blown, bona fide dream? For a moment I thought
I heard the angels starting to sing in the background of
my dream, but then a small grimy girl on a dilapidated
bicycle rode past my window holding a portable radio
against her ear and I finished waking up.

Harwood was talking to a man who was squatting
down counting money. As Harwood squatted down
himself to draw something in the sand, the man

peered at me from behind Harwood's knees and sent me a gap-toothed smile.

'Eez preety gull,' he said. 'Hi, preety gull.' He smiled again and waved. I waved back shyly and looked away.

'*Sí, ella es mi sobrina. La hija de mi hermana,*' Harwood said, without bothering to turn and look at me as he stood up again. Had Harwood driven us to a foreign country? Had I been asleep longer than I thought?

'*Sí, sí, sí.*' The man, still squatting, smiled up at Harwood now and winked. '*E bonita, y la sobrina. Muy bonita,*' he said. When he raised the fingertips of one hand to his lips and blew me a kiss I knew for certain I had landed in some strange territory. Possibly even in someone else's life.

Minutes later we had passed through a gate in the stucco wall and were traversing the world of Glen Echo itself. In my mind movie Barkley and Jack and I had always been the only patrons present, but this was not the case today. People were everywhere, studying maps, laughing, eating ice cream.

'Okay, Elray. Here we are.' Harwood seemed nervous, clingy even, as he reached for my hand. This was not good. I needed to separate from him enough to be alone.

'Let's see. Which way?' I mused, as if I didn't know. 'Harwood, no no. This way.' A moment later I stopped Harwood from making a wrong turn, and showed him the proper route to the little stone cottage that marked the entrance to the Tunnel of Love.

Then we were there, right at the doorway with the blue light. I felt strangely calm, still a little sleepy from the ride even. There was an old bench just outside the door and I eyed it slyly, wondering how inappropriate it would be to stretch out and take a quick catnap. I recognized this grogginess. It was the old, familiar preemptive numbness that Raoul and I had taught each other, the trick of dying before a big challenge. I looked over at Harwood and saw to my surprise that he was far from calm. In fact, he was sweating; it was a fairly cool day but he was definitely sweating. Heavily.

'Harwood? Are you okay? Maybe you should just wait for me by the car if this is upsetting you,' I said.

'Upsetting me?' Harwood swabbed at his brow. 'Why would this upset me? I'm fine. But how are you?'

'Fine,' I said, stifling one last involuntary yawn.

'Shut your mouth, little child. You'll let the flies in,' a gruff voice called out to me as I yawned. I looked around but saw no one at first. When I spotted the owner of the voice, standing in the half-light just inside the cottage, I snapped right out of my sleepiness. In fact, I nearly jumped right out of my skin.

It was a man. His hair was long and tousled and almost down to his shoulders, but the figure was unmistakably male. He was wearing an eye patch over his left eye, tied at a rakish slant. Had he been here nine years ago? He was such an eyeful, so eccentric, I couldn't believe I wouldn't have remembered him. He was wearing rubber waders that came up to his armpits, a quiverlike backpack full of fishing nets, a red and blue plaid flannel shirt buttoned tightly at the neck and wrists and waterproof gloves. A red baseball cap with ALPO scripted across its front had been pulled down over his head, and his ragged shoulder-length hair stuck out awkwardly below.

'Howdy, howdy,' he said. 'Did I say howdy yet? You behaving yourself? Probably not. Why should you?' His one eye was a deep green and he looked like he had swallowed a lightbulb, his skin was so bright. It was impossible to look at him for very long, or guess how old he might be. Was it possible, I wondered with sudden horror, that this man was my dead, burned-up daddy? He had all those fishing nets, and his hair looked fried. Humiliation, followed by rage, rushed through me as I recognized the ridiculousness of this thought. Get a grip, I told myself.

I was allowing myself to get rattled, violating one of the fundamental rules of invincibility training. When I had planned this trip to Glen Echo I had been prepared for it to be emotionally fraught. Simple logic suggested it had to be. If you returned to the place where your parents died violently, right on either side of you, if you reenacted the outing that took them away and landed them on the far side of a wall they could never climb back over, this would have to stir things up. In fact, that was the whole point. Now it was time for me to put aside the fears and thoughts that were side-swiping me. It was time to climb into a boat and set out through the Tunnel of Love, Tunnel of Closure, Tunnel of whatever it might turn out to be.

'Care for a smoke?' The bright-faced man was chatting with Harwood as he held out a pack of Lucky Strikes.

'Why, thank you,' said Harwood. 'Do you fish?'

We stood there, the three of us – Harwood, the bright-faced man and I – all smoking. Harwood and the man literally, their nicotine. Me, I had an interior smolder going. I found the casual chitchat of the two men extremely annoying. My organs felt like they might explode if I delayed another second.

'Okay,' I said, packing the single word with a resolve that surprised even me. 'You weren't here last time, Harwood, so I have to go on without you now. I'm going into the Tunnel of Love. See you on the other side. Maybe.' As I went charging through the cottage door, Harwood followed me.

'Elray!' He looked stricken. 'Wait!'

'She's fine. Have fun, kid. Ride's on me,' I heard the bright-faced man say. As I turned to look back I saw him take Harwood by the elbow, and then he turned and winked his one eye at me.

I marched over to a boat and jumped in and settled myself in the middle of the middle seat, just the place

I'd been in my mind movie. I checked the bottom. There were no leaks this time. Only then did it occur to me that I had no idea how to propel these boats forward; they had no paddles, no motors, no steering wheels that I was aware of.

I didn't have to wonder for long. Seconds later my boat was moving, lurching forward with a mechanical whine. As it pushed through a set of double doors and into the dark tunnel I distracted myself from the ride ahead by pondering the technical question of whether a one-eyed person could ever actually be described as having 'winked.' After all, his blink would be most people's wink, and vice versa, I reasoned. No, the bright-faced man probably hadn't winked at me, I decided. I must have just imagined that part. In fact, most likely I had imagined him altogether.

The Echo Chamber

As the boat moved steadily forward, pressing through the cool darkness, I closed my eyes. It seemed possible that I would never see the world or the people I knew there again. I shrugged my shoulders to practice nonchalance and concentrated on how every now and then the momentum of the boat paused for a split second and seemed almost to turn under on itself, as if trying to reverse direction. Each time this happened I was left hanging in a state of near weightlessness – the same sensation that comes just before an elevator comes to a halt and opens its doors. I let myself imagine that if I elongated the moments of weightlessness and strung them together they might carry me upward in an act of evanescence, evaporating me into the darkness overhead. Perhaps this was how my parents had departed? Maybe I would find them waiting somewhere up there?

My parents. Barkley, Jack. Jack, Barkley. The quiet swooshing of water noises all around me seemed to be whispering their names. It was strange. For so many years I had lived with a historical understanding of my birthday ride through this very Tunnel of Love and the irrevocable changes that ride had wrought on my life. But never had the event presented itself to me with the palpable, blood-altering sensations that usually accompany organic memories. I had my mind movie of the day, but by now this had become as predictably

191

scripted a show for me as *The Wizard of Oz* is for others. Now, as I settled back in my boat by myself, for the first time I remembered the event of my parents' death not as a packaged narrative, but from the inside out, through the muscles and blood and tissue that were my body. For the first time I knew that I really had been here on that day. That certain things really had happened.

I opened my eyes. My boat had splashed down a ramp and there she was, the giant Heidi, pumping her big butter churn. 'Yo-da-lay-eee-hoo!' Her scary yodel echoed through the dark tunnel, just as it always did in my mind movie, and I felt something much stronger than mere familiarity charging through me. It was as if an ice-cold, liquid form of knowledge had replaced the blood that ran in my veins. I was traveling on the old boat ride with my parents and on this new one without them at the same time; I knew exactly what was going to happen on each.

As I leaned back in my boat I realized that being here reminded me of something else, something besides my mind movie. It reminded me of lying in my little coffin in the attic, where I had so often practiced dying. I had a hunch. I turned my arm over and felt for the smooth, recently quite infertile crescent of my scar. Sure enough. Barkley was there.

DO YOU EVER WONDER WHERE YOUR DREAMS GO, ELRAY? she whispered. I'LL TELL YOU. EVERY NIGHT JUST AS THEY ARE RISING TO THE SURFACE YOUR FATHER SCOOPS THEM UP WITH HIS BIGGEST, MOST FINELY MESHED NETS. HE CARRIES THEM DOWN TO THE TERRIBLE, SLUGGISH OHNONO RIVER, THAT SLUDGE-ROLL OF THE SUBCONSCIOUS, AND THROWS THEM AS BAIT TO THE HUNGRY WATER PREDATOR. YOUR FATHER LIKES TO SAY HE IS ONLY 'HELPING THE DREAM SYSTEM TO FUNCTION, PROVIDING A PURGING EXPERIENCE OF THE PUREST KIND.'

BUT I AM THE ONE WHO REALLY PROTECTS YOU, MY SWEET. I STAND BY WITH MY BUCKETS OF PAINTS EVERY NIGHT AS YOUR FATHER STEALS YOUR DREAMS. I THROW MY COLORS ON

YOUR EMPTY SCREEN, SO YOU WON'T HAVE TO CONFRONT THAT TERRIBLE BLANK GLARE.

Interesting. What other pieces could I fill in? I wondered as I left Heidi and her mini-Alps behind and floated into another dark passage. And where was Barkley, exactly? Was it possible she was somewhere very nearby? Technically, I knew I was alone, but I couldn't shake the feeling of being watched. I touched the scar on the underside of my arm again, and this time I jumped.

CHECK OUT THE STRIKE AND DIP OF THE NEW TURF WE INHABIT! Jack shouted. CAN YOU SEE? EVERYTHING THAT WAS THERE IS HERE, EVERYTHING THAT IS HERE WAS THERE. BUT THE TANGIBLE AND THE INTANGIBLE, AS WELL AS CAUSE AND EFFECT, HAVE BEEN INVERTED. THE FEELINGS, THE INSIGHTS AND THE SEESAWING EMOTIONS OF MY LIE ON EARTH — THE LIFE I SHARED WITH YOU, MY CRUMPET — ARE MY PHYSICAL SURROUNDINGS HERE. THEY ARE MY ROCKS AND TREES, MOUNTAINS AND VALES, AND THUS RETRACE MY LIFE WITH YOU. EVERY DAY ON MY WAY TO THE LAB I WALK NEW PATHS OVER THE TIME WE SHARED.

I nodded to myself, determined to remain calm. There could be some real advantages to this afterlife inversion of the tangible and the intangible, I reasoned, trying very hard to distract myself from the here and now. Ideas must weigh in with a definite and satisfactory heft for the dead — maybe they could take a thought, toss it through space like a fat water balloon and actually hit someone with it. No sooner had I thought this thought than I heard a distant splash, followed by the rattle of Jack's laughter.

GOOD SHOT! he cackled. BUT NO FAIR GANGING UP. THE TWO OF YOU ARE STILL YOUNG AND ALIVE. I'M AN OLD DEAD MAN.

An old dead man who makes no sense, I thought as I shifted in my boat. A dead man who sees double. A tingle of discomfort was stirring in my chest. What if something truly supernatural takes place in here? I thought. I was used to hearing my parents' voices. I'd been doing that for years; it was nothing. But what if here in the Tunnel they decided to pull out all the stops, for old times' sake, and actually showed up in some visible form, all electrocuted and dead! I wasn't keen on this at all.

Another big splash echoed through the darkness. I'M LEAVING, Jack shouted. BY THE WAY, DID I TELL YOU I CAUGHT MY RESURRECTION PERMIT THE OTHER DAY? AND DO YOU KNOW THE SUCKER WAS ABSOLUTELY BONE-DRY WHEN I PULLED IT FROM THE DEEP!

HUSH! JACK DARLING, BE QUIET! It was Barkley's turn to shout, evidently. She interrupted Jack with a loud boom. HAVE YOU NO MANNERS? REMEMBER, WE'RE DEAD!

A moment later a loud rumbling, like the upside-down thunder of ice expanding at the bottom of a frozen lake, filled my ears. Was this some tangible, afterworld version of Barkley's anger? I wondered. The rumbling grew louder and louder and developed into a definite physical vibration right under my boat. Was it my turn to explode and die? It would make sense that my parents might try to pull me to the other side right here, where they already knew the way. As the rumbling eased up I realized that my boat had been climbing to the top of a hill and that I was now heading down a ramp. Down into the same tropical garden where I had watched the moon dance down to me.

I looked up, but there was no neon moon this time. Only flat painted stars and planets. Oh – and a purple rocket ship with a hand waving out the window on each side. I didn't remember the rocket ship from my mind movie. Was it new, had they redesigned this section of the Tunnel? Or had my parents been dying right here the last time, so I never noticed the rocket? I was trying hard to remain calm and scientific, not to get rattled, but my heart had begun to pound. Maybe that *is* my parents waving from the rocket, I thought as I slipped right into the irrational despite my best efforts not to. I looked down, away from the sky, which seemed like the most likely venue for an unwanted sighting of my dead parents, and concentrated instead on the tropical scenes that surrounded me. There were the palm trees with their bright birds and swinging monkeys – oh! I jumped in my seat and set my boat rocking from side to side as I spotted the snake coiled around one tree trunk. He was still smiling his big square-toothed smile.

'How about a little original sin, Eve?' Jack's last words as a live man echoed in my ears. Was I remembering it from my mind movie, or hearing it right now? 'PHAMPAM BIHRAM BACTI. I-OH-WAY PO-TA-TOE. QUE SERA, SERA.' I recited all three Invincibility Chants out loud, trying to get a grip on my rising panic. I did not want to be the author of another big out-of-control scream. This is where they died, I told myself, and where they may still reside. Say hello, and say good-bye.

'Hello and good-bye.' I tried to speak in a normal voice, but my salutations came out as a whisper. A split second later the boat began to rock from side to side again, this time of its own accord.

I grabbed the edges of my seat. I thought I might throw up. Someone had touched my shoulder. I shut my eyes. Worse. Someone was climbing into my seat from the seat behind, sitting down next to me on the left. Surely I was about to die. I squeezed my already closed eyes tighter.

'Elray, I'm here,' a voice said. 'I'm here.'

I stopped breathing and listened. I thought I recognized the voice. I cracked my left eye and let in a slit of the world. I couldn't believe it. I was right. It was Harwood.

'Elray, I'm here,' he whispered again. 'I wasn't going to let you go through this tunnel alone. You're okay. I'm here. Take my hand.'

I drew in a deep breath and opened my other eye and stared at Harwood. I couldn't decide if I was angry or relieved to see him. He had evidently jumped from boat to boat, Zorro style, through the empty boats behind me to catch up. I flashed him a weak smile, but I did not give him my hand.

'Elray?' Harwood asked. All I could do was stare back at him. Each of Harwood's pupils had a small face shining in its center – it was me, my face. I was in Harwood's eyes and Harwood was here in my boat, riding with me in the Tunnel of Love where my parents had died. He had made his way here, to sit beside me, because he cared about me. And that was a good thing, I told myself; I should let him care about me. He was my family. He loved me and I loved him. That's what families did. They loved each other. Families also died, I reminded myself. In fact, one had died right here in this tunnel. As I looked again into Harwood's eyes I could see myself waiting for the world to explode. Maybe if I kept staring into his eyes I could watch myself die there?

The rumbling sound started again as the boat headed up another hill, and then there were bright lights at the edges of my vision. This is it, I thought. I have practiced dying so often, but always with Raoul. Now it turns out I am actually going to die with Harwood. I reached for his hand after all.

The brightness was everywhere now, not just at the edges of my vision, and I had a sensation of velocity. But when I turned away from Harwood to look around I could scarcely believe what I saw. The world had not exploded. It was right here in front of me, all normal, with a blue sky and trees tossing in the wind and boring people going about their silly business. I had exited the Tunnel of Love and come back into the world. And I wasn't stuck in a big ugly scream this time.

'Harwood.' I looked at him in astonishment. 'We're alive!'

'Right.' He nodded as he gave me a shaky smile.

Our boat was shooting down a final ramp and slowing behind a line of empty boats that were headed back toward the entrance of the stone cottage. I felt inexplicably happy, ready for anything. Invincible.

I turned toward Harwood to read his face. Poor Harwood. He looked really shaken. I felt a stab of remorse for dragging him into this. Had the ride been hard on him? I wondered. Had Barkley tried to talk to him in there? Oh well. It was over now. Mission accomplished.

Then we were out of the boat and Harwood was squeezing me, lifting me right off the ground and practically crushing me in an embarrassing and very un-Harwood-like display. 'Oh Elray. You're okay, really? I'm so glad that's behind us,' he said. 'Let's get out of here.'

He was right. I felt finished with this place. Ready for something new.

'Elray.' Harwood turned to me as we were about to pass through the gate in the stucco wall, back to our everyday lives. 'Why did you bring us here, really?' he asked. 'What were you trying to accomplish?'

I smiled. I felt closer to Harwood than ever before, but there was no reason to go whole hog. 'I did it for one Person,' I said. 'That would be Raoul Person, my invisible friend. Sometimes he exists. Sometimes he doesn't. Because Raoul understands that if you're not living on the edge, you're taking up too much space.'

Harwood rolled his eyes and shot me a sideways glance. Then he stopped and squared me by my shoulders as he bent over to zip up my jacket. It was getting cold. 'Jesus, you can be such a tease,' he sighed and shook his head as he drew the zipper to my throat. 'Do you have any idea what a tease you and your mother can be?'

I smiled as I left Glen Echo for the second and last time. As we passed through the gate in the stucco wall someone called out to me.

'Hey, kid!' I looked over and there was the bright-faced man, the ticket taker in the Tunnel of Love. He was talking with the man who had blown me a kiss when I first came in. He looked much more normal in broad daylight, with my Tunnel adventure now behind me.

'So long, kid. See ya later. Tight lines,' said the bright-faced man as he raised a gloved hand in a farewell salute. As I waved back both men definitely winked, no doubt about it, right at me.

Stuck in the Mud

The weeks that followed my return visit to Glen Echo had an odd quality to them. My memories of this time seem permeated with a strange light, as if shot underwater. Depth of field is a shifting frame of reference; things that loom large turn suddenly microscopic when approached, and vice versa. Part of the strangeness was the upsetting secret that had been waiting in the house when we returned from Key West. Whatever it was, it had gotten worse. Ajax had almost daily weeping fits, and she and Rena and Harwood seemed to be constantly in conference behind closed doors. I could hear their muffled voices, but they refused to tell me what was going on.

Once Harwood bolted out of the room shouting as he stormed from the house. 'Leave it to me, why don't you?' he screamed at Ajax and Rena. 'I'll get rid of the bitch. I can handle this. No problem.' What was he talking about? Who was he going to get rid of? Could it be related to our long-anticipated court confrontation, for which we had an actual date in August? I felt shut out – a very dangerous sensation for an adolescent ego.

In fact, probably worse than the strangeness brewing inside my house was a parallel strangeness brewing inside me. During my ride through the Tunnel I had experienced the dual anxieties of explorer and survivor that any good invincibility test produces, as if I were paddling through a submerged shipwreck looking for artifacts – some prize to take away – and at the same time working just to resurface and live. It had been good to merge my interior trauma landscape with an exterior reality. It had been good to have a bulletin from my parents for what I suspected was the last time, however bizarre they sounded, whether or not it was really them talking. The challenges of the ride had to some degree resuscitated my sense of self, as intended. But in the aftermath of that day I had the distinct sensation that something inside me was growing at the same time that something was shrinking. The countermovements were disconcerting. In retrospect, I think I was suffering from that transitional patch the world calls puberty. I prefer to call it the Vertical Bog.

Like so many teenagers, I had a horizontal response to the Vertical Bog. I lay in my room by myself for hours and hours as a cloud of adolescent apathy, the kind I had sworn I would never be victim to, descended over me. Sometimes I'd slip upstairs to the attic and lie down in my little coffin. As I lay there I was mourning Raoul, of course. I wanted desperately to see him. I had sacrificed all dignity and tried to contact him twice, but he never returned my calls. Maybe it was payback. Months earlier, after seeing him at the soccer field, I had moved his empty coffin around the corner under a back eave in the attic where I wouldn't have to look at it. But lying up there in my own coffin I still felt him painfully near. Sometimes I could almost have sworn he was actually in the room with me. It was during these attic sessions, in part as an effort to escape the palpable presence of Raoul, that I discovered a new trick of letting myself drop only halfway into death, to a nice numb plateau where I wasn't quite anywhere. Perfect time killer for puberty.

'Little bird? What are you doing in that box? Where are you going?' Ajax followed me upstairs on one of my attic retreats one day, breaking the no-entry taboo on this top-floor space, and sat down beside me as I lay in my coffin. Her eyes were puffy. I suspected she'd had another of her crying spells.

I looked at her and managed a smile. Ajax was such a good old soul. I couldn't think how to explain to her that there was nothing to say, except by saying nothing.

'You're looking for something, aren't you, Elray?' Ajax decided to keep talking despite my silence. 'Well, that's okay. We all are, you know. We're all just trying to figure things out, just like you. I hate to break the news, but it's one of life's little tricks – there are always new questions. And sometimes the new questions turn out to be the same old questions. . . . Just figuring out who you are – that one has been a killer for me. Oh man, when I was your age I was so confused I used to stand in front of the mirror all day and wonder why the other person never said hello. Even when I was older – well, even now, to be completely honest – my sense of self comes and goes in fits and starts. Terrible disorienting patches of uncertainty hit me. But do you know what has really helped me, Elray?'

I still couldn't talk, so I didn't.

'Loving you. Loving you has been such a keel for me. Because I can see exactly how splendid you are, and it makes everything outside myself more important. I feel lucky to know you, to have you in my life, and then I forget about my uncertain self. Do you have anyone you think is really splendid, Elray? Is there anyone you really love? It helps so much to applaud or help someone else when you can't figure out who you are yourself. Or is there anything that intrigues you? Any mysteries to solve? I used to fall into books, all day and all night, when I couldn't find intrigue in the world right around me. Shall I take you to the library?'

'I'm okay, Ajax. Really. Don't worry,' I said, finally speaking. I sat up in my coffin and rubbed the back of my head and squinted into the late-afternoon sun that was slanting through the dusty attic. It wasn't that I took any real comfort from what Ajax had said; in fact, it made me extremely uncomfortable to have her talk to me in this way as I lay in what should have been my private coffin. The scene was so banal and so eccentric, it was worse than ridiculous. It was humiliating. 'I was just having a little rest. It's quiet up here.' I spoke with flat affect; I wanted to force normality on Ajax, on the scene. 'Thanks for the invitation to the library, but I already have plans.'

'Really?' Ajax's face brightened as she stood up. 'Where are you going?'

'Somewhere. Anywhere,' I replied. Then I clattered down the stairs and out of the house. After weeks of inertia, I actually did have a plan of action.

Et Tu?

Intrigue. That was the word that propelled me out of my coffin and out of my house that afternoon. I couldn't believe I had had such a passive response to the mystery of what had been going on since our return from Key West, couldn't imagine why I hadn't taken action to solve it earlier.

Ajax and Harwood and Rena had brushed aside all my inquiries, but Harwood, the least circumspect of the three, had given me a clue: 'A weird old woman has surfaced and she is trying to give us a hard time,' he told me one day. 'Don't worry – I'm dealing with her.'

I decided to tail Harwood wherever he went; I felt sure I would eventually catch him with the old woman, and then I could tail her. Piece by piece I would put the answer together. I left a note saying I'd gone to visit friends (it never occurred to me that Ajax and Harwood might scratch their heads at this first, and false, hint of teenage camaraderie), and then I hid in the back of Harwood's car. Sooner or later, I reasoned, he would come out and go somewhere.

I was right. It wasn't long before I heard the door open and the engine start, and felt the old bomber head down High View Street. It was late on a Saturday afternoon, and I had no idea where Harwood could be going, but the answer came quickly: Burka's, a corner liquor shop only a few blocks away. Harwood disappeared into Burka's, reemerged with a brown package after a few minutes and then crossed the street to Midget Groceries. He reemerged from the latter with a bouquet of daisies. Great, I thought. A date? Whomever Harwood might be courting, I was sure it wouldn't be the old woman. Strike one, I thought. When we then drove right back to our house on High View Street, it became strike two. I began to seriously doubt my espionage techniques. Harwood went inside. He did, however, leave his liquor and flowers behind in the front seat. I took this as evidence that he would be back soon, headed somewhere else.

Sure enough, within an hour Harwood was climbing back into his car, showered, shaved, in a crisp white shirt and smelling of bay rum. Abluted, as he would say. He's definitely headed for a date, I decided, and therefore definitely not on an outing that would yield the old woman. It was a hot day, and it was getting stuffy just lying there on the floorboards in the back of Harwood's car. It was too late to bail out, however. In for a nickel, in for a dime, I told myself as we headed down High View Street again.

At first I tried, from my position on the floor, to keep track of the turns Harwood was making. But after a few minutes I had to give up. Harwood was singing to himself in the front seat, belting out an old Hank Williams tune with embarrassing gusto. 'Hey, good lookin', whatcha got cookin', how's about cookin' somethin' up with me,' he wailed, adjusting the key a couple of times to find his best register. This was getting bad. I was suffering increasing anxiety that Harwood might discover me, and his singing made it so much worse; it would compound his fury. If he did find me, I would have to pretend I was unconscious, and later concoct some story about being mugged and dumped in the back of his car. At least then he wouldn't be angry that I'd heard him singing to himself.

My worry about being discovered distracted me so fully that I hardly noticed that we had arrived at

Harwood's destination until he was already parked and getting out of the car. I forced myself to wait a full minute or more before raising my head just enough to peer out the back window and follow my uncle's retreating figure. We were parked on a quiet tree-lined street with midsized homes, and Harwood was halfway up the walk of the house just opposite the car. I ducked down again, afraid that if someone came out to greet him they might spot me.

I waited a few more minutes before looking again. Harwood had evidently gone inside the house. He had taken the brown Burka's bag and the flowers with him. A good sign. Although the sun was nearly down, it seemed safer to wait until darkness proper had fallen before exiting the car. What if Harwood was picking someone up, taking that person elsewhere? What if the two of them came out and jumped in the car and drove away while I was outside prowling around? I waited, although I was starting to get seriously overheated now.

Finally I slid out of the car, on the far side where I would not be so easily spotted from the house. I walked quickly up the street and then circled back nonchalantly on the opposite side. My heart began to pound as I turned up the driveway of the house that held Harwood, and then ducked up onto its wrap-around front porch. I got down on my hands and knees and crawled up to a window and peered inside. The good news was that there were no curtains; I had an unobstructed view of the interior. The bad news was that there was not much to see. The immediate area was unlit, but appeared to be a sitting room of some kind. There were a couple of sofas, a coffee table, bookcases along the wall. Standard house fare. The room beyond was lit, and appeared to be a kitchen. I spotted Harwood's daisies lying on a butcher-block countertop, next to a bottle of red wine. I sat and waited patiently, like a spider watching its web.

And then suddenly I had action. Harwood moved

into view in the golden rectangle of the lit kitchen. He walked up to the bottle of wine and grabbed it. The sleeves of his white shirt had been rolled up and he now turned to the task of opening the bottle of wine. I could not hear the pop of the cork, but I saw that it was out as Harwood set it and the corkscrew on the counter. A moment later he was laughing at something, laughing very hard, and he held the just-opened bottle to his chest for a minute as he dropped his head slightly and surrendered to his mirth. He looked so relaxed and happy, I felt a little guilty about spying on him. But then my curiosity kicked in again.

Another set of arms had appeared beside Harwood, delivering two wineglasses. I couldn't see to whom the arms belonged because Harwood was in the way. He filled the glasses while the arms reached for the daisies and disappeared with them. From behind Harwood the arms and the daisies reappeared, the latter in a vase that the former placed on the center of the countertop. Then the arms, with their attached body still obscured, reached up to wrap right around Harwood's shoulders and neck.

Yuk. Whoever she was, they weren't wasting any time getting down to business. I looked away reflexively, the way I always did when people started to kiss in the movies, and wondered how Harwood could possibly think anyone would want to watch him doing this. Then I remembered that Harwood didn't think anybody would want to be watching him, that in fact he didn't think anybody was! I looked up again, re-embracing my role as spy, and almost let out a yelp as I did. Harwood and his date were still kissing, but they were walking side by side, straight toward me. Although my wish was to be elsewhere, to avoid being caught, I couldn't move. It wasn't just that to move would probably have given me away at this point – horror and disbelief had also paralyzed me. This wasn't just any date. This was a criminal tryst, an outrage, a betrayal. Harwood was kissing Rena! It was

Rena's body that Harwood's hands were roving over like hungry rats.

Their two bodies began moving toward me in erratic fits and starts, a few steps at a time. One of Harwood's hands moved behind Rena's neck and down the middle of her back as he drew the zipper of her dress down. Then the dress was slipping off her shoulders and they were tumbling together onto the sofa directly in front of my spying window.

I watched without wanting to, powerless to move, as a wave of nausea swept over me. I was disgusted and furious – not at the act of sex I was witnessing, but at the monumental betrayal it represented. Two people who I had assumed belonged almost exclusively to me had secretly belonged more to each other. It was not acceptable.

A low moan escaped me as I dropped to my stomach on the porch. Panic mixed with my fury and disgust as the possibility of being discovered hit me. I squirmed my way off the porch, down the steps and all the way to the end of the walk in a backward G.I. Joe crawl. At the end of the walk I stood up and set off at a dead run down the street.

I didn't know where I was or where I was going when I started, but instinctively I kept heading uphill as I zigzagged through the streets. Where I wound up was at the cathedral, my old stomping grounds, which was built on the highest point in the city. I walked into the familiar coolness, down the stairs of the west entrance toward one of the passageways to the crypts. I sat down in the St Joseph of Arimathea Chapel and looked up at the huge mosaic over the altar, the one where the angels are carrying Jesus' body out of its cave-tomb in the cliffside. I checked to make sure the angels' feet were still on fire; they were.

Everything was the same but everything was different. I dropped to my knees on the cold stone floor. I tried not to, but I couldn't stop myself: I began to cry. I cried and I cried, as I had never cried before.

When there were no more tears I stood up and wiped my face. The light, or lack of it, suggested that it had gotten quite late. I walked over to the door that led into the crypts, stopping to get a pencil and paper at the altar where you could write pledges. 'HELP. *JE SUIS PERDUE*,' I wrote in big block letters on the paper. Then I wiggled the secret loose stone out of the wall, stuffed my note inside the cavity and fit the stone back into place. I was sure that Raoul never checked our secret message center anymore; nobody would ever find my plea for help. But it made me feel less helpless, more hopeful, to have it stashed in there. I turned to Jesus and his angels and waved good-bye. Then I did the only thing I could do: I headed back to the house on High View Street. Back to the house I had always lived in, to the only place that I have ever called home.

Family Document:
Raoul's Diary

When I came across Raoul's diaries a few years ago, I read with amusement and delight through most of the entries. But this particular section made my blood boil. I ripped the pages out after reading them and was going to burn them, but in the end I decided not to. Now I'm glad I didn't. I reprint them here to punish Raoul, gently. No one likes to have his diary read.

DECEMBER 25. 8 A.M. Christmas morning. Today Elray and Harwood leave for Russia. Today I start my new life as a normal, red-blooded American boy, as Coach Bradelle would put it. Enough of the squirrelly world of crypts and Invincibility Chants. I bet Elray never comes back anyway. I wouldn't if I could explore Siberia with Harwood.

These are the bad habits I'm going to stop: 1) Brooding over Elray; 2) Apologizing for bad shots in tennis; 3) Thinking in rhymes. These are the good ones I'm going to start: 1) Chasing girls, lots of them; 2) Lifting weights; 3) Drinking booze. As Beelzebub is my witness, AMEN.

3 P.M. now. The brouhaha of gift-giving is over and we're in that soggy afternoon slump before the big family feed. Ugh. Mother gave Father some ugly ties and a book about the CIA; Father gave Mother an ugly necklace and an empty photo album. Mother and Father gave me a pile of stupid stuff, including a cheap little ant farm they forgot to buy the ants for. Oops. Thank God this only has to happen once a year.

I'm taking a break in my room, practicing new habit number 3 by sipping a big mug of eggnog I've loaded with rum. It tastes gross, like rocket fuel and cream mixed together. But it puts me in the mood to practice new habit number 1.

9 P.M. The jolly day draws to a close at last. At dinner

tonight Mother and Father agreed (after an awkward silence that coincided with everyone's first bite of Grandma's famous, rock-hard 'Banaboo Cake') to let me exchange the ant farm for a set of barbells. To bed now, with another shot − so to speak − of new habit number 3, a habit I think may be shaping up as something of a talent.

DECEMBER 26. 10 P.M. Today has been full of surprises. I awoke early this morning with my new-habits crusade on my mind, and I decided that to make a clean sweep of things I really should sneak into Elray's house while she is away and retrieve any of my possessions that are still there. No one ever locks the doors at her house, and I was pretty sure Ajax would be the only one home, because Elray and Harwood are in Russia. I figured it would be a pretty simple mission.

And so it was, at first. I slipped in at about 10:30 this morning, right through the front door the way I always do. I listened carefully before tiptoeing up the stairs to the attic, to our Heels headquarters. At first when I looked around I had an eerie feeling, as if someone might be watching me − but I am familiar with every hiding nook in that attic, and I checked them all. I was definitely alone. During my search I discovered that Elray had moved my coffin away from hers, stashed it under a faraway eave. This sort of hurt my feelings, ridiculous as that may sound. But it also strengthened my resolve.

I started going through the big stacks of our journals and films then. I had forgotten what an immense Library of the Invincible we'd compiled, and what I finally decided was that it would be wrong to break it up. Just as wrong as it would be to make off with the whole thing, lock, stock and barrel. I looked around for other artifacts from my time as a Heel with Elray that I might take with me, and then it hit me: My purpose in being there was not to retrieve anything, but rather to leave the last piece of that part of me behind. I was wondering exactly how I might do this when my eyes landed on my coffin in the dark faraway eave.

Working quickly, I stripped off all of my clothes – everything except my boxers. Then, using a big stack of cotton diapers that have been sitting in a box against one wall for as long as I can remember, I stuffed my pants and shirt and socks and shoes and constructed a dummy of myself. I laid the dummy in my coffin under the eave, placing a Washington Senators hat that I found on a hook by the door over the spot where my head should be. As I stepped back to admire my handiwork I glanced down and realized that something in the scene had excited me. Perhaps the sight of Elray's empty coffin across the room in the light-filled alcove by the dormer window and the memory of how peaceful she always looks when she is stretched out there like a dead Tree. She has no idea how smooth and perfect she looks when she is lying there dead.

As a final touch, I found a piece of paper and a red pen and in big block letters I wrote: 'QUE SERA, SERA. GOOD-BYE.' I pinned the note to the dummy's chest, and then my only problem was to find some clothes to wear. I searched through several boxes in the attic, but with the exception of the box of diapers, they all contained books. At first I was alarmed by the thought of making a pit stop in Elray's room on the second floor to find something to wear – but I quickly warmed to the challenge. (In fact it felt almost like old times, when Elray used to hide me away somewhere so that I could spy on her family, as I readied myself to creep down the stairs in my underwear.) Just before leaving the attic I decided to snitch one little memento after all. I tucked one of the old 78 records Elray and I used to listen to – a ragtime piano piece called 'The Insouciant Ghost' that we'd used as a sound track for *The Art of Dying* – under my arm.

This is turning into a very long entry. But today was a very big day in many ways, and a bizarre day, and I feel it's important to record the experience as fully as possible. Anyway, I was almost all the way down to the second floor when I heard voices, followed by the squeak of the second-floor bathroom door opening. I know that squeak well because I once spent an entire evening hiding in the linen closet directly across the hall from that bathroom, in one of the more boring of the 'nonexistence exercises' Elray concocted for me. Anyway, I heard the squeak, and the moment I did I scurried across the hall toward the same linen closet and I just made it inside the closet before the bathroom door finished opening.

My heart was pounding, but when it quieted a little I realized that it was Ajax, talking and laughing with someone. The door on that linen closet never quite shuts – it's swollen or the hinges are wracked – so I was able to peek through the crack along one side and get a pretty clear view of the following scene.

Ajax was the first to emerge from the bathroom – although I barely recognized her, her hair was so short. She was rubbing her scalp as she stepped into the hall, and laughing.

'Ooh, it feels so strange, I can't keep my hands away,' she said over her shoulder. 'Do you think it's maybe just a little too butch? Do I look like an axe murderer? What will Elray and Harwood say? Will they hate it?'

'Well it's too late now, isn't it,' said a second voice that I thought sounded like Rena, the lawyer woman. A moment later Rena herself, barefoot and wearing only a slip, followed Ajax into the hall. The two of them collapsed into laughter as they turned to each other, and then linked arms and walked to the end of the hall to admire themselves in the long mirror that hangs there.

'How are you today, Miss Guilfoyle?' Ajax asked, using her deepest man voice.

'Wonderful, dear *Mr* Mayhew,' answered Rena.

'What do you think, really?' Ajax turned from the

214

mirror version to the real Rena. 'Do I really look all right? Oh, look at all your lovely long hair,' she cried as she reached out and smoothed Rena's hair. 'Oh God. Mine's all gone!'

'Shhh now, don't fret,' Rena said as she took Ajax's face in her hands. 'You look very handsome, I swear. Look at yourself. Look.' Rena turned Ajax's face back toward the mirror, and then the two of them stared at Ajax's reflection. 'See?' Rena said. Rena bent forward and gave the reflection of Ajax in the mirror a kind of sideways kiss. Then she pulled back and she and Ajax exchanged a long look in the mirror.

'Okay?' Rena asked. She said it so quietly, if I hadn't been watching her reflection in the mirror I don't think I would even have known she had spoken. Ajax nodded and the two of them started back down the hall toward the bathroom.

As I describe it now the scene doesn't seem so strange, but earlier today, as I stood there in the closet and watched, it seemed worse than strange – it seemed almost sinister. Ajax, after all, is hardly normal. Elray always refers to her as an aunt, and I've come to think of her that way too – but we both know better. I've always had reservations about Rena as well. She is just too full of energy. Harwood, well he's cool, but he has one very obvious motivating priority – himself. He really can't be trusted to think about anything or anyone else. Obviously something very odd is going on in that house, and poor Elray is caught right in the middle of it. The more I thought about all this as I hid in the closet, the more upset I became. And then – and I blame this partly on all the time I'd just spent up in the attic, reviewing our invincibility work, and the weird mood this had put me in – I did something stupid. I blasted out of the linen closet and through the half-closed bathroom door to confront Ajax and Rena. I stood there in my shorts, holding a lonely 78 record as a kind of fig leaf, and I shouted: 'HELLO. I'M RAOUL. WHAT THE HELL IS GOING ON HERE?'

Ajax was sitting on the edge of the bathtub and Rena was standing in her slip in front of the sink. They both just stared at me in a way that made me instantly aware of how ridiculous I must look. As I bolted out the door and down the stairs, I heard Rena exclaim: 'Ajax, for Christ's sake! You might have told me you had a cute little visitor here!'

I was almost out the door when I slammed on the brakes and backed up and finally made my wardrobe pit stop in the hall closet. I grabbed the first coat I touched, slipped it on and hit the streets at full throttle.

So there is my day – or most of it, anyway. The rest of the story – how I had to wait behind the boxwood until I saw my parents go out and then get the superintendent to let me into our apartment (it is the second time in two months I have come home nearly naked) because like an idiot I left my keys in my pants that I left at Elray's house – is not so interesting. Besides, it's very late now and I'm falling asleep. But I wanted to record what happened today while it was still fresh. I am going to play 'The Insouciant Ghost,' with its big scratch, one more time and think about my strategies for tomorrow before retiring for the night. I've decided that I have to get my keys back from Elray's house. A farewell shouldn't confuse itself by looking like an invitation.

Oh yes. One last thing. The coat I pinched to streak home in turns out to be an old almost full-length fur. In its collar I found a yellowed name tag reading 'Amanda Baer Mayhew,' and in its right-hand pocket a pack of matches from Blackie's Bar and Grill and a Laurel Racetrack racing form dated August 13, 1939. A horse named Take It With You in the third race had been circled in red ink, which I've decided means that I don't have to return the coat. It feels like my prize. Think I'll just keep it, maybe give it to some lucky girl someday.

*   *   *

DECEMBER 27. 5 P.M. Today was anticlimactic, a big goose egg of nothing new after all the promising weirdness yesterday. Mother made me go with her to deliver some boxes of old stuff to Goodwill downtown, and it was noon before I could break free and head over to Elray's house. After scoping out the joint for an hour or more and seeing no activity, I decided to slip in the front. But big surprise: The front door was locked. So were the back door and basement door when I went around to check on them.

I hung out for another hour and a half but saw no activity, except for the mailwoman at about 3:30. I waited awhile and then snuck up on the porch to examine the mail. Nothing of interest. A telephone bill, a calendar of events from St Albans Parish and an assortment of catalogues, most of them for gardening supplies or baby equipment. I'll go back tomorrow, and if the mail is still there I'll know everybody's gone. What am I going to do about my keys?

Did chin-ups and sit-ups and push-ups this morning. Ran three miles. Tomorrow I turn in the ant farm and get my weights. Talked to Rachel Moskowitz, whom I met in the street on my way back from Elray's, and we agreed to go ice skating later this week. Ugh. Don't have it in me to booze. May have to rethink that habit – could prove damaging to my strength training, not to mention to my finesse as a spy.

DECEMBER 29. 11:30 P.M. Yesterday, December 28, was so dull I couldn't even be bothered to make an entry – football practice, and that was about it. Coach Bradelle told me I looked like I was 'bulking up nicely.' Ran past Elray's house after practice and it was dark. A new batch of mail in with that from the day before, but still nothing of interest.

Today, however, has been really amazing. Some very juicy developments. For starters, I ran into Rachel Moskowitz again on the way over to Elray's, but this time she was with her older sister Clair. Rachel and I talked about ice skating again, and agreed to head down to the Sheraton Park Hotel tonight, and then Clair volunteered that she would like to join us. Rachel's decent but Clair's a real dish, so of course I said yes, the more the merrier.

At Elray's I decided to fake gardening chores while casing the house for a way in. I had a quick and easy false start when I found a basement window that was unlocked. But then it turned out that the door at the top of the basement stairs was bolted on the far side. Another very unusual precaution. I must have really spooked Ajax when I dropped half-naked from the heavens the other day.

Now comes the real weirdness. I was trying the windows along one side of the house when I heard footsteps around the corner on the front porch. I dropped over the porch railing to the ground, and fortunately right there in front of me there was a little door in the latticework that encloses the area under the front porch. The door was slightly ajar and I slipped through it. Just in time too, because next I heard the footsteps moving right over my head, pacing back and forth, back and forth. I sat very still for a long time while the footsteps continued, and then, as my eyes adjusted to the light, I saw what looked like a table and chairs up ahead of me in the dark. I inched in that direction and discovered four beach chairs around an old stone table. Near the table, against the stone foundation of the house, was a shelf or bench of some kind where I could just make out the glint of bottles, or of something glass. I started to make my way over there when the footsteps overhead stopped and then resumed at a quicker pace, accompanied by a kind of chant. I couldn't quite catch what was being said, but then I heard it loud and clear: 'FEE FIE FO FUM. I'M QUITE SURE I SMELL SOMEONE!'

Just as I heard this I realized that the stamping overhead had stopped and my eyes caught a blur of something moving along the boxwood bushes on the far side of the lattice that ran along the front of the porch. Whoever had been on the porch was now beetling across the lawn and around the side of the house, straight toward me. I leaned back against the wall and shut my eyes and tried to lie still as the dead. Without planning to I let the old Invincibility Chants start up in my head: PHAMPAM BIH-RAM BAC-TI! I-OH-WAY PO-TA-TOE!

Seconds later I heard a loud 'HA HA!' and as I opened my eyes I saw the lattice door fly open. Stooping there in the window of bright light from outside was an extremely tall woman in a well-tailored tweed suit. Her hair was piled up on top of her head in a style that reminded me of the Elizabethan queens. At first I couldn't tell if the light was streaming in around her or maybe passing right through her, she was so thin and ethereal-looking. Something about her silhouette made me wonder for just an instant if I could be experiencing time travel backward to some earlier era.

'Yoo-hoo? Do we have a light in here, people?' she called out. 'ANSWER ME!' she shouted a second later as she stamped her foot impatiently.

I decided to remain motionless in my spot against the foundation wall. The woman moved forward a couple of steps into the darkness, talking to herself quietly the whole time, and then reached into her coat pocket and began to laugh. 'Yoo-hoo? Darlings? You can't hide from me,' she said. Then she brought something up out of her right pocket, floated her left hand across her eyes and held a lit lighter out in front of her.

'Andrew,' she called out. 'Are you here? I know you are. Where are you?' She kept her face tilted upward and her eyes covered as she moved slowly forward. Then she took her hand away from her eyes and looked straight in my direction and said: 'Young boy. Right there. Bingo.'

Moments later the flame of her lighter was right

under my nose, and her face was just on the other side of the flame, staring up at me.

'Who are you?' she asked. 'You're not Andrew. You're not Jack. Who are you? Where are the real boys? The ones who belong here? Is this someone's idea of a joke?' She looked around, as if she were expecting the guests at a surprise party to come stepping from the shadows. When she saw the table she motioned toward it with her head.

'Would you please sit down,' she said. 'And start talking. What do you think this is anyway? A silent retreat?'

I couldn't believe I was letting myself be ordered around by this strange woman, but I did as she suggested and moved toward the table and took a seat in one of the beach chairs. She settled herself in the chair across from mine, and as my eyes adjusted to the dark I got a better look at her. Her piled-up hair was a silvery-gray that suggested she was old. But the skin of her face was smooth and clear. She had elegant high cheekbones and perfect posture. As I studied her she closed her eyes, flicked her lighter on again, lit a cigarette and took a long pull on it. Then she opened her eyes and gave me a huge movie-star smile as she thumped her temple with the heel of her hand. 'Manners, please come home,' she murmured as she held her pack of cigarettes out toward me. 'Smoke?' she asked. 'Like to take a drag on a fag, my little friend?'

I really don't like to smoke, but again I obeyed. I said 'Thank you' and pulled a cigarette from the pack she held out. It was a Lucky Strike, unfiltered, and I almost choked on my first drag as she lit it for me.

'Pink lungs, eh?' she said, and laughed. 'Sweet little baby pink lungs in there? Who are you, anyway, Pinkie-boy? You're not Logan. No, course not. Can't be. Baby Logan is a she. Doesn't look a bit like you. Correct? ANSWER ME!'

I jumped, inadvertently, when she shouted at me all

of a sudden like that. I felt the hot tingling along the backs of my hands that I get in moments of crisis.

'No, I'm not Logan,' I said as I exhaled, and stubbed the horrible cigarette out on the table. 'Logan's away. Speaking of which, I'm afraid I have to leave now too. Good-bye.' I tried to stand up to leave, but I forgot how low the ceiling was and I hit my head on a porch joist and almost had to sit down again, it hurt so badly. I steadied myself on the edge of the table while everything went whirly for a few seconds – I think from the cigarette as much as from my bump. And then I felt her long fingers closing around my wrist.

'Not so fast, Tough Stuff,' she purred. 'Slow down, Mr Pony Express. I'm on an important mission here, and you're going to help me. Okay? Don't be frightened, I won't hurt you.' She flashed another of her dazzling smiles and exhaled a huge cloud of smoke. 'Promise.'

There was something about her that kept paralyzing me, something about the combination of her elegance and her rudeness that was disarming. Her eyes were an amazing bright green, and as I looked down at the left hand that still grasped my wrist I noticed a big ring – a giant emerald flanked by two huge diamonds – flashing on its fourth finger. A piece of white kitchen twine had been wrapped around the underside of the ring's gold band.

'Who are you?' I asked. I was genuinely curious. 'How do you know Elray? What are you doing here?'

'Who the hell is Elray?' she snapped back, and then quickly lit another cigarette. 'I don't know any Elrays. Goodness, what a name. So who's Elray? Come on, young boy, out with it.'

'Who are you?' I repeated. 'You tell me who you are, and I'll tell you who Elray is.'

'Oh my this is getting tiresome,' she said as she dropped my wrist and began to drum her fingers on the tabletop. 'Unless unless unless,' she said, and this time when her hand shot out she grabbed my face by my chin. 'Does this Elray person live right here, in this house, with the others? With – the family?' As she stared up at me I thought I saw tears gathering in her green eyes.

'Who. Are. You.' I asked this slowly as I pushed her hand away. She gave me a long stare back, and then she looked away.

'Oh dear,' she whispered. 'I don't know if I can carry on. Ouch. It *hurts*. I'm ready to come home, but nobody cares.' She stood up from the table, and as she turned toward me I saw that the tears were running down her cheeks now. A moment later she was gone, just as suddenly as she had come. She flew past me, out from under the porch and across the yard toward the street. I was a little slow to follow – but a few minutes later I looked all around the house and up and down the street in both directions, and she was nowhere to be seen.

I sat on the front steps of Elray's house for a long time then, wondering who the woman was and why she had been there. The mailwoman came while I was sitting there – she was an hour later than usual – and just smiled at me and handed me the mail. It was all bills, except for a letter to Ajax from someone in New York.

I finally left Elray's porch at about 6:30 and walked over to the Moskowitz house to pick up Rachel and Clair, as planned. The three of us headed down to the Sheraton Park. The skating, which for some reason I'd been dreading, turned out to be a lot of fun. For one thing Clair was looking amazing – she's very tall, almost as tall as I, and she was wearing a short black skirt and white tights. She has those legs that don't quit, and then her hair's so long too, and she looked to me like a flying dream as she went sailing around the rink. I had a hard-on practically all evening just watching her. Rachel looked good too, but with Clair there Rachel was definitely a contrast loser.

I had a few carefully planned collisions with each of

them, and one time I got pretty close to Clair's left breast. But the best was when we went inside the hotel to warm up for a few minutes. We were sitting in the lounge that overlooks the rink when Clair turned to me suddenly and said, 'This place is huge. Let's explore.' A second later she was up and moving down a long corridor in her socks. I was right behind her, in my socks, and somewhere way back there, still trying to pull her skates off, was Rachel, saying: 'Wait up, guys, wait up.'

I slowed down and looked back toward Rachel for just an instant, but when I looked forward again Clair was already miles ahead of me, slipping through a door on the right. I abandoned all pretense of courtesy and sprinted after Clair, down the hall and through the door, which, as it turned out, opened into a huge, empty ballroom. The light in there was very dim, but bright enough to give a little sparkle to the huge crystal chandeliers suspended overhead. I got that same hyped-up feeling I get when I am exploring a new cave. As I started to float through the dark room, Clair was nowhere to be seen. But I could tell she was in there somewhere, I could sense it. 'I know you're in here – I can smell you,' I shouted, and I meant it. An instant later I realized I sounded just like the crazy woman who'd cornered me under Elray's porch, and that gave me an idea. I started to prowl around the room then, muttering under my breath the way the woman had.

'FEE FIE FO FUM. I'M QUITE SURE I SMELL SOMEONE! You can't hide from me, darling,' I muttered as I started yanking the long white tablecloths up and checking under each banquet table. I made my way systematically through the room, looking under each table and muttering to myself as I went. When I had almost reached the far end of the ballroom, I looked up and saw the huge, ceiling-to-floor curtains that run the length of that far wall. There was a definite bulge in the long green expanse of the curtains. 'OH YES! I've got you now!' I called out. But as I headed for the bulge it began to move, rippling its way behind the curtains toward the far corner. I raced after the fleeing bulge, and just as it was reaching the corner where the curtains ended I flung myself at it and trapped it in my arms, behind the curtain and against the wall. 'Gotcha!' I whispered. 'Gotcha gotcha gotcha!' For one too-short moment I pressed my whole body against the anonymous lump behind the thick folds of green.

But then an instant later the lump, which was of course Clair, screamed – a high-pitched, terrified girl scream that I was sure would have the management in there in a matter of seconds. So I quickly opened the end of the curtains and tried to quiet her. 'Shhhh, shhh. It's okay,' I told her. 'I'm just playing. It's only me. It's me, Raoul.'

She was all curled up behind her wrists and hands and almost crying. I felt bad. 'What are you doing, Raoul?' she said.

'Shhh. Did I scare you? I'm sorry,' I said. 'Come out now, I'm sorry.' The truth was, I wasn't really sorry. I'd had too much fun. And it was satisfying in some way to see her so pathetic and scared. Plus it gave me a chance to be tender. 'Here, let's go now. Let's go find Rachel,' I said and I offered her my hands. 'Come on out, Clair. It's okay.' She hesitated for a second but then she took my hands, and even tried to smile. I smiled back, and I lifted her fingers – all ten of them – to my lips. The two of us exchanged a long look and then walked across the empty ballroom, holding hands. The whole way I was about to explode with a sweet sense of triumph. It was such an unexpected and odd victory. As I led Clair Moskowitz out of that ballroom tonight, and turned with her down the long tunnel of the hotel hall toward the lobby and Rachel, I knew for sure that I had bagged this girl. I knew for sure that if I wanted her, she was mine.

Well, now it's 2 A.M., and as I sit here and write this

I still don't know whether or not I really want Clair Moskowitz, or what I'll do with her if it turns out I do want her. But I like the general shape things are taking. As I think about the delicious stretch of Clair's legs between the hip and knee, I feel that the Elray games must finally be over, for good. I'm going to keep an eye on Elray, from a distance, because she needs someone normal watching over her. But my own life as a red-blooded man has truly begun. For this I owe the strange old woman – whoever she was – who followed me under the porch today. It was her performance that inspired the ballroom maneuvers that won me Clair. It was the beautiful but rude old woman who in-advertently taught me, after all my unsuccessful efforts to discover it for myself, the tremendous power and pleasure that can come of behaving badly.

Part Five

Lost and Found

Granny Rising

On an otherwise unremarkable day Ajax appeared before me as I sat in our dining room and in her most resonant and theatrical tones made this announcement: 'Elray, my dear. There is something I must tell you. A strange old woman has surfaced. A woman who is very much alive, but who claims she is my mother. Your Granny Mayhew.'

When Ajax first tried to break this news to me, I rejected the notion out of hand. I was sitting in the dining room of our house, peeling an orange and flipping through a fishing catalogue. I must have looked up at her for a second at the most before turning back to my catalogue. Children often find it hard to surrender their personal mythologies. I had spent many years in the affectionate company of my Granny Mayhew – but I was used to her as a private vision, not a warm-blooded living human.

'Ha ha ha,' I said. 'And Barkley and Jack are coming for dinner, I suppose. Shall I run out back and slaughter the fatted calf?' I was still in that obnoxious stage of adolescence when sarcasm seems to be the only motivating principle behind speech.

'I'm serious, Elray. It's true.' When I looked up again I saw that Ajax had her needle-nose face on. She was serious. 'I didn't believe it at first either,' she said. 'It seems impossible, I know. But she's written to me, and she's made a compelling enough case that she's my mother, your father's mother – your grandmother – that the courts may now get involved. She wants to see you, Elray. She demands that she be granted access to you. But I absolutely refuse.' Ajax burst into tears at this and ran from the room.

So this was the big ugly secret that had invaded our house. This was the mysterious old woman Harwood had talked of 'dealing with.' All the pieces began to fall into place. The woman claiming to be my grandmother had revealed herself to Ajax, it turned out, in a long letter that had been waiting when we returned from Key West. Ajax had immediately told Rena and Harwood. Not long after, just about every other literate citizen within a sixty-mile radius of my home learned about the miraculous resurrection of my allegedly dead grandmother, because of an interview that Granny decided to give a local newspaper after Ajax had repeatedly refused to meet with her. I, it seemed, was almost the last person on earth to learn that my Granny Mayhew had risen from the dead. I have since gone back and read the newspaper clippings about the bizarre story, all of which were carefully concealed from me at the time. Even though I now know the answers to most of the unknowns – about Granny Mayhew's mysterious reappearance and how it would impact on my life – I still find the story intriguing.

LOST AND FOUND
Woman Returns from the Dead
to Claim Orphaned Granddaughter

CASE OF THE LIVING DEAD?
Woman Wants to Reunite with Family
Thirty Years After 'Death'

These were some of the headlines that heralded what was referred to as the 'puzzling reappearance' of my father's mother. What was 'puzzling' everybody, of course, was that the same Amanda Baer Mayhew had made headlines three decades earlier as the sole and tragic victim in the fire that had broken out in Blackie's Bar and Grill late one New Year's Eve. Now, years and years after her family – my father, my uncle, and my grandfather, that is – had laid her to rest and set about the business of piecing together a life without her, here came a woman who insisted that she was Amanda Baer Mayhew and that she had never died in that long-ago fire. The story Granny gave reporters was that she had suffered a severe head injury that had condemned her to thirty years as a wandering amnesiac. Until one day she picked up an old Baltimore paper in a library and stumbled across a report of the Glen Echo accident that had killed my parents. The printed names of Ajax and my father, her little sons who had been twelve and eight at the time of her supposed death, had brought everything rushing back to her, she claimed.

'When questioned by authorities,' one news article reported, 'the woman demonstrated a flawless knowledge of personal and family history that would seem to support her claim as the allegedly dead Mrs Mayhew. However, Andrew Jackson Mayhew, the sole surviving son of Amanda Baer Mayhew, remains skeptical and in fact has so far refused to meet with the woman who claims to be his mother.'

'Forensic experts are stymied by all the contradictory evidence, most especially by certain dental samples that were taken as conclusive proof of Mrs Mayhew's death at the time of the fire,' another account exclaimed. They all had their own way of working it in, but not one of these stories failed to mention the little tidbit about the remnants of Granny's teeth that had been found thirty years earlier in the ladies' lounge of the restaurant, only a few feet from the kerosene heater that had exploded and caused the fire. 'The woman who claims to be Amanda Mayhew has refused to submit to a dental examination,' one account solemnly reported.

This then was the public status of Granny's

attempted reemergence when Ajax first made her existence known to me. After her initial announcement, however, Ajax became strangely reluctant to broach the subject again.

'All right already. What's the rush anyway?' Ajax would say to me every time I argued that it made sense for me to meet the woman claiming to be my Granny Mayhew. 'She's been dead all your life until now, and you've done just fine, haven't you? Do me a favor and just assume she's dead for a little while longer, okay? I was premature in mentioning her to you. I'm sorry. I should have waited a little longer.'

'Can I at least read the letter she sent you?' I would ask.

'No. Never. It's disgusting,' Ajax would answer. 'I can't explain it right now, but things have gotten complicated recently. We must proceed very carefully. Trust me. Besides, we should be putting all our energies into preparations for the trial.'

After repeated and failed attempts at settlement, our long-awaited court battle – our showdown for justice against the amusement park – had finally been scheduled for a date in August. Rena was in an agitated state over this, and frequently talked about the 'war strategies' we needed to review in preparation for the event. I had come to believe the trial would probably never happen, that indeed the whole notion was just another subplot in the strange and abstract obsession with my family that seemed to have seized Rena. I no longer cared, about a trial or a settlement.

In fact, the more I thought about it the more I realized that the prospect of retrieving my Granny Mayhew from the dead might be the only thing I could allow myself to care about anymore. I had proved to have an impressive talent for losing people. I had lost my mother and father a long time ago, of course; but recently I had lost others as well. Harwood and Rena were gone. Although they both still pretended that nothing was going on, I had seen for myself that they had abandoned me for each other.

Raoul, it had become painfully clear, was also gone. I had tried three more times to contact him since completing my Glen Echo pilgrimage: twice by loitering for hours on the street corner opposite the entrance to his apartment building, and once by telephone. The second time I waited on the street, I had seen him eventually, but he had been with someone – a girl. The way he rested his hand on her shoulder as he ushered her through the door to the apartment building sent a rush of blood to my cheeks, and I sprinted straight to the Bishop's Garden, where I hid in the boxwood for two hours.

Two weeks later, when I worked up the nerve to call Raoul on the telephone, his mother answered. When I asked for Raoul she said, 'No, I'm sorry. He's out. Who's calling please?'

'Stump,' I replied, before I'd even had a chance to think about it. Then I hung up.

At about the same time that Ajax broke the news about the woman claiming to be Granny Mayhew, I had learned that the girl I had seen with Raoul was Clair Moskowitz, a sleek, older girl who lived just a few blocks from me. I had also learned that she and Raoul were seeing quite a lot of each other. 'They're like totally in love,' I had overheard a girl named Brenda telling someone at my school. It was a preposterous, maggoty notion – as ludicrous as the image of Harwood and Rena groping around together – and I had decided to push all four of the silly lovebirds out of my heart, out of my mind, to the wasteland where only the most boring stories belong.

Granny Mayhew, on the other hand, and the prospect of actually laying eyes on her after so many years of only imagining her, began to seem the opposite of a boring story. I decided I was as eager to meet my no-longer-dead grandmother as Ajax had claimed my no-longer-dead grandmother was to meet me. As it turned out, I wouldn't have long to wait.

The Solace of Secrets

I have always been partial to secrets. I can see that
now. While growing up I treasured my secret
exchanges with Barkley and Jack, and delighted in the
irony of my home life with an aunt whom the rest of
the world mistook for an uncle. For a long time I
cultivated the sweet secret of Raoul, my allegedly
imaginary but actually very real best friend. Then, just
when all these hidden pockets of mine began to disappear, leaving me flagstone-flat and bereft of all
mystery, along came Granny Mayhew.

After failing to get to me through Ajax and Harwood,
the woman who claimed to be my grandmother took
more direct action: She snuck into my house and
materialized unannounced at the end of my bed one
afternoon. I was dozing there at the time, adrift in a
slag heap of magazines and books I couldn't be
bothered to read, and the first thing I noticed was a
sweet, almost lilac smell. It had a pharmaceutical tinge
that made me think of hypodermic needles floating in
glass jars. When I opened my eyes I saw a very tall,
very erect woman standing at the end of my bed. A
green velvet hat with one long peacock feather was
perched atop her piled-up hair like a boat under sail. I
stared at her for a few seconds and failed to recognize
her, either as someone I should know or even as anything real. She was just another figment of my bored
adolescent imagination, I decided. A kind of weird

hybrid of the actress Hedy Lamarr and Robin Hood. I had had all sorts of strange hallucinations parading past me lately – Hansueli had assured me they were quite common. 'Typical escape fantasies uf adolescents suffering dee unbearable trauma uf everyday life,' he had said. 'Nutting to worry about.'

Moments later, however, this particular fantasy of mine touched me very gently on the toes. Blood went flushing through my body as it hadn't in weeks. As I drew myself into a ball and took another look at the vision at the end of my bed, it began to speak.

'Don't scream, Logan,' the woman said in a rich, almost liquid voice. 'I am your grandmother, Amanda Mayhew. Your own flesh and blood. I am so eager to get to know you, to make up for lost time. I hope we can be friends.'

I gave her a good look and decided it was not possible, any of it. It was not possible that this mythological-looking creature could be flesh and blood, much less my dear, dashing dancer of a dead grandmother. It was not possible that I would not scream, instantly.

'A-A-A-A-AAAAY-JAX!' I did scream. Seconds later my visitor was standing at the head of my bed and had placed a hand across my mouth to silence me. She's surprisingly strong, not to mention agile, I thought. And then it finally sank in.

'I've been looking for you,' I said as I pushed her hand away. 'You are my Granny Mayhew?' It still seemed impossible to me, but the woman was already smiling and nodding a solemn yes with her hands crossed over her heart. 'But Granny Mayhew was . . . I always thought she looked . . . It's just that you are so . . .' It was going from bad to worse, so I decided to shut up.

'What? So strange-looking and old? Is that what you're trying to say? Go ahead, you won't hurt my feelings,' the woman said as she shrugged her shoulders and pulled out a pack of cigarettes. 'But what did you expect? Think about it. I've been dead about twice as long than you've been alive, darling.'

'Of course, absolutely, you're right,' I said quickly. 'And actually you look beautiful – just different from what I had imagined. Well, Ajax did say you used to dance a lot. Right? By the way, I wouldn't smoke in here if I were you. Bad idea.' I was still hunched in a ball, and I stared down at my intertwined fingers and toes as I made this last suggestion. When I finally looked up again, I was stunned. The woman who claimed she was my grandmother had begun to dance. Her arms dipped and turned and rotated through the air gracefully while her feet went speed-bombing recklessly through a Morse code tap language all their own. Her face was tilted upward and radiant, almost as if it had a spotlight on it. After a sequence of increasingly dramatic maneuvers, she came sailing straight toward me in one last, big leap and landed on one bended knee on the floor right in front of me with her head tipped way back. We sat for a moment in silence and then, with a quick snap, she was standing again and staring intently at me. Her face was flushed and her already bright green eyes seemed to have switched to high beam. In that instant I made up my mind: Whether she was my grandmother or not, I was going to claim this woman. I wasn't sure if I approved of her or not, but she was wild. And she was mine.

'Granny Mayhew,' I said. 'That was great.' A second later her tall elegant frame was seated right next to mine and she had wrapped her arms around my shoulders. We exchanged a tight squeeze. After a minute she pushed away slightly and looked at me.

'You can call me Mama Baer,' she whispered. 'That's what your daddy called me.' Then she pursed her lips and blew me a kiss.

After her first dramatic visit to my bedroom, Granny Mayhew and I began to meet almost every day. Although we never discussed it openly, we both understood from the beginning that our meetings would of course be conducted secretly. Our first rendezvous spot was the crawlspace under my house. Granny had surprised me at our first meeting by suggesting this location herself.

'Meet me tomorrow afternoon, at the little table under your porch, at five o'clock?' she whispered to me as she prepared to sneak out of the house. I was curious as to how she knew about my crawlspace, but I just smiled and nodded and hurried her on her way.

The next day as the two of us sat in our crawlspace chairs amid the cricket-chorus of evening, I confronted her. 'How did you know about this crawlspace? Who told you about it?' I asked.

Granny, who was smoking, leaned back in her chair and released a huge cloud of smoke. She was wearing a well-fitted gray flannel dress with a long row of over-sized buttons running right up the front from the hem to the collar. Very *Philadelphia Story*. 'I've been here under the porch many times before,' she said. 'I was always looking for you, but all I ever found was the boy.'

'The boy? What boy?' I asked. I hoped the awful hunch that had seized me was wrong.

'The one I thought might be your dead daddy or Andrew – what is it he calls himself now? Ajax? Terrible name. A lapse of logic on my part, of course. That kind of thing happens when you get old, Logan. I forgot that one boy's dead and the other's no longer a boy. No longer a boy and yet not a man. Goodness. Who could have called that one? Not me . . .'

'What boy? What was his name?' I interrupted her.

'Never got his name, he never got mine. Mutual standoff. But we've talked a couple of times. He tracked me down one day and asked me a million questions about you. As if I knew anything. He suggested that I stay away if I was a "troublemaker." Bossy little chap, he was. But pretty boy, almost too pretty. Gray-green eyes with specks of light in them and cheeks like pink leather, with a fine white scar running up one, as if he had had a toothpick embedded there. He had pink lungs too. Little turnip practically passed out when he tried to smoke a cigarette the first time we met. He knew all about you, I could tell. But he wouldn't help me. Not one bit.'

It had been Raoul, just as I'd suspected. The toothpick scar was a giveaway. It had come from a wound he had suffered about a year and a half earlier, during an Invincibility Exercise we devised one afternoon in the crypts. The exercise involved sending each other, blindfolded, deep into the crypts to retrieve a specific object. We were to accomplish our respective missions within thirty minutes, without ever removing our blindfolds – at any time under any circumstances. Raoul had been merciful. He had asked me to fetch a single candle from the torch room – a relatively simple sortie through a straightforward section of crypt. I, on the other hand, had assigned Raoul 'the third bottle from the left in the Devil's Saloon,' the Devil's Saloon being our name for the row of empty Dewar's scotch bottles that sat high on a wall in one of the remotest corners of the next-to-lowest crypt.

Our point of departure and return for this exercise was the gargoyle room, and it was there that I was sitting – triumphant, gloating, my candle trophy alight and held on high – when Raoul finally stumbled in, ten minutes after our thirty-minute time limit. I had been about to shout something derisive about his having overshot his time, but one look at him silenced me. His face and neck and upper torso were covered with blood, and a huge tear in his left pant leg was flapping back and forth over a badly scraped knee.

'Home again, home again,' he said as he lifted his blindfold and held an empty Dewar's bottle toward me. Five seconds later he was on his knees. 'Hey Tree, I think I cut myself somewhere,' he said. 'Can you help?'

In the Glee Club bathroom upstairs I stripped off

Raoul's shirt and, in an exercise that felt like a cross between surgery and an archeological dig, I slowly washed the blood off his face and neck and shoulders. All that blood, we discovered, had come from one razor-thin incision that ran down Raoul's left cheek. He had no idea what had put it there. The cut needed stitches, but it certainly wasn't anything life-threatening. I'm ashamed to admit that a little later, after my initial rush of concern, instead of feeling sympathy for Raoul, or guilt for having been the one who had sent him on the mission that had wounded him, I felt only envy and resentment. Not only had he undertaken and accomplished a tougher assignment than I, but he had earned himself a splendid badge of courage – a dashing facial scar that he would wear for the rest of his life. Raoul always made me feel like a runner-up in the invincibility Olympics.

As I sat in the crawlspace with Granny Mayhew and remembered the war-worthy sight of Raoul's bloodied torso and the warm murmur of his voice thanking me again and again for taking care of him, I felt a rush of heat and sadness. I thought of our parting on the morning after our river swim, and saw once again the haunting image of Raoul disappearing half-naked into the sunrise. Pushed away by me. My sadness curdled to fury. Hadn't he humiliated me enough already, with his superior invincibility and courage and honesty? Now it turned out he had been rooting around in my private crawlspace unbeknownst to me. Even worse, he'd had the gall to meet my dead grandmother before I had. I thought of the very last glimpse I'd had of Raoul – guiding Clair Moskowitz through the door of his apartment building like some greasy mobster on a date. I snatched one of Granny's cigarettes and lit it and started puffing away like there was no tomorrow.

'Exactly when was he in here, anyway?' I just managed to get my question out before a coughing fit derailed me.

'Easy now, easy now,' Granny said as she bent

forward and began to rub my back. 'Here, give me that nic stick. You don't need it, darling. Not yet.' She pulled the cigarette out of my fingers and stuck it in her mouth, alongside another one that was already there. 'Logan, tell me about this boy.' (Granny always used my given name, which no one else ever used. 'Elray is a monstrous moniker. I won't be using it,' she had announced.) 'Looks like we've hit a nerve here, doesn't it?' she said as her two cigarettes went bobbling about in front like insect feelers. 'What's his name? How did he maneuver you to a place where he can hurt you so much? What are we going to do about it? I want to hear all about it. I want to hear all about everything. Do you understand? I have so much lost time to make up for. I want to hear all about everything that has ever happened to you.'

Pas de Deux

I took Granny Mayhew at her word that afternoon, and during the next few weeks I confided in her as I had never confided in anyone. Perhaps my openness with her had something to do with a lingering uncertainty I had as to whether or not she actually existed, as a living and breathing mortal. Or perhaps it was because Granny contained, in one tidy if bizarre package, so many pieces of my life that I had thought were forever lost. My secret exchanges with Barkley and Jack, for instance. My little crescent of scarred flesh, faded to a silvery headstone-white, was now nothing but a mute memorial to the busy switchboard that had once been. Granny Mayhew provided a new secret link to my parents. She had been my father's mother, however briefly. Technically, she still was.

Granny also served as understudy for Raoul, my secret friend and coadventurer, and – less obviously, I suppose – for the surrogate mother I had looked for in Ajax. I became obsessed with the two-way task of teaching my newfound relative everything there was to know about me and extracting everything there was to know about her. One of my first strategies was to take her to the crypts, where, over the course of several outings, I gave her a tour of all the major landmarks, along with a condensed history of the adventures Raoul and I had shared.

'Lord have mercy!' she exclaimed on the first of

241

these expeditions. 'Such subterranean tendencies you have, darling.' Although our explorations involved a great deal of climbing and crawling and snaking through tight places that should have been taxing for a woman of her age, Granny never complained or let on that she was having anything but the time of her life. Once she stopped and put her finger to her lips as we were about to emerge from the crypts into the St Joseph of Arimathea Chapel. 'Fee Fie Fo Fum, I smell someone,' she whispered as she turned and winked at me. 'He's here. The boy. Raoul.'

'Not possible,' I said, but my heart was racing at the suggestion. We searched the chapel; there was definitely no one there. I decided to show Granny the niche behind the loose stone that had been my message center with Raoul, and when I pried it open there sat the note I'd left so long ago. Or so I thought. 'Help. *Je suis perdue*,' I expected to hear Granny read, but she surprised me.

'You're not lost. You're fine. I'm watching,' she read. 'Yuk,' she said, looking up and wrinkling her nose slightly. 'What's that about? Bit treacly, don't you think?' I snatched the note away from her and looked around the chapel again, spooked now. Then I led Granny back outside, to the bright and obvious day.

On sunny days later that spring, as the Washington weather turned briefly but irresistibly perfect, I would sometimes cut afternoon classes at school in order to rendezvous with Granny. 'Tallyho, young blossom!' Granny would hail me as I approached our meeting place a few blocks from my school. 'Ready?'

'Ready,' I would answer. Then we would climb into Granny's little blue convertible Dodge Dart — 'Cleopatra,' Granny called her — and ride off into the fluid spring air like two mermaids in a seashell. Usually we would weave our way through the downtown streets, visiting the haunts that Granny had frequented as a young woman. As we went slowly past the bombed-out business section down at 7th and F streets, Granny would recite the names of all the snazzy clubs and elegant hotels that had been there when she was young and footloose. But Granny would always send Cleopatra roaring at high speed past the intersection of 15th and K streets, where a medical building now occupied the former site of Blackie's Bar and Grill. I could never get her to slow down there, let alone stop and reminisce as she did at every other spot that-sparked some memory.

'I shall not talk about that place, that event. Ever. I wrote it all down for Andrew. Once was enough. Read the letter,' she'd say. 'It's all in there.'

The house on O Street where Granny had lived with my grandfather and father and Ajax was another story, however. It was one of my favorite stops, and on warm days we would take a picnic and park ourselves on the steps of the little yellow church just opposite. Granny would sit and eat and tell me stories from those long-ago days. It was here that I learned how she and Amos Mayhew, my grandfather, met and fell in love.

'It was on a cold November night outside a little jazz club on E Street in this very city. I was dressed as a bumblebee and he was with another woman,' she told me. 'If either one of us had had even a pinch of common sense we would have understood that based on appearances alone we should grant each other a wide berth. But life never works sensibly, does it? You know that, Logan. And when you are as young and foolish as I was then, you don't even want it to. It took fully thirty seconds for your grandfather and I to launch ourselves into a dialogue that would last us some thirteen years.'

'What were his first words to you? Do you remember?' I asked.

'Of course I do,' Granny answered without hesitation. 'He said, "I'm deathly allergic to bees, but may I offer you a light?" As I've mentioned, I was dressed as a bumblebee. I was working with a tap revue at the time, and we were performing in the club that night.

I had slipped outside during a break for a smoke.'

'What did you say to him?' I asked. Once Granny got rolling, the merest prod would keep her going.

'I told him the truth. "I have a paralyzing fear of fire," I answered. "But I accept. Thank you." Your grandfather cupped his hand around one side of his lighter and I cupped my hand around the other side. I closed my eyes and leaned forward with my cigarette into the little temple of our two hands, where a tiny flame was burning, and I knew I was gone. I was head over heels. He reminded me of Clark Gable. Only taller, and thinner. Better-looking.'

'Interesting. You and Grandpa confessed your fears when you first met,' I said. 'In a way, Raoul and I did that too. Who was the other woman? You said he was with someone.'

'Oh my, she was a beauty, a society dame who had a neck that stretched skyward like Jack's beanstalk,' said Granny, stretching her own neck out to illustrate the look. 'She kept shifting from foot to foot, saying, "Amos, I'm freezing. I think I'd like to go home now." When he finally turned to her and looked her up and down as if he barely knew her, I was encouraged. "Excuse me for a moment," he said to me, and then he stepped to the curb and hailed a cab and helped her into the backseat and sent her on her way. Just like that. It was probably the first and last impulsive and ungallant move your grandfather ever made in his life, and therefore actually a piece of false advertising. But it sure worked like a charm on me.'

The stories of those early days in my grandparents' courtship seized my imagination with the tenacity of the best of fairy tales. My grandfather, the finely groomed elegant society giant, came to every show at which my grandmother, the lanky and languorous tap-dancing bumblebee, performed for the next two weeks. After each show he wined and dined her, and all her backstage buddies too. He could joke and drink and backslap with the best of them. He always picked up the bill.

When my grandmother had a break in her performing schedule, she made a contrapuntal guest appearance in his world. 'I am nothing if not a quick study, Logan,' she told me. 'I understood without needing to be told that I should applaud demurely at the opera, and plaster on a Mona Lisa smile during poetry readings. At the dinner table I spoke in confident and round tones as I ordered beluga, quenelles, *rognons, canard* and a slew of other delicacies whose identities remained entirely mysterious to me – even after I'd carefully consumed them tiny bite by bite, upside down and backward, holding my fork in my left hand and my knife in my right as everyone around me did. Your grandfather sat beside me, beaming all the while. It was his turn to tumble into love, his turn to make the fatal mistake of believing he could have me on his terms.

'Oh, be careful in life and in love, Logan,' Granny said, grabbing me by my wrist. 'It started as sheer, infectious fun between your grand-father and me – a little improvisational number in which we switched hats and tossed cherry bombs into each other's hearts. Before long it was a binding contract of expectation and obligation.'

When Granny's tap group opened another show at another downtown club, my grandfather was much less enthusiastic in his attendance, but not in his attentions. Although he appeared in the audience only twice in that two-week period, flowers were delivered to Granny backstage every evening, and every night a sleek black automobile was waiting for her outside. Sometimes my grandfather would be waiting there too, in the backseat, with a whiskey in one hand, the newspaper or some work documents in the other and a big smile breaking beneath his bushy broom of a mustache. But more often the backseat would be empty, so Granny would slide into the front seat alongside the driver and off she would glide to meet her lover at some prearranged destination – a quiet restaurant in an obscure neighborhood, or the polished cigar box of a dining room in his own elegant bachelor quarters.

'One winter night – I still remember this so vividly – your grandfather's car eased to a stop alongside a private yacht that was anchored right here,' Granny told me one afternoon when we had motored down to admire the cherry blossoms at the Tidal Basin between the Lincoln and Jefferson memorials. 'A violinist was standing on the bow of the boat serenading me as I approached, and I did a little tap riff right up the gangplank and then landed like Persephone in your grandfather's arms.

'I've always liked to think that that was the night your Uncle Andrew was conceived, Logan, but who can say. Had to be sometime around then, so why not say yes, it was right there in the cabin of that yacht on that same starry winter night, in a circle of leafless cherry trees with two dead presidents watching.'

Six months after the November night when they first met Granny was married to Amos Mayhew in a quiet civil ceremony at the local district court. Ivy, his maid, was their witness. Granny was three months pregnant with her first child – my Auntie Ajax.

'I went in the next day to the theater where I had just landed a big role in a musical about Joan of Arc and resigned. Oh dear. I know it may sound like we had a less than glorious start, Logan. But this is the way most lives are shaped: in part by improvisations of the heart, but more by the clumsy, haphazard world of fact and circumstance and time logged. Of course, I could never have admitted such a thing to myself back then. Instead I threw myself into my new life, told myself it was just what I had been looking for all along. I had come east three years earlier on a crusade to escape the crushing monotony of my poor midwestern roots. Well, what more thorough escape could I have found than the utterly alien culture that I landed in when I married Amos Mayhew?'

'What was so alien about it?' I asked. 'It sounds pretty nice to me.' I often felt the need to defend my grandfather, since he was not there to defend himself, during these stories.

'Oh, don't misunderstand me, we had our good times,' Granny said, patting my arm. 'Others have hit upon more enduring forms of love, but I can't believe that many come across anything better or more intense than the happiness your grandfather and I first found with each other. Of course, one could argue that what sparked us was nothing more than the inevitable cross-circuitry that pops and crackles between people as radically different as the two of us. Your grandfather was third-generation Washington blue blood and a lawyer with the Justice Department. I – since the truth can now, at last, be told – was your basic back-woods urchin from Beetlebay, Missouri. People often mistook me for something grander, but in fact I was just a good-looking bit-part dancer in a second-rate tap revue.'

'Did you always live in the O Street house? How did you pick it?' I asked. I had never before considered that you could choose a home; I'd assumed that houses chose you.

'Oh yes. It had belonged to Amos – to the Mayhew family – for years,' said Granny. 'I moved into a house filled with the chicly shabby hand-me-downs from three generations of Mayhews. You know what I'm talking about. You're living with them now, Logan. All those muted paisley throws over the worn backs of bottle-green armchairs. Everything in the deliberately haphazard style perfected by the old and urban rich. It wasn't my style.'

When Granny started strolling down memory lane she sometimes got a little whiny – and about the strangest things. 'When I married Amos I had to go cold turkey on a lifelong habit of eating most of my meals on my feet – either in front of an open re-frigerator or beside a street vendor,' she complained one day. 'I had to totally remake myself. I had to plan well-balanced, sit-down meals, and order my groceries from a local grocer who delivered the goods himself, packed in wooden crates and wrapped in layers and layers of tissue as if they were Christmas ornaments and not just lamb chops and potatoes he was bringing. It was very traumatic.'

'I love lamb chops. Yum yum. Tell me about the babies, about Ajax and my father,' I would say, trying to distract her and calm her down.

Granny told me about the day Ajax was born, and explained how the new baby was installed in a back corner of the house with a French mademoiselle. 'I found him such an enchanting-looking little creature, but I hadn't a clue of what to do with him after the initial squeeze and kiss each time we met,' she said. 'Rather than get it wrong, I left him alone. I took refuge in the privacy of my bedroom, where I passed the day reading magazines and practicing tap routines in front of my closet mirror. By the time your grandfather got home from work, I have to confess, I was usually primed with a martini or two. And ready for mischief. I would greet him in the hallway, before he'd even had a chance to remove his hat and coat. Often I would have cooked up a costume of some kind during the course of my afternoon.'

'Sounds pretty fun to me. What would he say when he saw you?' I'd ask. I wanted Granny to keep talking. I loved the scenes with my grandfather in them.

'Oh, he'd say something like "Goodness, look at you, Little Baer." That was the nickname he had created for me from my maiden name.' During these exchanges Granny would pretend she was reluctant to continue and only humoring me at first. But I began to understand that she loved acting out the scenes as much as I loved hearing them. She would change voices for the different parts, and throw in appropriate gestures.

'Then what?' I'd ask.

'Oh, then he'd say, "What are you, Little Baer? A gypsy? Titania, the Fairy Queen?" And I'd answer, "Oh nothing in particular, Amos. Just another housewife. Your housewife." And he'd say, "Well, and a mighty exotic one at that. Come here. Sit down. Let me look at you." We would go sit in the library and Amos would have his first martini while I had my second or third. Sometimes I'd try to suggest that we go out – for a meal, or for a show. But Amos almost always refused. He'd say, "I've been out all day, Little Baer. I just want to stay right here and look at you. The finest entertainment a fellow could possibly want is seated right here in this room with me right now. Why budge?"

'You see, Logan, this was the part I hadn't figured on.' When Granny reached a certain point in her stories she would pause and grab my arm – a gesture that I learned was a surefire signal that she was about to try to extract a nugget of philosophy from her experience. 'I had convinced myself that marrying Amos would be the perfect escape from the crushing monotony of the life I'd been born to. But what I had failed to understand was that he was trying to escape the crushing monotony of his own life, and that his escape route was me,' she announced. 'So there I was, trying to recast my life within the context of his world, at the same time that he was recasting his world within the context of a single human – me. It was a formula that did not leave us much elbow room. I am someone who can barely stand to live inside my own skin, let alone have someone else move in there with me.'

At moments like this I would nod my head sympathetically, as if it all made sense to me – and indeed, much of it did. But what I really wanted was for Granny to keep talking. There were so many more stories I wanted to hear. I wanted to hear stories about my father, and I wanted to hear about the fire that was supposed to have killed her. I wanted to solve the puzzle of the teeth – I was dying to hear the story of her teeth. But I had to be subtle.

'Love and marriage seem to be very tricky, Granny,' I said. 'Very very tricky.'

'Tell me about it, oh young one.' She'd start up again. 'One of the saddest lessons I've ever learned is that while it is a wonderful thing to love someone madly, it can be a terrible thing to be madly loved. For years your grandfather and I battled over who would have the upper hand in this matter. But it was almost always he – with his superior patience and intellect and capacity for devotion – who triumphed. It was he with his gentle brown eyes and his unflagging admiration and his infinite ability to forgive and forgive and forgive who drove me stark raving mad in the end.'

'When my father was born, didn't that help?' I asked, trying to nudge her toward stories I wanted.

'Your father Jack was born almost four years after Andrew, and what a darling boy he was. What a sweetheart. Unfortunately, by then I was already a monster – as wild-eyed and hostile and impulsive as those big gorillas who perform such a sad pantomime, moping and raging around their cages at the zoo,' she confessed. 'By then my habit of a slightly premature evening cocktail had slurred into a pattern of inter-mittent all-day drinking, and I'd abandoned my afternoons of practicing tap routines in front of my mirror – a physically demanding if mindless pastime – in favor of a new and far more thrilling obsession. By then I was hooked on the horses. But that, darling Logan, is a story for another day.'

Whenever Granny used that phrase – 'a story for another day' – it meant she had reached her limit for reminiscence. Then we'd lean back and light cigarettes. Under Granny's tutelage I was learning to smoke. Granny made it look so cool. We'd change the conversation to my life, what was happening at home and at school, and to general observations.

'Life and the way we live it shape us in ways we can't control,' Granny told me. 'I don't necessarily like what I've become, but I am what I am. I'll tell you one thing, though: I can stand what I am better since I've met you.'

When we ran out of conversation Granny always ended our sessions by teaching me a song-and-dance routine. My favorite was a song called 'Fascinating Rhythm' from the Gershwin musical *Lady, Be Good!*

Got a little rhythm, a rhythm, a rhythm
That pit-a-pats through my brain;
So darn persistent, the day isn't distant
When it'll drive me insane.
Comes in the morning, without any warning,
And hangs around me all day.
I'll have to sneak up to it
Someday, and speak up to it.
I hope it listens when I say . . .

She taught me the Fred Astaire dance routine to the song, and the two of us would sing and dance right down the middle of the street together. It was exhilarating. My life felt bigger.

Perdue, Encore

One Friday in mid-May Granny picked me up at our usual spot, but instead of heading downtown or over to O Street for more stories from her past, she drove straight to my house on High View Street. As far as I knew she hadn't been back inside our house since her first, surprise visit, and recently she and I had even stopped using the crawlspace as a meeting place. Ajax had been curious about where I was spending all my time after school lately, and the risk of getting caught had seemed too great.

'What are you doing? Are you crazy? Ajax is in there,' I said to Granny as she parked Cleopatra and opened her door.

'No he isn't,' said Granny. 'Andrew hasn't been home during the day all week. He's been elsewhere. I've been watching; I know. Come on, let's go. It's time for me to see these films. I need to see the films you and the boy Raoul made. Show me.'

Something about Granny's manner had changed. There was an unfamiliar brusqueness about her. During our sessions I had told Granny all about the Library of the Invincible films, just as I had told her about almost everything else that I could think of that had ever happened to me. But I had resisted actually showing her the films, using the logistical problem of how to do so without getting caught as my excuse. I think part of my resistance stemmed from my reluctance to view the films again myself. With everything so dead and discredited between Raoul and me, there seemed little point. At the same time, part of me felt protective toward the old archives, the celluloid transcripts of what Raoul and I had once been. They were just about all he and I had left. To show them to a stranger, even a stranger who was a newly resurrected grandmother, seemed like a terrible breach of trust. Maybe even worse.

But there Granny stood on that May afternoon, her green eyes shining, her long-fingered hand reaching for mine as she headed up our front walk. How could I not show her the films if she really wanted to see them? What were the films anyway but some silly fluff put together by a pair of adolescents? Only an indulgent grandmother would even feign an interest in such nonsense. I grabbed Granny's outstretched hand and we clattered up the front porch steps together.

The first thing I did was to make sure that Granny had been right about no one being home. It took me several minutes to convince myself of this and to calm my heart, but finally I was ready. Beckoning for Granny to follow, I climbed the creaky wood stairs to the attic, former headquarters of the Invincible Heels. As I pushed the attic door open for the first time in several weeks, I was overcome by a sensation of sepia; the afternoon sunlight that came slanting through the windows gave the big attic space a polished, antiquated glow, and the musty but lived-in air that filled my nostrils seemed the very essence of nostalgia. The muscles in my throat tightened as I stepped into the room, and for a moment I was convinced that it was I, and not the woman just behind me, who looked out on life from a perspective of seven decades.

'The boy's somewhere in here,' Granny announced primly as she stepped over the threshold into the room. 'Definitely a boy somewhere in here.' Was it possible that Raoul's lingering presence in this attic was palpable to everyone, and not just me? I moved

Granny across the room to the viewing chair that had been Raoul's and got to work setting up the movie screen and projector. As I threaded the first frames of *The Art of Dying* into the projector, I was surprised to find that I was shaking slightly. I knew it couldn't be in anticipation of what I was about to see – I'd seen the film a hundred times. I was, I realized, shaking with excitement because for the first time there would be an audience for my work. For our work, I should say.

Granny sat on the edge of her chair with her impeccable posture and watched the film while I sat on the edge of my chair and watched Granny. She barely moved a muscle or blinked an eye, even though the bulk of this first film was an extended shot of Raoul and me lying dead in our coffins. When the room brightened from the white glare of an empty screen, she turned to me and spoke.

'Fantastic, darling. Really great,' she said. 'Really, it was truly fascinating. Please, show it again.'

'Oh come on, you're just being nice. That was our first one, it was really pathetic,' I objected. But my face was already blushing with pride. 'Let me show you some of the later ones – they're a little better.'

Over the next two hours we watched all the films – *The Art of Dying*, *Cryptograms*, *Domesticating Fear* and *Free Heeling* – while Granny nodded and applauded demurely and raved about what 'treasures, precious, precious treasures' they all were. I was a little suspicious of her sincerity at first, but slowly I let my ego puff like an adder in my chest until, but by the time I was loading *Free Heeling* into the projector, I was speaking with all the pomposity of an Oxford don.

'In this last film you'll note a slight departure from the very controlled, ritualized environment of our earlier efforts,' I announced. 'We take our credo and hit the streets – literally. Okay, here we go. Roll 'em.'

At first Granny sat spellbound, as she had for all the films, while scenes of Raoul and me on our Wednesday night Invincibility Walks unfolded on screen. But about midway through she began to fidget, and occasionally to shake her head. By that time I too had become unexpectedly disturbed by the images on screen. I had seen them all many times before, but as I watched them again that afternoon I felt the same tension I had felt on that night long ago when the man who called himself Bill Rogers had reached through the dark to expose me as a failure and a fraud.

I could hear the man's footsteps on the audio track, following me. I could hear his mumbling, and because I had been there I could sort the mumbling into the phrase it was: 'My name is Bill Rogers. My name is Bill Rogers.' Over and over. A moment later the picture began to skip crazily from side to side, as cameraman Raoul broke into a run. The camera tumbled to the ground, a fallen soldier, and the screen froze on a sideways shot of empty street and night sky. Angry shouts filled the room, and only then did I realize that the shouts weren't all part of the sound track. I was screaming, screaming 'Raaaaoul!' in stereo, from the film's sound track and from my own live throat.

Granny Mayhew reached out and took my hands. 'That will do. You may turn the projector off now,' she announced quietly. She smoothed the hair away from my face, off my cheek and forehead, and as she did I felt the wet smear of tears I hadn't realized I'd shed.

'It's okay, Logan,' Granny whispered. 'I'm here now. Don't worry. I've come home.' I nodded, not trusting my voice yet. 'Poor Little Bear,' Granny crooned, patting and squeezing my hands until finally I couldn't take it anymore.

'I'm okay, I'm sorry,' I apologized. I stood up. 'Let's get out of here,' I suggested. I felt humiliated.

Granny nodded and stood up and we headed toward the door. But just as we reached it, she paused. 'He's definitely in here!' she whispered as she whirled around. 'The boy!' She went marching back into the recesses of the attic, and as my eyes followed her to

255

the far corner where she was headed, I froze. Stretched out in the corner dormer where I had hidden his coffin lay Raoul. Dead dead dead as a doornail.

Or so I thought. Of course, he was not dead. In fact, I suffered only about five seconds of belly-flipping horror before a vision of Granny destuffing what was a dummy of Raoul chased away my horror and ushered in confusion, fury and shame.

'What's this all about?' Granny asked as she held up Raoul's T-shirt and jeans and a handful of the cotton diapers that had stuffed them.

'I have no idea,' I answered as I walked over and grabbed Granny by the elbow, anxious to get her out of the house now. 'Let's go. Quickly,' I urged her. 'Ajax will be home any minute.'

Granny smoothed her silk suit and glanced at her watch. 'I'll leave,' she said. 'But something has to be done about all of this. This is not an acceptable life for my one and only granddaughter. I'm angry now.'

I walked Granny downstairs and outside to Cleopatra and watched as she drove off. When she turned the corner at the end of the street I headed back up the walk, only to find Ajax sitting on the porch steps in her workout clothes, watching me as I approached.

'Where have you been, Elray?' Ajax asked.

'Oh, nowhere,' I answered.

'Who were you talking to in that car over there?' she asked.

'Nobody,' I said.

I tried to make light of the matter, to shrug it off. But an hour later, as I sat on our front steps by myself, the little note from Raoul that read 'QUE SERA, SERA. GOOD-BYE' crumpled in my hand, it finally hit me. I knew how completely I had been ruined.

Family Document:
Granny's Letter

I tried to get my hands on this letter for years. I knew Ajax had to have it stashed somewhere, and every now and then I would ask her about it. But she always refused to discuss the matter. 'Nasty stuff,' she'd say. 'Not for tender eyes.' It is one of the treasures I eventually found in my aunt's desk drawer.

December 31

Dear Andrew:

What you are about to learn may shock you, so sit down.

Andrew, I am your mother. I am Amanda Baer Mayhew – and I am not dead. Technically speaking, anyway. I am very old, but I am alive.

I announce myself to you after so many years with the hope that you will listen to me, try to forgive me and maybe even help me. Your brother Jack is dead; he and I will never speak again. But you and I still have a chance. I am determined to tell the story I have never told before. It is not a pretty story, but it is a true one. And if I can tell it to you truly now, in as much detail as I can muster, that should count for something – to both of us.

It all started one day when you were still a toddler, Andrew. I don't know how much of this you will remember, but I was not perhaps the best of mothers. When you were still very young I developed a pattern of shutting myself in my bedroom for most of the day, where I would drink whiskey and listen to music and practice old tap dance routines in front of the mirror. Not nice, but true. Anyway, on this particular day I'm speaking of I was in my room and I twisted the dial on my bedroom radio and landed by chance on a station that broadcast exclusively from a local racetrack. At the moment I tuned in the announcer was in a state of extreme agitation. 'Oh my Lord! Here comes Hamlet's Ghost!' he was screaming. 'Ladies and gentlemen, can you believe it! Hamlet's Ghost is closing in. Yes, Hamlet's Ghost is almost neck 'n' neck with Fine by Me!'

The urgency in that announcer's voice hit a nerve in me, Andrew, and everything in my life changed. I sat up in my chair and leaned toward the little radio speaker as a tingle came rushing through my bloodstream like a drug. It was not just the suspense of the race that stirred me. There was something else. Only minutes earlier I had been standing in front of my mirror in my old bumblebee outfit – as it happened, the very same costume I had been wearing on the night I first met your father – do you remember that story? I had been standing there improvising a slow and sad dance while reciting a slightly altered version of Hamlet's famous soliloquy. 'To be a bee, or not to be a bee. That is the question,' I murmured as I dipped and rolled through the air, doing my best imitation of a bug in a quandary. (No doubt this sounds ridiculous, but believe me, this is the way people who are lonely and lost and have too much time on their hands tend to behave. Especially if they've had a half bottle of Rebel Yell, Kentucky's Finest, for lunch.) Anyway, there I had been minutes earlier, doing my bumblebee Hamlet, and now here was this announcer screaming about Hamlet's Ghost. As I leaned toward the radio I knew as surely as I had ever known anything in my life that this horse, this Hamlet's Ghost, was going to win the race. The knowledge registered in me with a click, and as I moved to the edge of my chair to listen to the rest of the race it felt as if my power switched from the 'off' to the 'on' position. A long-dormant piece of me came flickering to life.

Hamlet's Ghost did win that day, against all odds and by a single stride. I spent the rest of the day listening to the station, taking notes and then placing imaginary bets on all the subsequent races. By the time I slithered downstairs for my evening meal with your father when he got home I had racked up an imaginary profit of $740.

'Goodness, you look lovely, darling,' I remember your father said to me as we sat down together that evening. I could tell by the way he stopped eating and leaned forward to stare that he had really detected something new in me. 'What is it?' he asked. 'Are you pregnant again?' I just laughed and took a big sip of red wine.

'No no, oh no,' I answered. 'I've just had the most marvelous day. Been reading Shakespeare.'

Bad habits are much easier to launch than good ones, Andrew. By the end of that week I had located the daily racing forms, and soon, convinced by my success on paper that I must indeed have a psychic talent for picking winners, I had located a bookie to help make my imaginary bets real. With real money riding on the races, what had been a new form of amusement was bumped up to the status of full-blown, life-altering compulsion. I started living the brutal extremes of an addict. Simple, normal composure and manners began to slip away from me. Impatient with any form of time other than the three-minute segments when I had a race running, I would yell at the radio commentators, Maury and Joe, whenever they blathered the requisite fill between heats or segued in and out of dumb advertisements for soaps and beer. 'Yeah, yeah, yeah,' I would shout as I hustled across the room to fix myself another drink. 'Let's go go go.'

One day, when the station's signal blacked out during the middle of an important race, I became so enraged that I attacked my little humpbacked radio, kicking it over and over with the steel toes of my tap shoes until a small explosion followed by a loud buzzing convinced me it was dead. Of course, I could have gone out and bought myself another radio – I had

261

done very well that week, clearing over $500 in the first three days. But instead I seized the opportunity to dig deeper into my compulsion; I began making daily field trips, by trolley, to the track itself.

From then on it all happened so quickly. The moment I set foot inside the scruffy interior of the Laurel Racetrack Clubhouse, with its low ceilings and dirty tile floors, I felt right at home – like a germ among germs, waiting to be told which healthy body I had been assigned to invade. The shiftless, purgatorial air of the place, with its heavy cigar smoke and its dingy yellow light, suited me perfectly. In the clubhouse bar I found a fellowship of mute and distracted souls who drank, like me, to smother the insufferably hollow time between races. In the bar I also found Blackie, an owner and trainer who not only shared my appetites for the bottle and for betting, but who also was everything your father could never be – short, impatient and vulgar.

Blackie and I fell into each other's company the way two hyenas might fall together over an abandoned carcass – our partnership was a sneering, self-serving and presumably temporary affair. I was a relative newcomer to the track and its seductions, and I found the grimly seasoned Blackie a useful guide and a fascinating source of inside information. Drinking with Blackie and arguing with him over our respective picks helped me get through the dead time between races. From Blackie's point of view, I suppose, I appealed as the standard companion/victim package – an audience for his nonstop self-aggrandizing spiel, as well as someone to get mad at and to try to boss around. Blackie and I were soon spending almost every day together – from 10 to 5, Monday through Friday, at any rate – in our little cesspool of a world at the track.

During all this time your father remained oblivious to everything – the booze, the betting, the trips to the track and, of course, Blackie. Or I should say that I, with the tunnel vision typical of an addict, allowed myself to believe that he suspected nothing. What he didn't know couldn't hurt him, I told myself, and what I did during the day while Amos was away in no way interfered with the 'life' we shared once he got home. Looking back now with the perspective of old age and comparative sobriety – yes, Andrew, I have been trying, so hard, to reform my errant ways – I can see that it was only your father's extreme discretion and good manners that allowed me to sustain this fantasy. He was, after all, fronting me substantial chunks of money on a regular basis during this period; although I thought of myself as a sizzling success at the track, in truth I was constantly running on empty. I would make some foggy reference to 'home improvement projects' when I requested cash advances, but your father never once asked when or in what way these mysterious 'improvements' might manifest themselves. He simply opened his wallet and forked out the dough. In an even greater act of graciousness, he never once made the slightest reference to what must have been the quite obvious and devastating effects of my churlish, round-the-clock drinking. He smiled and offered to help me upstairs when I slumped over my plate at the dinner table. Not once did he hesitate to fetch me a final nightcap if I requested one – not even on the nights when I could barely speak clearly enough to request it.

Such a man is a saint, I can hear you saying, and such a woman can only be Satan in drag. And for the most part you are right, of course. But Andrew, you are also just a little wrong. For such a man is also a terrible and selfish tyrant. Your father's compulsion to adore me was as willful and destructive as – and not entirely unrelated to, by the way – my own more sordid compulsions to drink and gamble and generally misbehave. There seemed to be nothing I could do to shake his blind devotion, and therefore there seemed to be no real connection between that devotion and me

– its purported object. Amos appeared to be ready to let me squander every penny he had and embalm myself with booze before he would tamper with his precious vision of me as perfection itself. And for that I will never forgive him. I was in real trouble, in desperate need of help – and Amos just kept flashing that big handsome smile of his at me, and calling me his 'Little Baer.'

I'm wondering if you remember any of this? My story has not been pretty so far, and it gets worse. But I am determined to carry on. It is time for me to tell it, to put it all on the table.

You were about ten, I think, when I hatched my master plan. You may perceive it as a plan of escape, and it certainly had elements of that. But I maintain that it was also an act of self-sacrifice. We were all of us in a situation that could not go on – something had to give. I saw that I could be that something.

I was still drinking and gambling and hanging out with Blackie in those days, although I no longer spent much time at the track itself. You boys were getting too demanding, with your heavy schedule of school and social activities. Besides, you were big enough to talk, to say where I had or had not been. So in body at least I was more or less there during the day, clumping through life as your mother. But in spirit I was a burned-out husk of nothing. I remember I had a constant buzz, the kind that tired refrigerators make, ringing in my ears twenty-four hours a day and the metallic taste of anxiety on my tongue at all times – from the booze, I suppose, in combination with the betting. I had burned through some unknown but enormous sum of your father's money with my compulsive gambling, and I hated myself for it. But I hated your father even more for letting me do it, and for refusing to hate me in return.

My buddy Blackie, meanwhile, had managed to amass a tidy pile of cash for himself, and he had used that cash to open his own restaurant downtown: Blackie's Bar and Grill, on the corner of 15th and K streets. It was there, to the garish and poorly lit red and black interior of Blackie's Bar and Grill, that I began to migrate almost every evening. On many evenings your father, more stubborn than ever in his devotion, would insist on accompanying me.

'What a clever find, Amanda my dear,' he had remarked the first time we were seated together in one of Blackie's oversized red leather booths with its window-box display of ugly orange plastic flowers. 'The place has a certain, uh, backstage quality, doesn't it?' I of course knew that Amos was longing all the while for the wise and quiet dust of his library at home, and knowing this made me resent even more the tall, elegant figure he cut amidst all the short, flush-faced, beef-eating men.

More often than not Blackie himself would insist on taking our order, for the unabashed perversity of it, I suppose. Two New York strips, with creamed spinach and baked potatoes. Hearts of lettuce salad with Russian dressing. We almost never varied our meal, but Blackie would come over every time anyway, jumpy as a horse in the starting gate, and ask: 'Evening, Mr Mayhew. What'll it be for you and the little missus tonight?' Amos always had one scotch followed by one glass of red wine, and I always had old-fashioneds – as many as I could swallow in the allotted time. Eventually Amos would pay the bill and we would slump home, Amos to his library and me to bed.

Sounds pretty desultory, doesn't it? Well it was, I can assure you. I had become a walking corpse, a somnambulist at best, and the hopelessness that filled me was so dreary and leaden that the only plausible course of action was the one I finally chose.

My inspiration struck, as inspiration so often does, in a most unlikely time and place. I was seated on a sofa in the ladies' lounge at Blackie's Bar and Grill, enjoying a smoke and marking a racing form so that Blackie could place some bets for me later. I had just perched my second cigarette between my lips and was lifting my lighter – a sleek little silver number Amos had given me before we were married – when the vision struck. Amos had had the lighter engraved with a dancing bumblebee and the phrase '*MAY OUR FLAME BE ETERNAL, MAY DEATH HOLD NO STING*,' and as the flame hovered only inches from my nose I was reminded of the first words I had said to your father on the cold night when we met so long ago: 'I have a paralyzing fear of fire.' As it happened I had opened with a true confession. I don't know if you remember, Andrew, but an overwhelming fear of fire has always plagued me, and has caused me all sorts of embarrassment. Campfires, Christmas trees – even dinner candles – have been known to ignite agitations in me that render me helpless.

As I sat there in the ladies' lounge that night and stared past the dancing flame of my lighter, my eyes settled on a spot on the far side of the room where a little pool of something liquid had puddled on the floor just beneath the kerosene heater. A split second later my phobia exploded. It was as if the line of my vision had actually carried the flame of my lighter to what I assumed must be the highly flammable fluid on the floor. Panic raced through me like a brushfire. Mesmerized by the vision of my own gruesome and fiery end, I could not move.

I am not sure how long I sat there in the ladies' lounge, paralyzed by my fantasy of flaming death, but it was long enough so that Amos finally sent one of the waitresses in to check on me. Zelda was her name, and as she gently pried the still burning lighter from my grip and patted me briskly across the cheeks her hands felt so hot I was sure they had burned me. The truth was, I myself had gone icy cold. Zelda helped me to my feet and back to the table, where Amos was patiently waiting. By the time I looked up at him and smiled, my fantasy had already metamorphosed from phobic attack to inspiration. I saw exactly what I could do to solve the unbearable dilemma of my life. I could die, and in a most appropriate manner. I could die by fire, thereby setting Amos and you boys free.

The nitty-gritty of how I set about planning my death probably doesn't interest you, Andrew, but there were a few twists that surprised even me at the time.

The first big revision came when I realized that I was not ready to commit suicide. Sadly, it was neither fear of death nor love of family that kept me from taking my own life – but rather my compulsion to gamble. Every time I tried to settle on a date for my execution, I found my plans thwarted by some very exciting upcoming race that I simply couldn't bear to miss. Finally I decided that I could solve everyone's problems just as effectively if I only appeared to have died. Then, in the privacy of my alleged postmortem nonexistence, I could carry on my all-important life's work – gambling – until I had won back all the money I had ever squandered, and more. Once I had accomplished this, I would set up a huge and anonymous trust fund for my sons. Then, if I still felt like it, there would always be plenty of time for a real suicide.

The second major revision came when I realized I needed help staging the fire that was going to allegedly kill me – I needed someone who would keep all the trains (especially pyrophobic me) moving on time. Blackie had been my underworld accomplice in so many gambling ventures, he immediately occurred to me as the logical choice here too. Besides, it was his joint I was planning to set on fire, and unless I was mistaken there was an angle we could play that would make the tragedy very profitable to both of us. I knew that business had been slow at the steak house in recent months, and one night, when Amos and I had been one of only three parties at the restaurant all evening, I confronted Blackie as he sat cursing into his whiskey glass at the bar.

'Cooking for people, what a raw deal,' he muttered. 'Restaurants! Shit, you can have 'em. Horse goes lame, you shoot it. Restaurant goes lame, might as well shoot yourself.'

In about forty-five seconds I laid out my scheme. We burn the place down, tragically knocking me off in the process. Blackie collects the insurance money, I get my freedom. All I ask from him is total cooperation and discretion as my accomplice, and a 20 percent cut of the insurance money to set me up in my illicit afterlife on earth. Blackie's little pig eyes were sizzling like two pools of hot bacon grease by the time Amos joined us at the bar, and I knew I had found a willing partner for my crime.

The third significant revision in my scheme was the one that took me most by surprise. During the weeks when Blackie and I were plotting together, ironing out all the little technical wrinkles in our scam, something began to irritate me – something so low-grade and so familiar that I couldn't quite identify it at first. Then one day as I sat next to Blackie on the sofa in the ladies' lounge in his restaurant, going over for probably the hundredth time the exact timing and mechanics of our carefully planned tragedy, I looked up at him and realized with horror that he was speaking to me with something akin to tenderness. 'Now I want you out that window and long gone by that point, you understand, little miss?' he said. 'This is the most important part, so we're going to rehearse it over and over.'

Blackie, whom I'd thought I could trust to act the rat in any situation, was showing signs of genuine affection. With my luck, that affection would blossom into devotion. Oh God – the very thought of it created a panic in me as great as any I had ever felt in the face of fire. I looked up at Blackie once more, just as he squeezed his face into a sour little smile and spoke of the 'joyous reunion' we would have after my 'tragic death.' It was in that instant that I realized I would have to die for Blackie too. At first I was afraid this might mean forfeiting my cut of the insurance money, but I quickly thought my way around the problem. Taking advantage of the devotion blooming in Blackie, I asked that he give me a smaller cut of the insurance money – only 15 percent – but that he give it to me immediately. 'We won't be able to contact each other for a while,' I explained. 'Too risky.' Blackie saw my point and forked over the dough.

My next challenge was how to convince Blackie that I really had died. Operating on a theory of irrefutable evidence that I pieced together after studying a series of crime reports and murder mysteries, I decided to sacrifice several of my teeth to the challenge at hand. In a series of appointments made with different dentists over a period of three months, using five false identities, I had five back teeth pulled. I test-scorched my teeth in our fireplace at home before planting them in the ladies' lounge on the day Blackie and I had designated as my execution date. As you know, the teeth worked like a charm. Although experts were a little confused about the exact mechanics of a fire or explosion that would consume all but these scattered remnants of me, the dental evidence was taken – as I had hoped – as irrefutable proof of my end. The explosion of the kerosene heater and the evacuation of the restaurant must have gone flawlessly and precisely as planned, for the restaurant was burned right to the ground, with no other victims than the unlucky, pyrophobic me. Your father cut a poignant figure as the bereft husband and single father – as I had known he would – and even the greedy and unscrupled Blackie gratified me a little by losing his cool when workers discovered my teeth on the third day after the fire. Evidently he went storming through the ruins of the restaurant, kicking at charred timbers and screaming, 'That stupid bitch – she was supposed to go out the goddamn window. Idiot! Stupid fuckin' dead idiot!'

I'm sure Blackie regained control of himself quickly

enough, but when fire investigators later voiced their suspicion of deliberate arson, pointing to evidence that trails of kerosene had radiated through the building like the arms of an octopus from the ladies' lounge, one of the cleanup crew remembered Blackie's odd little tantrum. The insurance company then revealed that Blackie had beefed up his fire coverage on the restaurant five times during the last six months, and Blackie's goose was cooked. Deep-fried in his own greed. He was found guilty of deliberate arson and attempted insurance fraud, and held accountable for heavy damages to Amos and you boys because of my death. I kept track of all these developments as best I could from the little town in Mexico where I landed in the wake of the accident, and it comforted me to know that a little cash might be headed your way because of my alleged demise. As for Blackie, I told myself that justice couldn't have dumped on a nicer guy.

So there, Andrew, are the sordid details of how and why I left you motherless at the tender age of twelve. Does it shock you? Can you see at all that I was only trying to do what I thought would be best for you and Amos and Jack? Can you see at all that what I did probably was best for all of you? The three of you went on to have a relatively normal, happy life with an only slightly diminished family grouping. I had nothing – no family, no past I could acknowledge, not even a full set of teeth. Just a ready supply of cheap tequila and rum, and the comforting conviction that even if I was whiskey-bent and hell-bound, at least I wouldn't be dragging anyone down with me.

I know you must be wondering why I am writing all this to a son who has considered me dead for thirty-one years. A son who has done just fine, probably better, without his sad sack of a mother. Why am I introducing myself to you now, and telling you all of these gory details? you must wonder.

For years I have been following all of you, keeping

tabs on what you're up to. The fact is, I couldn't live with my family, but I can't quite live without them. When Amos was on his deathbed, I snuck into our old O Street home one last time, to say good-bye. He was already in a coma. He never knew I was there – but I felt better. I have followed the two of you boys as best I can from my self-imposed exile all these years. I have kept track of your lives, have even photographed you from a distance from time to time. It gets weirder. I was there nine years ago on that day at Glen Echo when Jack and his wife died. Looked him right in the eye before he died, even took his picture.

Oh what a sad day that was for me! I know you may find this hard to believe, when you consider that I have been alive but out of touch for thirty-odd years. But I can tell you, there's not a mother in creation, not even the bottom-of-the-barrel brand like me, who wants to outlive her children. I wept fat bitter tears when I heard about Jack's accident that day – and my guilt at being alive was compounded by the eerie feeling that he had somehow inherited a real version of the gory death I had only faked for myself.

For nine years, ever since that day, I have been watching all of you, wondering how I can return. Every day I seem to remember more and more of what life we did have together, of the way your little faces used to look up at me with love. When I remember that part I could cry. I am so sorry, Andrew. I truly am. I couldn't say that to you back then, but I am ready to say it now. And I am ready to say a whole lot more if you will only let me.

I am an old woman – nearly seventy – and I surely will be dead soon. Very soon. But for the first time I sense an opportunity to rectify some of the wrong in my life. For the first time I feel ready to talk, to you and to others. I know it's late, to put it mildly. Jack's already dead and gone. But for some reason I feel more hopeful of reaching him than I have ever felt before. Perhaps if I could manage to talk to you, my living son, together we could find a way to talk to Jack, who is dead. If he would listen to me for a minute, if he would let me try to explain a few things, maybe he would help me accomplish something here with my remaining time.

Tell me, is there any chance I could return to what's left of my family? Is there any chance I could be of some help to Jack's daughter, my granddaughter? Or even to you? I am anxious to make amends somehow, Andrew. I really am. Will you try to forgive me? I beg you. Forgive the mother who loved you but failed you. Please. I have missed so much already. Let me have my few last years with you, and with Logan, Jack's daughter. Give me another chance?

Remorsefully yours,
Mama Baer

Part Six

The Case Is Cracked

Shifting Sands

After my afternoon in the attic with Granny I shut
down, on almost every front. Granny had canceled our
meetings herself, claiming that this was temporarily
necessary because of 'legal developments' and that it
wasn't right for me to miss so much school anyway.

'You know, darling, when you can't get what you
want in life by being nice, sometimes you have to up
the ante and get a bit nasty,' she said to me on one last
afternoon when I found her waiting for me after
school. 'We resort to this as babies, and again, I'm finding, in the gray infanthood of old age. Sorry, but I have
some not so pretty work cut out for me now. I don't
want you watching too closely. Here. I brought you
something. Hold on to it,' she said as she handed me
an envelope. 'Adieu, dear Logan.' Then she slid into
Cleopatra, blew me a kiss and motored off.

In the envelope I found a faded Polaroid of me and
Barkley and Jack taken on our last day together at Glen
Echo. It was the twin to the one I had from that day
myself, except that in my picture Barkley had her blue
cotton candy hidden behind her back. In this picture,
the one from Granny, Barkley was holding the cotton
candy above the unsuspecting Jack's head, like a big
beehive of hair. Granny had told me that she had been
watching us for a long time. Here was proof. I set the
two Polaroids side by side on a shelf in my room, to
make a little movie.

Granny disappeared from my life after that afternoon, but the lessons I had learned from her lingered. As she herself liked to say, bad habits come more easily than good. Thanks to Granny, I was smoking regularly now. And even though I was no longer roaming the city with her, I saw no reason to stop skipping school. I had become addicted to the feckless, grifting quality of my illegal afternoons. I was sure the excuse I had forged for my absences from school – that I was undergoing intensive pretrial therapy – would remain solid for the rest of the term. In fact, though, just a week after my last meeting with Granny, I was called into the principal's office and suspended, without due process of any kind.

'We're on to your little game, Elray. A person who shall remain unnamed but who clearly has your best interests at heart tipped us off,' Mr Herder, our principal, announced as he folded his bifocals and stuffed them into his jacket pocket. I couldn't keep from staring, fascinated and repulsed, at all the tiny little warts that were scattered across the pouchy flesh beneath Mr Herder's eyes. 'I'm aware you haven't had the easiest life, but we wouldn't be doing you any favors if we let you get away with this kind of thing,' he continued. I nodded solemnly and wondered for probably the hundredth time why he didn't have the warts removed. 'Now take this note home to your parents – your, uh, uncles, that is. And tell them we'll be calling them to set up a conference.'

To my surprise, Ajax was very upset by the news of my suspension. She spent two days trying to track down Harwood, who had been away on assignment in the Basque country of Spain for three weeks. When she got hold of him she broke down and sobbed for several minutes until at some point she realized that she had been disconnected and that Harwood was no longer on the line. Then she slammed the phone down and turned to me with a frightening look in her eye.

'Elray honey, we're going to have to get to the bottom of this one all by ourselves,' she announced. 'Something's been bothering you lately, hasn't it? Hmmm?' I shrugged and said nothing. 'Please, talk to me about it,' Ajax pleaded. 'Won't you please tell me what is going on?' Still I said nothing. 'Oh, it's all my fault, isn't it? I've been so busy lately with – all my projects. I haven't been home much during the days, I know. But I've made a point of being here for you when you get home from school. Half the time you don't get back until almost dinnertime anyway, so I can't see how that should make a difference. But we're going to do things differently from now on. I'm going to sit and help you with your homework every after-noon like I used to. And we're going to plan some outings together. And you're going to let me know where you are at all times, do you understand?'

The worst thing about my suspension was its timing. I had only two weeks of school left before summer vacation, and had been looking forward to the long, empty, unsupervised dog days of summer in Washington. Now that Ajax's alarms were abuzz, I knew there would be no hope of that. She would make sure every day bristled with back-to-back activities.

Sure enough Ajax inflicted the ultimate torture and enrolled me in summer camp. Day camp – tennis and swimming and 'community services' for boys and girls. At Luckwell Friends – Raoul's school. When I tried to protest, Ajax became as fierce as I'd ever seen her.

'YOU ARE GOING. Got it? You are still a minor, after all, and I am still legally in charge here. GOT IT? Besides, you'll love it once you start – that's the way it always works. Children resist the new and unknown, but it is a parent's duty to push them out there anyway. Separation anxiety and all that.'

I shrugged. I knew I could solve my dilemma by simply skipping camp every day, just as I had been skipping school. It was on my third day of doing exactly this that I came tiptoeing into my house and stumbled upon the first thing that had piqued my curiosity in a while.

It was a hot June afternoon and Ajax was lying on her stomach on the sofa in our living room, talking to herself. Or so it seemed. I had slipped into the house and was trying to slide up to the attic undetected when, halfway up the stairs, I heard Ajax speak and then spotted her prone body on the sofa.

'Oh, she's such a snake,' Ajax said. 'Such a slimy, slithery serpent. I always knew it instinctively. I swear I did. I just never had to face it before because – well I mean after all, she was dead for so long.' Ajax appeared to be lying there naked from the waist up. This was extremely unusual. So unusual that I decided to descend a step or two and peek over the railing for a better look.

'Ah, but no good deed goes unpunished, does it,' Ajax was groaning. 'Let's face it, I'm an idiot. Go ahead, say it: Ajax, you're an idiot.'

I couldn't believe my eyes. Ajax was lying there naked from the waist up, and what was truly shocking about this was the vision of her back. In the more than nine years that we had lived together I had never seen her back before. It was broad and powerful-looking – and deeply tanned. I couldn't see her chest, but Ajax's back sure didn't look like the flip side of something that would have breasts. As I realized this, I also realized that in the more than nine years that we had lived together I had never bothered to think about Ajax in this way. I had never dissected the actual mechanics of her adopted versus her given sexuality. I took another long look at her back, and as I did I heard another voice.

'Darling, you're not an idiot. Not about this, anyway.' It was Rena, I was almost sure. As the body that proved me correct wandered into my frame of vision, I sat down on the steps and stared. Rena was wearing only her underwear – a black bra and black panties –

and black high-heeled shoes. She was rubbing something between the palms of her hands as she made her way toward Ajax. She looked much chunkier than she did in her clothes.

'Here we go,' Rena said as she sat down on the sofa and began to massage whatever was on her hands into Ajax's back. 'How's that?'

'Oh, you angel.' Ajax sighed. 'Feels heavenly. Pure bliss. Thank you so much.'

'My pleasure,' Rena murmured. 'Do you know, your workout sessions are really paying off. I can see quite a bit of new muscle articulation in your back.'

'Oh, I'm sure!' Ajax snorted.

'Seriously, you'll be a regular Tarzan soon.'

'Please, don't even suggest such a thing. That's hardly what I want.' Ajax lifted her head slightly to say this, and then let it drop again. 'Just some spot toning, you know. Enough to maintain the fight against – ugh – gravity. Ooooh, yes. Right there – oh, that feels wonderful!'

As I sat spying on the two of them from the stairs, I couldn't decide whether I should feel confused, horrified or entertained. I felt something like excitement stirring in my chest. This was getting weird, truly weird. Rena was really leaning into it now, massaging Ajax's back and shoulders with long strokes that brought muffled groans of delight from Ajax, who had buried her face deep in the cushions of the sofa.

'Let yourself relax, darling. Forget all the nasties. Try to stop worrying about your mother for a minute,' Rena said to the ceiling. 'We'll get rid of her, I promise. If she's as bad-hearted as you say she doesn't stand a chance anyway; she'll be her own worst enemy. Trust me, I've seen how these things work. Besides, you've done a perfectly spectacular job with Elray – anyone can see that. Every girl should be so lucky.'

'Oh God, I don't know,' Ajax groaned. 'What I can't figure out is WHY. Assuming she is my mother – and to be honest I still have my doubts about that – why is she doing this? Why is she coming forward after so many years? What good can come of my meeting her now? It's too late. And what can she possibly hope to gain?'

'Don't be so naive, sweetheart!' Rena gave a snort and collapsed onto Ajax's bare back. 'What motivates every low-minded selfish snake? No offense intended to your dear mother, of course. Well? Why, money, of course. Filthy stinking lucre!'

'Money? You think she's doing this to get money? But that doesn't make sense. I don't have money.' Ajax twisted her head sideways to look at Rena.

'Shame on you, Ajax!' Rena shouted as she sat upright and raised both hands toward the ceiling. Perched atop Ajax in her black underwear and high heels, she looked like some kind of new age witch riding a sea beast. 'Have you forgotten about the buried treasure, about the fabulous pot of gold that the amusement park is going to have to hand over after our brilliant performance in court? THAT'S what dear Granny Mayhew wants to get her hands on. And that is why we're going to flatten the greedy antique. Shove her down the stairs, put a little cyanide in her Geritol – not literally, of course, but we'll do whatever we have to do to send her back from whence she came. We'll make her vanish.'

I had already moved downstairs and across the hall, and as Rena finished this last speech and collapsed back onto Ajax with a big sigh, I stepped into the open doorway to the living room and confronted the two of them.

'Hi. What are you talking about?' I asked, trying to be as casual as possible. 'What's going on here?' They both jumped and screamed. There was a frantic scramble of limbs as Ajax struggled to sit up while Rena struggled to get off her. Finally the tangle of bare flesh was sorted out, and Ajax was left sitting primly on the edge of the sofa, two cushions clutched to her chest, while Rena scurried, like an oversized spider, across the room to a pile of discarded clothes that lay on the floor.

'Elray, my God! You scared me half to death! What are you doing here? Why aren't you at camp?' Ajax said breathlessly.

'I told you, I don't want to go to camp. I won't go to camp,' I said. 'What are YOU doing here?' I stared first at Ajax and then at Rena.

'Rena and I were just having a little legal conference, about some private matters,' Ajax said. I kept staring and said nothing. 'It is brutally hot today, in case you haven't noticed,' Ajax continued. 'We were trying to cool down a little. Rena was kindly administering a eucalyptus-oil back rub. They're very refreshing – have you ever tried one? Toss me my T-shirt, would you, Rena?' Rena, who had zippered herself into a sleeveless green linen dress, lurched across the room to retrieve a crumpled shirt from the far end of the sofa and tossed it to Ajax. 'Thank you,' Ajax muttered, but she made no effort to put the shirt on.

'What "private matters"?' I asked. 'What "private matters" were you discussing? They sounded like they were MY private matters. Tell me about them.'

Ajax and Rena exchanged a look, and then Rena spoke for the first time since I had surprised them. 'I think you might as well, Ajax,' she said. 'Elray's bound to find out sooner or later, and she might be a big help to us if she knew now. Go ahead, tell her.'

I looked expectantly at Ajax, who was still clutching the cushions to her chest. 'Tell me,' I demanded. 'Tell me whatever it is you have to tell me.'

'All right, Elray.' Ajax sighed. 'Here it is. I have denied your Granny Mayhew – or a woman who claims to be your Granny Mayhew, I should say – any access to you. In retaliation the tweedy old fossil has sued for custody of you. She claims that Harwood and I are totally unfit as guardians, and that she has evidence galore to prove it.'

'Custody?' I asked. 'Of me?'

'That's right, baby,' said Ajax. 'The selfish witch couldn't be bothered to raise me, her own child. But now she says she deserves to have you all to herself.'

Trial and Error

So it was that in August of that summer, thanks to Granny Mayhew, Ajax and Harwood and Rena and I finally found ourselves in the court setting that we had been anticipating for so long. The only problem was, we were there for the wrong reasons, fighting the wrong battle. I had been surprised by how ambivalent I felt toward the question of my own custody when the news of Granny's lawsuit was broken to me. I'm afraid I must have wounded Ajax when I failed to fall to the ground in a fit at the notion that she might be removed as my caretaker. But the fact of the matter was, I hadn't felt that I'd been under anyone's care for a long time. As I saw it, I looked after all the adults in my life – Ajax and Harwood and Rena – as much as they did me. Even Hansueli had wound up taking more advice than he'd given. I had stopped seeing him regularly years ago, and now only got together with him occasionally, more as friends than anything else. At our last meeting two months earlier, when he had complained to me about how lethargic and unhappy his wife had become, I suggested that perhaps she was missing the fine life they'd had in Spain.

'Maybe you should take her back to the land of lovely summer-evening boat picnics,' I suggested. 'I'd be depressed too if I'd moved from that to this.' A month later Hansueli moved his family to Málaga. I received a postcard of the view to Gibraltar from him, with a message thanking me and inviting me to visit anytime.

For me the topics of Granny Mayhew and her custody demands were complicated by the fact that I wasn't yet prepared to confess that I'd ever met my grandmother. I was clinging to my clandestine meetings with Granny as one of my sole surviving secrets, and this made the issue of either approving or disapproving of her rather difficult. How could I feel strongly about someone I had never met?

Ajax had managed to summon Harwood home from his world travels in late June, shortly after I learned of Granny's lawsuit. Harwood's initial reaction to this new dilemma, as to most domestic crises, was to shrug the whole matter off as nonsense. Ajax and Rena, he implied, were just do-si-doing around the barnyard like a pair of Chicken Littles. As usual.

'Tell me again what's so awful about this woman, your mother?' he asked. 'Why is it we can't just grant her visitation rights?'

'Yeah, good questions,' I chimed in. 'Tell me again too.'

'How about the fact that she's a compulsive drinker, smoker and gambler, for starters,' Ajax shot back at us. 'How about that she abandoned her children – either she abandoned me and Jack, or she actually died, which makes her even creepier, because then she's a ghost. You want Elray hanging out with more spirits? That surprises me, Harwood. Besides, Mama doesn't want visitation rights. She wants Elray – lock, stock and gold pot!'

I found the suggestion that Granny Mayhew might be a ghost a pleasing notion. That might explain why Ajax had been reluctant to introduce me to her in the first place – and it fit in with the curious way Granny had appeared and then just as suddenly evaporated from my life. I hadn't heard a peep from her since the day she told me we would have to stop meeting. I had taken the bus down to some of our old haunts a couple of times, thinking I might find her waiting on the steps of the O Street house or sipping a beer in the Old Polo Bar and Grill. But these excursions never yielded the slightest clue that she had existed or would ever appear again.

As the court date for the custody suit approached, I found myself curious to see this phantom grandmother of mine once again. A week before our trial date, however, I suffered a disappointment when Ajax and Harwood and Rena sat me down and explained that of course I would be spared the torture of sitting in the courtroom through my own custody trial. 'You'll be asked a few questions – by me, and by the lawyer who represents the woman who claims she is your grandmother,' Rena explained. 'Then you'll be excused until the very end, when there may be a few more questions. Then it will be over.'

'But I want to be there,' I protested. 'I need to be there. It's my life we're talking about. Besides, I want to see Granny Mayhew. I want to see what she – what she looks like,' I lied.

'I'll get some pictures,' Harwood offered. 'Then, when this is all over, if it seems appropriate, maybe you can meet her.'

'Over my dead body,' Ajax growled. There seemed to be nothing I could do to convince the three of them that I deserved to be present in the courtroom throughout the trial. But then, on the day before our opening session, an obvious solution to my predicament came to me. I was walking back from the bus stop on Wisconsin Avenue, heading home from the fencing lessons I had started after Ajax and Harwood insisted that I take on some 'instructional activity' in lieu of the summer camp they had finally allowed me to boycott. It was about five o'clock in the afternoon, and so hot that even the crickets sounded miserable as I waded through the muggy streets. As I passed Rosedale, a big private park on my left, I remembered a picnic Granny and I had shared there earlier that spring. Granny had arrived, as she did for many of our meetings, decked out in an elaborate costume. On that day she was a dead ringer for Lana Turner. 'Disguise is one of the most freeing exercises in life,' Granny had told me. 'I've been hiding for so long, I can't break the habit.'

Ajax and Harwood and Rena had said that they didn't want me in the courtroom after my initial appearance in the witness stand. And as far as they would know I would not be there.

The next day I was on the witness stand in family court, answering questions directed at me by Granny's lawyer, a Mr Sammy Slanner. Upon entering the courtroom I had looked around for Granny herself, and had been disappointed not to spot her anywhere. But then in the last few minutes before the trial opened, a tall figure wearing a raincoat and a voluminous head scarf sat down at the far end of the second row and pulled a wad of knitting from a brown basket. I couldn't see the figure's face, but the posture was unmistakable. It was Granny. A moment later the court was called to order and I got my first glimpse of Sammy Slanner. My nightmare had begun.

From his opening question onward I found the process of Mr Slanner's cross-examination disconcerting, not because of what he asked me, but because of Mr Slanner himself. The problem was, he appeared to have no nose. No nose, a barely recognizable mouth and two free-floating eyes that seemed on the verge of drifting right off the top of his forehead. The poor fellow had obviously had a nasty accident of some kind, and I felt bad for him. But his monstrous appearance worked to his advantage as a cross-examining attorney. Every time I looked at his jigsaw puzzle of a face I was overcome by the urge to organize the drifting or missing pieces back into place. Although Mr Slanner spoke in a normal voice and seemed to have a rational brain, it was impossible to look at him and not wonder, to the exclusion of all other thoughts, what could have happened to him.

I was barely aware of the substance of Mr Slanner's questions at first, or of the robotlike answers that I gave back. As I recall he focused heavily on my day-to-day routine with Harwood and Ajax, and despite all my coaching I must have slipped up occasionally when referring to Ajax, because there came a point about midway through the morning when Mr Slanner paused and limped to the witness stand.

'Elray,' he said, folding his hands on top of and leaning forward against the cane he carried. 'Elray, I'm going to ask you something, and when you answer you mustn't worry about anything except telling the truth, to the best of your knowledge. In the course of our conversation this morning you have referred to your Uncle Ajax as a "she" several times. Why do you do that?'

I stared at Mr Slanner and then glanced across the courtroom to the spot where Ajax and Harwood and Rena were seated, not sure which was worse: the close-up vision of the creature before me or the prospect of the dressing-down I would surely receive later if I had in fact blown Ajax's cover. My glance across the courtroom was not lost on Mr Slanner. His following glance toward my family was, in fact, my first solid evidence that he was not blind.

'Tell us, Elray,' Mr Slanner said as he leaned toward me again. 'Why do you sometimes refer to your Uncle Ajax as a "she"?'

'Objection,' Rena shouted, jumping to her feet. She had been objecting all morning, but with limited success. 'Mr Slander is asking the child for impossible speculation on an irrelevant point.'

'Overruled,' drawled the unhappy gray donkey of a judge I had privately nicknamed Eeyore. 'Miss Mayhew, you may answer.'

'Perhaps you misheard me,' I said quietly. But then, instead of stopping after the briefest possible answer as Rena had coached me, I squirmed under the eerie scrutiny of the faceless Mr Slanner and began to babble my way through a series of red lights. 'You must have misheard me,' I repeated, 'because I no longer use the pronoun "she" or the prefix "Aunt" in reference to Ajax. None of us do. Not in public anyway. And this is a public place – most trials are public in this country, as I understand it.'

'Am I to understand, then,' Mr Slanner said after a long pause, 'that in the past and in private you – and others close to you – have spoken of and still do speak of your "Aunt Ajax"?'

'I'm not sure,' I whispered. 'She's just Ajax. My Ajax.'

Another long silence followed while Mr Slanner retreated to review some notes at his desk. Then he turned to me once again. 'This is not a pleasant process for you, Elray, I'm sure,' he began. 'But to make it as easy and brief as possible, I'm now going to ask you a series of very straightforward questions that you should be able to answer with a simple yes or no.' I nodded, grateful that he was at least standing a little farther away. 'Okay, let's begin. Can you tell me, have you ever seen your Uncle Ajax wearing a woman's dress?' he asked.

Ha. It was a trick question. But I would give a trick answer. 'Yes, when I was filming a story –' I began, but Mr Slanner interrupted me with a raised hand: 'Remember, a simple yes or no is all we need,' he said. 'Let's make this quick and easy. Second question: Has your Uncle Ajax ever urged you to drink dirty water from flower vases, citing the special nutritional properties therein?'

'Yes,' I said softly, after a short silence.

'Was there ever a period when your Uncle Ajax allowed you – excuse me – encouraged you to wear a knife concealed under your sock to school?'

'Yes.' I found myself staring across the courtroom again, not at Ajax and Harwood this time, but at the tall, bescarfed figure who was still knitting quietly in the second row. At Granny Mayhew, my Judas. She had pulled every detail of my life out of me and then betrayed me.

'Have you ever wandered the streets of downtown Washington after midnight without an adult chaperon?' The trick questions continued.

'Yes,' I whispered.

'Speak up,' Judge Eeyore scolded. 'Speak into the microphone please.'

'Have you ventured on such night escapades on more than, say, twenty occasions?' asked Mr Slanner.

'Yes.'

'Has anything frightening ever befallen you on these escapades?'

'Yes.'

On and on the questions ran, exposing all the precious secrets of my life in a clinical and ugly light. Slanner smeared everything. He asked me about the crypts and about my snakes and about the crawlspace and about my conversations with Barkley and Jack.

'Have you ever practiced dying in a small home-made coffin?' he asked.

'Yes,' I had to answer.

'Has your Uncle Harwood ever allowed you to consume alcohol in his presence?'

'Yes.'

'Was he also drinking at the time?'

'Yes.'

'Have you ever both been drinking while driving?'

'Yes.'

And then, finally, there came the double whammy with which Slanner closed his questioning: 'Have you ever witnessed your Uncle Harwood engaged in sexual activities with someone?'

'Sexual activities?' I asked.

'Yes, sexual activities or what appeared to be sexual activities.'

'Yes, I guess so,' I finally answered, looking up to stare Harwood straight in the eye.

'Are any of his sexual partners here in the courtroom today?'

'Yes,' I said softly, after a long pause.

'Could you please identify them? Name them if possible. Point to them and describe what they're wearing.'

'That's not a yes-or-no question,' I turned to Slanner and argued feebly.

'This is the last thing I'll ask of you, Elray,' said my ruthless, faceless inquisitor.

'Rena Guilfoyle, my lawyer,' I said. 'She's sitting right there, in the blue dress.'

'Thank you for your honesty and courage. I have no further questions,' Mr Slanner said quietly. Then the courtroom was filled with one of those enormous silences that always seem to follow moments of irrevocable damage. I glared at Granny as she sat knitting, furious at her betrayal. Then I turned toward Harwood and Ajax and Rena again. They had not moved since my last statement. Harwood was staring at me, Rena was staring at the floor and Ajax was staring at Rena.

'We will take a one-hour recess for lunch now and return at two-fifteen,' the judge announced. 'Court dismissed.' I slid from the witness stand, my heart suddenly breaking with sadness and remorse. I edged across the courtroom toward Ajax and Harwood and Rena. I walked and then I ran toward my family, the only real family I had ever known. There they sat, my own dear family. The same dear family that I, so single-handedly and heartlessly, had just blown to bits.

The recess that followed was one of the most dismal sixty minutes of my life. We all sat outside on the courthouse steps – Ajax, Harwood, Rena and I – in the sweltering summer heat, unable to speak. Ajax had packed us a nice picnic lunch of vichyssoise and shrimp salad, but nobody could eat. Finally, just before we had to head back in, Ajax spoke up.

'I don't understand what's going on here,' she said. 'I literally don't understand it.' Everyone looked at me, but I said nothing. I knew all too well what had happened, and I knew all too well that it was all my fault.

'I wonder if there's any point in my continuing,' said Rena, sighing.

'Are you crazy?' Harwood snapped. 'We don't have a choice.'

'Elray, just tell me one thing.' Ajax turned to me and laid one of her big hands on my shoulder. 'And pretend you're on the witness stand, telling the whole truth and nothing but the truth, when you answer,' she said. 'Do you want to live with us? With Harwood and me?'

I felt a huge ache fill my head and throat, and then I fell sobbing into Ajax's arms. Like an idiot baby. 'Yes, I do,' I wept. 'I'm sorry, I'm so sorry. And I do, I do. I do want, I must stay with you.' Ajax held me tightly and stroked my head the way she used to when I was little, and then I felt more hands on me, patting my back and squeezing my elbows, as Harwood and Rena crowded around. We had a big sad family huddle, right there on the courthouse steps, like a bunch of migrant workers in a tear-jerker Depression movie. And then we stood up and marched back into the courthouse en masse, with the shaky gait of determined survivors.

I can barely remember my next session on the witness stand, during which I answered questions directed by Rena. I could go back and read the transcripts, I know, but I have never really wanted to. We were neither one of us in any shape to perform cleverly, or even coherently. In fact, given what I know now, I am surprised that Rena had the courage to carry on at all. Our mutual goal was one of damage control, and with no rehearsed script to work from we set about trying to concoct a convincing picture of the familial love and bliss that had filled the house on High View Street. Rena would field me something obvious, like 'The crawlspace gatherings, the meetings under the house that Mr Slanner referred to so briefly. Have those occasions ever been depressing or scary to you in any way?'

'Oh no, no, no,' I would answer eagerly. 'They have always been a lot of fun – we celebrate my birthday for the second time, and tell stories about my dead parents and drink champagne and—'

'Oh, how nice. And what about your meals – well, your breakfasts and your dinners anyway, since your lunches are probably mostly taken care of by the elite private school for girls that you attend.' Whenever Rena felt my answer was dragging on too long or straying into dangerous territory, she would interrupt me with a non sequitur of some kind and tap her cheek with her index finger to send our prearranged signal that I should shut up immediately.

'Objection!' Mr Slanner would scream at such moments. 'Once again Miss Guilfoyle is failing to let the child finish!' The judge would sustain or overrule, as he saw fit, and Rena and I, grateful for the interruption, would regroup and prepare to pick our way gingerly ahead. Using this strategy of innocuous if boring exchanges, we made it safely through the afternoon, until I thought Rena must be finished. She had been standing before me quietly, reviewing her notes for a long time, when she looked up and asked me one last question.

'Tell me, Elray,' she said, staring at me intently. 'Have you ever witnessed your Uncle Ajax engaged in sexual activities, or what might appear to be sexual activities of any kind, with anyone?' I stared back at Rena for a long quiet moment as I tried to read her angle on this one. I considered the afternoon earlier that summer, when I had spied from the stairway as a half-naked Rena gave a half-naked Ajax a back rub. Then I plunged ahead, telling the truth and nothing but the truth, to the best of my knowledge.

'No, I have not. Never.'

'Thank you very much. I have no further questions.' Then Rena smiled and nodded her head as she began to gather her papers. The judge said something I didn't hear, and everyone was standing up. My first – and as it would turn out, my last – grueling day on the witness stand was called to an end.

Pass the Mustard

The evening after our first day in court Ajax and Harwood and Rena and I sat glumly at High View Street, eating the picnic we hadn't had at lunch, saying almost nothing. I was dreading the sledgehammer I knew had to drop any moment, when Harwood and Ajax and Rena all demanded to be told where Mr Slanner had come up with such bizarre information about crypts and night walks and homemade coffins. Was it all true, they would ask, or had I perjured myself deliberately in an effort to escape their custody?

To my relief, as the evening wore on the amnesty that Rena had granted me in her questioning that afternoon seemed to carry through – not once did anyone attempt to interrogate me on any of the details. I seized the first opportunity to retire to my bedroom, where I fell asleep to the muffle of pacing and shouting downstairs. It felt like old times.

The next morning I stood on the porch and waved good-bye to Harwood and Ajax as they headed off to meet Rena at court. It was their turn to squirm on the stand, and despite my pleading they had refused to allow me to spectate.

'Who knows what nonsense the slimy Mr Slander will trot out today,' Ajax said as she buttoned up the khaki jacket of a summer suit she had borrowed from Harwood. She looked handsome. 'I won't have you dragged through such rubbish unnecessarily.'

My anger at Granny Mayhew's betrayal of confidential information made me more determined than ever to be present at the custody trial, so the moment Ajax and Harwood were safely out of the house I set about putting together what I thought would make a foolproof disguise. I decided to be a law school student. 'Older' and 'bookish' were my two working precepts, and after an hour of rummaging through closets I climbed atop the toilet in the upstairs bathroom for a full-length review of myself in the mirror over the sink. I wasn't sure whether or not the figure staring back at me resembled a law student, but it certainly didn't resemble me. I had dressed myself in low-heeled sandals, tight black jeans, a purple T-shirt, one of Ajax's old blond wigs and wire-rim glasses. The front of my T-shirt bulged over a falsely amplified bosom; long silver earrings that resembled miniature wind chimes swung from my ears and my face was caked with makeup. After deciding I had perhaps gone a little long on the 'older' and a little short on the 'bookish,' I dug a lightweight knapsack out of Harwood's room and slung it over my shoulder. Perfect.

As I gave myself one final look, exhilaration – not unlike the jazzy rush I used to feel during Invincibility Exercises – went zizzing through me. In that moment I knew this was the day to accomplish a little errand I had been contemplating for some time. I ran upstairs to the attic to the spot where Raoul's clothes – the clothes he had used to make the dummy that Granny Mayhew had discovered and then torn limb from limb – were lying, folded in a little pile in his coffin. I packed the clothes into the knapsack and sauntered downstairs and out the front door.

It was a cool day for August – it was almost nine o'clock in the morning but still possible to breathe outside. As I headed down the street in disguise I loaded my mouth with an entire pack of gum that I had grabbed off a table in the front hall. (Rena had been trying to stop smoking recently, and much to Ajax's annoyance, she left stashes of chewing gum all over our house.) As I strolled along I quietly hummed 'The Insouciant Ghost' and experimented with what voice would best complement my disguise. Before I'd had time to think better of it, I was standing on the front porch of Clair Moskowitz's house, ringing the doorbell.

'Hello,' I said to the woman who opened the door. 'Clair here?' I cracked my gum a few times in the silence that followed.

'Yeeeees,' the woman answered slowly. I just loved the way she was looking at me. 'But I'm not sure she's up yet; let me check. Who shall I say—'

'Who's here, Mom, is it Raoul?' And then there was Clair herself, pushing past her mother toward me. She looked sleepy and soft and like she'd be easy to knock the crap out of in a fistfight. 'Hi,' she said. 'Who are you? Do I know you?'

'Oh I'm nobody, honey, nobody,' I answered, digging into a thick southern drawl. 'But I thought maybe next time you see that li'l ol' Raoul Person person, you could give him these.' I pulled the wad of Raoul's clothes from my knapsack and thrust them into Clair's arms. 'He leff 'em at my house the other night, silly ol' boy.' I gave my gum one last loud pop and quickly walked away.

I couldn't keep from laughing through most of the bus ride to the courthouse. Clair had looked so useless standing there in her flowery nightgown, holding Raoul's clothes out as if they were bloody body parts, her mouth hanging open. I felt reckless and wicked, in a mood to pick pockets and torture small dogs and generally abuse the world as I found it. I stuck my wad of chewed-up gum onto the back of the leather jacket of the man sitting in front of me as I rose to exit the bus. Granny's right, I thought; disguise is very freeing.

As I marched up the courthouse steps I squared my shoulders, forcing my big fake chest against the front of my T-shirt. Inside the courthouse I stopped long enough to buy another pack of gum at the concession stand in the lobby and then slid down the hall toward Room 113, where day two of my custody trial was already under way.

The room looked strangely dark from the far side of the rippled glass door as I approached, and a few moments later, as I eased the door open and slid inside, I found out why. The lights were out and a film was playing on a small portable screen that had been set up at the front of the room. It was not just any film. A tingling sensation ran up the back of my neck, and my fine invulnerable, bully mood went sailing out of me with one sharp gasp as I realized that there, flickering at the front of the room for anyone who cared to look to see, was my film. Raoul's film. The *Cryptograms* film that the two of us had made together.

As I slumped into a seat at the back of the room I was overcome by the same tangle of emotions I had felt when Granny had watched our films a few months earlier. My wish to keep them entirely secret was pitted against my desire for an appreciative audience. I loaded my mouth with the pack of gum, shut my eyes and tried to dissolve into the sugar burn that now spread across my palate. I concentrated on dropping, straight as a pebble and whimsical as a feather, to some other place. Some place outside my little life, some place outside this world, some place beyond light and vision and family – and way beyond this courtroom.

When I opened my eyes I was there – elsewhere, that is. Everything around me was cast in the same black and white hues that filled the little screen at the front of the room where *Domesticating Fear* now played. From a great distance I watched as snakes I had once owned encircled the person I had once been.

When *Domesticating Fear* ended and segued directly into the *Free Heeling* night-walk adventures of Elray and Raoul, those would-be Invincible Heels, I let myself float even farther away. By the time the final frames of this film spluttered to an end and the lights came up, I had drifted so far that the courtroom itself was nothing more than a distant screen where scenes from other people's lives were playing in black and white.

In the center of the screen, sitting erect and immobile on the witness stand, looking more statue than human and more male than female, was Ajax. Prancing back and forth in front of her was Mr Sammy Slanner.

'Well, Mr Mayhew,' said Mr Slanner in a shrill voice. 'Can you tell us, have you ever seen these films before?'

'No, I have not,' Ajax the statue answered in a big bass boom worthy of an oracle. Nothing, not even her lips, moved.

'But were you aware that your niece was involved in making the films? I mean surely these movies represent hours and hours of time, time spent in rather disturbing pursuits, if I may say so. Did you know your niece was making the films? Did you approve of her playing around with coffins and snakes and walking the city streets all hours of the night?'

Ajax closed her eyes, giving the first sign that she was in fact animate. 'Your question, Mr Slanner?' she asked.

'Did you know Elray was making these movies, or involved in the kinds of activities they depict?'

'No, and no. I did not.'

'Well, what do you think, do you approve? Do you find the films disturbing in any way?' Slanner squeaked.

'I find the films intriguing, and very moving, Mr Slanner. Elray is a complicated and a wise child. Even wiser than I had thought. She pushes at and over edges most of us ignore. We all could learn from her, from these films.'

Ajax, bless her odd soul, was pulling the equivalent of a Lady Fustian on the topic of the films. Even from my faraway seat in another universe I could recognize this, and feel pleased by it. I felt pleased and grateful, both for Ajax's dignity and for the fact that she had said nice things about the films made by the person I had once been. I saw that some color had flooded back into the figure of Ajax – her eyes shone their clear green and her face had taken on the pink tones of human flesh. Everyone else remained black and white, or something in between.

'I can't remember ever meeting him. You say his name is Raoul? I'm happy he exists.' On and on Ajax went, fielding snide questions from Mr Slanner. As time crawled by in the same way it always does in black-and-white courtroom movies – minute by minute on the face of a plain clock mounted high on the wall – I felt that perhaps Ajax and Harwood had been right: There was no point in my witnessing this. Everyone knew about the films now, and they knew about Raoul. They knew about Harwood and Rena. What was left to uncover? The rest was so predictable – they would pick on Ajax about her sexuality, if they hadn't already done so this morning before I arrived. They would beat on Harwood about his drinking, about his long absences, about his bachelor habits. I didn't need to see any of it. There really was only one further stage of testimony that interested me, I realized. I wanted to see Granny Mayhew on the witness stand. I wanted to see what the double-crossing, cigarette-smoking, conniving old relic had to say for herself.

'Yes, she was recently suspended from school,' Ajax was bravely carrying on. 'It was very, very upsetting to us. She has always been such an excellent student.'

'What was she suspended for?' asked Slanner.

'I guess she'd been cutting classes in the afternoons

– she'd manufactured a fake excuse. There was also some suspicion she'd been smoking. The first I knew of it was when Mr Herder, the school principal, called. These are difficult years, you know, these teenage years . . .'

As the significance of Slanner's last question sank in I felt myself starting to slide back from my voluntary exile to the reality of the situation at hand. With sudden clarity I understood for the first time that I had to tell Ajax and Harwood and Rena about my secret relationship with Granny Mayhew. As soon as possible.

I looked down with some embarrassment at my bulging chest and reached up to snatch off the silly earrings I was wearing. Approaching anyone in my current disguise was out of the question. I told myself to calm down. There was plenty of time to regroup. Harwood still had to go before Slanner, and then presumably Rena would be cross-examining Ajax and Harwood. I slipped out the door and headed down the hall toward the ladies' room.

Minutes later, standing in the wiggly underwater light of the fluorescent-lit bathroom, I stared at myself in the mirror over the sink. What was it I wanted from all these people who were making such a fuss over me in the courtroom down the hall? Ajax and Harwood. Harwood and Rena. Rena and Ajax. It made me smile to think of the different configurations they had taken around me during the many adventures – not to mention just quiet afternoons – we had all shared. Ajax and Harwood and Rena. And then, of course, there was Granny. Yes, double-crossing Granny.

Returning to my mission of the moment, I slid into a stall and began to strip away whatever elements I could of my disguise. The wig and the false chest, for starters. I was preparing to emerge and scrub the makeup off my face when suddenly the bathroom door flew open. I climbed up onto the toilet so my feet didn't show. A few stalls down a door was slammed shut.

'Bloody ladies' lounges. I hate them,' the new arrival announced.

I heard a flicking noise and then 'Go baby, go go go!' It was Granny Mayhew, trying to get her lighter lit. I wondered if she was covering her eyes for this procedure, as she usually did. A few seconds later the odor of burning tobacco came to me.

Yes, it was Granny Mayhew, administering nicotine. No question. I tried to decide on my most strategic play. Was there any advantage to revealing myself right now? Should I drop to the floor and wriggle like a lizard into Granny's stall? Now or never, now or never, I told myself. But at that very moment the bathroom door flew open for a second time.

'Holy Mary Mother of Christ,' groaned the newest arrival. It was Rena. She was standing at a sink, splashing water on her face – or so I gathered from the sound effects and from the little slice of her back that I could see through the crack along my stall door. 'This cannot be happening to me,' she groaned. I remained motionless, my heart pounding. It seemed to me Granny was remaining pretty quiet too. I wanted to crouch down and take a look across the floor toward her stall to see if she had also pulled her feet up out of sight, but I didn't dare.

'Oh, Rena Guilfoyle, you've got yourself in a fine mess this time, you have. Look at your fat green face. Pathetic, that's what you are. Oh Jesus yes, this is getting bad.' Rena had been talking to her reflection, and with these last words she leaned down to take a big slurp of water from the faucet she'd left running. She rinsed the water back and forth vigorously in her mouth, and spat it out. 'Oh Lord, here we go. I hate this,' she mumbled and lurched toward the toilet stalls. She banged once against a door that I guessed must be Granny Mayhew's stall, and then moved down the line, to the stall adjacent to mine.

'How is it these stalls are always empty but locked,' I heard Rena ask herself. 'Like socks lost in the dryer. Oh Jesus, oh God . . .' She made a kind of strangled, coughing sound and spat once. Then she was quiet for a few minutes, just breathing and moaning lightly every now and then. I felt bad for her. It sounded like she was going to throw up. But I didn't dare reveal myself.

Finally she was finished. She spat a few times and blew her nose. 'I wonder if this is developing into an all-day hazard for me. How splendid. No smoking, no booze, unlimited puking – how do people do this?' She exited the stall and headed back to the row of sinks, where she turned on the water and began to wash her face and hands and noisily rinse her mouth once more.

'All right then,' she announced as she finally turned off the water and began to rummage through her purse. 'Back to the battlefront.' She turned and with another whoosh, just as abruptly as she had arrived, she was gone.

Seconds after the door had closed, Granny waltzed up to one of the mirrors, where she adjusted her big flowery head scarf and blew her reflection a kiss. Then she tap-danced right out the door, leaving me alone again. The moment had come for action.

A Girl Gets to Her Feet

Nothing could have prepared me for the scene that would unfold after I returned to court, no longer in disguise, to my same seat at the back of Room 113. Rena was on the witness stand when I entered, and Mr Slanner was standing a few feet in front of her, giving her one of his walleyed looks. Evidently he had just finished asking a question, for a moment after I sat down Rena shot to her feet.

'OBJECTION, your honor,' she screamed. 'And excuse me, but this is really such a highly unorthodox situation I find myself in. As the defending attorney I must object to the question Mr Slanner has just posed to me, the testifying witness. The nature of my or anyone else's friendships with family members has nothing to do with the custody situation under review here. I ask that the last question be dismissed.'

'Miss Guilfoyle, I am most sympathetic to the unusual nature of your dilemma — believe me, this is an odd one for me too,' the judge drawled. 'But ma'am, we're just going to have to take it step by step, together. As to Mr Slanner's question, I believe you yourself opened up the issue of possible motives behind so-called "affections," Miss Guilfoyle, with your own cross-examination focus on Amanda Mayhew's potential interest in any liability awards that may be coming to the child. It therefore seems appropriate that you should now answer Mr Slanner's question. Objection overruled.'

'Repeat the question, please.' Rena spat this out as she settled herself again in the witness chair. She was still looking a little green around the gills, poor thing.

'My question, Miss Guilfoyle, is whether you, in the several years you have been employed as an attorney for Miss Logan Mayhew, have ever had an intimate friendship with one of the girl's guardian uncles.' Slanner walked right up to the witness stand and shoved his nonface at Rena as he said this.

'Haven't we been through this?' Rena said with a sigh.

'Please. Just answer the question to the best of your ability,' the judge growled.

'It depends what you mean by an "intimate friendship,"' Rena began. 'When you work very hard with people on a long project, over the course of years and years, yes, it is inevitable that you get to know them rather well, intimately even . . . I'm not sure . . .' Rena trailed off as Slanner retreated from the witness stand and bent over in conference with Granny Mayhew. She was pushing a legal pad toward Slanner. Slanner took a few minutes to read it and then, after a few more scribbled words from Granny, returned his attention to Rena on the witness stand.

'Let me try a more direct tack, Miss Guilfoyle,' he said, folding his arms smugly across his chest. 'Are you, to put it bluntly, pregnant?'

Rena stared at Slanner as even the green around the edges seemed to drain from her pale face. 'Pregnant?' she asked.

'Yes, pregnant. With child. Knocked up,' Slanner snapped back.

'Objection,' Rena asked more than stated as she turned to the judge.

'Overruled,' the judge replied.

'Pregnant. Goodness, what a notion,' Rena murmured. 'I mean, who's to say—'

'A doctor, for one, could very easily say, Miss Guilfoyle,' Slanner interrupted her. 'But for now – well, let me rephrase the question slightly, to see if that helps you: Do you have any reason to believe that you are possibly, even probably pregnant right now?'

Rena was quiet for so long I thought perhaps she wasn't going to answer. 'Yes, possibly. Probably,' she finally whispered.

Slanner moved forward to lean against the witness stand. 'And if in fact you were to prove pregnant now,' he asked, 'would it also probably be true that the father of your child was in this courtroom?'

'Yes, yes. Probably,' Rena said quietly. She was staring down at her hands, which had wound themselves into a tight knot.

'Could you please then point out for the court and identify by name who, if you are probably pregnant as you say, the father of your child would probably be?' Now it was Slanner who was whispering, with the sibilant hiss of a snake.

Rena stared at her hands a moment longer and then looked up at Slanner. 'No, I COULD NOT,' she announced with her wild Irish smile. 'I could not and I cannot and I will not identify the father of my child, you horrible man!'

A little vacuum of quiet followed the sound of that last statement, and then it was as if an epidemic of reckless behavior spread through the room. The first outbreak came from Harwood, who leapt to his feet and shouted, 'Tell it, Rena baby! Tell it!' I looked over toward Harwood just in time to catch a glimpse of Ajax, pale and quiet, shaking her head. I looked down toward the front of the courtroom where Granny's bescarfed head was calmly perched above her thin square shoulders. Something had to be done, immediately. A moment later I was running down the aisle of the courtroom.

'My grandmother has a confession to make!' I shouted as I approached Granny and pulled her to her feet. 'And so do I.' I heard the knock knock knocking of the judge's gavel trying to restore order and saw security guards entering at the back of the room. I had to act quickly.

'Good afternoon, Your Honor,' I said. 'It is I, Elray Mayhew, and this is Amanda Baer Mayhew, my once dead grandmother. She has been sneaking into my house and taking me on secret outings where she has taught me many new things – like how to smoke cigarettes and how to skip school. We've had dozens of secret meetings over the last months, during which she has dragged all sorts of private information out of me that she is now trying to use against my dear uncles. But does that mean she deserves custody of me?' The judge stared at me dumbly and I began to panic. Obviously he didn't believe me; he thought I was making everything up. 'Here's something else Granny taught me,' I announced as I made a rash decision to forge ahead and pull out all the stops. I grabbed Granny's hands and looked her in the eye and began to sing.

'Got a little rhythm, a rhythm, a rhythm, that pit-a-pats through my brain,' I sang softly. *'So darn insistent, the day isn't distant when it'll drive me insane. Comes in the morning, without any warning, and hangs around me all day. I'll have to sneak up to it someday, and speak up to it. I hope it listens when I say . . .'*

Granny just stared at me during most of this verse, but as I raised my volume and launched into the first chorus, her lips began to move and her feet began to dance across the floor in synchronized step with my own. By the second chorus the two of us were singing together, dancing our way up and down the little space at the front of the courtroom, dipping and twirling and spinning in each other's arms like a pair of birds on Broadway.

'I know that once it didn't matter, but now you're doing wrong; when you start to patter, I'm so unhappy.

Won't you take the day off? Decide to run along, some-where far away off, and make it snappy! Oh, how I long to be the man I used to be! Fascinating rhythm, oh, won't you STOP PICKING ON ME!'

We finished with a big leap through the air that landed each of us on one knee with our arms out-stretched on high, our heads bowed toward one another. We lifted our heads as a spattering of applause broke out, punctuated by the rapping of the judge's gavel and finally by the unmistakable tones of Rena in full throat.

'MISTRIAL!' she howled. 'I DEMAND THAT THIS BE DECLARED A MISTRIAL!' She was pounding her feet up and down as fast as she could against the floor of the witness stall, the way sports fans in bleachers do in tense moments of near triumph. 'MISTRIAL!' she screamed again as she lowered her head and began to shake it back and forth in tempo with her feet.

'GRANTED!' the judge roared back. 'AND COURT DISMISSED! Now get the hell out of here, all of you loonies. Right now, this minute, before I have every last one of you arrested!'

Forty minutes later we were all of us – Ajax, Harwood, Rena, myself and even, at my insistence, Granny Mayhew – packed into a taxicab and headed for High View Street. At first when we were all stand-ing outside the courthouse Ajax and Harwood and Rena had objected to the idea that we do anything but spit at Granny and walk away. But then, Ajax and Harwood and Rena weren't calling the shots anymore. I was. That was something I had learned for sure in the course of the trial. It was a strange feeling. Our trial, at least in the legal sense, was over. It had been declared defunct by the judge, and the issue of my custody was no longer a matter of public debate, thank God. But what a busted-wide Pandora's box the last thirty-six hours had been! The hugeness of what remained un-explained made it impossible for any of us to speak.

Ajax and Rena and Harwood had loaded themselves

into the backseat of the cab, leaving Granny and me to share the front seat with the cabdriver – a strange character who had long greasy hair, wore a dime plastered to the middle of his forehead and kept a low chant going nonstop. As he raced through the city in wide, reckless swoops, all of us and all of our unanswered questions tossed back and forth from side to side in the crowded taxi.

About halfway home, Granny reached over and grabbed my left wrist. At first I resisted – I was still furious with her. But I recognized her gesture as prologue to an important statement and I looked at her as if to say, 'What?'

'I didn't know what else to do, Logan. I didn't know how else to get everyone's attention. I've been dead so long. I want to be alive again,' she said, brushing away tears. She was a damn good actress. I knew that. But it was working. I felt responsible for her. In fact, this cabload of people – all of them, with the exception of our nut-cake driver – they all needed me. It was I who had custody of them.

Family Document:
Rena's Confession

In the months that followed the trial that exposed all of us so mercilessly, I often wondered how much Ajax knew about what had been going on between Harwood and Rena. It was a worry to me that Ajax might have been kept in the dark and somehow taken advantage of in the overall scheme of things. It was therefore a great relief to me to discover, along with the other goodies stashed away in Ajax's desk, this letter, sent from Rena to Ajax before the custody trial began.

Dearest Ajax:

MEA CULPA, MEA CULPA, MEA MAXIMA CULPA. That's the chant that used to start inside my head at the corner of High View and 33rd, as I turned down High View and headed for your house. That is the corner where the Mannings' big white poodle always runs down the walk and stands barking from behind his iron gate, and sometimes it seemed to me that the dog was barking backup: MAXIMA CULPA, MAXIMA CULPA, MAXI-MAXI-MAXIMA CUL-PA!!

Pretty obvious hint, wouldn't you say? A normal, intelligent person might take that hint and change her course. Not I. Even with my guilt cutting up like crazy right in front of me, doing the blessed boogaloo big as day in my brain, I could not keep myself from returning again and again to the very situation that had brought it on. To the house – your house, Ajax – where, week after week, I put on my brightest smile and dug myself deeper and deeper into a pit of sin.

How did I let things run so far and so astray? You know, I was so intrigued by all of you, and I really did believe I could help. You and I had sparked each other like a brushfire from the very start, so that was fun. And then Elray . . . Well, she was irresistible, with her big doubting eyes and that deep gravelly voice that came rumbling so incongruously, after long periods of silence, from her small child self. The things she used to say and the sound of her saying them would have kept me coming back to that house even without everything else that started.

Yes, the initial attraction was the delicious challenge of the basic situation. Your case was the first whiff of fresh air I'd had since coming to the States. The only assignment I had been offered that hadn't sounded toe-curlingly tedious. And we were definitely going for big game on this one – or at least the way I saw it we were. I don't think the rest of you realized this at first or even realized that we had embarked on anything as wild and unpredictable as a safari. But all of you caught on quickly enough, and as it turned out all of you had a natural talent for the hunt. Even Harwood. Ah yes, how easily I can see it now. Especially Harwood, I should say – despite the fact that he was always the most resistant, muttering his disapproval at the floor before looking up to take aim, deliberately and coldly like any good hunter. Centering me in his sights for a short and heavy second, and then shooting me bull's-eye dead with one of his rough looks.

And of course I, possessed by the hunter's need not just to hunt but at the same time to be hunted, welcomed each of Harwood's attacks like a glimpse of prey. I luxuriated in the sensation of being targeted. And even as I took a hit I would already be narrowing my eyes in calculation, doing my hunter's slide rule on the departing shape of Harwood as he stomped from the room and sometimes out of the house.

But I'm getting ahead of myself here, aren't I? I'm getting way ahead of myself. It is so easy to see now how I fell into my sin. I can slip to the heart of the matter in the tiniest of spaces, the space that separates one sentence from the next.

You must believe me, Ajax, when I say that I saw none of this then. Then I saw only the promise of a good fight, the raw challenge of a bizarre situation and the opportunity for possibly netting some justice from this mean world.

'You're an angel to stick with us through all this, Rena. Just an angel.'

Oh Lord. Why is it that when I try to think about everything that's happened, I always end up at that silly remark you made to me one day in one of our sessions? I suppose it is the logical place to begin, because it was your remark, Ajax, and the train of thought it sparked in me that made me first bite the apple, so to speak.

Your remark was innocuous enough in itself. But in the silence that followed it I remember feeling vaguely insulted and at the same time disappointed to hear such cutesy pitterpat drop like cheap candy from the mouth of someone who I knew understood the bigger things in life. I decided to ignore the comment. It was, I told myself, a fine spring day and a pervasive sense of the goodness of life did fill the air. I congratulated myself prematurely on my largesse.

What caught up with me a second later, what transformed your little inanity into a fulcrum that pried open a whole world I had meant to keep locked away from myself – from everyone – was your timing. You had spoken during what I can now see was a kind of sacred moment for me: the moment just after Harwood had leapt to his feet and, toreador style, drilled me with one of his deadly looks. Yes, Harwood had just slaughtered me, absolutely and divinely, with a look of hatred and disgust. I'm sure your words were meant in part to defuse the violence of that look and to repair any injury. But the more I repeated your words to myself, the more I hated them. They made so obvious what I already knew too well. For the fact was, at that moment I was about as far away from angels or angel behavior as it is possible to get. At that moment I was nothing but a little black beast. And as a little black beast I could see the real truth about what drew me back, again and again, to the room where I then sat. It was lust. Rapacious and ruthless lust, nothing more.

You know how all those self-help groups that are meant to make you drop whatever bad and destructive habits you have acquired insist that the first step toward recovery is a proprietary approach? You must claim the bad habit as your own? As I watched Harwood leave the room that day and realized with horror that I was actually trembling with physical desire at the sight, I seized on this popular wisdom and determined, on the spot, to make my admission my salvation. I sat there, and I let myself get weak in the knees with a fantasy that Harwood might turn back suddenly and loom over me, his rude mouth bearing down to swallow my own. I sat there, quaking at a fantasy of being kissed by a man who was not just a client but a client who seemed to hate me. And even as little beads of sweat broke out on my temples from the heat of my imagined passion, a little voice was reasoning with me: So this is what we have here, it said. What we can see, we can conquer.

That night at home I stood in front of my bedroom mirror and lectured myself sternly, as I would any client: 'What we have here,' I said, 'is a pure and simple case of lust, given a classic topspin by the age-old impulse for self-destruction. Is it not an old story? Animal appetites are suppressed and suppressed, and then, when circumstances that qualify as the most highly inappropriate and potentially most disastrous come along, these appetites are given free rein.' I stood in front of the mirror and lectured to myself in this way for a long time. I smoked a lot of cigarettes in the process, to combat the little shivery chill that runs up my back when I talk out loud to myself and when, occasionally, for some reason I have to fake a tele-phone dialogue over a dead phone line. At some point I turned to the whiskey. I'm not sure exactly when, but I know I was well into it by the time the doorbell rang.

Believe me, Ajax, I am in no way trying to excuse

my behavior, but only attempting to give an accurate picture of the sorry state I had cooked myself into when I tell you that the doorbell rang and I knew that it was the devil, come to carry me away. I had just devised a plan to smother this awful lust I had let infect my soul, and after reviewing my plan one last time I had stood in front of my closet mirror and lifted my whiskey glass on high. 'As God is good I swear to this plan,' I had proclaimed. 'Or may the devil come this instant to fetch me and carry me away.'

I find it painful to recount this next bit – to myself or to anyone. But that is why I am writing to you tonight, isn't it. To get these things out. So, with apologies to you and to my preferred version of myself, I will push on and admit that the instant I heard that bell I headed into the little bathroom that adjoins my bedroom and clambered out the window. (Jesus. Really. This part is so degrading. As if one could in fact elude the devil should he come knocking on one's door.) I wedged myself through the bathroom window – and this also is embarrassing, but I was barefoot and wearing only my slip and my smallies at this point – and into the branches of a sweet gum tree that grew conveniently just alongside. It was not the first time I had practiced this maneuver, or it might not have sprung to mind so quickly as an escape route. No, I had actually been out this window and down the same tree at least five or six times before to convince myself that it provided a quite adequate means of fire escape. (I'm sure I have bored you with the grisly stories of the five members of my extended family who have died by fire – it is a strain of tragedy you and I share, after all. I hope you won't consider it a pathetic bid for sympathy when I pause to say that I always, always make sure of escape routes from the upper floors of my homes.)

Anyway, there I was in the tree, and once I had calmed down a little I realized that I had brought the whiskey bottle out with me. This was a happy mistake.

The devil was beginning now to make a real ruckus out in front of my house, and I decided it might not be a bad thing at all to just sit in my tree for a while, have a sip or two and try to live my life deeply enough in the next five minutes to compensate for the fact that the remaining forty-odd years of it were about to be brutally lopped off.

Since this letter is meant as a kind of confession, I may as well go ahead and explain that sometimes – very rarely, but sometimes – when I drink an odd thing happens to me, Ajax. I become another person – a character I idolized as a child: the warrior Cuchulain. This metamorphosis overcomes me less and less often as I get older, and it is no longer much of a problem because these days it is mostly only my language that changes. But when I was younger, at university and such, I had some very embarrassing evenings when I actually performed as if I were Cuchulain deep in the heat of some mythical battle. I have never understood why drink and becoming Cuchulain conspire in my blood in this way. What I do understand is that when I am Cuchulain, I get very brave and very daring. Which quite often amounts to getting very foolish too.

As I've admitted, I was already well into the whiskey by the time I climbed into the tree. (To be completely honest, I've been having a few here tonight too. Otherwise I could never be writing to you like this.) Anyway, as I sat there taking great slugs of hooch and listening to the devil raging on my front porch, it happened. I became Cuchulain as I had not been Cuchulain in a long long time. In retrospect I like to think that being stationed treetop, on a fine spring night with the crickets out there whispering their war secrets to me, may have had something to do with my metamorphosis. Whatever it was, I know that I slipped down that tree in nothing flat and when my feet touched earth they met the ground with the fearless tread of a warrior. I was Cuchulain, on a mission to do away with the devil.

I won't bore you with an account of how brilliantly I maneuvered my way to the front yard and through the bushes to the side of the porch, or how, with the power and stealth of a jungle snake, I levitated myself up and over the rail of that porch. I needn't tell you any of this or about how the blood was pounding like a million tom-toms in my ears, because all that really matters from this point on is what you no doubt have known all along. That is, that it was not the devil who sat crouched there on my front porch. Not strictly speaking, anyway. Strictly speaking it was only Harwood. He was big as day and a devil of sorts in my book, but still only silly mortal Harwood.

Relief is what I should have felt, or shame if I'd had even half my wits about me. But rage is what came pounding through me with the boom boom boom of the tom-toms that was my blood. It went shooting through my system and made my fingers fidget at the ends of my outstretched arms, so itchy were they with the urge to strangle. I came roaring at Harwood from the shadows of the porch – half Cuchulain, half myself – ready to tear him limb from limb.

Luckily for Harwood, he looked up from his crouched position in the nick of time. He looked up and then he did the only thing he could do. He decked me. He executed a quiet backhand across my mouth – a backhand that brought the sticky warm taste of blood to my tongue – and then neatly and deftly, like a machine in a factory doing a job it did every day, he caught my folding body and there I was, just another woozy woman in her underwear in his arms.

Oh Lord, I don't know if I can bear to tell it all. I don't know if I can even bear to remember, not with all that's happened since. Surely you can imagine any bits I leave out more vividly than I could ever relate them? But no, I'm going to try to press on. Before I do let me swear that it is an absolute truth that Harwood had come to my house that night to fire me. Something I'd done in our session earlier that day – the very thing, in fact, that had caused him to stand up and skewer me with that look of his and then leave the room, thereby triggering your 'angel' remark, which in turn exposed to me the ugly knowledge of my own lust – had been eating on him for hours. He had worked himself into a pretty fine stew by the time I came charging from the shadows, and he also by that time was not – if you will trust me as a judge on such a matter – entirely sober. One angry drunk can be ugly, my mother always used to say. But two angry drunks guarantees disaster.

Again, I'm not trying to make excuses for anyone's behavior but simply trying to expose the physics of the situation, the vectors that were at play. Harwood had resolved to fire me from Elray's case, and I, only minutes earlier in my bedroom, had sworn to myself that I would resign from the same case immediately. Throw in several shots of booze, a rasher of rage and lots of lust and you can see that neither of us stood a chance. We were both moving too powerfully in too many of the same directions. The magnetics of the situation were inevitable. There was nowhere we could end up but in each other's arms.

'I knew it! I knew you were here somewhere, you witch!' These first words of Harwood's came from behind clenched teeth that swam in a fuzzy haze about two inches from my face. 'What have you been doing all night, Rena? Gabbing with Barkley and Jack? Tell me. Have the three of you been putting together some big schemes, making everything just peachy-keen for Elray?'

That was the thing that had bothered Harwood earlier, you see. You know how uncomfortable he is with the whole notion of Elray's alleged communication with her parents, how he is unable to just let it be whatever it is for Elray and then use whatever she chooses to share of it as grist for our mill. I've never understood why this is – have you? I suspect it has something to do with his attachment to Barkley and the terrible ways that he misses her. Have you noticed how quiet and intense he gets when Elray shares messages from her? Then he explodes into some fiery speech about our 'sleazy fortune-teller tactics' and leaves the room. Just as he did on the afternoon I'm describing.

I can hear you, Ajax. You're thinking that I'm having a hard time getting to that afternoon and to the larger points here, that there's an awful lot of to-ing and fro-ing and a great willingness to leap on any diversion whatsoever. But let me point out that this was not a premeditated or in any way deliberate sin that Harwood and I slipped into. I for one am still greatly puzzled by it, still examining the forces that forged it. Harwood insists to this day that his only thought in coming to my house that night was to fire me, once and for all. I can't shake a guilty suspicion that my own rude desire, which that very day had come crawling from my subconscious, had something to do with his being there.

Isn't it strange, how silly and seemingly irrelevant the details are that stick with one after some of life's most intense experiences? When Harwood first held me in his fierce grip and spat his rage flat in my face, I remember I felt curiously distant from the chaos around me and became obsessed instead with a single item only inches from my face. Clutched in Harwood's left hand was a postcard addressed to me. A postcard I'd seen lying on the porch along with the rest of my mail when I first came home, but which I hadn't bothered yet to retrieve. So that's what the devil had been doing there, squatting on my porch. The bastard had been reading my mail!

The moment I realized this, Cuchulain came roaring back through my veins, and I twisted sideways and took a big bite of Harwood's chest, shirt and all. He tried to drop me, but I was still attached at the mouth, so when I went down he had no choice but to come with me, howling with pain. Then we were both there on the floor of the porch and he had my shoulders pinned and he was shouting 'You're off this case! Do you hear me? Fired!' in my face. And I was screaming right back at him: 'I've already quit, you prying mail thief. I'm finito, finished. Do YOU hear ME? Bye-bye. BYE-BYE! Now give me that postcard, or I'll bite your balls this time.'

Harwood paused for just a second and cast a quick look down at the region of his anatomy under threat. Then he glanced upward to the postcard that was all scrunched up now in his left hand. There was blood, my blood, on his shirtfront.

' "Bye-bye?" ' Harwood repeated my phrase and then turned a quizzical look on me. 'Did you just say "Bye-bye"?' He seemed incredulous.

'Yes,' I whispered. I could hardly breathe.

The corners of Harwood's mouth were twitching slightly, and I noticed for the first time a sequence of small scars, in dots and dashes like a Morse code, under his lower lip. A moment later it was as if all the blood in his body changed direction, and in doing so gained momentum, like a swimmer doing a racing turn at the end of a lap. His face became smooth and fierce and his neck and shoulders seemed to stiffen and swell, as if he used to have feathers there and couldn't break himself of the habit of trying to spread them. Then there was that Harwood mouth of his, bearing down to swallow me just as I had imagined it might only about eight hours earlier. But this time it was really happening. Our two mouths became all that was left of the world. We tumbled to the left, we tumbled to the right and then we tumbled all the way down each other's throats.

Afterward we lay in our spot under the sweet gum tree, the spot Harwood had carried me to after discovering that the front door was locked and I didn't have a key. I reached over and casual as any good magician pulled the bottle of whiskey out from between the two roots where I had stashed it a little while earlier, when I was Cuchulain and off on a mission.

'Care for a pop?' I asked and offered him the bottle. I could see by the look Harwood gave me before accepting that he was impressed. He took a big swig from the bottle, narrowing his eyes as he swallowed. Then he moved the bottle toward my lips, but paused halfway.

'Let's take care of this first,' he said, reaching for my slip, which lay on the ground nearby. He moistened a corner of my slip with whiskey and then gently, almost tenderly, dabbed at the cut on my lip that he had put there with his backhand. 'I'm very very sorry about this,' he said. 'Have I said that yet?'

'No, but don't worry about it,' I answered. The whiskey was stinging terribly, making me aware of the cut, which I had almost forgotten. 'It's nothing, really. I've had far worse. How's your chest?'

Harwood looked down at the purple circle of bruise on the left side of his chest where I'd bitten him and smiled. 'It's my medal,' he said and touched it lightly. 'My Purple Heart.' Then he took another long pull on the bottle and lay back to stare up into the canopy of star-shaped leaves above us. 'I've heard that first fucks can be bloody,' he said. 'But Jesus, Rena, you really put a new twist on it.'

Now I've told you how it started, Ajax. I've told you in such embarrassing detail so you will know I've told you everything. There can be no secrets between us. You can see for yourself how selfish and indulgent and totally irresponsible Harwood and I both were. I'd like to be able to say that the two of us allowed ourselves to surrender to each other that first night under the sweet gum tree because we believed we were no longer officially linked in any business matters. Harwood had just fired me, and I had just sworn that I'd quit anyway. But if this was the case, why did we never once, either of us, mention this matter again? Why did I arrive as scheduled for my next session at your house a day and a half later, and why did

Harwood seem not only not surprised to see me there, but even perhaps just a tiny bit relieved? Even stranger, why did he and I play our accustomed roles in that session, as if nothing had happened less than forty-eight hours earlier on a fine spring night in the moon-shadow of a sweet gum tree? During that session Harwood fumed and snorted with disgust at every tack I took, and in response I poured it on thicker, dying all the while for one of his deadly looks.

He gave me the look eventually, and stomped out of the room as expected. But that night, and on many nights thereafter, he was there on my front porch, anxious to give me something else altogether. As anxious to give it as I was to take.

Now Ajax, I have made my confession, I have told the sordid tale in all its sordid detail. Knowing what you now know, can you tell me, please, which was the greater sin: to have started this thing or to have continued it in the face of all the improprieties? But most of all, knowing what you now know, can you possibly forgive me? Will you believe me when I say that Harwood and I are absolutely finished? Will you grant me absolution? Will you give me a second chance? Please.

Yours if you'll have me, Rena

Part Seven

Do-Si-Do

Full House

Rena was pregnant. That was the most significant piece of flotsam to wash ashore from the wreckage of my custody trial. I suppose Rena decided there was little sense in denying it – after all, we had seen her on the witness stand, and her silhouette was bound to betray the truth in time. It was just bad luck that she'd been found out as early as she had. If only Rena had gone to the ladies' room to the right of our courtroom instead of the one to the left, if only Granny hadn't happened to be in that same ladies' room at the same time, if only Rena hadn't been one of those people who compulsively talk to themselves when they think they're alone. If only one of these ifs had been otherwise, Rena's life – no, all of our lives – might have proceeded differently.

But life will fall out as it falls out. As far as I was concerned, Rena's bad luck was my good luck. Both my home life with Ajax and Harwood and my relationship with Granny had survived the courtroom fireworks, which was a major coup. My private affairs had been subjected to the indignity of public scrutiny, but then so had those of Ajax and Harwood and Rena and Granny. As it turned out, in their company I was the contrast gainer. My own shocking secrets were nothing alongside those of my elders, and the most riveting shock of all was this notion of a baby growing inside Rena.

'What do you mean you don't know who the father is? How is that possible? Have you really been doing that brisk a business? And been so careless to boot?' Harwood bombarded Rena with these questions as we sat around the living room sipping iced tea with mint the first evening after my trial had gone bust. This direct and public questioning of Rena was typical of a newly relaxed attitude about talking in front of me that would characterize all the adult exchanges in our household from the trial forward. With so many secrets about all of us blown so sky-high, and with my custody now seemingly secure, I suppose everyone found it silly to tiptoe around me the way they used to.

'Slow down, Captain Morality, before you make a hypocritical fool of yourself,' Rena had snapped right back at Harwood that night. 'Just buzz off and mind your own business, why don't you.'

'Mind my own business? Rena, you know perfectly well why I'm asking about this.' Harwood rose from his seat and was moving across the room toward Rena, somewhat threateningly, as he spoke.

'David, leave her alone. This is hardly the time or place,' Ajax said quietly as she escorted Harwood back to his seat next to me. She was still dressed in the khaki suit she had borrowed from Harwood, and after depositing him in his seat she stood there and flicked at the sleeves of her jacket, as if smoothing ruffled feathers. 'Don't you know ANYTHING?' Ajax leaned forward to spit this at Harwood in a stage whisper. 'If Rena IS pregnant, then it is IMPERATIVE that she remain calm at all times – starting right now!' As I watched Ajax scold Harwood I wondered if she knew what I knew and what Harwood must be thinking about – that there was at least some possibility that it was a Harwood baby that was growing inside Rena.

Then there was the dilemma of Granny Mayhew, who at my insistence had come home with us after the trial for a sort of debriefing and clearing of the air. In the days that followed I found myself in a kind of secondary trial as I stood before Ajax and Harwood and Rena and defended Granny's right to walk among us. Ajax was the most vociferously opposed to her presence – Rena and Harwood were still too consumed by the riddle of their own relationship to give anything else much thought – so it was to Ajax that I made my strongest appeal. I spoke of Granny's advanced age, her dwindling time, the responsibility of families for their own senile. I made shameless and false reference to my scar and to the long-dormant voices of my dead parents, claiming that the oracle on my forearm had stirred to life for the first time in years to issue this order: TAKE GRANNY HOME WITH YOU. EMBRACE HER AS YOUR OWN.

'Yeah, uh-huh.' Ajax had looked at me sourly. 'And pay no attention to the little girl behind the curtain, right?'

Not one of my arguments moved Ajax from the stance of absolute rejection she had adopted toward Granny. 'She's a conniving, dishonest, selfish old bitch,' Ajax announced to me one afternoon a week after the trial as the two of us sat with Rena at a table on the front porch, playing poker. 'She happens to have poisoned my youth, but I don't see why she should be allowed to poison yours.' Granny herself was sitting alone at another little table not eight feet away, playing solitaire, and she looked up and nodded as Ajax spoke.

'Good point, Andrew,' Granny said. 'I really haven't been quite the storybook mum, have I. Oh, and you always such the model son. Poor baby, so tragic.'

'Stay out of this,' Ajax growled at Granny. 'Legally, you are trespassing right now, you know. I don't have to let you sit on this porch if I don't want to.'

'Legally I just might turn out to be the owner of this old Mayhew house,' Granny countered. 'Watch out.'

'Ajax, she's your own mother. The only one you'll ever get,' I scolded as I interrupted the two of them and rearranged my cards. I had just picked up the

327

queen and the jack of hearts for a winning spread, and as I slipped the jack into place between his two brother jacks and sister queens my heart skipped a beat. Was it possible that this jack had just winked his one eye at me? I stared down at the card and thought I saw him wink again, with one eye that blazed a bright green.

'Yes, the only mother you'll ever get,' I repeated sadly. 'Do you have any idea how lucky you are, Ajax? She was dead and gone for so long, since you were a child, but here she is again. You could spend whatever time she has left on earth together if you wanted to, but instead you want to send her away. I can't understand that. Do you know what I would give to have Barkley and Jack come walking up those steps right now?' As I stared at Ajax, tears − not real tears that were connected to any ache in my throat or heart, but water tears like the kind that come when you peel onions − ran down my cheeks and spilled like liquid guile onto the shiny faces of my cards. I peeked at my jack, but he had gone as still and flat as every other card. Then I looked up at Ajax and Rena. 'Full house,' I announced as I spread my winning hand out on the table.

'Oh you scoundrel, you rogue, you monster child!' Ajax cried. Her tone was meant as one of mock outrage, but her voice was edged with sadness. I caught her brushing at the corner of each eye with the back of her hand. 'How do you do it every time? How do you always win? I'll never play with you again, I swear,' she said as she tossed her cards onto the table.

'She cheats, I'm sure of it. She must cheat. She's got an extra pack under the table or something,' Rena muttered, joining in on the outrage act. I smiled sweetly as I scooped up the cards and began to shuffle them. Not another word was said about whether Granny was welcome, that day or ever again, by any of us. There was nothing more to be said. I had already won, and we all knew it. I had won, and by the end of that month Granny would move into the house on High View Street with Ajax and Harwood and me.

Less than two months after Granny moved in, Rena came to live with us too, and for the first time every bedroom in our big rambling house was occupied. It was Ajax who had laid the groundwork for this, insisting that in her pregnant condition Rena needed 'a family' to take care of her. From the very start I was delighted with the idea. I found Rena's pregnancy fascinating. Rena was already noticeably larger than she had been at the trial. Every time I looked at her she seemed to be eating something. Her angular face had taken on a kind of soft, vulnerable look, as if it might be serving as a periscope window through which the baby inside was peering out at the world.

I was not the only one who found Rena's creative condition fascinating. Ajax was constantly concocting special 'high-protein shakes' for the mother-to-be and reading out loud from pregnancy books, keeping all of us informed as to exactly which cells were forming in what portion of the tiny fetus week by week. Granny, whose courtroom foil of knitting had stuck as a habit, had produced a small mountain of baby sweaters and socks and blankets in a rainbow of pretty unisex pastels, and even Harwood expressed a mild curiosity from time to time in what he had dubbed 'Rena's Unknown Soldier.' 'Anybody kickin' yet?' he would ask, or 'How's the little Lost Dauphin?'

At the family dinner in October when Ajax, after weeks of dropping heavy hints on the matter, had finally come right out and proposed that Rena move in with us, all gazes had turned expectantly on Harwood. I think everyone just assumed he would be the one to snort and then howl with disapproval. In fact, Harwood remained silent and noncommittal on the subject, and it was Rena who finally spoke up with misgivings.

'Oh, it's so sweet of you to offer, I'm so touched,

329

really I am,' she said, sounding more like Dorothy from *The Wizard of Oz* than the fireball Irish attorney I had come to know. 'But you know, I think it would be very bad business for a lawyer to be living with her clients when litigation is still in process, don't you?'

'Well, that's easily remedied,' Ajax countered. 'Let's just wrap it up then. Let's settle. The other side has been wanting to for years. So let's go for it.'

It was true. For almost a decade now the attorneys representing the amusement park had been pressing for a settlement out of court, and we – with Rena as our fearless guide and advisor – had steadfastly refused. Perhaps we all felt that it was somehow nobler to dig dig dig for our treasure than simply to open our paws and take what was being freely offered. Money per se was not really a problem, as my grandparents and parents had left small trust funds that covered the modest needs of our household. And one very real drawback to settlement was that it would put an end to what had become an important and unifying thread in our family life – our sessions with Rena. As I looked around the table that evening and saw that not one of us seemed too horrified at the notion that we might now abandon our 'treasure hunt,' it struck me how long we had all been together and how much we had all changed. What was it we had really been digging for all those years anyway? Was it recompense or treasure, or was it something else? Had we found it, or had we simply grown older and tired and given up? It was impossible for me to say at that moment. The only thing I knew for sure was that as a group we, like most things in life, had demonstrated a tendency toward accretion. There were more of us. There was no arguing that, I thought as I looked around at the faces of Ajax, Harwood, Granny and the fertile, soon-to-subdivide Rena. For someone who had been left all alone in the world at the age of six, it seemed to me, I had quite a large and complicated family.

For that matter, I thought as I looked down at the

scar on my right forearm, I had never really been left entirely alone in the first place. How much of the so-called communication from my parents had come from them, I wondered, and how much from me? I couldn't say. They always seemed to come knocking in moments of crisis, I had to admit. Indeed, at that very moment, as we sat there and discussed the question of where the pregnant Rena should live, I could swear I felt a palpitating drumbeat strike up in my right arm. As I laid the fingers of my left hand across my scar I felt a whooshing, rhythmic pounding – like the wash cycle of a washing machine, or a heart beating underwater. Was it the pulse of my own blood that I felt? I shifted my left hand so its palm lay directly over the scar, and as I did the wailing ragged voice of a screaming baby filled my ears. I had never experienced such a raw and urgent expression of absolute need. I looked across at Rena's expanding figure and shot to my feet.

'Of course we should settle, as soon as possible,' I announced, embarrassed by the urgency I could hear in my voice and by the stricken look I could feel on my face. 'I have no intention of ever entering another courtroom as long as I live, if I can possibly avoid it. And of course Rena must live here with us, where we can take care of her and her baby. Babies are very very needy creatures. They cry a lot.'

Anxious to give the impression of having had the last word on the matter and to escape whatever dynamics had sent the wailing baby cries through my arm, I fled from the room. I ran outside into a cool October night where the warm colors of an Indian summer day still lingered beneath the gentle dark. I drew in huge gulps of the delicious, biseasonal air and marveled at the miracle of autonomy. I belonged to all of them, to all the people who were still sitting around the dining room table inside, and yet I was still only myself. I stretched my hands out against the night sky and wiggled my fingers back and forth, as if to prove this. I opened and shut and opened and shut the lids of my eyes, as if this were the wing-stroke that could carry me anywhere I might want to go. Then I set off.

I went sailing through the night, pumping my legs and windmilling my arms as though it were the rushing waters of a river and not flat macadam that I navigated. I set off on a long and looping journey to nowhere in particular, delighting in the sensations of motion and independence and in the certainty that whenever I was ready, I had a busy bustling home to which I could return.

Swing Your Partner

Ten days later – almost ten years to the day after the accident that killed Barkley and Jack – I watched from the sidelines in a small, poorly lit conference room somewhere downtown as the attorneys for Glen Echo Amusement Park and Rena Guilfoyle shook hands and I officially became worth two million dollars more than I had been a moment before. If it seemed odd that a simple handshake should close so many years of scheming and planning, it was no odder than the emotional flatliner that registered inside me at the thought of my new wealth. Two hundred, two thousand, two million – I had lost two parents, and any of these sums would probably have sounded equally arbitrary to me as recompense. The important thing was that the matter had been settled. The world had made formal apology for its cruelty. We could, life and I, move on. In theory.

Two days before the settlement meeting, Rena had moved into the spare bedroom adjacent to Ajax's. Originally she had intended to hold off until all the papers were signed, but we had convinced her that this was silly and unnecessary.

The day after settlement was my sixteenth birthday. In addition to being taken on the skydiving outing that Harwood had promised me to celebrate the occasion, I was told that Ajax and Harwood had invested in a new Plymouth and that I would officially inherit the old black Chevy station wagon that had been the family car for as long as I could remember. The mere sight of Black Beauty, as we called the old machine, filled me with sweet intimations of mobility and adventure.

Two days after my birthday was Halloween and Ajax's birthday, an event my aunt usually preferred not to acknowledge. This year, however – it was Ajax's forty-fourth, if I am counting correctly – Granny and Rena put their heads together and we surprised Ajax with a combination dance party and Creole feast at which Ajax, Harwood, Rena, Granny, myself and Harwood's eternally partying statues carried on into the wee hours. At the very end of the evening Granny came forward shyly with a heavy package for Ajax. 'It's the one thing I took with me when I died. I'm ashamed to say I did sell off a few pieces in moments of extreme need. But most of it remains. You should have it now,' said Granny. Inside was the Mayhew family silver, or most of it. Even Ajax had a hard time disguising her pleasure.

Finally, on the blown-out day after Ajax's birthday, came my tenth Crawlspace Day. As I've said, Crawlspace Days, like Cracker Jack boxes, always contained some surprise. This one did not disappoint.

The day started slowly – partly because of the late-night exuberance at Ajax's party the evening before, which had been alcohol-fueled for everyone except Rena and me, and partly because the sound of torrential rains spread like an extension of night through all our shade-drawn rooms, giving us an excuse to stay in bed.

By noon, my housemates had come shuffling, like so many walking wounded, downstairs to the dining room, where Ajax was already administering hair-of-the-dog mimosas. Harwood was the last to appear. As he stood in the doorway he looked all crooked, as if he'd been torn to pieces and then stitched back together by an amateur seamstress. Rena stared at him for a moment as he stood there rubbing the inside-out-looking surface of his blue-gray, unshaven chin.

'Quick, another mimosa,' Rena said. 'This one's in critical condition.'

'Ugh, no, take that away.' Harwood put his hand out to ward off the drink that Ajax offered, but then a second later he relented and grabbed it. 'Oh hell. Can't make things worse,' he muttered as he tipped the glass and drained it.

Over the next hour and a half I watched as, mimosa by mimosa, the moods and looks of my elders gradually revived. Between the excitement of Rena's moving in, the legal settlement and Ajax's and my own birthday celebrations, the champagne had already been flowing pretty steadily in our house all week. But that morning it reached flash-flood levels as cork after cork went flying across the dining room with the giddy pop pop pop of decorum breaking down.

Ajax, who had been the official party planner and bartender, announced that the orange juice was all gone and that she was 'sick as Simon' of refilling everyone's glass every five minutes anyway, so 'would everyone please just grab your own bottle and do-si-do.' After a five-cork salute, accompanied by a sloppily executed rendition of a round called 'My Dame Has a Lame, Tame Crane,' Ajax placed five freshly opened bottles of ice-cold champagne in a line on the sideboard, like so many dance partners, and bade us each step forward. Rena and I had been lagging behind the others, trying to nurse our champagne all morning, but when our turns came we too stepped forward and claimed a bottle, to avoid spoiling Ajax's minuet.

Ajax raised her bottle on high as she beat against it with a silver spoon. 'Now, my dears, the moment has come,' she announced. 'For this is no ordinary day. This is Elray's TENTH ANNUAL CRAWLSPACE DAY. You each have been armed, so now on with your headgear and then LET'S GET GROUNDHOGGIN'.'

With this Ajax produced from under the table a traditional Crawlspace Day miner's helmet for each of us, including – touchingly – a bright blue one with orange flames painted on the sides for Granny. Five minutes later, with our helmets strapped to our heads and our bottles clutched to our breasts, we fell in line behind Ajax and marched, a ragtaggy corps of pajama-clad warriors, out the front door through the still heavy rain to the musty old crawlspace under the house.

If any of us wondered why we were letting Ajax lead us through the muck and mud that day, we understood the moment we entered the crawlspace and switched on our helmet lights. Ajax had outdone herself. Balloons and streamers brightened the low-ceilinged space where the stone table, with linen napkins and the reclaimed Mayhew silver, was set for five. A side table was laden with cheeses and fruit and an enormous white birthday cake. The necks of several more champagne bottles were sticking out, like a gaggle of curious geese, from the depths of an ice-filled tub. Stacked on a blue blanket that was spread against the back wall lay a lode of brightly wrapped presents. Ajax had thought of everything. There was even a small battery-run heater humming in one corner, to fight off the chill.

'Happy Crawlspace Day, Elray my sweet.' Ajax turned to me shyly and kissed me on each cheek as she spoke in a voice that had collapsed from a drill-sergeant bark to a schoolgirl mumble. 'I love you very much, you know,' she practically whispered.

'I do know. And I love you too,' I whispered back as I wrapped her in a big squeeze. As we sat down, our kinetics as a group suffered the inevitable awkward-ness that comes when high spirits pause mid-spree and relocate to a new setting. This was soon overcome as I began to tear open my stash of bonus birthday presents. As I uncovered one lovely gift after another, I reached more and more frequently for my champagne glass. Soon the whole crawlspace was a happy, twirling merry-go-round ride.

'Oh God, this is beautiful!' I cried as I pulled an old and well-worn leather jacket from a box Harwood had pushed toward me. 'Oh, I love this, I really do,' I whispered, burying my nose in its wise and buttery folds. It was true, I did love the jacket. I loved the jacket, which had once been Harwood's, just as I loved the little black lace-up tap shoes Granny gave me, and the books and the records and the sweet-smelling soaps from Ajax and Rena. I loved all my presents, and I loved all the people who had given them to me, but most of all I loved the splendid, spinning sensation of this moment that had expanded to embrace us all in my crawlspace.

'Here's to all of you on Crawlspace Day,' I announced, hefting my now half-empty bottle on high. 'And may every child who gets orphaned land as luckily as I.' As my tablemates murmured their modest thanks and took big slurps of champagne, Ajax bent down and began to fumble around under the table.

'Wait, dearie, you haven't finished your presents,' Ajax said as she produced a large box wrapped in black paper with gold stars. 'Here's one more. This is from all of us, from your adoring fans.' As I took the big heavy package into my lap and began to tear at its wrappings, I felt a blush of self-consciousness. I was tired. I had burned through my natural fuse for opening presents, short-circuited on gratitude. Still, I tore away the paper, making appreciative grunts, until I sat staring down at the words written in big black letters across the top of the exposed box: EASTMAN KODAK MODEL 1503 35MM 'REEL-LIFE.'

I was genuinely impressed. This was a substantial present, a very costly one, not to mention a truly professional, very grown-up piece of equipment.

'Is this really . . . ?' I asked, trailing off as I pointed at the still unopened box.

'Yes dear, the man in the shop said this is the

absolute top-of-the-line small-production thirty-five millimeter on the market today,' Ajax said as she swallowed a mouthful of champagne hastily and drew a big breath. 'You can do just about anything with it, he said, and we were all so knocked out by your films. Weren't we, Rena? Harwood? And we think you deserve the best. You simply must do more – you've a natural talent for it, you really do. Everyone who's seen the films has said so. In fact I've been wanting to tell you about an idea I've had for a little project. Well—'

'Simmer down, Ajax,' Harwood interrupted. 'Let Elray enjoy all her presents and let all of us enjoy Crawlspace Day. Your "little project," whatever it is, can wait. We haven't even had the cake yet, for Christ's sake.'

'Quite right, of course,' Ajax apologized as she reached for the cake and set it on the table before her. As Ajax struck a match and began to light the candles, Granny – who had been sitting quietly for some time – shot out of her chair with a gasp.

'Could you possibly warn a soul when you're about to do something crazy like light a multitude of candles? We could all explode, detonate right here on the spot, as much alcohol as we have in us,' Granny complained. She had smacked her helmeted head against the underside of the porch, she had jumped so high out of her chair, and then had staggered backward to the rear wall, where she stood cowering, her hands lifted in a peekaboo cover over her eyes.

'What'sa matter, Mama?' Ajax asked wickedly as she lifted the lighted cake and pushed it toward Granny Mayhew. 'Don't you like the pretty candles?'

'Oh, stop it,' Rena scolded, leaning forward and laying a hand on Ajax's shoulder. 'Here, that's Elray's cake. Give it to her. Be a dear and blow the candles out now, Elray, would you?'

Ajax placed the cake in front of me and then, accompanied by Rena, launched into a rousing chorus of

'Happy Crawlspace Day.' Granny kept her station along the wall, her back to us now, and hummed a show tune loudly to herself.

You didn't have to be a genius or even sober to sense that things were beginning to unravel. The beautiful spinning moment had lost its balance and was now clunking lopsidedly, like a washing machine with all the wet towels on one side. Still, I leaned forward and blew out the candles on my cake and let out a happy squawk.

'Well done!' Rena congratulated me and turned toward Granny. 'They're all gone now, Granny. Elray took care of them. Come on back and have a piece of cake with us.'

'What's all that about?' Harwood asked, nodding in Granny's direction as he accepted a large slice of cake. 'What's her problem? Champagne finally get to her?'

'My mother suffers from an irrational and psychotic fear of fire,' Ajax said primly, as if she were Mary Poppins giving a lecture on how to hold a teacup. 'She always has. 'S quite ludicrous really. That's why I painted flames on her helmet.'

'You shouldn't tease, Ajax,' said Rena. 'I've had several rellies go up in flames, you know. Death by fire is far more common than you'd think. It happens all the time. That's why I always – ALWAYS – make sure of an alternate exit when I spend the night in a strange place. Granny's no fool . . .'

'I have a healthy respect for the powerful element of fire,' Granny called out from her corner. 'That's all. As well you or anyone might if you'd been nearly roasted to a crisp in a flash conflagration as I nearly was.'

'Oh Mama, really. You know very well you've been phobic about fire all your life, since way before Blackie's,' Ajax called back. 'We all knew it. As children, we used to have to light her cigarettes for her. Can you imagine? That's why we all felt so sorry for her when it looked like she'd been pit-roasted, bagged by her own demon. Little did we know.'

'Is it true? Are you really scared of fire?' Harwood asked. For some reason this seemed to intrigue him.

'Petrified,' Granny answered after a long pause. Then she came scuffling back to the table. 'There. Satisfied?' she added as she turned to Ajax. 'Are you happy now?'

'Praise Jesus, we must drink to this,' Ajax cried as she grabbed a fresh bottle of champagne from the ice tub. 'Granny's come clean with an honest answer on something. This IS cause for celebration. Chin chin, everyone,' Ajax said as she filled our glasses to the brim with fresh bubbly. As we lifted them on high and then to our lips, it felt for a minute as if our world had righted itself and was back on its magic axis again.

'Granny's sprung a secret, shared a little something special with all of us. It's our turn. This is what Crawlspace Day is all about. Discovery and revelation, surprises, secrets. Digging to bury the lost and digging to uncover the new.' It struck me, as Ajax slipped so glibly into this little speech, how much she reminded me of someone – was it Rena? After all those years of being coached by Rena, had the style rubbed off on Ajax? Or was it perhaps my father, or what I thought I remembered of him and his lecturing tendencies? Ajax was certainly looking more and more like Jack these days, now that she no longer wore dresses or wigs. She'd joined a fitness club, 'to battle the dread middle-age wobblies,' as she put it, and her body looked different. The soft, matronly layer of pudge that had always encased her big frame was no longer there, I realized as I studied her in the patchy light of the crawlspace. It must have taken a lot of discipline to get rid of all that flesh, but it was definitely gone. You could see that much clearly now as she sat there in elegant white silk pajamas under a maroon, amoeba-patterned silk bathrobe. Beneath the layers of silk her shoulders squared off with real authority and the rest of her body seemed to fall into rank, logically and obediently, below. Ajax, I realized with a

340

champagne-blurred splotch of surprise, was looking almost dashing.

'Okay, so who's next?' my handsome aunt was asking as she looked around the table. 'Harwood, how about you? Share a secret with us. Stun us, make it something big.'

'Oh go away,' Harwood said as he waved a hand at Ajax. 'I don't have any secrets or phobias or hidden urges. Not everyone can be as twisted a nutcase as all you Mayhews seem to be.'

'Come come now, there must be something you could say that would surprise those of us who think we know you so well. Think for a minute; throw us a scrap, Davey-boy.' Ajax wasn't letting up.

'Yes, come on. You've got some secret pockets in there, I know you do,' said Rena as she leaned forward and laid a hand on Harwood's forearm. 'Reach in and relinquish one little nugget, Harwood.'

'Okay, okay,' Harwood said as he lifted his glass to his lips and drained it once more. 'Here's a little piece of news. Nothing earth-shattering, but something none of you knows yet. I've been offered a full-time staff position as a photographer for *National Geographic* magazine. Of course, I probably won't accept it.'

'THE *National Geographic* magazine? The slick yellow one with all the gorgeous pictures? David, that's so splendid!' Ajax filled our glasses again. 'To Harwood, our very own world-class shutterbug!' We toasted Harwood, then Rena leaned over and gave him a big kiss, which seemed to please him. Before I could ask Harwood where the magazine was based and if this meant he would be leaving us, Ajax had moved around the table to me.

'All right, Elray,' she said. 'Your turn. Throw us a little something. Share.'

'Share? What's left?' I asked. 'You guys rifled through my entire stash of secrets at the trial.'

'Don't be so coy. You've got plenty left,' Granny said as she stuck a finger into her champagne and began to dislodge the bubbles that clung to the sides of her glass. 'Let's see. What about Raoul?' she asked, looking up at me suddenly with ice-green eyes. 'What happened to him? What was he all about?'

'I don't know,' I said, staring back at Granny. 'What about your teeth? Would you like to talk about your teeth?'

'Not nice,' said Granny, shaking her head. 'I'm very old. Old people often lose their teeth.'

'People can lose a lot of things,' I said. 'Mothers, fathers. Friends. Even babies.' I looked across at Rena and made an alcohol-impaired decision. 'But you want to hear a secret? I've got a secret for all of you. Would you like to hear something wild, something kind of spooky?' I lowered my voice and leaned in toward the table, as if it were a campfire. All the others leaned in with me, on cue. Yes, they all nodded, yes we want to hear. 'Sometimes . . .' I began in a whisper, and everyone leaned in a little tighter. 'Sometimes, Rena, I can hear your baby crying. Right here, in my arm. Clear as a bell. Right where I used to hear Barkley and Jack.' I pointed to the scar on my forearm. Everyone stared at my arm for a moment, and then Rena and Ajax exchanged a glance.

'Really? You can hear it?' Rena whispered back finally. 'You can hear my baby?'

I nodded.

'What does it sound like? How do you know it's mine?'

'I can tell,' I answered. 'It's yours all right.'

'Ever happen to mention who its daddy is?' Harwood spoke in a normal voice that made us all jump, it seemed so loud and out of place after our whispers. Like a helicopter descending on a circle of druids at worship in a quiet grove of pines.

'It sounds like a hundred babies,' I said, ignoring Harwood's attempt to sabotage the mood we were all trying to build. 'It sounds as if it could have a hundred different fathers or none at all.'

'Huh, figures. That makes sense,' said Harwood with a laugh. 'About what it's going to get, I guess. A hundred fathers or none. Same thing, actually.'

'Can you tell if it's a girl or boy?' Ajax asked. She and Rena were ignoring Harwood too.

'It's both, it's everything,' I whispered, not knowing what I meant by this, but liking the sound of the words anyway. 'It's everything a baby can be.'

'It's a poor little fatherless bastard, is what it is,' said Harwood, jolting us all for the third time with his deliberate obnoxiousness and becoming the first real piece of evidence that we had all had too much to drink. 'It's going to be a poor little fatherless bastard unless Rena here snaps to. Come on,' he said, leaning his face toward Rena. 'This is the time for the sharing of great secrets, and it's your turn, Rena. So tell us who knocked you up, honey. Who jammed that little bun in your oven?'

'Jesus, you are a pig,' snapped Rena as she pushed Harwood's face away with the flat of her hand. 'Buzz off, you big drunk. Go get ugly on someone else.'

'I'm not trying to get ugly, Rena,' Harwood said in a singsong voice filled with mock hurt. 'I'm just trying to get you to share a little secret on Crawlspace Day, like everybody else. So fess up. Who's the lucky stud who power-planted his seed in you last June? Huh?'

'Oh, you've done your math, have you? Very impressive. Well, let me tell you one thing, Harwood, since you keep asking.' Rena turned on him viciously. 'There isn't a day goes by I don't pray to the good Lord it isn't your mean, blighted seed that's rooted itself in me. And that's the truth.'

'Ah, then it might be! It might be my mean, blighted seed!' Harwood crowed as he began to beat the edge of the table with his fists. 'Now we're getting somewhere – although you still haven't told me anything I hadn't pretty much figured out for myself. How about the real secret now – who else MIGHT it be? Hmmm? How many cowboys went riding with you last June, Rena?

Hmmm? Five, ten, twenty? "Rollin' rollin' rollin', keep them doggies rollin'. Rollin' rollin' rollin' . . ."' Harwood burst into song, but not for long. A moment later Ajax had pitched a glass of champagne right in his face and was leaning menacingly across the table.

'Shut up, you idiot,' Ajax said quietly. 'You're drunk, and you need to shut up. You're making a fool of yourself.'

'Me? I'm making a fool of myself? Compared to what, Ajax?' asked Harwood as he reached for his napkin and began to wipe his face. 'Compared to you in your silk pajamas and toenail polish? Or Granny here with her fear of fire and ridiculous high hair? Or Rena with the little bastard growing in her belly? Or even Elray, who says she has a baby boo-hooing in her arm? You tell me who's the fool here, Ajax. You think about it and you tell me.'

'You want to hear a big secret, Harwood? Is that what you want?' Rena broke the silence that had followed Harwood's last words. 'I've got a big secret I'll share with you, David. With everyone. I'm going to announce right now, Ajax; I'm not going to wait,' Rena said as she turned and took Ajax's hand.

Ajax stared at Rena and then nodded. 'Go ahead,' she said.

Rena took a deep breath and a big sip of champagne and finally she spoke. 'Ajax and I are going to get married,' she said. 'We're in love.'

No one said anything for what seemed a long time, and then we all began to splutter at once. Granny started clapping and said, 'Well done, my son. How exciting!' while I got stuck on 'But . . . but . . . but . . .' for so long that I sounded like an outboard motor. From across the table Harwood produced an incoherent mumbling that finally erupted into the first concise and coherent reaction.

'WHAT?' he screamed. 'What the hell are you talking about, "married"? It's impossible. She's a she and you're a she. It doesn't work. In fact, it's an obscene

344

suggestion. Jesus, you witches have really gone too far this time. If this were April first instead of November first I'd go along with the joke, but under the circumstances—'

'Technically, as far as any court that would issue a marriage license is concerned, Ajax is male,' Rena interrupted him. 'And technically, as I believe you know, I am female. Technically there is absolutely no reason why we should not get married, and morally – and let me just point out, Harwood, that as usual you seem to have overlooked the important news here – morally there is every justification for our union, since, as I said, we are very much in love.' Ajax and Rena smiled at each other as Ajax reached over with her free hand to squeeze the Rena hand she was already holding.

'Very well put!' Granny Mayhew exclaimed. 'Spoken like the brilliant attorney that I've always known you must be, daughter-in-law-to-be. Andrew, you are full of surprises. I love that.'

Ajax rolled her eyes and blushed slightly at this while Harwood just sat and stared at Rena. I didn't know what to think or say, so I watched. Finally Harwood shifted his weight backward in his chair and began to speak in a voice that sounded hollow and dangerous, as if it were traveling toward us from the rear of a gun barrel.

'This is the ultimate power trip for ball-busting broads like you, Rena, isn't it?' he said. 'The ultimate tribute to your Circean charms: to convert the poor, befuddled faggot. To resuscitate the dormant seed of virility that must lie somewhere inside even the most raging and dedicated of queens. You get off on this, don't you, Rena? You get off on the notion that you are so irresistibly sexual, so alluringly female that even Ajax here, who has struggled all her life to be a woman, will now do an about-face and – for your sake alone, just to get closer to you – struggle to be a man.'

'You don't know what you're talking about, David,'

Ajax said quietly. 'If you can't say something nice, just keep quiet.'

'As usual you're dead wrong, Harwood,' Rena said with a sudden, festive laugh that seemed to blow up out of nowhere. 'Totally off target. Who said anything about converting "the poor, befuddled faggot," as you so flat-footedly put it? Not that it's any of your business, but if you must know, I'm the one who's been converted. I've become a lesbian.'

We all sat motionless in silence for two seconds before Granny came to our rescue. 'Congratulations!' she said as she reached over to pat Rena on the back. 'Good for you, my girl! That's very plucky, I must say. I like a gal who can be so adaptable. And at your age too – exactly how old are you again, Rena dear?'

Rena turned to look at Granny but didn't bother answering. We were still waiting for something, I'm not sure what. Probably for Harwood to finish exploding, or for Ajax to step in and resume the role of camp director she had been playing all morning, or for Rena to let out another wild laugh and scream, 'Just kidding! But I sure gotcha that time, didn't I?' None of them did any of these things, however, and when Harwood finally broke this latest silence, it was in a quiet and defeated voice.

'You've lost me,' he said. 'I'm not even going to try to follow this one anymore.' He lifted his glass. 'Best of luck to you. As for me, I don't want to think about any of it. Not now.'

'Yes, here's to Ajax and Rena,' I chimed in, following Harwood's lead. 'Are you guys really going to get married?' I asked. The longer the notion survived as a real possibility, the more exciting it began to seem. I had never been to a wedding. 'Will you have a big party and everything?' I asked. 'Who gets to wear the white dress?'

'Slow down, silly,' said Ajax as she reached across to straighten my helmet, which had slipped sideways on my head. 'We've got plenty of time to figure all that out, and you can help. I promise. But right now is Crawlspace Day, and you're the one we should be toasting. To Elray! To Elray and Barkley and Jack!'

'Hear, hear!' Rena said. 'Let us raise a glass to all the Mayhew and Harwood family members – past, present and future!'

'Hear, hear!' Granny joined in. 'And as a Mayhew who's been born again, so to speak, I would like to propose a special toast to the Mayhew who is yet unborn.' This time it was Rena's turn to blush as we all raised our glasses and nodded toward her belly, and it was Harwood's turn to let loose with a strange laugh.

'That raises an interesting question, doesn't it,' he said, as he refilled his glass. 'If you do marry Ajax as you say you plan to, Rena, what surname will you give your mystery babe? Mayhew? My my, this IS getting twisted.'

'Leave it alone, why don't you,' Ajax muttered. 'You're the one who just said you don't want to think about any of it right now. So leave it alone.'

'How right you are. I really don't want to think about it,' Harwood agreed. 'But I do have one question,' he added as he leaned across the table and grabbed Rena's wrist. 'One question that should be easy to answer, my little androgynous, switch-hitting siren. Is there any chance, any possibility at all, that this baby growing inside you is the child of that overripe, forbidden fruit sitting next to you? Is there any chance that you have been impregnated by your cross-dressing, male lesbian fiancée – Elray's Auntie Ajax?'

Rena stared at Harwood and stretched her lips back in an expression that was more a show of teeth than a smile. 'You know, Harwood,' she said as she began to pry his fingers from around her wrist, 'in a world where I can fall in love and get married, I have to figure just about anything's possible. Now, if you'll all excuse me,' she said, turning to the rest of us, 'I'm going to head upstairs and rest. Thank you for the lovely Crawlspace Day, Elray. Ajax. Granny. It's been wonderful, but I think I've hit my limit. It's time for a little toes-up.'

Thus ended my Tenth Annual Crawlspace Day. We had all hit the wall – absorbed as much alcohol and food and information and emotion as our systems would take. One by one we excused ourselves from the table and headed, in a bent-back shuffle, for the crawlspace exit. All of us, that is, except Harwood, who sat in his chair and watched us.

As I stepped from the crawlspace into the side yard, I had to blink against the light. The rain had stopped. The sun was shining now on a world that looked freshly painted, its colors wet and clean. Rena is right, I thought as I watched Ajax and Granny and Rena pick their way, linked arm in arm, across the soggy lawn. Anything is possible in this world. Anything is possible.

Birth of a Notion

Technically the season was late fall, but in the months following my tenth Crawlspace Day the mood in our house on High View Street was more akin to that of spring. We all seemed to be budding. And if the prevailing mood in our High View house that fall can be likened to spring, as a group its occupants resembled one of those conventions of spring robins that blanket tender young lawns, with all the birds standing shoulder to shoulder, pecking intensely at one square inch of turf while avoiding even the slightest eye contact with one another. With near-comic narcissism, as if each of us believed ourselves the lone and noble harbinger of a brave new season, my housemates and I all burrowed into newfound obsessions.

Rena was literally blooming, of course. In late November she and Ajax slipped off to City Hall and tied the knot in a quiet civil ceremony with Granny Mayhew and me as witnesses. The newly-weds were fixated on each other, and on the baby growing inside Rena.

Granny was starting over as Ajax's mother, and testing her talents as grandmother and mother-in-law for the first time. But more important, she had auditioned for and landed a part in a musical presentation of *Arsenic and Old Lace* that was being staged at the National Theatre downtown. Every day she went skipping out of the house like a schoolgirl, a knapsack of rehearsal accessories slung over one shoulder, and disappeared into the city. Usually she was gone right through dinner, and sometimes it was one or two in the morning before I heard her come tiptoeing upstairs to bed, humming show tunes.

Harwood had taken the job at *National Geographic* magazine – the first full-time staff position he had ever surrendered to, he confessed over a last supper of sushi and sake that the two of us shared on the eve of his first day at work. Within twenty-four hours of reporting to the job, Harwood had been sent to Antarctica to shoot a story on blue whales, and from then on he was rarely around our home for longer than two days at a stretch. When he was, he logged most of his time in a comalike sleep – either because he was suffering a wicked case of jet lag or because he preferred to avoid all of us.

I, not wishing to be outdone, hurled myself at my own new toy, my movie camera. The seeds for this had been sown by the very, very underground premiere of the invincibility films at my custody trial, and by the minor fuss that resulted over my so-called natural talent as a cinematographer. Shoving aside the inconvenient fact that Raoul had coproduced the Library of the Invincible, I rolled like a sea otter in the sappy compliments about the 'singular cinematic vision' behind the films. I let myself get giddy with the first tingle of competence I had felt in a long time.

Ajax was my most fanatical supporter. It was she who had masterminded the gift of the camera on my tenth Crawlspace Day, and as it turned out, the 'little project' that she mentioned briefly on that day would eventually become the focus of my first serious film effort. But by far the most significant response to my films in the aftermath of the trial came not from Ajax, but courtesy of Melba Cairns, a walleyed blonde who was the court reporter at my trial. Melba, as luck would have it, was married to the head of the film department at American University. Evidently she thought my films intriguing enough to merit a mention to her husband, and one day in mid-November, after he'd made a brief telephone call to introduce himself, the doorbell rang and there stood Albert Cairns himself.

Although I hadn't a clue as to who he was when he first appeared, I took one look and decided there was something innately heroic about the figure before me. Perhaps it was the black leather jacket that encased his upper torso with all the polish of a suit of armor. Perhaps it was the subtle hum of paradox he exuded: his black jeans crumpled around his ankles in a way that made him look expandable – as though he had only collapsed himself temporarily to this, our normal human scale – while his oddly under-sized spectacles suggested that he could be reduced to some other, far more diminutive dimension. He gave the impression, in other words, of being at once both large and microscopic. His ice-blue eyes were back-lit and peered out upon the world at wildly independent angles. This disarmingly skewed effect was compounded by his feet, which appeared to be permanently set at about ten past nine. I took one long, soaking look at this man and decided he was divine.

'You're amazing.' The ridiculous greeting fell from my open mouth as I stood there staring through our out-of-season screen door at Albert.

'You're Elray,' he said back. 'I recognize you. I'm Albert. May I come in? 'S cold as a box-office flop out here.'

Minutes later the two of us had made a full tour of the first floor of my house, my mysterious visitor in the lead and me following behind, answering whatever questions he posed. At one point I stepped aside as he walked around Harwood's statues for several minutes, studying them with his crazy, crooked vision.

'Your work?' he asked, rubbing his chin.

'My uncle's,' I answered.

'Interesting,' he nodded. 'Very Paleolithic. Very

missing link. Can I have something to eat?' We moved to the kitchen, where I served my guest a big bowl of cereal and two pieces of toast with butter and honey. It was only after he'd polished these off that Albert finally got around to the topic of why he had come.

'Melba says you've got scary raw talent,' he announced. 'A liquid eye like Jean-Luc Godard. Melba's usually right. Can I see your films? Talent excites me.'

Two hours later, after an attic screening of all the invincibility films, Albert gave an impromptu lecture on film in general and pronounced my own footage 'effin' beautiful.' It was there, with this endorsement, that my relationship to my so-called talent was drop-kicked from the subliminal to the ridiculous. I might just as well have donned a black beret and started carrying a folding director's chair everywhere, so taken was I with my new status as filmmaker extraordinaire.

At that moment the only thing that rivaled my infatuation with myself was my infatuation with Albert Cairns. By the time I waved good-bye to him from our front door that day, I had agreed to appear, with my films, as a guest lecturer at one of his classes the following Thursday. Ten minutes after his quixotic figure had disappeared over the horizon at the end of our street, I was wearing my own leather jacket – the one Harwood had given me for Crawlspace Day – and my own black jeans. Like all who suffer truly obsessive crushes, I wanted not just to be near my beloved; I was desperate to become him.

Over the next few days I ate almost nothing – in his attic lecture Albert had mentioned that 'vision is heightened by hunger' – and I wandered the city with a new purpose: to 'practice my eye,' as Albert had described it. I parked myself on street corners for hours and stared at the negative space defined by the edges of tall buildings. I watched for the tunnels and washes and flat sheets of light that were layered through the ordinary world around me, defining bright pages of a strange story waiting to be told. I studied crowds of pedestrians as they approached, looking always for the protagonists among them, and for what is was that made them so.

When I had exhausted the visual effects of a scene, I would shut my eyes and let the noises and smells wash over me; then, with my eyes still closed, I would try to give these sensations fresh visual expression. Downtown, with its clanking fuming traffic, translated into a short-order kitchen during the breakfast rush on a morning when the toaster was on the blink, burning all the toast. In the formal gardens of Dumbarton Oaks, where the busy purr of insect life hung in pastel-quiet air, I closed my eyes and saw a pointillist rendition of a huge family picnic.

In every scene that I saw or imagined, I searched for what Albert had referred to as the 'forgotten spinning wheel.'

'It's got to be there. Whether implicit or explicit, it's got to be there, in every single story,' he had spluttered as he paced back and forth in my attic, silhouetted against the empty movie screen. 'The forgotten spinning wheel, the trap that bagged Sleeping Beauty. Ineluctability – that's what makes the story roll. And that's what is so superb, so fantastic about these films you have made, Elray. You absolutely have it, you've captured it in the most primal, visual way. Every shot sizzles with clarity and mystery at once. Do you realize that?'

I had nodded hesitantly at the time, anxious only that Albert keep talking, keep saying flattering things about me, keep moving his noble self back and forth across the floor right there in my attic, where I could sit and stare at him. But during the next week, in the course of my long city walks and at night as I lay wide-eyed in my bed, I had no idea why the films should have elicited such excitement from Albert or anyone else. Equally if not more troubling was my other guilty secret, the knowledge that I personally had nothing to do with whatever it was that was excellent in the films. Raoul and I had made the films together, and clearly Raoul was the source of any genius. I was a prop, an extra, a grip with no grasp.

As my lecture date at American University approached I became more and more agitated. I was the emperor at the moment when he first senses but is not quite ready to accept the truth about his 'new clothes.' On the Monday before the fateful Thursday appointment, I finally called Albert to cancel my lecture. But the moment I heard his voice I realized that the real reason I had called was for exactly that – to hear his voice.

'Elray,' Albert said in his raspy gurgle that had a touch of the thug in it. 'How funny. I was just thinking of you.'

'Oh, really?' I could hardly speak.

'Yes, really. I was reading this morning's front-page piece in the *Times*, about the recent discovery of ancient cave paintings in southern France. It reminded me of you, of how I discovered you.'

'You mean Melba,' I corrected him.

'Who?'

'Melba. Your wife,' I answered. 'Technically it was she who "discovered" me – or discovered the films, anyway. I don't think there's much to discover in me.'

'Sure there is. You're my new rising star. Speaking of stars, did you watch the sunset last night? Did you notice the light?'

'Mmmhmm, yes I did.' My heart began to race, as if I were a contestant fielding a ten-million-dollar question on a TV game show.

'Well?'

'Pink-grapefruit light. Underbelly light. Interior-of-a-conch light. Last Supper light. There were a lot of ways to see it, a lot of stories to tell.'

'Good girl.' Albert sounded genuinely pleased. 'Are we still on for Thursday?' he asked. 'Why don't I swing by your house and pick you up, so you don't get lost. How does that sound?'

I paused, and then surrendered. 'Sounds fine,' I answered. 'Just fine. Thursday. I'll be here.'

I've heard that hard-core panic can embolden even the timid to fearsome feats. In my case, terror of the humiliation I would suffer at my upcoming lecture inspired me to do something I would otherwise never have considered. I called Raoul. I really felt I had no choice. I no longer hoped – or even wished, for that matter – to cancel my engagement at the university. As far as I could tell this was my only means to the only end I now coveted: spending more time with Albert. I had already girded myself to go through with my guest-lecture stint, and now worried only about how I could minimize the damage to my dignity. I considered feigning laryngitis, or saying simply: 'These films speak for themselves.' But I knew that Albert, who saw language as a kind of performance art, would probably dispose of me like a bad zoom shot if I went mute. No, I had to actually have something to say. I had to understand what made the films what they were. I had, therefore, to call Raoul.

'Hello? Hello? Who's there?' Raoul answered after two rings. His voice sounded impossibly deep. Could Raoul have become a full-grown man? The notion seemed so unfair, I was temporarily unable to speak.

'HELL-O-HOH?' Raoul's big voice came booming through the phone in a tone that sounded final, as if he were only seconds away from hanging up.

'Hi, Raoul? Yeah. Hi, it's me. It's Elray.' My own voice sounded flat and dirty and all used up after Raoul's vigorous roar.

'ELRAY? This is ELRAY?' Why did he have to shout my name like that? Now I was the one on the verge of hanging up. But the thought of Albert's inquisitive, crooked stare stopped me. I was desperate, I needed help. It was already Tuesday; I had no time to waste.

'Yes, surprise surprise, Raoul, it's Elray. Listen, would you ever be willing to meet me and watch the invincibility films and discuss them with me? I'm doing a study on "Partnership in Art" for my art class this year and, well, I'm supposed to draw on personal as well as historical examples wherever possible.' I got right down to business, lying like a big dog all the while.

'Wait a second, slow down. You want me to do what? "Partnership in Art"?' He sounded skeptical. 'What has that got to do with the invincibility films?'

'Well, not much, I know. We were hardly partners and they were hardly art . . . But I'm really up against a wall on this one – not much time left. It would help me so much, Raoul. And it won't take long, I promise. We can meet anytime that's convenient for you. Anytime in the next day and a half, that is.' I couldn't stand the way I sounded, but Raoul seemed to enjoy it. He hedged for a few minutes, made me beg some more, gave me a hard time about having procrastinated as usual and then agreed to meet me at seven the following evening on what he insisted would be 'neutral territory' – Conference Room C on the first floor of the Sheraton Park Hotel.

'How do you know this Conference Room C will be available tomorrow evening?' I asked. I was not looking forward to lugging the projector and films all over town.

'Because it always is. Trust me,' Raoul said. 'Hey, Elray,' he added.

'What.'

'You sound so weird. You sound so . . . so normal.'

'Yeah?'

'Are you? Are you normal now, Elray? Because that would be weird.'

'I don't know. You tell me, Raoul. I'll see you tomorrow. Conference Room C.' This time I did hang up.

Close Encounters

Raoul and I converged on Conference Room C at the same time from opposite directions at seven the next night. We were both wearing – guess what – leather jackets and jeans. My jacket was Harwood's hand-me-down, lovely and old; Raoul's was brand new, but nice enough anyway. He looked huge in it; he was huge.

'After you,' Raoul said as he twisted the knob and pushed open the door to the conference room. 'It's "available," you'll notice.' It was true, the room was unoccupied by people; but it was stuffed to the gills with furniture. Mattresses, mostly, I realized as my eyes adjusted to the lack of light. For some reason I thought immediately of the bedroom in the storybook *Madeline*, where twelve little beds were lined up in two rows of six.

'In an old house in Paris that was covered with vines, lived twelve little girls in two straight lines,' I began to recite.

'What?' Raoul asked.

'Nothing. What kind of conferences do you suppose they hold here?'

Raoul laughed. 'None, dummy. They've been using this room as storage while they renovate the rooms upstairs. Nobody ever comes in here. I found it several months ago.'

'They store everything here? What an odd way to do things. Don't you think?'

'I don't know, Elray. Why don't you drop them an interoffice memo on efficiency.' Raoul sounded almost annoyed. Probably because I hadn't displayed enough delight over his 'find.' But I didn't care. I was here on business. I had work to do.

'Okay, which is the best viewing wall?' I asked, scanning the room. 'Probably this one here with no doors. Right?' I waded across the mattresses with the projector.

Two minutes later I had flipped the projector on and threaded the conglomerate reel with all the invincibility films. Raoul had already sprawled himself over a pile of mattresses, and as the opening frames of *The Art of Dying* came into focus I crawled over and made a nest for myself nearby.

'Here we go,' I said. I felt strangely nervous, as if my whole system was going tic tic tic rattle tic with the projector. This had been a terrible idea, I decided, to come here with Raoul to watch these films. But it was too late now.

'Yep. Here we go. Dropping. Be both pebble . . . and feather when you drop . . .' Raoul was reciting the lines along with the film's sound track, in a voice that sounded sludgy and drugged – either that or my ears were losing their hold. Yes, something was slipping – and then I realized what it was. It was the two of us. We were dying, the same way we always had. I turned my head toward Raoul and was not at all surprised to see that he had stretched himself out straight and still as a corpse. Exactly as he was on screen but without the coffin. A wave of something sweet and lost washed over me, and I cast a downward glance at my own body. I could feel it changing density, stiffening, dropping. I told myself I shouldn't surrender to this – I was here for other reasons. But dying was so easy, so familiar, so cozy. I closed my eyes and for one last time let the still black water fill my lungs, my neck, my head, my eye sockets . . .

'Here. We. Go,' I gurgled, happy to know I might

never speak again. It took all my effort then to roll my head in Raoul's direction, and this time I was surprised – but only mildly – to find that he had changed his position. He remained as straight and stiff as a corpse, but he had moved over and was lying right beside me now. I stared at him, and for a moment I thought I heard someone trying to speak to me from far away. Then I realized it was not a voice that had registered – it was the distant sensation of touch. Something was touching me; it was Raoul's right hand, holding my left hand. Our fingers packed around each other.

'Let's dance.' Raoul turned to me with his liquid black stare and said this in a sludgy, wrong-rpm voice. 'Let's. Go. Dance. With the dead.'

It sounded good, and I wanted to squeeze yes to Raoul the way I had by the river so long ago. But I had dropped too far out of myself. It didn't matter. The two of us were already spiraling off, falling and rising at the same time, together, into the peculiarly dense weightlessness of a dead man's float. I wondered how far we could drop, linked like this. I wondered if we would ever resurface, or if we might act as anchors, weighting each other down into a permanent oblivion. It really didn't matter; I really didn't care.

'Elray.' Had Raoul said my name? Was it possible he could still speak? 'Elray, Elray, Elray.' Yes, he, or someone, was saying my name in a quiet sighing tone. I couldn't see anything anymore but I could still hear.

'Elray, I've been dying for you,' the voice whispered. 'Literally. Just dying. For years. Did you know that?'

I didn't know what to say, or even how to speak.

'I've been dying for you. But not now. We're not alone. Someone's watching. Have you noticed? Can you smell?'

I searched for the place where my sense of smell might have been, if I still had one. I searched, and found nothing at first. But then, ever so faintly, I crossed the trail of something – a pungent, almost funky seaside smell. Like the rocky coast of Maine at low tide. And then another, more acid scent, like oil paints or turpentine or both.

'Someone's here,' the voice that I knew must be Raoul said. 'The dead are watching. Let's dance with the dead.'

I was not sure exactly what he meant by this, but no sooner had the suggestion been made than we were doing it. Swooping and swirling, pirouetting wildly, wrapped now in a tight embrace, we plummeted through the blind, fathomless atmosphere of some other place.

We had a brief but lovely and reckless dance, and when it was over the two of us shot upward together, still wrapped in each other's arms. Back toward the surface of life. I flinched as oxygen spread through my lungs and light came stabbing back at my eyes and a thunderous pounding began to echo in my ears. It was the throb of blood and living tissue; it was the pounding of Raoul's warm body arched against my own. His face was only inches from mine, and I watched as flecks of color and light displaced the liquid black of his eyes. I watched him, and when he was fully alive he sent me a smile it was impossible not to return.

'Old habits die hard,' he whispered after a few minutes.

'Yes,' I whispered back. 'Die and learn.'

On screen we had risen too. *The Art of Dying* was over and our reincarnated selves were up there handling snakes and other reptiles in the various scenes of *Domesticating Fear*. Gingerly, awkwardly, Raoul and I edged out of our tight embrace, but still we held hands.

'So what is it exactly we were doing in these films?' I asked, somewhat abruptly. I was fully alive again, fully myself, and feeling very self-conscious. I thought of Albert and my lecture, and a mix of panic and chagrin swept over me. What had I been thinking, what had I been doing? I hadn't extracted a single piece of useful information from Raoul yet. 'What was it we did in *The Art of Dying*?' I asked. 'What was your favorite thing we did?'

'What did we do?' Raoul sounded confused.

'Yes, what was the most artful part, do you think?' I asked.

Raoul was silent for a while and then he shrugged his shoulders. 'It wasn't what we did, Elray – it was what we didn't do. With us the big thing was always what we DIDN'T do. At least it was for me.'

'What we didn't do?' It was my turn to sound perplexed.

'Exactly.' Raoul tightened his grip on my hand and edged toward me.

'But I don't understand you. Show me – tell me what's the best thing about this scene, for instance. This scene we're watching right now.' On screen I was standing in the bamboo patch, lowering a big boa constrictor into a cloth sack. 'What makes this scene . . . sizzle?' I tried to remember the language Albert had used when he praised the films.

"Sizzle"? This scene?' Raoul turned his focus to the screen. 'Why, it's just as I said. The best thing about this scene is not what's there – it's what isn't there. The best thing I see in this scene is the way your blue jeans fit – the way you have a . . . a buffer zone of air all around each of your legs inside each of your pant legs. That's what really "sizzles" here – the way your legs don't quite fill your pants. That's what's hot.'

I stared at Raoul. He had gone mad. Either that, or he was being obnoxious, trying to make fun of me. Making fun of my skinny legs. It never occurred to me, not for an instant, that his comment could be construed as a compliment, or even as the opening salvo of a come-on. I withdrew my hand and sat up.

'Raoul, please. Be serious. Help me out here; this is why I asked you to meet me. I'm perfectly willing to admit that it was your talent that carried these films. I'm just asking you to share a little. Help me to understand – or remind me, rather, what it was we were doing. Artistically.'

Raoul sat up and scratched at a flattened patch of hair on the back of his head. He rubbed wearily at his face with his hands, as if he had paused on a forced march to splash off over a roadside puddle. Then he looked up at me with a heavy sigh.

"My talent"?' He spat the words as if they tasted bad. 'What are you talking about, Elray? I don't know why you always have to get so agitated and intense. I don't have any talent – not for making films, anyway. *You* might have a little, if your camera work here is anything to go on. But I wouldn't say either one of us will be making an Oscar acceptance anytime soon. We made these films when we were children, you know. They're very meaningful to us, to you and to me. But time passes, things change, people move along. Stop picking at the films. They were great – they ARE great. But they are over. We made them a long time ago.'

Raoul was right, of course. I can see that now. But at that moment I still needed the films, desperately – my entire future seemed predicated on them, and on my understanding whatever there was to be seen in them. I wouldn't let up. 'What do you mean my "camera work"?' I asked. 'Talk to me about my camera work. Show me.'

Raoul sighed again and pinched the bridge of his nose. 'I don't know, Elray. I really don't know what you want sometimes. But let me try. Let me try once more, and then let's get out of here. Okay. Your camera work.' He straightened up and stared at the screen and then launched into rapid-fire-lecture mode.

'Okay, now take a look.' Raoul gestured toward the screen, where he was now pictured sitting in a bathtub feeding raw hamburger to a two-foot caiman. 'This is a scene you shot, obviously. Surely you've noticed that whenever you're behind the camera everything looks a lot better in these films. Which may seem to contradict what I just said about you in your blue jeans – but not

362

really. Because that was a scene that I filmed, and therefore the best thing about it is that you are in it, the way you look in it.

'Anyway, this is a scene that you shot, and it is distinctly superior,' he continued. 'Notice the oblique angle you use, which creates the illusion that Ralphie the caiman is almost as big as I. Notice the simplicity and the fluidity of the sequence of shots you choose, and notice most of all the . . . how shall I describe it? The reticence with which you film. Once again, you accomplish so much by what you do not do, by what you do not show. Are you following me?' Raoul paused and looked at me quizzically. I stared back at him, unsure if I had really just heard what I thought I'd heard. Unsure if he was serious, or launched on high satire. It didn't matter. I was taking mental notes on everything he said. I was going to use it all.

I stared at the screen with new eyes as Raoul continued to analyze the camera work, scene by scene, unveiling my 'talent' to me. Had I really done – or refrained from doing – all the marvelous things he attributed to me? Now that he had pointed it out, I could see the difference between the scenes I had shot and those filmed by him. I had never noticed before – in fact, even as I was filming I had never really thought about angles or sequences of shots or any of the techniques he was praising. I had just held the camera to my eye and tried to tell the story.

Raoul paused for a minute, and I looked at him. 'Raoul,' I began hesitantly. 'Why is it, if you were aware of all this "camera work," as you call it, and I wasn't – at least, not until you explained it to me – why is it that you weren't doing it and I was? How is that possible?'

'I don't know.' Raoul shrugged. ' "Genius does what it must, and talent does what it can." Right? Not that I'm quite ready to grant you "genius" status, but there does seem to be something innate about your film work. You've got a touch of the noble savage when it comes to the camera, I guess. Kills me to admit it, Tree, but I think it's true.'

I could have kissed Raoul, he had made me so happy. Granny had raved about the films, and so had Ajax and Harwood and Rena and Albert, but it was Raoul's grudging praise that made me proudest. It was Raoul's articulation of my talent that made it real, that made it mine. I looked at him as he sat cross-legged next to me on a lumpy sea of mattresses, still pale and hollow-eyed from our recent death, and I knew he was the most remarkable friend I would ever have. Long ago he had thrown before me the glorious challenge of my own invincibility. Now he had held up a mirror and transformed my image of myself. He had handed me my life.

'Raoul.' I whispered his name hoarsely, afraid that noise or movement might wake me up, might prove this all a dream. 'Raoul, you have been such a help to me. More than a help – an inspiration. More than an inspiration even – an angel really. An angel. What can I do for you, Raoul? How can I thank you?'

He stared back at me with his calm young face, so familiar to me it could have been my own, and shook his head sadly. 'What I want I can't ask for,' he said. 'It has to be given. And you don't have it to give, not yet. I can tell.'

'What do you mean?' I asked, confused by his riddle. 'I'll give you anything I have. What do you want, Raoul? Tell me.' He reached over and took my two hands and turned them palms upward. Then he rested the fingers of his own hands lightly on top.

'I'll think of something else,' he said. 'I'll think of something I can ask for. Okay?'

I nodded, eager to prove my own generosity.

'Okay, tell me, Tree,' he said. He leaned toward me, and I could feel his warm breath against my ear. 'Tell me,' he whispered. 'Who was watching us die?'

I flinched, his question was so bold. It felt like a violation, really. You weren't supposed to drag things from the dark side to the bright like that, drag them right into conversation. No one had ever said so explicitly, I just knew it.

'What are you talking about?' I said. It was a statement of disapproval, and an obvious evasion. I knew it and Raoul knew it, and I was ashamed of my dissembling words as they hung in the air. I was especially ashamed after all Raoul had just done for me. 'Oh, you mean just now, just when we were—' I mumbled feebly, trying to make amends but only making things worse.

'Never mind,' Raoul interrupted. 'Forget it.' He had pulled away from my ear and withdrawn his hands from mine and was already standing up. 'It's getting late,' he said. 'I've got to go.' I watched him stretching awkwardly, rubbing at his face as if this might rid it of the color that had risen to his cheeks, and I understood that he was as embarrassed for having asked his question as I was for dodging it. I began to feel even worse.

'Raoul.' I stood too, and reached over to touch his shoulder. I wanted to fix things, as quickly as possible. 'Raoul, whoever was watching us . . . I'm not sure, I think it might be my parents. Barkley and Jack. They're waiting for me. They love it when I get close.' I stared at my toes. Everything I said only made things worse, it seemed. 'I don't know, Raoul,' I finally said, sighing. 'I don't know what I'm doing.' There was a long silence, and I was sure that if I looked up I would see that Raoul had left. I had spoiled everything, I had done everything wrong. Even the discovery that my potential 'talent' was potentially real seemed dreary at that moment. I threw myself facedown on the mattresses and let a long groan rise out of my chest. But then, mid-groan, I stopped.

'Shhhhhhhhhh.' Raoul had not left. He was right there. His hands were on my shoulders, massaging them gently. 'I'm sorry I asked that question,' he whispered warmly into my hair as he pressed his face against the back of my head. 'I shouldn't have. You didn't have to answer. Shhhh. I'm sorry, I'm sorry. Elray?' He was turning me now, turning me the way you would turn a corpse that lay facedown. Tentatively, hopefully, looking for vital signs. 'Elray?' He said my name so quietly, so tenderly, as he turned me over.

'Raoul.' I spoke as gently as he, and with a small smile. 'Don't worry, I'm okay.' His face was so close to mine it wasn't his face anymore, it was ours. His face moved toward mine while something – something like a rope – was extracted deliciously from the midsection of my body. The rope was hope, I realized. And my hope was to kiss Raoul. My blood was thundering through my veins. And then the mouth that was about to become mine spoke.

'Elray,' it murmured. 'You are beautiful.' My thundering blood went quiet. The rope of my hope snapped and fell away. My breath turned to lead in my lungs. Clair. I had forgotten about Clair. What a fool I'd been. I saw as clearly as if I'd filmed the scene myself that Clair Moskowitz and Raoul had reclined together on these same mattresses in this same room. It was obvious.

I sat up and shoved at Raoul. 'I've got to go now,' I said.

Raoul looked genuinely upset. 'What is it, Elray?' he asked. 'What . . . What's wrong?'

'WHERE IS CLAIR!' I screamed this right in his face and then I jumped up and started to pack up my projector and films. Raoul was saying something behind me, but I couldn't hear him. He kept talking but I didn't listen or react at all, until I felt his hand on my back. Then I whirled on him.

'Don't touch me!' I snapped. 'I have a boyfriend, you know. He would be very angry if you touched me. He's older, and bigger.'

'You have a boyfriend?' Raoul pronounced the question with a tone of incredulity that infuriated me further.

'Yes. Yes, I do.' I dug deeper into my lie. 'Alberto. That's his name.'

'Alberto. Oh, I see.' Raoul nodded sadly, as if the name legitimized the whole notion.

'Yes, Alberto. Well, it's none of your business really. But yes.' I was beginning to feel silly. Why was it that Raoul always inspired the most ridiculous lies in me? I wanted to go home.

'Well, anyway, thanks for everything,' I said as I tried to gather myself and stuck my hand out for a farewell shake. 'You know, for the analysis of the camera work, and all that. And good luck on your own, um, projects.'

'Sure. No problem. Thanks.' Raoul just stood there, staring at me, until finally I turned and walked away. I was almost gone, almost out the door, when he spoke one last time.

'Hey, Elray,' he called. I turned my head but not my body toward him. 'Elray, I just wanted to say . . . For what it's worth? You're definitely not normal yet. You're still weird.'

'Thanks, Raoul.' I smiled at him. 'So are you.'

Losing Power

My appearance as a guest lecturer at Albert's university went brilliantly, thanks to Raoul and the gift of confidence he had presented to me during our odd encounter in the room full of mattresses. I had walked away from that meeting filled with a dull ache – an ache as useless as an underwater scream. But I had also walked away suffused, beneath the ache, with a bright sense of myself. Less than twenty-four hours later, as I stood onstage in the American University auditorium and stared out at a sea of expectant and unfamiliar faces, I still didn't have a lot to say about my films. But at least I believed I had every right to be standing there. This, combined with a few performance tips I had gleaned from Granny Mayhew at the last minute, got me through my ordeal.

'Memorize a couple of great lines – preferably somebody else's,' Granny had advised me when she arrived home late on the eve of my lecture and found me rehearsing my opening remarks in front of Harwood's statues. 'Hold them in your back pocket and deliver them strategically. To plug the holes. You'll be amazed, Logan. Also, never underestimate the power of silence. Remember, your average audience cannot distinguish between an unspoken wisdom and an unthought wisdom.'

That night I picked through *The Oxford Dictionary of Quotations* for a few pithy remarks. The next day I dropped these remarks, as needed, into the big hollow silences that came rolling up as I stood there at the lecture podium. When someone asked me about my inspiration for the 'stark format' in *The Art of Dying*, I cribbed from the Reverend Sydney Smith: 'A good question.' I nodded. 'But think of it this way: Death must always be distinguished from dying, with which it so often is confused.' A hush spread through the room and no further questions were asked about that particular film. Finding myself in a similar bind while answering questions about *Domesticating Fear*, I stole from Dryden: 'He has no hope, who never had a fear,' I pronounced. 'He has. NO HOPE. Who never had a fear.'

Although I couldn't see him because he was sitting behind me throughout my lecture, I could sense the happy thrum of Albert's approval at each of these remarks, and this too fed my new confidence. When *Free Heeling* finally came to its accidental and inconclusive conclusion, I loosed some modified Swinburne on the perplexed-looking crowd. 'Night is the shadow of light,' I intoned. 'And Life, of course, the shadow of death.' After a long moment of silence, wild applause erupted. Then Albert was right there by my side, squeezing then patting then squeezing my shoulders as he said 'Thank you, thank you Elray' over and over again.

Two days after my lecture date, I, Elray Mayhew, who all my life had had only peculiar and private friendships with a few family members and Raoul, seemed to be a full-blown member of a full-blown clique quite apart from my family. It was, to be honest, more than I had bargained for. Albert, with his crazy cubist face and his abrupt, almost insolent interest in my 'talent,' fascinated me. I had a fantasy about the two of us – a naive and abstract fantasy in which Albert the Wise would lead me, his brilliant ingenue, through a beautiful pas de deux of pure art. What I had failed to realize was that Albert, like so many self-declared men of artistic vision, was not looking for a dance partner. He was the type of guy who needed a whole troupe.

Hence the clique. The jockeying, cooing circle of Albert's obsequious admirers. Students mostly, men and women alike, they tumbled and rolled and fell all over themselves in their efforts to be both near him and envied by each other. At first, before I detected the redundancy of their hopes, I found it a giddy and thrilling experience to be embraced by this throng; I mistook their intense, hair-splitting scrutiny of me for genuine interest. In retrospect I have tried to tell myself that their sheer numbers defeated my powers of levelheaded assessment. How else can I explain why it took me so long to recognize them for the fools they were?

Immediately after my lecture I started running with Albert and his gang – as if to do so were actually an invigorating and expanding way to spend this, my one and only life. I met with them for private viewings of obscure films in shabby student apartments all over town. I sat in smoky, dank corners of underfurnished and overpopulated bars, nodding sympathetically as one or two or a whole tableload gave vent to some extreme enthusiasm or despair – not one among them had any receptors, it seemed, for feelings of the middle range.

At each of these gatherings, there was a tacit understanding that until Albert arrived we were all of us on hold, saving our real selves for him. Albert was our Sun King. Only he could fill the void at our center. Only he could inspire our motley gaggle to the gravity and grace of a full and orderly galaxy.

Whenever he was among us, it was Albert who held the floor, scattering shot in his staccato and minimalist style. I was his newest – and youngest – prop that fall. I can see that so clearly now. He turned to me constantly, as a dandy would to a hand mirror, for a fresh and flattering reflection of himself.

'Tell us, Elray,' he might say as he held court with a

group of us in some soggy bar. 'What do you see in that corner, over there?'

'Over there? Why, a fat woman, drinking at the bar,' I would reply.

'Take it somewhere, give us more. Run with it,' he would prompt.

Knowing that what Albert really wanted from me was a script, I would begin to roll. 'I see a fat and disappointed fishwife drinking herself blind on Brandy Alexanders. She is here all alone tonight. Her husband, a simple but good-hearted fisherman, is also all alone tonight. But at home. He is propped in front of the television, his entire head wrapped in thick gauze bandaging.'

'His entire head is bandaged?' someone would take my bait. 'But – can he see the television?'

'No, he can't. But knowing that he is bathed by its pale green glow seems to soothe his pain.'

I cringe even now at the pretension of the supposed creative exercises at those gatherings. I, at least, have the excuse of my youth and inexperience; Albert, however, was in his mid-thirties and really should have known better. I don't know why I never wondered why a man of Albert's age would spend so much time with a crew of university students, let alone with teenage me. Who knows how long I might have drifted along if Ajax, who was getting more and more outspoken as she grew accustomed to her new public profile as husband and father-to-be, had not been so prompt to call a spade a spade when she met Albert for the first time.

That meeting occurred at a Christmas party that I had uncharacteristically decided to host for my new friends – 'the filmerinos,' Rena called them. In fact, the entire Christmas season had been unusually hectic in our house that year, because everyone in our expanded household of five seemed to have fallen simultaneously into a new sociability. We were all clique freaks.

Whenever he was in town Harwood had taken to hanging out with a circle of all-male photographer friends from the *Geographic* – a group of single, exceedingly vain, aging 'boys' in their late forties or early fifties who referred to each other as 'son' and told nonstop stories over nonstop beers of their worldwide adventures as world-class photographers. Granny had organized a group of octogenarian dancers and singers, the true survivors of show business, into a troupe called the Old Gray Geese. As their performance schedule geared up, the Geese began to gather regularly in our house, where they practiced their routines and reminisced about the old days and complained about the side effects of their heart medications.

Then there were the Ajax and Rena gangs. The newlyweds had enrolled in a Lamaze course together shortly after Rena's obstetrician had finally settled on a due date of March 14. ('Ah, the terrible Ides!' Harwood couldn't resist portending every time the date was mentioned. 'Shall we name the little bugger Caesar? Or Brutus? Or how about Harwood? What do you say, Rena?') But after only two sessions with the official class, Ajax, who had taught herself Lamaze some years ago when she first inherited me, had dropped out in disgust at the 'sodden little idiot of an instructress' and had begun to offer an alternate course of her own, right in our house. Two thirds of the original class had mutinied in favor of Ajax, and every Tuesday evening they could be found, puffing and panting like beached seals, scattered among Harwood's party-guest statues in our living room.

As a kind of offshoot of her Lamaze class, Ajax had started a counseling program for a group of women who were residents at a local institution known as the Florence Crittenden Home for Unwed Mothers-to-Be. It was typical of Ajax that in her joyful anticipation of having a baby with Rena, her mate for life, she had developed a sympathy for those who were in similar, but less fortunate, circumstances.

'Can you imagine having such a momentous event looming in your life and having no one to share it with?' Ajax had remarked to all of us after her first visit to the Florence Crittenden Home. Soon she was spending three or four afternoons a week there, playing the role of a 'surrogate sharer' in various exercises and trying to prepare the unwed mothers-to-be for the 'unparalleled challenges and joys of raising children alone.'

By the time Christmas rolled around it had seemed only natural, so to speak, that Rena and Ajax should throw a Lamaze class Christmas party at our house. And when the Crittenden gang got wind of the Lamaze party, they demanded a fete of their own. Soon after this Granny and Harwood had followed suit and organized Christmas parties for their newfound friends.

Finally, although I was the last to do so, I succumbed to the same errant social urge. Surrendering mainly to pressure from Albert, who had been asking for some time that I 'introduce us all to your unusual family,' I organized my own Christmas party, for my film gang. It was at this party that Ajax met Albert for the first time and sallied forth with her snap judgment on him.

'Have you met Elray's new guru?' Ajax said as she pushed Albert toward the very pregnant Rena. Rena was reclining on a pile of pillows on the floor at the time, in the comfortingly rotund company of Harwood's statues. 'Most amazing case of male arrested development,' Ajax hissed in a loud stage whisper as she reached down to help Rena to her feet. 'Check it out. Worst case I've ever seen.'

''S quite a statement,' Rena muttered back as she struggled to rise. 'Especially coming from someone who shares a house with the dreaded Dave Harwood, of *National Geographic*-slash-arrested-development fame.' Only then did Rena turn her wide Irish smile on Albert. 'How do you do, Elbert,' she wheezed at him in her overoxygenated pregnant voice, deliberately mispronouncing his name, I was sure. 'Tell me all about yourself, please. Elray here seems to think you extraordinary.'

'I work as a lens, a seeing aperture on the world,' said Albert.

'You work as a lens?' asked Rena.

'Yes. I translate the world,' Albert said, then nodded as he began shoveling hors d'oeuvres off a small plate and down his gullet.

'Hmmm. Translate into what? For whom?' asked Ajax.

'Into art. The universal language. Do you speak it?' said Albert.

No sooner had Albert stepped into my house and under the scrutiny of those who knew and loved me best than he was stripped of all his fine gloss. I resented this in Albert, but I resented it even more, of course, in Ajax and Rena and Harwood and Granny.

The original plan for my party had been to serve a buffet dinner and then, once everyone's plates were loaded, to have a screening of three new 'pieces,' including a Christmas short by Albert called *Soot Yourself*. But by the time Rena and Ajax appeared from our kitchen with dueling platters of poached salmon and asparagus for the buffet tables, I was in deep despair. I could not allow this intermingling of my two worlds, with all its terrible degenerative effects on each, to continue for a moment longer. As my guests squawked appreciatively at the food and began to divide into two feeding lines, I slid down to the basement on a mission of ambush. I walked to the back where all the fuse boxes were, and hunted until I found the electrical main.

'Let there be dark,' I whispered, and with the quick and ruthless touch of an executioner, I yanked the switch off.

From my spot in the basement it sounded as if the house itself let out a huge gasp the moment the lights went out. It had been a close call. But no one would be watching any films tonight, or even taking more than a gentle, candlelit look at each other. I could imagine how Ajax and Rena must be already moving to the rescue, to our stash of candlesticks on the high sideboard in the dining room. All the guests would be shifting and crowding into two groups, huddling in the glow from one or the other of the two fireplaces, as if the loss of light had made things cold as well as dark. The food on their plates — minutes ago yet another predictable holiday repast — would taste remarkable now, as all meals do when you are camping or at war or otherwise deprived of one or more of the amenities we have come to take for granted. Everyone would turn gratefully to this food and begin chatting with each other in a more attentive, less critical mode made possible by the accident of their impaired vision. And then everyone would go quietly home. Or so I sincerely hoped.

I was tired, I realized with a yawn. There was just too much going on. Albert and all my new acquaintances were turning into silly pumpkins all around me, and Ajax and Rena and Harwood and Granny were giving new meaning to the term 'family baggage.' My 'talent' was a joke. The sound of babies crying in my arm, the strange intercom to the mysterious nursery that I had confessed to on Crawlspace Day in an alcohol haze, had become more intense and almost painful at times in the last few weeks. Beneath all these discomforts there lay another deeper ache, a thudding sadness. A sadness begot of the unthinkable fact that Raoul could be still alive but not my friend.

I climbed up on one of Harwood's workbenches and stretched out on my back. I closed my eyes and folded my hands and tried to fall elsewhere, the way I would have half-died in the old days. I was drifting for a while, thinking about Raoul and how handsome he'd looked the last time I saw him, when I realized that the darkness was changing, brightening. Had I fallen asleep without realizing it? Was it daybreak already?

I sat up and surveyed the scene. The room was brighter, but not because the sun was rising. The light was coming from one of the miner's hard hats we all wore on Crawlspace Days. Ajax was wearing the hat. Standing behind Ajax were Granny, Rena and two others whom I thought I recognized as members of the Florence Crittenden crew.

'Elray?' Ajax called out to me as she raked me with the beam of light from her hat. 'Elray? My God, but you gave me a scare! What on earth are you doing?'

'Could you please not shine that light in my eyes,' I grumbled. 'I was trying to take a little rest. What about YOU? What are you doing, might I ask?'

'Power's out upstairs,' Rena said. 'We came to check the fuse boxes.'

'I already looked at them – they're all just fine,' I said. Technically this was not a lie. 'All five of you came to check the fuses?' I asked. It seemed like a strange way to attack the problem, by committee.

'Oh well, Granny was having a pyrophobic attack,' Ajax explained. 'You know, all the candles and everything. We had to get her out of there.'

'Oh, and do you remember Tamara and Angela?' Rena asked as she gestured toward the two other pregnant women. 'From the Crittenden Home?' Tamara was very dark and Angela was very pale; they looked like negative images of each other as they stepped forward with their big bellies and smiled at me. 'We've all been working together on building up our confidence and our self-reliance, you know,' Rena continued. 'So important to have both, don't you think? Especially if you're going to try to raise a little baby all by yourself. Well, as it happens, both Tamara and Angela are terrified of the dark, and this little power outage seemed like the perfect opportunity to exorcise that silly fear. Show them just how easily it can be squelched.'

'Of course,' I said, nodding. 'You must domesticate

your fears. Nothing to fear but fear itself, and all that.'

'Elray! Oh, yes yes yes. I'm so glad you've mentioned *Domesticating Fear*. The film, that is.' Ajax was rushing toward me with her miner's helmet still alight, leaving the others in dark shadows behind. 'You know, I've been meaning for ages to talk to you about this idea I have – an idea for a little film project that I think you could do so brilliantly. You've been so busy, what with school and all your new friends, I hadn't wanted to bother you. But since you mention it now yourself . . .'

For several minutes Ajax and Rena and I sat in the chilly basement, talking about the possible uses of film as a 'confidence-building' tool for women from the Florence Crittenden Home for Unwed Mothers-to-Be. Ajax was especially excited, and determined to sell her idea to me.

'Just think of the ways you have used film to bolster your own courage and to expand your own sense of invincibility,' she argued. 'And then think of what you would be doing for these women – not to mention for their unborn babies – if you were to boost their confidence in a similar way. They are all simply riddled with the most inane fears, you know.'

'It's true, it's true,' Rena joined in. 'One of them, a sweet woman named Darlene, is absolutely undone by midgets. Falls apart every time she sees one, even if it's on TV. Calls them roly-polies, and gets completely – and I mean COMPLETELY – rattled every time she sees one. Can you imagine?'

'Hmmm. That is pretty interesting.' I nodded. I was surprised by the enthusiasm I felt for Ajax's proposed project. I liked the idea of examining other people's problems instead of my own, drawing a bead on other people's fears. And this practical application of film, as a literal tool for whittling away fear and carving character, seemed so appealing after all the artsy la-la-poof talk of Albert and his crew.

'So what do you say?' asked Ajax. 'Will you give my

project a try? Will you come to the Home with your camera?'

I looked at Angela and Tamara as they stood waiting at a discreet distance, a pair of shy hippopotami. 'Okay, yes. I'll try,' I answered quietly.

'Fantastic!' Ajax screamed as she wrapped me in a bear hug.

'Brilliant!' Rena added and blew me a kiss.

'Hip hip hooray,' Granny called out glumly.

'What do you say, Elray?' Ajax asked a moment later. 'Shall we turn the power back on, or stay with the soft-candlelight look?'

I looked up at Ajax. 'How did you know?'

'Actually,' she muttered sheepishly as she offered me her arm, 'that was just a wild guess. And for once I was right?'

I nodded.

'Well, I wasn't so right about your friend Albert.' Ajax seemed determined to push on. 'I shouldn't have made those cracks about him, and I apologize. I talked to him some more, after you walked away, and you know he's really a very intriguing man.'

'Yes, yes, I'm sure,' I said, waving my hand in an effort to silence Ajax. It was too late. Albert had already been killed. 'Let's go up now, and let's leave it dark. More fun,' I said. I let myself lean against the side of Ajax's substantial torso and reached out for Rena's hand. The three of us made our way across the basement, a most unholy trinity. We gathered the others before us like our lost sheep, and headed in a herd back upstairs.

Part Eight

Coincidence Can Be Stronger Than Gravity

Of Rats and Men

The day began as simply and predictably as any other in the pearly-gray string of days that was February that year. The sun pushed meekly through a balding haze of clouds at exactly 6:12 A.M., and dawn broke here on earth – without any show of color or heat or even much light, as I recall. I am able to remember this, and to state categorically that there was no reason to think this day would be any different from those that came before or after, because I happened to be up and watching that cold winter morning. Poised behind my movie camera. I was waiting, in fact, for those first rays of enfeebled February daybreak to fall like dirty dishwater across the back parking lot of the Florence Crittenden Home for Unwed Mothers-to-Be.

For almost two months Ajax and Rena and I had been making our therapeutic films, trying to exorcise the wild assortment of bugaboos that afflicted the unwed mothers-to-be. We had been having great fun and a fair amount of success with our efforts, curing problems as diverse as a bad stammer and a neurotic phobia about sour milk. Even though the filming itself often involved getting up and in position before dawn – to catch the best light and to pack the work in before I had to head off to school – I was enjoying the project. I think it must have been the first time I had experienced the effortless gliding high that comes with sustained hard work at something you do well.

On that particular morning we were filming a scene that we hoped would help purge a young woman named Vanessa of her irrational fear of rats. The date was February 14 – Valentine's Day – a fact I probably would never have remembered if not for the surprising events that came later. Ajax was with me in the parking lot that morning, tending the caged live rats that were to be costars in our film, and Rena was also somewhere nearby, trying to coax Vanessa into the large, velvety-brown rat suit that we had created for her. Our strategy to vanquish Vanessa's phobia was two-pronged, and involved scenes where she identified with as well as scenes where she bullied the animals that inspired such terror in her.

Although I spent the next hour and a half filming a pregnant woman disguised in a rat suit as she prowled near a Dumpster and then chased a small band of rats across the empty parking lot, what I remember most vividly from that early-morning shoot are the sweet warm bites of a freshly baked doughnut that Ajax brought me to eat between takes, and the bitter, reviving mouthfuls of hot coffee with which I washed them down. Bits and pieces of the center-stage action also remain, of course; I can, for instance, remember the moment when I looked at Vanessa through the camera lens for the first time and immediately saw what none of us had noticed as we watched her struggle into her costume – that the puffy white snow boots on her feet bore no resemblance to rat paws. And I remember how we then traded footgear, Vanessa and I, she putting on the brown Irish brogues that I wore to school every day, and I slipping into the squishy white snow boots. And of course I remember the moment just before our last take of the morning when Vanessa got stuck in the mud.

'Let's loose these last two rats and call it a wrap,' I called out to Ajax as she stood by the Dumpster, preparing to free the last of the rodents we had purchased at a pet shop.

'Queen Rat! Are you ready?' I shouted for Vanessa, who had disappeared into the bushes at the back of the parking lot a few minutes earlier (Could it have been to pee? These pregnant women seemed to pee every other minute). 'Yoo-hoo, Vanessa! One last scene and we're finished.' A long moment of cold winter quiet followed, and then a tragic howl cut through the stillness. Ajax and Rena and I pelted across the parking lot and into the woods behind, where we found Vanessa, ankle-deep in a nasty patch of icy mud. Her rat head was bowed against her rat chest, and her shoulders shook with violent sobs.

'What is it, honey?' Rena asked after she'd picked her way right through the mud and put her arm around Vanessa.

'I'm stuck!' Vanessa wailed as she looked up and turned her tear-streaked, whiskered face to Ajax and me. 'I'm stuck. In the mud. Oh, your shoes, Elray! Just look at your SHOOOOOES!'

'Oh baby, please. Don't break my heart. Not on Valentine's Day,' Ajax said with a big smile. 'Here, come on out of there.' She offered Vanessa her hand. 'And for goodness' sake – don't worry about Elray's shoes. Not for a minute. We can clean them, can't we, Elray?'

I stared at my shoes and nodded as Rena began to whisper soothing things to Vanessa: 'Of course we can, of course we can. Hush now, honey, I know just how you feel; the strangest things can seem so sad when you're pregnant.' Then came a series of small sucking sounds – upside-down and backward noises, like wine bottles reswallowing their corks – as Ajax and Rena and Vanessa maneuvered themselves out of the mud and back to solid ground. And all the while I just stood there staring, saying nothing – for I was in the early phases of a brainstorm. A brainstorm that, if successful, might solve something that had been bothering me for some time. A brainstorm begot of the coincidence of Ajax's mention of Valentine's Day and the vision of Vanessa stuck in the mud.

We were all quiet for a minute or two, and then Rena spoke to me in a tone that was almost brusque. 'What is it, Elray?' she asked. 'Whatever is the matter?'

'Nothing. Oh, yes, well, nothing,' I stammered as I caught myself staring and looked up at all of them with an apologetic smile. 'But, I was just wondering . . . Do you think I could borrow that rat suit tonight? I have a party to go to, and absolutely nothing to wear.'

Some twelve hours later, at about 7:45 that evening, I was buttoning myself into the rat suit. On my feet I wore my still very muddy Irish brogues – at my insistence, they had not been cleaned – and tied to my arms and to the top of my head were bundles of sycamore twigs.

Parties, I had learned by then, were not my forte. But for all sorts of reasons I felt compelled to attend the one I had been invited to that evening. For starters, this particular fete was hosted by my drama teacher, a Miss Ziggy Potter, who was new at my school that year and quite frankly about the only reason I still managed to drag myself through the grim green halls of the Cathedral Academy at all. Ziggy, who had a cloud of wild blond hair and was about three decades ahead of the rest of the world in her blend of irreverent humor, had taken a special interest in me after learning about my experiments with film. She knew Albert, evidently. ('Oh God, yes. We go waaaay back, Albert Cairns and I,' she had said. 'Way, waaay back. Cockeyed Albert – do you know his walleyed wife Melba? "The groupers," I used to call the pair of them. Can you imagine being a fly on the wall in their kitchen? Wouldn't feel safe anywhere!')

Ziggy had pulled me aside in the hall at school one day earlier that month to tell me that she was going to throw a costume party in honor of Valentine's Day, with the caveat that all guests come disguised as an idiom used for a mood or a state of mind. 'Albert and I have discussed it, and we think it would be fantastic if you would film the party. It should be so rich visually. Positively yeasty. Doesn't mean you don't have to wear a costume yourself, mind you. But you would get to hide behind your camera most of the time. And I'll pay you, of course – pay you for your film and for your efforts.'

I had agreed – it did sound interesting. But then I had forgotten entirely about the party until the evening before Valentine's Day, when Albert called me to remind me about it. Ever since my Christmas party, when Ajax and Rena had demystified Albert for me as quickly and as simply as they might have trussed a holiday turkey, I had been seeing dramatically less of him. It wasn't that I didn't still like him, it was just that he had tumbled so abruptly from the heroic to the human. I found it almost embarrassing to look at him. That, and then I was so busy with my new film projects for all the unwed mothers-to-be. But life wouldn't be life, would it, if it weren't a seesaw act? And as my obsession with Albert had diminished, his with me had increased. He called me almost every day, looking for some excuse for us to meet.

'I think I'm going to be Under the Weather tomorrow night. How about you?' This was how Albert, in his inimitable style, announced himself when he called me on the eve of the Valentine's Day party.

'Huh?' I'm afraid I responded rather dully. I wasn't sure who he was – not to mention what he was talking about – at first. 'Albert, is that you?'

'Yeah. Yeah, it's me. I said I'm going to be Under the Weather tomorrow night. Either that, or Out to Lunch. I can't decide. What do you think, Elray, which would be better?'

I didn't answer. My understanding of what Albert was talking about was just beginning to take hold, and as it did a wicked case of preparty angst was coming on.

'Or hey, maybe I should just dress up as Taken for Granted,' Albert said loudly into the phone. He was hating my silence. 'That would have a certain poignancy, don't you think? Hello?'

'Oh God. Ziggy's costume party.' Finally I'd spoken. 'I'd forgotten about it. Thanks a lot for reminding me, Albert.' Then, without meaning to be rude, I hung up.

After Albert's call that night I spent several sleepless hours flopping around in my bed, trying to think up a costume for myself. Eventually I surrendered to sleep, and when my alarm clock rang at 5 A.M., I rushed out the door to my sunrise shoot with Vanessa and her rats without giving the matter of Ziggy's costume party another thought. A few hours later, as I stared at Vanessa standing ankle-deep in the mud in her brown velvet rat suit, the problem of my costume suddenly resurfaced and solved itself, all at the same time. I stared at the mud-stuck Vanessa and I saw exactly how I would dress that night. I would be a Stick-in-the-Mud. All I would need would be the rat suit and the muddy shoes and a few simple props – why, my conceit even suited me temperamentally.

Ziggy lived in a slightly ramshackle Victorian on a quiet street just six blocks from my house, so I decided to walk to the party. As I headed out in full dress, I paused outside our living room and listened for a moment to the familiar rumble of voices coming from within. Harwood had only just returned from Costa Rica that afternoon, but already he and Ajax and Rena were sitting around, ensconced in cocktails and the latest round of what had become their ongoing fight. I considered stepping in to say good night and show off my Stick-in-the-Mud disguise, but about one minute's worth of eavesdropping convinced me it would not be wise. They were already pretty far gone.

Their argument was over the issue of issue, so to speak, for Harwood had been agitating for a DNA test on Rena's baby. Both Rena and Ajax had been horrified by the 'barbarism of this predictably pig notion,' as Rena put it. And Rena had flatly refused.

'Isn't it just like a man,' I heard her complain to Ajax as I stood there, a Stick-in-the-Mud stuck in the hall, 'to want to document ownership as a prerequisite of caring.'

'Oh, they're all alike, I swear. I don't think they can help it,' Ajax answered. 'Possession is the gateway to obsession, and vice versa. I've seen it so many times, I can't tell you. But don't you worry, dearie. No one will be jabbing any needles into this precious babe of ours.'

A loud, braying snort exploded from Harwood, followed by the rattle of ice as he drained his drink and set his glass on the table. 'Pleeease,' he groaned. 'I'm just getting over a case of the Costa Rican Curse – my stomach's not ready for this.'

'You're so perceptive, sweetie.' Rena had ignored Harwood and was cooing at Ajax. I could just imagine the way the two of them must be sitting there, patting each other, trying to drive Harwood around the bend. 'Not many even dream of finding what we have,' Rena whispered.

'That's it. I'm outta here,' Harwood announced. I took this as my cue to slip out into the dark and star-studded February night.

Outside the air was cold, and edged with a sweet moistness that suggested a possible frosting of snow later. I drew in a few deep-cleansing sniffs and then, bracing my coatless shoulders against the chill, headed off. As I picked my way along the dark side of the streets I discovered that my costume, while simple in concept and design, was no joy to inhabit. The twigs that I had tied to my arms and head, to encourage a sticklike rather than ratlike interpretation of the brown suit, were rubbing against me uncomfortably. The brown cowl that I wore on my head (I had removed the rat ears) was too big and kept flopping into my eyes. The thick mud that I had slathered on from my ankles to my knees had dried now, and kept flaking off in big, discouraging chunks that marked my progress along the city sidewalks – a dirty, urban version of Hansel and Gretel's breadcrumb trail. Finally, to compound my discomfort, I was lugging my camera and a big bag of film accessories. Why, I cursed myself as I bungled along, had I refused Albert's offer to give me a ride?

By the time I struggled up the sagging wooden steps of Ziggy's front porch and rang her doorbell, I was the embodiment of my costume: a grumpy killjoy. My mood was not improved when Ziggy, packaged in a pink crepe gown with crisscrossing pink ribbons and a little sign on her chest that read 'Bundle of Joy,' threw open her door and shouted: 'Elray! Come in. But sweetheart – WHAT ON EARTH ARE YOU?'

'Your photographer,' I growled at her as I pushed past and took refuge in the first dark corner I could find. A minute later Ziggy delivered me a glass of something she referred to as a 'highly illegal glass of Attitude Adjustment Punch, please don't tell a soul or I'll get fired,' and for the next half hour I stayed in my corner, sipping at my drink, fussing with my camera equipment and taking surreptitious peeks every now and then at the guests as they came floating in and out of the room. One of the first things I noticed, with relief, was that many of those present were, like me, easily recognizable as themselves and not so easily recognizable as anything else.

'Harold! Okay, let me guess, let me guess.' I put the camera to my eye and began to film as a woman wearing a pea-green jumpsuit and a paper crown of red flames greeted a man in a red union suit who had festooned his body with several sets of deer antlers, like giant necklaces. 'You are ... you are ... The Predatory Urge?'

'Close, but no cigar, Sue.' Harold shook his head and smirked.

'Okay, I know, I know! You're – Killer Instinct? ... Animalism? Bestiality?' Sue kept at it, making several good but incorrect guesses. I was impressed by her resourcefulness. Finally she gave up. 'All right, tell me,' she said. 'You're just too clever, that's all.'

'I'm HORNY, Sue.' Harold doubled over with laughter at his joke, and the deer antlers clunked against each other. 'Get it? HORNY.'

Sue burst into giggles too, and adjusted the paper flames on her head. 'You know, we'd actually make a great couple, you and I,' she said with a suggestive flick of her hips. 'Can you guess what I am?' She struck a pose in her pea green. Harold rubbed at his chin.

'A Bacterial Infection? A Head Cold?' he asked, and then doubled over with laughter again.

'A HEAD COLD? You numskull!' Sue swatted at Harold. 'I'm a Jealous Rage. Can't you tell?' Filming a few exchanges like these and taking regular sips of punch did wonders for relaxing me. Soon, camera in hand, I was ready to venture forth from my corner and into the next room, where music was playing and some of the guests were already dancing, jerking themselves around with the blend of self-consciousness and abandon that infects people when they wear costumes. The first thing I noticed as I edged my way into this crowd was the preponderance of Cupids and red hearts. Evidently many had been inspired to give a Valentine's Day twist to their disguise – I had spotted at least three versions of Brokenhearted on the dance floor.

The second trend I noticed was far more alarming. For there seemed to be young people, people my own age, at this party. I had never imagined this would be the case. I had simply assumed I was Ziggy's one and only student invitee. I felt betrayed, cheapened almost, as I took a closer look at the gyrating bodies and recognized three of my classmates from Ziggy's drama course.

Reacting with an instinct to hide, I threw my camera to my shoulder and peered through the viewfinder; from this vantage point, I told myself, I could plot my escape. But as I peered out at the crowd from the comforting distance of narrative that my lens provided, what seized my eye was not a possible exit but rather a potential heroine. Twirling across the center of my viewfinder with untold grace came a beautiful two-headed girl. Her left head, which sprouted at a slight angle from her central, lithe neck, had raven-black hair and dark, elsewhere eyes; her other head, which was clearly the dominant member of the set, had long honey-colored hair and big, popping blue eyes. I began to film her and a moment later, as if on cue, the music dipped and my two-headed beauty executed a perfect James Brown swoon. She tipped herself backward into oblivion and then righted herself, with a syncopated pop, at the last minute. Her blond head flashed a huge, dazzling smile at her dance partner, whose back was to me, while her left head stared moodily off into space. Yes, the blond head was definitely the dominant half. . . . Actually, I realized a split second later with considerable horror, the blond head was someone I knew. The blond head was Clair Moskowitz.

Some moments of humiliation burn so badly they never really heal, and so it has been with the blast of embarrassment that came scorching through me when I first realized that yes, in fact, Clair Moskowitz was out there – out there and dancing with my Raoul. Even now the color rises to my cheeks, the tips of my ears burn and my throat goes dry as I relive the nightmare in slow motion. On that night I peered through the magnified perspective of the viewfinder at Clair and watched as she stalked across the dance floor, a two-headed Diana. She lifted her arms – one sheathed in black, the other in white – to shoulder height in a gesture that to her was probably just another dance maneuver. To me it was obvious that the two-headed archer had just drawn her mighty bowstring and was taking aim. A second later, Clair's eyes fastened on the camera and bore through the lens and into me. 'Raoul.' I could not hear it, but through the lens I saw Clair's lips say his name. The arrow came tearing through my chest. 'Raoul,' she said again, her eyes never swerving from their fierce path through the camera into me. 'Look,' she said. Then, placing her huntress hands on his shoulders, she spun Raoul toward me.

Or was it Raoul? For a split second I was not sure. A white face was floating atop a column of black. I was reminded of a nun. Or a penguin. A black, cone-shaped head assembly shot upward from the face and ended in a long, looping coil of wire. Like a dunce cap with an antenna. I zoomed my lens in slowly on the left side of the face, and there it was: the telltale scar. The toothpick, running vertically in the left cheek. I had no idea what his costume was meant to be, but this face at the far end of my lens – no doubt about it – belonged to Raoul.

Without bothering to lower my camera or reverse my zoom, I did an about-face. My only thought was to flee. What must they think, Raoul and Clair? Why, it was bad enough to be at the same party, but to be caught filming them – as if I were compiling evidence. As if I cared.

'Elray!' I had not taken two steps when I heard someone shout my name. At first I ignored it, assuming it must be Raoul. But then the shout came again. 'ELRAY!' Right at my ear. I lowered my camera and there was Albert, looking absolutely crazy. He was dressed in a mummy suit – no, a straitjacket and white pajama pants – and decorated from head to toe with what look like tiny Christmas ornaments. Little colored orbs dangled from little pieces of string all over him.

'Albert!' I was actually happy to see him, for the first time in weeks. My full-throttle panic was ebbing slightly, just enough, possibly, to let me live. 'Albert, oh there you are!' I said as I grabbed at his arm (which of course I couldn't find, because it had been shrink-wrapped against his side by his straitjacket). 'Come here, Albert. Quick, come with me.'

The vision of Albert brought me out of my personal

purgatory and back into the world at large. For he looked truly weird. There were more little balls hanging on strings from his hair, I noticed, and several running in a necklacelike row down a string that was dribbling from one ear. His face was paled with mimer's white, and his off-center eyes jumped around the edges of it – like another pair of balls that might come falling out on strings at any minute.

'Albert?' My face must have conveyed my confusion about the theme behind his special effects, for Albert interrupted me before I could say another word.

'No, no. Let me look at you first. Let me see if I can guess you,' he said impatiently. A little wad of spittle had collected in one corner of his mouth, and his nose must have been running slightly, for a trail of exposed flesh ran down the whitened slope of his upper lip. I experienced a fleeting urge to toss him a bone to gnaw.

'Hmmm, this is a tough one,' Albert said as he walked around me and looked me up and down. 'I don't want to be rude – now don't get angry if I'm wrong – but this would be just like you and your self-deprecating ways . . . Elray, are you a Piece of Shit?'

I looked down at myself with fresh horror, wrinkled my nose and shook my head.

'Okay, okay. I didn't think so, not really. Let me try again; you look great, you really do, not like shit at all. Just inscrutable, you know, as always . . .' Albert was talking more to himself than to me, and circling me now like a predator. 'Let's see, we got twigs, mud, fuzzy brown. A Self-Flagellating Chipmunk. No, no, that's not mood . . . not idiom, either, come to think of it . . . Aha! I've got it now. Busy as a Beaver! That's got to be it. Am I right? Huh? Busy as a Beaver?'

I looked at Albert and shook my head. 'I'm a Stick-in-the-Mud,' I said quickly, anxious to end the insult of his guesses. 'But I'm really just here to film,' I added.

'A Stick-in-the-Mud? Oh yes, of course, I can see now. How clever.' Albert nodded his head enthusiastically, and all his little ornaments jiggled. 'Yes, Ziggy told me you'd be filming. Good idea – great stuff, huh? Very telling, isn't it, what people will come up with when they're encouraged to disguise themselves. Very, very revealing. '

'Speaking of which . . .' I butted my head in Albert's direction. 'You are?'

'Oh come on now, I'm easy. Piece of cake.'

'Piece of Cake? Oh yes, of course. With white frosting and sprinkles. It's a very imaginative . . .' I leaned toward Albert mid-sentence. 'Shall we get out of here?' I suggested. My back was tingly, I was so painfully aware of Raoul and Clair somewhere in the room behind me, possibly moving closer as we dawdled.

'I'M not a piece of cake!' Albert roared at me, his wild eyes going wilder until I thought they really might escape their sockets this time. 'My COSTUME is a piece of cake, you ninny. TO GUESS. So try. Take a guess, Elray. What am I?'

'Gosh, Albert. I don't know, I'm not very good at this sort of thing.' I looked at Albert as he stood there, his eyeballs and his ornaments all aglitter, and I found I was grateful he was in a straitjacket. What I wanted to say to him was 'Lunatic. You're a lunatic.' But I didn't. Instead I took a closer look. The little strings reminded me of tampons – perhaps he had opted for a highly interpretive disguise. 'Toxic Shock Syndrome?' I ventured. And then, when Albert shook his head no, I surprised myself with another guess. 'String Fever?' I asked, embarrassed by my feeble pun.

'Wrong. You give up yet?'

I nodded.

'I'm Losing My Marbles, Elray. Can't you see? Losing. My. Marbles.' Albert twisted his straitjacketed torso back and forth so all the balls tossed and turned at the ends of their strings. 'I was going to use real marbles, but it was impossible to attach them to the strings,' he explained. 'I tried drilling holes in a few – no fucking way. Then I hit on the idea – well, actually

393

Melba did – of little Christmas balls. Ever tried to buy Christmas paraphernalia in February, Elray?'

I shook my head. 'Where is Melba?' I asked. 'I'd love to talk to Melba. Let's go find Melba.' If Albert didn't take the hint soon, I was going to have to bolt by myself.

'She's not here,' Albert said. 'Melba takes law courses at night. No parties for Melba – but OH MY GOD!' At least one of Albert's eyes was staring over my shoulder with what registered, even on his beyond-the-fringe face, as amazement. 'What have we here? Get your camera up, Elray. We've got ourselves a live one!' I was scared to look – I thought I knew what I'd see. I turned slowly and sure enough, there was the two-headed Clair, sailing straight toward us. Her long body came undulating across the room in a kind of cat suit that was split down the middle, white on the left side and black on the right. Before I could pull myself together to flee, she was upon us. I braced myself for battle, prepared myself mentally for a showdown of some kind – but within a matter of seconds it became clear that Clair had no interest in speaking to me. She brushed right past me and hurled herself at Albert.

'Ix-scuse me,' she said. 'But er yoo Elbert Cairns? The feeyulm miker?' Her voice was shockingly nasal, her accent totally cracker. I stared at her in disbelief. It was like opening a big blue box from Tiffany's and finding a little pile of raccoon turds inside. 'I've heard soo mooch abayout yoo, Elbert. Kin we towk?' I looked from Clair to Albert. Albert seemed oblivious to any vocal disorders; in fact, he looked entranced. He was struggling to get out of his straitjacket.

'Here, help me get out of this thing, would you, Miss . . . uh, Miss . . . ?'

'Mus-co-weetz. Clay-yair Mus-co-weetz.'

'My pleasure, Clair.' The moment Albert had freed an arm he thrust a hand forward. 'And your, um, silent partner?' He nodded toward Clair's second, dark-haired head.

'Whut?' Clair looked confused for a second, and then she understood. 'Ow, ow, oooow!' she howled. 'You're towking 'bout Ra-chewell. She kin be a iddy-bit shy sometimes. Ra-chewell! Sigh hilloo to Elbert.' Clair dipped her second head toward Albert. Then she leaned her first head into Albert's face and whispered: 'Ah am SCHIZOID tonight, case you couldun guess. It was my fri-yend Raoul's i-jea. Closest I'd evah get to bein' com-plee-cated, he said.'

'I never said that – Clair's just drunk.' It sounded like Raoul was talking right there at my elbow. My heart started jamming in my chest. I slid my eyes sideways. Yes, it was definitely Raoul. Raoul was standing right beside me, in his strange black costume.

'I A-YAM NOT DRUNK!' Clair objected. 'Why, I haven't had a drop all night. Cooorse, Ra-chewell here – she's bin a liddle fee-yesh. As u-shul . . . Just-a glug glug glug.'

Albert was staring at Clair with a look I recognized: a look of utter, near-clinical fascination. 'Clair, shall we get Rachel a little coffee?' he suggested, offering her his one free arm.

'Charmin'. Please don't squeeze the . . . charmin' idea.' One moment Clair was giggling uncontrollably at her own nonsense, and the next she and Albert had disappeared together into the crowd. Leaving me standing there – I couldn't believe life kept doing this sort of thing to me – with Raoul.

I waited for at least thirty seconds, and then I turned ever so slowly to face him. I took so long, I think, because I was half hoping Raoul would be gone by the time I looked up. But there he stood, staring down at me from under his peculiar dunce cap with the crazy, coiled antenna. I made myself stand unflinching under his gaze, although I felt hopelessly unglamorous in the wake of the tall and bodacious Clair-cum-Rachel. Eventually I managed to speak.

'Hi.' Actually we both spat this out, in unison, and then we both fell silent.

'Nice camera.' Raoul was the first to speak again. He gestured toward the fancy camera that was staring down at the floor from my left hand, artful as a dead chicken.

'Yeah, thanks. I'm filming the party, recording the costumes. You know, for Ziggy.'

Raoul nodded again. 'Good idea,' he said. 'Great scenes.'

This time it was my turn to nod. 'I'll say. Boy, your girlfriend . . . Clair . . . Raoul, is she your girlfriend?' I couldn't believe my audacity, but I was genuinely curious. 'She is a wild one, isn't she? Her voice . . . I didn't remember it—'

'It's fake,' Raoul interrupted me.

'What?'

'The southern accent's fake,' he said. 'Clair just landed the part of Stella in a production of *Streetcar* Ziggy's doing at our school, and I think the whole thing has kind of gone to her head. Her part in the play – and the costume and the booze too, of course.'

'Oh, I see.' I tried to hide my disappointment. 'So Ziggy teaches at your school too?'

'Yeah. Anyway, to answer your question, Clair's not really my girlfriend,' Raoul continued. 'She's kind of a dink, really.'

'A . . . dink?' I wasn't sure what he meant.

Raoul nodded, and we exchanged a long quiet look.

'Well, she's a pretty tall and good-looking dink,' I finally said. And as I spoke I could feel a crazy but familiar energy beginning to course through me. I knew exactly what it was. It was the bubbly old bang of invincibility – so sweet, so ruthless, and oh so mine. I looked up at Raoul as my invincibility came pounding home, pounding down my pike. I looked up into Raoul's gray-green eyes and I felt an expansive rush of generosity toward everything in the world – including the beautiful but dinky Clair.

Raoul shrugged. 'Tall dink, short dink. Fat dink, thin dink. A dink's a dink,' he said with a quiet smile. And then he leaned right up against my ear. 'Hey Elray,' he whispered. 'Can I ask you something?'

I peered up at him and nodded.

'Elray, what the hell are you?' Raoul was positively grinning now. 'I mean, what the hell is this getup you've got on?'

I glanced down for a second at my rat suit and my twigs and my mud and I experienced a brief dip in my surging confidence. But then I looked back at Raoul, with his coil of wire dangling stupidly from the top of his weird hat, and all my systems were full speed ahead again.

'I'm a Stick-in-the-Mud,' I announced, without a moment's further hesitation and with something that might almost have passed for pride. 'A Stick-in-the-Mud,' I repeated.

'A Stick-in-the-Mud? No! Elray, why that's perfect! PERFECT!' Raoul seemed genuinely thrilled by my answer. He grabbed my two hands, camera and all, and began to squeeze them in his own. 'Do you know what I am?' he asked. 'Guess.'

I looked Raoul up and down as he stood back and struck a pose. His body was encased in a kind of black cylinder, and on his head was the cone-shaped black hat. He was like a black rocket with a looping wire antenna springing from its snout. I hadn't a clue what he was supposed to be. 'A Bad Trip?' I asked. 'A Spiraling Depression?' Raoul shook his head.

'Come on, Stick-in-the-Mud,' he said. 'You of all moods should recognize me.'

I shook my head and shrugged my stick shoulders.

'I'm a Wild Hair, Tree. Can't you see? You're a Stick-in-the-Mud and I'm a Wild Hair. Isn't that great? Come on. Let's dance.' Raoul grabbed my hands and pulled me toward the dance floor, and to my amazement I did not resist. I let Raoul, the Wild Hair, pull me, the Stick, from my mud pit and guide me onto the dance floor. We shuffled around the room for a few minutes in a simple and shy embrace, oblivious to the music or to the other dancers or to anything much but each other. And then Raoul turned to me mid-step, removed his Wild Hair hat and said with astonishing earnestness: 'Elray, let's leave.'

Trading Places

Outside it was snowing. Big fluffy flakes were drifting earthward as whimsically as feathers, as steadily as if some sky-bound giant had decided to empty his down comforter onto our world. Raoul and I stood in the middle of the street outside Ziggy's house, admiring the snow and the way our footprints had followed us through it, down the walk and into the street where we were standing. They were like a map of the moment — as fresh as the snow, as tender as the twist of Raoul's fingers in mine, as inevitable as our rediscovered appeal for each other.

'Look at these snowflakes, Elray. They're the size of potato chips,' Raoul said. He had tipped his face skyward, closed his eyes and opened his mouth.

'Hmmm. Like big butterflies,' I agreed, reaching out with my free hand to catch at one.

'Or big wet kisses.' Raoul squeezed my hand and drew me closer. 'Come on,' he said. 'I'll walk you home.'

We had shuffled only a hundred yards or so down the street, hand in hand and wrapped in the warm cocoon of quiet that a big snow creates, when a burst of laughter erupted from somewhere behind us. Pausing in our tracks, we looked back and I saw Albert and Clair — immediately recognizable because of Clair's two heads. They were standing together in a small amphitheater of light under a streetlamp outside Ziggy's house, dancing. Or something like that. They were tipping backward, at any rate, and then popping forward with howls of laughter.

'No, no, no!' Clair shouted at Albert as he leaned backward and then snapped forward awkwardly, his ornaments a-jiggle. 'Not like THA-YAT. Like THIS. Do the DI-YIP!' Then Clair leaned backward and executed the perfect James Brown swoon again, with the syncopated pop, that I had seen her perform on the dance floor.

'She's good at that.' I turned to Raoul, curious to read his face.

He shrugged. 'She practices a lot,' he said. 'Come on. Let's go.'

We walked on, leaving Clair and Albert to their antics. The garish sound of their fun faded quickly, snuffed by the all-embracing silence of the snow. Then it was Raoul and I alone in our world once again, moving through the dark city streets, loping down the long blocks the way we used to. But headed this time for an entirely new place.

We rolled down the streets and through the night with the pulse of our happiness pounding like a prize in our intertwined hands. Before I knew it we were standing on the front walk of my house. The snow seemed to be slowing. And the trees were singing, I realized with a start. Either that or the stars behind the clouds had opened their throats. The night had somehow found a voice.

'Raoul, do you hear that?' I asked.

Raoul took my two hands in his and tipped his head sideways and listened for a minute. 'I can't hear anything except my heart,' he said. 'It's going like a jackhammer. Elray?'

'Yes?'

'I'd like to be your friend again, but I'd like to exist this time.'

'Exist?' I wasn't sure what he meant.

'Yes. For you, of course, but for your whole family too. For Ajax, and Harwood and Rena.'

'Oh, oh, oh.' I couldn't help laughing. It seemed so long ago, the way we had stashed Raoul in my house in our pursuit of the so-called invincibility of nonexistence.

'I would like you to exist,' I said, reaching out toward Raoul's face. I wanted to touch the toothpick scar on his left cheek, run my finger down its smooth white surface. But as I watched my right hand stretching toward him I felt my big happiness draining out of my toes, dissipating like body heat into the cold snow. I pulled my left hand out of Raoul's grip and whirled around so that my back was to him.

'Elray?' Raoul was behind me, questioning.

'Raoul,' I began, my voice nearly breaking. 'Raoul, I have to tell you some things. You're not going to like them. Or me probably, once you hear them.'

'What, Elray? What is it? Tell me, please. Right now.' Raoul had placed his hands on my shoulders and he was trying to turn me around. I resisted for a minute, and then I faced him.

'Raoul,' I announced gravely. 'Obviously I do not have a wooden arm.' I thrust my right arm toward him and pulled back the rat suit sleeve to expose the warm, live flesh of my forearm. 'Look. It's real. It has ALWAYS BEEN REAL. I know you know that. But I still need to confess it.' I said it all in a rush and then, like an idiot, I began to cry.

Raoul stared at me for a second, and then he laughed and stepped forward and wrapped me in his arms. 'Shhhhh, shhhhh, be quiet,' he whispered into my ear. 'I knew that, silly little Stump. You don't need to cry. I knew your arm was real. What can you be thinking? I've known that for a long time.' He placed his hands on my shoulders and pushed me away again and held me there at arm's length. 'Where do you think you live, anyway?' he asked with a big smile. 'In a Flannery O'Connor story?'

I looked at Raoul, and through my tears I could see he was still smiling. But there was more. 'Raoul,' I began, 'I never went to Russia.'

'You didn't?' He looked so perplexed I decided I'd better get it all over with right away.

'No, I didn't. And I've only been through the Tunnel of Love once. *After* you'd suggested it. And I've never had a boyfriend named Alberto.'

Raoul paused, and then he grabbed my right arm. He pushed back my sleeve and began to plant kisses up and down my forearm. 'It's real, thank God,' Raoul muttered, looking up at me between Gatling rounds of kisses. 'Thank God, it's real. Oh thank God, she's not a freak! Oh what a relief!' He was smiling. I had admitted everything and he was still smiling. I began to smile myself, just a little.

'Okay, okay. Stop now. Raoul, that tickles!' I pushed at Raoul's head, tried to get his face up where I could see it. It was hovering before me, a map of my heart, bending down toward me. A moment later Raoul's mouth met mine.

A kiss.

My blood stood still and my heart ran aground as I prepared myself for an explosion of light and sound. I waited for the world to catch on fire, and for a moment I believed I must be burning already or possibly turning into light. A second later I understood that I needed to breathe, to replenish the oxygen in my lungs. And then, when I finally pulled back and drew in a huge swallow of air, I heard it. The scream. It was a great big enormous scream. The kind of scream that is more a signpost than a sound. A marker for when the world as we've known it gets permanently altered in some way.

For the first few seconds, because of my full lungs and because of my historical precedent with kisses and screams and annihilation, I assumed the noise was blasting from my own throat – yet again. My instinct was to silence myself by clamping my hand over my mouth, but I had forgotten that my mouth was half-attached to Raoul's. For Raoul was still kissing me – or trying to, anyway. Evidently he had not heard the scream. Evidently, I slowly realized, I was not the one screaming.

'Elray. Elray . . . finally . . .' Raoul slurred his words like a drunk in the first moments after I managed to pry our heads apart. But a second later he must have seen the look on my face. 'What's the matter?' he asked abruptly. And then, as the enormous scream finally registered: 'WHAT IS THAT?'

'It's coming from inside my house,' I answered. And then, realizing that what I'd said was true, I ran up the front steps and across the porch and through the door, heavy with dread.

I'm not sure what I expected to find inside, but the situation that confronted me obliterated any response but action. The moment I entered the front hall I was in a scene of total mayhem. Both Granny Mayhew and Rena were laid out on the floor before me, stretched flat on their backs, and both were howling at the top of their lungs. It must have been the discordant harmonics of their two yowls that had created the huge scream I'd heard outside. Ajax was kneeling between them, while Harwood paced back and forth talking to someone on the telephone.

I stood in the doorway until Harwood spotted me and pulled me into the room. Ajax wrapped me in a big embrace as I approached.

'Oh thank God. Oh Elray, you're here,' Ajax said.

'What's happening? What's going on?' I asked.

'Rena's in labor, sweetie. Her water has broken. And Granny – oh God, we think Granny is having a stroke. Or a fit. Or a heart attack. Or something. She was fine a little while ago – they both were. We were all—'

'Have you called an ambulance?' I interrupted Ajax.

'Oh yes, they're on the way. Should be here soon. Very soon, I hope. I do wish they'd get here – do you think they could have the address wrong? I hope I didn't say Half-Moon Street. You know I do that sometimes when I'm not thinking . . .'

'Have you called a doctor?'

'Yes, Harwood's on the phone with them.'

'Them?'

'Yes, Rena's doctor on one line, Granny's on the other. Come talk to Rena and Granny, Elray, help me keep them calm. Jesus, why does everything always have to happen all at once?' Ajax, despite her surface panic, seemed to have all the essentials under control. I held her hand and went to kneel with her on the floor between Rena and Granny.

'Logan, darling,' said Granny as she looked up at me with a smile. Both she and Rena had stopped screaming for the time being. 'I think the Black Ducks have got me.'

'Don't be silly, Granny,' I said. 'Nobody's got you. Nobody but me. Me and Ajax. We have you.' Granny looked younger and smoother than ever. Pain became her. 'Where does it hurt, Granny?' I asked.

'My chest, my heart, my lungs. They're on fire.' Granny resumed her moans, and as she did, Rena, who had been quiet, also began to get worked up again.

'Oh Lord, here we go. Yes, yes. JE-SUUUUUS! That hurts! It does!' Rena groaned. Beads of sweat had broken out all over her brow, but she was shivering, as if chilled.

'Maybe you should try to get Rena to walk a little,' I suggested to Ajax. 'Isn't that supposed to help? I'll stay with Granny.'

'FORGET IT!' Rena roared. 'I heard that. I'm not moving – I can't. I'm about to die. OH GOD!'

'Actually, with her water broken I think it's better to keep her horizontal,' Ajax whispered to me. 'The baby might be breech. And it is a month early. I think we want to keep it in there until there's a doctor around.'

I nodded. 'How long has this been going on?' I asked.

'Not even fifteen minutes,' Ajax answered. 'It was amazing – everyone was just fine. We were all sitting in the living room when Granny came in from her show – the Gray Geese had a Valentine's Day performance tonight. And Granny was just showing us some steps from her new routine when she and Rena were stricken – right at the same time. Granny fell to the floor and grabbed her chest and Rena jumped up and started screaming, 'I've peed everywhere! What's happening?' Of course, it was her water breaking . . . Your Uncle Harwood's been just great. So calm – he's made all the phone calls, bless him.'

I looked up at Harwood. He was still on the phone, looking down at his wristwatch. 'Yes, uh-huh,' he said to whoever was on the other end. 'That's right. Contractions seem to be coming at about eight-minute intervals now. What? Okay, okay.' He cupped his hand over the receiver. 'Try some breathing exercises,' he called out to us.

'Okay. But with whom? Which one?' Ajax called back.

'With the birthing mother, not with the tired old matriarch, I would venture a guess,' Granny whispered. 'Go on, save the young women and children. Don't worry about me. I've had a long if unhappy life – What are you doing here?' Granny asked as she suddenly tried to sit up and stared over my shoulder. 'Who invited you?'

I turned around to look, and there was Raoul. I had forgotten about him. He was standing there in his Wild Hair costume, sans hat, the snow still piled on his shoulders.

'Everyone, I'd like you to meet my friend Raoul. Raoul Person. He exists.' I said this to the room at large, and then I turned to Raoul. 'Raoul, meet my family.'

Rena stopped her huffing and puffing long enough to open her eyes and take a look. 'Oh heavens, it's the film boy,' she said. 'How do you do – please excuse me for not rising.' Then she turned to Ajax. 'What's he wearing?' she asked, tears running down her cheeks. 'I swear, I can't keep up with the fashions of young people these days. I'm so old.'

'Raoul,' Harwood called across the room. 'Had any CPR training? Yes? Well, go scrub up in the kitchen and then get back here. Pronto.'

A second later Rena opened her throat, in full scream once again, and the very pictures on the wall began to reverberate. I looked down at Granny and I saw that her face was turning smooth, her eyes liquid and dark. It was a look I recognized from my practice sessions in the coffins with Raoul.

'Granny, wait! Don't go anywhere.' I grabbed her hands. 'Ajax!' I called across the hall. 'Ajax, Granny's in trouble over here. Real trouble.' When I looked down at Granny again she was almost invisible, she was so quiet. 'Wait, Granny. Don't go yet,' I pleaded. 'Wait. I'm coming with you.' I stretched out on the floor beside her. I held her hand and closed my eyes and prepared to die.

'You can't do this. Go away.' I thought Granny had said this, but when I opened my eyes she looked even quieter than before and it was Ajax who was speaking to me.

'Elray,' Ajax said. 'Please get up. There's too much going on already. You'll give *me* a heart attack. Stand up.' Ajax was holding a little felt bag, clutching it to her chest.

'I'm going with Granny. Just for a while,' I said. I looked over at Raoul, who had returned from the kitchen, all scrubbed up. 'Raoul will escort me. Raoul will make sure I come back. The two of us will bring Granny back too.' A second later Raoul was stretched out alongside me, holding my hand.

'Guys, please . . .' Ajax pleaded, tears streaming down her face now.

'Take care of Rena and her baby. We'll be fine,' I said. 'Right, Raoul?' Raoul nodded and squeezed my hand.

'Mama?' Ajax bent over Granny and showed her the little bag she was holding. 'Mama, I have something for you. I found it just the other day, when I was cleaning out a closet in the baby's room. I was going to give it to you tonight, for Valentine's Day – I don't know why, kind of a stupid idea, I know. But . . . But . . .' Ajax had broken down and was sobbing now. 'Here. I think this is yours.' Ajax reached into the bag and pulled something out. She placed it in Granny's free hand, the one I wasn't holding. I know I should have been half-dead already, but I couldn't keep myself from looking – I was too curious. I sat halfway up just in time to see Ajax hand Granny a little plastic bag of charred teeth. Granny wrapped her hand around the teeth and smiled. She definitely smiled. Then she spoke.

'Thank you,' Granny said quietly. 'Perfect. Irrefutable. Now out with the old and in with the new.' She closed her eyes and began to hum. '*All of me . . . why not take all of me,*' she sang softly. '*Can't you see, I'm no good without you.*' Then her feet began to twitch, as if they were dancing to the music. But not quite. That's when I knew it was time to lie down and die with her.

Raoul and I stretched out and fell together, with each other and with Granny, down the old familiar chute. Granny fell much faster and more expertly, I noticed. Her hand quickly melted out of my touch and became just a scent – a residual fragrance of tobacco and lilacs. I tried to keep up with her but she was just too nimble and too quick – being a dancer, she was doing all kinds of tricks I'd never seen before; I couldn't possibly follow. She slipped away just before I ran aground of the same haunting smell of seaweed and wet paint Raoul and I had intersected with briefly in the room full of mattresses. It was mixed this time with other smells. Smoke and wet ground and rotting fruit. I thought perhaps we'd gone too far, but then I felt Raoul's steady touch pulling me up. Hauling me back to the world of light and sight and sounds. Unbelievably loud sounds.

As I resurfaced in the hall Rena was howling at the

top of her lungs to my left, and Ajax was screaming too, right in my face. She was holding my shoulders and calling my name over and over, the same way she had in the crawlspace on the day of my own Big Scream so long ago. Harwood was shouting into the telephone as he paced back and forth, looking first at Granny, who was stone-still, and then at Rena, who was like a volcano preparing to erupt.

It's a wonder we even heard the doorbell ring when the ambulance arrived – or maybe we didn't. Maybe the medical technicians didn't bother to announce themselves but just took the screams as their welcoming anthem and came on in. I don't know – I can't remember. What I do remember is that it was a tremendous relief to see them, all dressed in white like angels, and loaded down with the stainless-steel equipment with which modern miracles are performed. I sat up and looked at Raoul. Then the two of us stood up together and lurched across the room with the unsteady balance of the recently dead. We hovered at the edges, holding hands, while the technicians quickly took charge.

Two of them moved to Granny with their equipment and began working on her chest, trying to jump-start her. Two others were with Rena, talking to her quietly while they loaded her onto a stretcher. Within minutes we were all in the eerie icy whiteness of the outside world, moving en masse across the snow toward two ambulances with blinking lights – like aliens from another planet loading their wounded into their spaceship for the voyage home.

Granny was gone. I knew there was nothing to be done. I felt a stab of sadness as the medical people loaded her into one ambulance and prepared to drive off with her – she had always been such a loner. But at that moment the rest of us were determined to squeeze our way into the other ambulance with Rena – and the ongoing show. Raoul was about to be excluded at one point when Rena, after catching a quick glimpse of my face, howled: 'We can't go without Raoul! Get Raoul in here! I won't go without him! Oh damn! Here it comes. THE PAIN! THE TORTURE! THE TORMENT!'

Finally we were all loaded and on our way, the ambulance sliding through the snow-clogged streets like a shuttle bus on a slippery route between this life and some other. The driver never bothered to turn on the siren – perhaps he figured the bloodcurdling sound of Rena's wails was siren enough. It was all the rest of us sitting in the back with her could do to weather those wails, with their life-shattering urgency. Raoul and I were sitting on one side of Rena while Harwood and Ajax sat on the other. It was a tight squeeze, and the four of us kept exchanging looks over the heads of the ambulance staffers who were working on her. In a moment of sudden quiet, when Rena stopped groaning, one of the attendants spoke quietly.

'Okay, folks. I think it's show time here,' he said. 'Yep, this little baby definitely wants out. Okay, Rena – is it Rena? Rena honey, I know we've been telling you not to – but now I think you better push. How about giving us a little push?'

Ajax let out a big groan, and Harwood jumped up and rapped on the window that separated us from the ambulance driver. 'Hey buddy!' he shouted. 'Could you put a nickel in it? This is supposed to be an EMERGENCY vehicle, remember?'

'Sir, it's very snowy, very treacherous driving tonight,' a voice came to us over the intercom. 'I'm in the business of saving lives, not taking them. I'm sorry, but I'm going as fast as I can.'

A second later the world went dark. Utterly blank and empty and quiet for a merciful interval of I can't say how long. Whatever happened, it was a huge relief while it lasted. But then as suddenly as it had come, the darkness was over. The world exploded into chaos again with a loud howl from Rena. At the same time I stood up in the crowded ambulance and let loose with what I knew must have been the loudest scream any of us had heard all night. My arm – my right forearm – had caught on fire. It was a stinging, burning tyranny of pain. I grabbed at the right sleeve of my rat suit to take a look – but there was nothing to see. Only the same old scar on the same old arm. I rubbed it in an effort to drive the pain away, and only then, as my fingers brushed against the scar, did I realize that it was the babies who sometimes lived in my arm who were screaming – not me. The second I realized this the screaming and the pain in my arm began to fade, and for the first time I noticed a terrible throbbing in my forehead. I lifted my fingers to my brow and felt the thick, slippery mistake of fresh blood.

The ambulance was stopped and pitched at a radical tilt. We had had an accident of some kind – not too serious; everyone was still moving, it seemed. The attendants were reorganizing their equipment to compensate for our new angle. I turned to look at Rena, and the moment I did I heard her bawling again – not with pain this time, but with joy. And then a moment later I heard her baby, crowing like a rooster. A fat and feisty cry. Triumphant, scrappy, alive.

I lurched across the ambulance toward Ajax and the bundle she was holding. Ajax looked up at me and smiled, tears running down her handsome cheeks.

'Just look at him,' she said, holding the baby toward me. 'Isn't he incredible? Isn't he beautiful?'

He was. As beautiful as newborn babies get. All fat and ruddy and lusty, with eyes that were strangely bright and wise. Eyes that seemed – I realized as I moved in for a closer look – an amazing shade of green. A green I'd admired in others' eyes. In my father's, for one. In Granny Mayhew's, for another. In Ajax's.

I looked over at Harwood. He was kneeling beside Rena's stretcher, his head bowed as if in prayer. I wondered if he'd seen the baby yet.

I wanted to congratulate Rena, but I felt a huge and heavy fatigue spreading downward from my throbbing head and up from my ankles, threatening to knock me over. There was nowhere to fall. There were bodies and doctors wall to wall, the birthing and the watching and the working folk all crammed together in this wild, wheel-based juggernaut that our lives had become. I considered curling up somewhere for a quick nap. Just for a minute. But suddenly all my thoughts of rest were obliterated. The pain and the screaming had returned to my arm. And Rena was howling with pain again too.

I moved toward Rena as quickly as I could, but I couldn't get to her. Everyone else had crowded around. Ajax, Harwood, the medical people – even Raoul.

'What is it?' I shouted frantically at their backs. 'What's wrong? Please, someone. Let me see!' Raoul turned to me finally, his face radiant, his touch as gentle as sleep as he drew me near.

'Rena's having another baby, Tree!' he whispered, as if there were any need to be quiet with all the noise around us. 'There's a second baby in there!'

No sooner had Raoul told me this than the pain and the howling in my forearm ceased and Rena's cries turned to hiccups of happiness. A moment later I heard a second baby voice – a different baby voice – come gurgling through all the chaos, tumbling over itself like brookwater, washing away the pain and the blood and the death and the fatigue. Raoul steadied me as I moved toward Rena's stretcher. He kept me on my feet as I looked down and saw the most magnificent baby girl. She was all guile and style and attitude.

'Look at her – what a beauty.' Harwood was entranced. 'Just look at that baby – Elray, she's the spitting image of your mother.' Harwood turned to Ajax with a wicked grin. 'This one is ALL MINE.'

'She's all OURS, David,' Ajax corrected as the medical attendant gently laid the baby girl on Rena's chest. 'They both belong to all of us. And aren't we blessed. What a miracle they both are.'

411

'A-MEN to that,' said the medical attendant as he went about his business, mopping up blood and taking pulses. 'Twins. Lordy, it's a first for me. Where are we, anyway? Noah's Ark?'

I looked around at Ajax and Rena and Harwood clustered together admiring the two babies, all five of them aglow. Somewhere ahead of us in the night, Granny had embarked on her own journey. I wondered if she was still clutching her irrefutable teeth. And standing a few feet from me, beaming down with a smile that I hoped would become my vin ordinaire, was my lost but found Raoul.

'No, not Noah's Ark,' I said, shaking my head and speaking to no one in particular. 'But maybe the Garden of Eden.' For as I looked again at my naked baby cousins lying side by side on Rena's chest – Valentine and Rosie, she would name them, before we even reached the hospital – I could have sworn I saw them exchange a look. It was a look I had seen somewhere before. An age-old, world-wise, cunning look. A sleight-of-brow glance that managed, in the mere two seconds that it lasted, to say: 'Hey, we made it! Gimme five. Now. How about a little original sin?'

Epilogue

Dear Rosie and Valentine, Valentine and Rosie:

So there is the story of how you first came to me, when I was sixteen, delivered amidst screams as big as the scream that carried my parents away. You arrived in disguise as my baby cousins, but I always knew you were more. What a delight the two of you have been. We haven't had a Crawlspace Day, you and I, but we have had our own share of secrets and adventures. And I think we have all understood that you embody pieces if not all of just about everyone I have ever loved. Your wisdom both frightens and comforts me, now as much as ever.

I write to you today, Rosie and Valentine, to wish you a happy eighteenth birthday. Has it really been eighteen years since that slippery ride through the snowy night that landed us in each other's lives? Eighteen years since that most amazing show of human alchemy, where Granny went POOF and the two of you went BOOM? (Or BOOM! BOOM! I should say.) Sometimes it feels impossible, but then when I pause and think about all that has happened, I know that it must be true.

I write to you today to say 'Happy Birthday,' but also to send you this story I have been compiling for the last year. The two of you are eighteen now, and I am thirty-four. We are all of us old enough to talk frankly — or as frankly as we find pleasing or useful, at any rate. And that is why I am sending you this story about Barkley and Jack and Ajax and Rena and Harwood and Granny and myself – about all of us. I have written it in part for myself – how I longed to have such a story about my own parents when I was a child. But I have also written it for the two of you. For both of you, and for the newest member of our family – Raoul's and my sweet baby boy, Achilles. It is a story about the dips and thrills of losing and finding so much. About the dear people we have all known so well. About letting go and holding on.

As I sit here now at my desk in my library on High View Street, preparing to send this manuscript off to you, I am struck by how far-flung our lives, all of which took root so firmly in this house, have become. The two of you have flown the coop and are capering about doing God knows what (please, don't tell me) on your respective campuses. I just returned yesterday from Patagonia, where baby Achilles and I had an almost illegally good time filming the last scenes of *To the Edge and Back*. Raoul is in China, on one of his archeological digs, and Harwood – our eternal uncle, who keeps returning home like life-sized postcards of himself – is over there with Raoul, making pictures for a magazine piece. As you no doubt know, our blessed Ajax and Rena, never ones to be outdone, decided to take Raoul and Harwood's travel plans as an excuse to make a little China trip of their own and have set off on a cruise down the Yangtze River. I'm sure they are soaking up life as only they can.

Achilles and I are here alone, enjoying the unusual quiet in our big home. Outside the February light is fading, and – oh, I've just noticed: It's beginning to snow. A serious, road-clogging snow. How perfect! I'm going to rise from this desk, brush off the nostalgic ache that this birthday toast to you has brought on, and walk out in the world. I'm going to wrap myself and the baby in Granny's old mink coat, the one Raoul stole when he was sleuthing through this

414

house so long ago and then returned to me when he proposed. I'm going to make some footprints in the snow. I'm going to walk across our front lawn, and who knows – maybe as I do I'll hear a mighty rumbling and the ground will crack open and there will be Raoul and Harwood and Ajax and Rena, tunneling home from China. Digging their way home for dinner.

Happy Happy Eighteenth, my dear wild ones. I miss you and I love you and I hope to see you soon.

Your everloving, everlasting Elray

THE END

A SELECTED LIST OF FINE WRITING
AVAILABLE FROM BLACK SWAN

77115 5	BRICK LANE	Monica Ali	£7.99
99588 6	THE HOUSE OF THE SPIRITS	Isabel Allende	£7.99
99946 6	THE ANATOMIST	Federico Andahazi	£6.99
77105 8	NOT THE END OF THE WORLD	Kate Atkinson	£6.99
99863 X	MARLENE DIETRICH LIVED HERE	Eleanor Bailey	£6.99
77131 7	MAKING LOVE: A CONSPIRACY OF THE HEART	Marius Brill	£6.99
99979 2	GATES OF EDEN	Ethan Coen	£7.99
99686 6	BEACH MUSIC	Pat Conroy	£8.99
99767 6	SISTER OF MY HEART	Chitra Banerjee Divakaruni	£6.99
99836 2	A HEART OF STONE	Renate Dorrestein	£6.99
99985 7	DANCING WITH MINNIE THE TWIG	Mogue Doyle	£6.99
77142 2	CRADLE SONG	Robert Edric	£6.99
99935 0	PEACE LIKE A RIVER	Leif Enger	£6.99
99954 7	SWIFT AS DESIRE	Laura Esquivel	£6.99
77182 1	THE TIGER BY THE RIVER	Ravi Shankar Etteth	£6.99
77125 2	TRICKS OF THE LIGHT	Alison Fell	£6.99
99890 7	DISOBEDIENCE	Jane Hamilton	£6.99
77001 9	HOLY FOOLS	Joanne Harris	£6.99
77082 5	THE WISDOM OF CROCODILES	Paul Hoffman	£7.99
77109 0	THE FOURTH HAND	John Irving	£6.99
77005 1	IN THE KINGDOM OF MISTS	Jane Jakeman	£6.99
99867 2	LIKE WATER IN WILD PLACES	Pamela Jooste	£6.99
99996 2	EVA'S COUSIN	Sibylle Knauss	£6.99
99977 6	PERSONAL VELOCITY	Rebecca Miller	£6.99
77106 6	LITTLE INDISCRETIONS	Carmen Posadas	£6.99
99780 3	KNOWLEDGE OF ANGELS	Jill Paton Walsh	£6.99